RING MASTER

k.j.packer

Honour and shame from no condition rise;
Act well your part, there all the honour lies.
                                    A. Pope

North City Press
Norwich

First published in Great Britain in 2017 by
North City Press
www.northcitypress.co.uk

A CIP catalogue record for this title is available from the
British Library

ISBN 978-0-9954743-1-4

Printed and bound by ImprintDigital, Exeter,
using FSC-certified products.

*In memory of the real
"Female Blondins"*

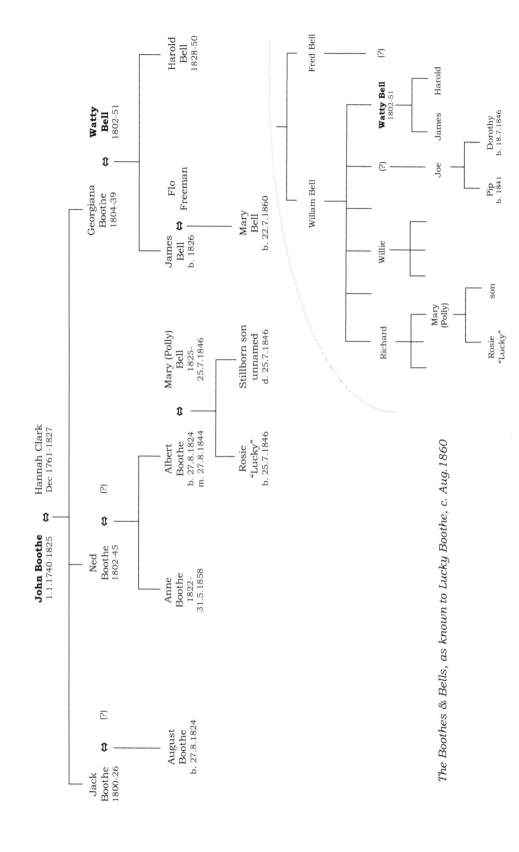

The Boothes & Bells, as known to Lucky Boothe, c. Aug.1860

Part One

One

I have it on good authority it was Ellie Scott named me and raised me with all the love a mother might her own. It should've been my father did both, but my coming into the world hadn't been the best of occasions for him, taking his wife and the son he'd yearned for – my twin that never drew breath. For years my father called me Rosie when he bothered at all, but the name he refused to hear was Lucky – Lucky Boothe of the Boothe and Bell Travelling Shows. Now, that might sound grand, but I tell you it weren't. The story goes my birth ended our better fortune, not a few laying the blame at my feet. And if Ellie Scott had hoped naming me would bring her luck she was to be mistaken.

A day to my seventh birthday, we were at Dartford Fair. As I was soon to learn, we were but a hop and skip from where my life had once begun and stretched ahead of me like the rope I'd one day become enslaved to.

It was the day everything started to change.

Ellie was just married, so she was all abloom and cooing over her husband, though she'd vowed to me she had love enough for us both.

– You'll be all grown the morrow, barefooting the embers and supping ale and the like, Ellie told me when she waved me off from her waggon that morning, hugging me to her and kissing my neck so it tickled.

I was heading onto the fairground to look for cousin Dorothy, but before I could reach the first stall, I met my aunt coming the other way. She was Anne Boothe, my father's sister. Till that day, not she nor my father had played much part in my life.

– Morning sweetheart, my aunt said, dropping to her haunches and running a finger through my locks. That's quite as busy out there as I've ever seen it. Reckon I could use a young lady's hand with the gingerbread.

There was a glint in her eye when she said it and that was all the asking I needed. It was my first time helping her.

– There'll be no time for chit-chatting, she said, showing me to the waggon she shared with my father, and passing me an apron.

Indeed she hardly spoke another word that day, except to hurry me or send me for more ingredients. Yet she sang like a bird in a cage, and every so often I heard a name I recognised, so I knew they were songs about our family.

I thought her quite odd – too tall and thin, like the stick insects she showed me in a glass box at the head of her bunk.

– You can look but don't touch, she told me, scraping a shock of hair from her eyes.

She worked harder than any man I'd ever seen, and soon the air tasted of vanilla, and the waggon floor was sticky with flour and treacle, so my father fumed when he stopped by for his hat to keep the sun at bay.

All day I scuttled between a half-dozen of our waggons that had ranges, tending the fireboxes and shuffling hot trays like playing cards, my eyeballs burning with the heat. And all the while my aunt stood at the window, smiling and singing at the buttercups, and kneading the mixture that seemed to grow in her hands as though from a magic pot. She let me touch the dough, just once, and when I rolled it in my fingers it felt like warm flesh. But it weren't till the sun left her face and sank below the meadow that she rubbed the flour from her hands, stopped her singing, and spoke to me again.

– Go take a piece to your Ellie, she said, which I did.

Ellie's new man was a Cooke, so that was now her name too, but I never called her it. His family had charge of the fairground that year, my father not able to raise the money in time for the lease – the first time I was aware of that happening. Ellie was put to work helping with a new tent the Cookes had brought. It was a huge thing, grey as their elephant, longer than it was wide and not a bit inviting when it was empty. No one had seen its like before, and the Bells were saying it wouldn't pay. Though it would never be my place to say, I reckon they were too hasty building it up on their first attempt and that was what caused the pulley to come loose.

As I entered the tent, Ellie's pearly eyes met mine and she smiled. I'll always remember that smile, showing her dimples and the crow's feet she was surely too young to have had. As I shuffled towards her she took a step backwards, making room for whatever she was expecting of me – a flourish of a curtsy perhaps. But she'd not needed to move, as I dipped my head like a Chinaman and held out the cake tray. It was then that the pulley fell from up high, and when I looked again her smile was gone and there was confusion in her eyes. Then her face collapsed like an old jack-o'-lantern, her mouth folded on itself and her breath was taken from her.

The screams weren't mine, but they brought my aunt running. She found me cold as a statue still holding the tray, with blood in my hair and Ellie lying in a heap at my feet, everyone round me bawling and wailing. My aunt wiped her hands on her apron before she took mine in them, pulled me against her and whispered everything would be all right. But I tore from her grip and fled into the fair – in shock I suppose. I lost myself amongst the hundreds of stalls and show carriages, and the encampments of living waggons laid out in circles like ripples on a lake, slipping every hint of my aunt approaching, though all she'd wanted was to hug me.

That night and next day, there must've been a whole lot happened that I can't now recall, as I wandered as though sleepwalking through fog. It would've been all a panic back at the tent, that's for certain. I know I turned that moment over and over in my head till I couldn't bear it no more. Every waking minute I saw Ellie's face as she took her final breath, and I've remembered it ever since. Perhaps I found shelter and food; perhaps I took from others the comfort my aunt would've given me if I'd let her find me. Or maybe I was alone, which was how I felt the following evening when I found myself back at the Cookes's tent, exhausted and bothered by the heat.

The show had to go on of course, so they'd been busy those hours. In front of their new tent, they'd built a facade of wood and canvas, grandly painted in red and yellow and edged with gold. There were huge murals brought to life in the blaze of a hundred tallows. I could make out a serpent coiled at an Indian girl's feet, coloureds with spears and blowpipes hunting tigers, and a strongman pulling a waggon with a chain between his teeth, his face glistening, the paint not yet dry. I searched for a likeness of Ellie, thinking they might've painted her somewhere, but there was not even a sketch – as though her death had been kicked clean in the dirt.

They were showing the full-house sign, so their dancing girls were gone to get ready for their next routine, no longer needed to attract a crowd. There was a set of steps as wide as a stage leading to the entrance, where a pair of velvet drapes hung, with a Cooke showman standing to either side. Each time they drew the curtains to allow in a latecomer, I angled for a glimpse, till finally one of the men called to me.

– Ain't nothing here for you, Lucky Boothe, he said, though the din of chatter from inside told a different story.

– But my cousin will be in there and it's my birthday, I replied, but he was deaf to my words, not a care for how I was, after seeing Ellie die and all.

I stole into the shadows and took a slow walk round the outside. I scoured every inch of the canvas for a shard of light escaping a ripped seam or poorly laced join, a chink through which I might watch or intrude, but they'd pitched the tent perfectly second time round, every wall staked taut without a gap even to let a rat through, as if they'd wanted to seal Ellie's spirit inside. Then two thirds round when I'd almost given up, I fell upon a narrow wooden door set into the canvas, unguarded and almost invisible in the dusk. I pushed it and it gave, and in a trice I was inside, standing behind the cashier who was too busy counting the takings to notice me. I ducked through a curtain, into the darkness beneath the seating stands, and was hit by the stench of the animals that had bedded there earlier. Footsteps thudded above my head. I crawled on till I stumbled out beside the left wing of the stage, almost falling into a knot of gents shouting at one another as though on opposite sides of the tent. As I edged away, one of them leaned towards me and jabbed my chest with an unlit pipe.

– Quickly now child, take a seat, said he, showing me a smile missing all its back teeth.

I might've hesitated, looked at him a moment too long. He might've raised an eyebrow. I know I found a place at the front, on the low forms where the apprentices were sat, and sure enough Dorothy was amongst them, her head in her hands. With our birthdays just a week apart we were to have shared our rite, our first fire-walk out of childhood. But it was forgotten now after the accident, and I supposed it was that, as well as Ellie's death, that was upsetting her. I wanted to reach her, but there were too many others in the way. And the band was already tuning for the anthem, so she wouldn't have heard me anyway above their racket, even if I'd made it to her. Instead I looked round at the inside of the tent, unrecognisable now in its glory, dripping with silk and velvet, aglow in naphtha, hundreds of faces looking back at me, and I so wished one of them could be Ellie's.

The band managed seven verses and I sat through them all whilst the folk behind me stood and sang as though a single raucous voice. Then it was as if a hand touched every head in the crowd, though truly it was just a twitch of the stage curtain that did it, silenced them all. It was tugged again and a great cheer went up when Sir Cooke, Ellie's husband, thrust out his head, his painted face the last I'd expected to see that night. He licked his lips and rolled his eyes like a lunatic, then lunged through the curtain to the front of the stage, losing his tricorn to a child in the second row, a sullen thing in her finest turnout. Her governess returned it at once, and Sir Cooke slapped his own arse, stuck a finger in his ear, and pretended to eat from it. And of course, the crowd clapped and whooped and loved him with all their hearts; how could they not? He placed the hat on his foot and flicked it into the air above him, let it drop to the floor, pretended to cry, and did it again before catching it on his head the third time. Yet first time every time he could've caught it, even now with Ellie lying dead in his waggon.

So this was the Cookes's homage to Ellie, a clown's tears for all of their loss. But did he let his mask slip? Not a chance. He had not a stitch out of place. Every button he'd polished to a gem, every crease he'd pressed sharp as a blade. Enough rouge on his lips, and no more. And that brooch he wore at his breast, a delicate thing like a tiger's claw – Ellie had worn it all nine days of her marriage, given her by her beloved new husband, worn by his mother, and her mother before her.

Sir Cooke's routine lasted but a few minutes, a blur of knockabout, fumbling with props, tripping over himself and dragging a tune from an old chanter. He climbed a ladder, crashed to the stage and played dead till the crowd could bear it no longer and screamed at him to be up and doing it again. So he jumped to his feet, and with another manic smile turned and sprang like a hare into a life of mourning.

I'd barely had time to return my thoughts to Ellie, and the crowd had only just begun cheering, when there was hush again, pulling me out of my sorrow.

It was now that I saw Him for the first time – though of course I couldn't know then what he would one day become to me.

Without ceremony he stepped from the wing, dressed in white flannels and cap, a blue waistcoat piped with gold, his feet in calico slippers. His skin was darker than I'd ever seen on any man or woman, though not as dark as the coloureds in the paintings at the entrance; it was more like butterscotch, I decided. He carried an umbrella in one hand and with the other lifted the clown's ladder to centre stage. Once he was in position, he looked left and right as if to cross a road, made a show of taking a deep breath and then stepped onto the first rung. The crowd fell quiet as he climbed, and in the hush I could hear whispered counting, marking his progress. At the top he paused before stepping off, yet unlike Sir Cooke he didn't fall.

You may ask – how could I've not spotted it, a rope shimmering in the limelight like a skein of silver? It stretched from behind the stage and across it, to where it was guyed not six feet from where I was sat, before it rose steeply over the crowd to the Gods.

Cos I didn't yet know of such things, was how. Seven summers in the fairs and I'd never seen a tightrope, let alone a tightrope walker. And if Ellie hadn't died, I mightn't have seen one then – if I'd been nursing the soles of my feet after my first fire-walk, and rinsing the taste of ale from my mouth, Ellie's arms wrapped round me to keep me warm.

There was polite applause as the walker teetered for a moment, like a spinning top finding its balance. Then silence, and into it a taunt thrown by my neighbour.

– You could've scrubbed up for us Ali Baba, the apprentice said, bringing laughter from everyone round me.

I didn't laugh with them, though I might've reddened, but the walker ignored us all anyway and took his first steps. As he approached the front of the stage he flicked open his umbrella and began twirling it above his head like a maiden would. He raised an upturned palm to his shoulder, and as if to answer the heckler, performed a kind of cakewalk, his face without expression. He stepped forward again and then – I'm quite certain I remember this, though perhaps it's just cos I know it now – his feet began to flow along the rope like water over sand. He clutched the air, showed the whites of his eyes, and stared at the floor as though at a pit of snakes. I must've risen to help him, for a hand on my shoulder stayed me. But soon he was all smiles again, tipping his beret to the ladies in the circle. He came alongside me then, hovering like a hummingbird plucked from paradise. I could see the sheen on his trousers and smell talc on his feet. And he met my gaze, as if to say – this is for you sweet child; no better a rite than this to ease your pain.

He put his back to us now, moving further along the rope. He walked upon tiptoe, light as a fairy, dancing as though on a broad plank. The crowd took to their feet and cheered till their throats gave out, as if the Queen herself had appeared on the rope with all her children heaped upon her back. When he was almost out of sight, he glanced over his shoulder and blew us a final kiss. Then in a flash of magnesium he was gone – swallowed by the stars is what I thought – leaving me to my sadness.

Two

In an instant, my father was standing over me with blood in his eyes. I'd not felt his hand on my wrist – not till he hauled me from my seat – so he might've had it there a while. He dragged me from the tent in view of the crowd, limping ahead of me into the moonless night, and so to his waggon, though my legs were good enough to walk by myself. He pushed me up the steps and inside, clipping the back of my head with his palm, and fumbled to light a candle.

– You sleep here now. Your aunt will have to head to toe with me, he said, pushing me again towards my aunt's bunk that was too short for her anyway.

He snuffed out the candle before it'd barely taken and left at once, locking the door from the outside, not thinking to leave me a bed pot; I was that confused not knowing what I'd done to deserve such treatment.

I awoke in daylight, the mattress a little damp, to the sound of our encampment pulling down. I could make out angry voices cursing my father; it seemed we Boothes and Bells were to return to the City. Yet no one wanted to leave so soon, or to break the cycle they were used to: always it was Dartford round my birthday, and Blackheath after that; then in August to Hampstead and the dying days of Bartholomew Fair; then St Giles in September, and a run of mop fairs at the back end of the year. But as my father was still the head of our shows – the Boothes by birth and the Bells cos he'd married my mother – whatever he said went. So we were to travel to Mile End, which we usually only did in winter.

My aunt slid open the shutter from the bed-quarter that she now shared with my father, and climbed down in her nightgown, her hair untied and falling about her shoulders. She wished me a good morning, her voice sounding as rough as if she'd been out all hours round a fire. I sat up in the bunk and reached out to her. Her eyes flooded with tears as she bent towards me, as I let her give me that hug at last, and she brought me to my feet. She helped me into dry clothes and got dressed herself, then we stepped outside, and we had just long enough to squat, wash our faces and share a hunk of bread, before the waggons began to roll and we had to jump aboard again. My aunt grabbed whatever possessions my father had forgotten to load, but with no time to find a place for it all, she piled it on to my bunk, first covering the damp patch with an oilskin. I helped her with the last of it, before we took to her bed and tucked ourselves under the covers.

As we set off, my aunt began to sing with what voice she had left. That's all she did for a while, and since helping her with the gingerbread, I expected no more of her than that. But then she did start to speak to me.

– I'm sorry about Ellie, she said. That was a dreadful thing to happen. You must try and put it from your mind. I'm here now and I'm going to look after you.

I lay my cheek on her breast and it felt warm beneath her shift. She stroked my forehead as she spoke, her words muffled by her heartbeat, and soon I was lulled into a daydream.

We'd been travelling like this for some time, feeling every bump and twist, when my aunt left the bed and began rummaging beneath the bunk that was now mine. She drew out a suitcase and took something large and flat from it, then removed several sheets of brown paper to reveal a stiff canvas with no frame. She brought it to me, holding up the painting for me to see. It showed a woman from the side, against a night sky. She had dark hair to her ankles and her stomach bulged under a white dress. She was standing straight as a tree, her arms outstretched, her head tilted away towards a sliver of moon, so her face couldn't be seen. I thought she was floating, till I made out the slim cord upon which she was balancing.

– It's your mother, my aunt whispered. She was a tightrope walker like the fella last night. It's time you knew that.

I felt sure this was the first I'd heard of it, though it made me wonder if my Ellie had told me when I was too young to remember.

I sat up and took the picture, my fingers clutching the edges of the canvas. I wanted to see my mother's face, and I turned the painting over thinking I might catch it on the other side. My aunt started to speak again, but then without warning the waggon ground to a halt. I looked towards the window, and to my aunt; she didn't rush to see what the matter was. She took the canvas from me, replaced it in its wrapping and stowed it in the trunk before beckoning me to the door. I never saw that picture again; I don't know why not.

There didn't seem any reason for our stopping, and I didn't recognise the lane we were on. I'd not travelled with my father before; Ellie had taken me everywhere with her. My father was at the roadside and a few others were approaching – including James, who I call uncle, though my father and he are cousins, as was my mother and James. As I stepped down from the waggon, my uncle removed his cap and dropped his eyes. I didn't know him so well then, though he'd been fond of Ellie and had always treated me kindly.

– I'm so sorry about Ellie. It's good you're with us now, he said, running his hand over my head.

As more of the showmen gathered, my father began to speak, fiddling with his copper bracelet. I couldn't make out his words to begin with but I knew they must be important, for the men all lowered their heads and murmured back at him. They followed him onto the verge and stood beside what looked like a lump of rust in the long grass, then each of them took something from their bag or pockets and placed it on the ground in front of them. I could see a handful of poppies and a penny loaf, and a boy's cap.

My aunt touched her fingers to my neck and whispered to me,

– This is where your mother passed away sweetheart. You know she would've loved you more than anything in the world.

I squinted at the verge a moment, trying to see what it was that was surrounded by the offerings.

– Did I have a brother? I said suddenly, just loud enough for my aunt to hear.

– What do you remember? she asked me.

I remembered a fragment of a story, is all, from a fireside perhaps, but I didn't say that to her.

– He was lost here too, she said softly, squeezing my hand.

She didn't say this was the place I was born, but I knew it's what she meant.

As the men stepped backwards I saw my aunt wipe a tear from her face, before she led me across the lane to take their place on the verge. She knelt and kissed the grass, but it felt odd to me to do the same, not certain if I was meant to be copying her. I was wearing a thin scarf round my waist, and I pulled it free and started ripping the end of it. My aunt tried to stop me, till she realised what I was doing. I arranged the torn pieces on the grass in front of me, one each for my mother and brother, and the third for Ellie. That's what I told myself. And now I could see what lay there – an iron rim and a charred remnant of a horse shaft, the signs of where a waggon had been burnt.

When I rose again, I glanced behind and saw that every showman had his eyes upon me, except my uncle; his gaze was fixed on my father, who was staring at the ground. My aunt hugged me to her and let out a cough, and the men all looked down as my father lifted his head. He took a step away, and then one by one the showmen began returning to their waggons, and I thought – whatever strange ceremony this is, it must now be at an end.

With the midday sun upon us, the convoy started to roll again, and I knew we were travelling away from Ellie. I knew too that I had no choice in the matter. Uncle James stayed for the funeral, and I'm sure he would've taken me with him if he could have. But once more, I took to my aunt's bed, where she told me my mother's story without me having to ask.

– I swear, since your mother's last walk, I've not seen a crowd as big as gathered last night, she began. Thankfully it was the Cookes' doing, so your father can't be blaming any of us for bringing a tightrope walker to the fair. He mightn't have wanted a scene, but there were plenty eyebrows raised when he grabbed you, she told me.

It was only years later that I came to understand why so many fairfolk had turned their heads, how they'd known why my father was in a rage, why the likes of that walker had not been seen on any fairground my father had had charge of since I was born. Cos since that day of my birth, the story of it had been told round every encampment fire from the King's Road to King's Lynn, and in countless taprooms besides, though never in my earshot. They'd all had their own take on it – the Boothes and Bells and plenty others besides – and they needed nothing more than a pint of porter and a stranger passing to be weaving another version of the story. Yet it was only my aunt knew the whole of it.

– Your mother was performing as usual, she went on. She must've had a thousand watching her that day, throwing her flowers and tossing coins at her feet. Not one of them saw her start out though, limping as she took to the rope, telling me that her leg was just stiff from how she'd slept. I never did find out what she done to it; she wouldn't tell me that. But once she began walking, no one could tell there was anything the matter; graceful as a swan on water she was. When it was over, they cheered her as they did that boy last night, and just like him, she disappeared in a puff of smoke at the end of it. It was only me and your father saw what happened next. She slipped from the rope and fell six feet, and I could tell she was hurt, though she didn't say so. She said she should see the midwife before leaving, as if she'd just remembered it. I've never fathomed your father's rage; he turned his back on her and told her we wouldn't wait, that she could bloody well follow us when she was ready. But there was no way I was leaving her.

My aunt paused for a moment to catch her breath, before carrying on even more excitedly – telling me how my father had then set off from Dartford towards London, by all accounts too quickly for some of the show carriages to keep up. My mother did start to follow, but only after she'd sent for Katherine Scott, so she must've known what was coming. That was Ellie's mother, who'd been like a midwife to the show-women for as long as could be remembered. Ellie was then sixteen and it was the both of them my aunt found parked up at the edge of the fair in an old bowtop waggon with a leaking roof. Once my mother had changed from her costume and bandaged her foot, she set off in her own waggon with my aunt at the reins, Katherine and Ellie following behind, chasing after my father and the rest of the Boothes and Bells. But it was to be in vain. They made just three miles before the sun set on them and my mother started to cry out.

My aunt began to sob as she told me that bit, and I said she could finish the story another day, though I was desperate to hear to the end. But I reckon she'd had it inside her so long – like a belly of worms – that now she was ridding herself of it there was no stopping her. So finally, she told me about my birth.

– It was on that same verge we've just left behind, she said. There wasn't a peep of moon, and Katherine and I could barely see to help your mother. You came quick enough but not your brother, and that's what did for them both. Sweet Polly, I used to call her; I was the only one called her that and not Mary. Right in front of me she passed away, and there was nothing Katherine or I could do. I wish I could tell you it were different, tell you that she met your eyes and glanced upon your brother if only for a moment, but I reckon you'll do better hearing the truth, so one day you might understand what I've told you. I should've taken you on then but I was hysterical from losing Polly, so I weren't fit to care for you. I was so angry at your father, I thought of leaving the fair for good. There was nothing for it but for Katherine to take you.

That's what my aunt told me.

Seems there was no question of my father caring for me; he'd lost too much by my coming along. Born in blood, he used to say of me, as if my birth had been my fault. Right away he gave up the drink and his daughter as if they were one and the same, my aunt said.

I don't recall seeing much of my father or aunt in the years that followed. It seems Katherine only lived another few months. She was already old – Ellie being her youngest by nigh on thirty years. So it was Ellie then took me on. A right pair of orphans we must've been, her father being long gone.

For the little I remember of it, I'm sure they were happy years, till the day Ellie died. Then all at once it changed – seeing the tightrope walker, being taken in by my aunt, witnessing that ritual of my father's for the first time. In the years after, I made that my memorial for Ellie too. I'd plan my offerings weeks or months before, picking spring flowers

17

and pressing them inside my aunt's books, or collecting strands of wool from hedgerows and twisting them into figures.

Leastways, that's what I did till it all changed again.

Three

The way my aunt talked about her father, Ned Boothe, I reckon there was none other she loved as much, though she never mentioned her mother and I never felt I could ask her. She knew all his stories by heart, yet she still read them to me from the journal he'd kept all his days. I remember the book as being twice as big as my hand. It was bound in stiff leather the colour of blood, with two letters stamped in black on the front: N and B, my aunt told me they were. Inside the cover was a sketch of a man with the longest of legs, wearing striped trousers and nothing above, standing on a large ball. The pages were as thick as new leaves but yellowed and creased, and they were crammed edge to edge with tiny writing. My aunt said he'd a neat hand, my grandfather, but a poor grasp of the language, so she'd had to fill in the gaps when she read to me. It meant she never told a story the same way twice, which was how it'd always been round the fire and in the taproom, so she might as well have done without the book after all. Not all the pages were full though; a good third of the book was blank. My aunt reckoned her father had had a whole raft of other stories to tell, but didn't live long enough to write them.

– So now they're lost if they've not been passed down, she told me.

That weren't altogether true though; we had the Bell's Penny Theatre too. Every Christmas at Mile End, they put on a play telling the story of the year just gone. They painted a huge backcloth showing everything that had happened, and acted out the drama of our lives in front of it, though certain things would've been better left to memory. Once every ten years at the Winter Fair, they displayed all the canvasses that had survived. I had to wait till I was fourteen to see them for the first time when I could remember them.

The tale most told of Ned Boothe was of him taking the shows to Weston Hill one dreadful summer. I might've thought it a tall one had I not heard it first from my aunt when I was but nine years old, on the eve of our own fateful visit to that wretched fair. She'd not told it to scare me; she was just that terrified of returning.

She'd been a child herself when it happened, a dreadful night that had stuck with her much as Ellie's death had with me, and she didn't need her father's journal to remember it. The fair had passed well enough, she recalled, with much gingerbread and ale sold and plenty of showgirls treading the boards. And that's what started it – word reaching the slums there was fun to be had on the hill. But when the horde arrived, the firkins were dry and the belles already towelling away their powder masks. So they tore down branches and thrashed every door, window and skull in their path. Scores of our shows were burnt and a good few livelihoods lost.

Come morning, my grandfather rounded a mob of his own and went a-lynching. The dozen or so he caught might've been the ringleaders but possibly not, and later my aunt wondered how he could've recognised anyone from that confusion. But it weren't so much the act she remembered, though it was a vile thing that wouldn't even be done to a knacker. It was how she'd just stood, watching, and learning a terrible lesson about her kin. The memory still haunted her all those years later, when my father told her we were to meet another convoy at Reading and travel to Weston Hill again.

Our own tale was no happier. We rolled for five days under black skies, through mud and torrents, abandoning our peepshow after it sank to its axles, which should've been enough to turn us round, try our fortune elsewhere. But my father pressed on, our waggons cowering behind the grander carriages of Wombwell's Menagerie. Day after day the thunder came. My head churned with my aunt's story, and it was the first time I remember feeling vulnerable in that fragile home.

We arrived on the Saturday night, the rain still lashing and turning the hill to a quag, so I didn't leave the waggon till morning. The church bells awoke me before my father did. He'd been outside all night and he opened the door head to foot in mud.

– Get your dog ready. You're showing in an hour, he told me.

There weren't time to light the stove and the ground was too wet for a fire, so I went hungry. Though it was summer, it felt cold as a February morn. I found Bess tucked behind the wheel of a neighbour's waggon and it took a while to coax her; she was the collie runt I'd had since I was seven. My father showed me to the tent – a sorry thing with no sides and the wind whipping through, but away from the central ring where the gypsies were gathering their horses.

I had a ten-minute act with Bess, which I'd been taught when I was first given her and hadn't changed since. I never much liked the attention; I didn't feel then that I was born to perform. We did three shows every hour, with ten minutes between each. I wore a yellow dress and a bonnet I never grew into, and Bess had a collar of flowers – silk ones when we didn't have fresh. She remembered the routine better than I did, always knowing which trick followed the last. She could turn somersaults and stand on her front paws, and even tell the time, though I didn't like the teaching for that. She could jump through hoops too, and there was a special one I held with a gauntlet and set alight. But the custom was pitiful that day and we couldn't keep an audience. The only relief came when Dorothy stopped by during a downpour, though it was such a shame she did. She ducked under the canvas and shook her red locks, spraying rainwater into my face.

– I've only made two shillings and my shoes have had it, she said, having to stoop these days to peck my cheek, she was growing that quickly past me.

She'd been performing with Bess's sister Grace. She'd only left her a moment to come and see me; she should've just brought her. I knew something was up when I saw a crowd gathering on the far side of the market. Dorothy spotted it too, and I saw the dread in her eyes before I understood. We locked Bess in the menagerie and rushed towards the fray. We arrived at a ring of men several deep, some stripped to their waist as though about to wrestle, all yelling and barging for a view. I didn't recognise a single one, so I reckon they were all locals. Slight that we were we slipped into the crush without being noticed. I took Dorothy's hand as we got deeper, and then I heard the words that set me rigid.

– That bitch is from the fair for sure, came the voice, and I prayed Dorothy hadn't heard.

I crouched, and through the legs of the crowd saw a circle of dirt and Grace being held without a struggle – the poor thing, clueless as to what was coming to her. Then a terrier on a chain, baring its teeth, was let forward to within inches of her face. I felt myself pushed and looked up to see Dorothy stepping over me. I grabbed at her waistband and managed to hold her, then pulled her to the ground beside me.

– There's nothing we can do, I told her. They'll lynch us if we try and save her.

I seized her to me, clamped my hand over her mouth to stop her replying, then pulled her backwards till we were clear of the mob. We scrambled to our feet again before the fight got underway, though fight is hardly the word for what it must've been – no fairer than pitching a cripple against a lion.

Back at our encampment, Dorothy rushed to her waggon. I wanted to join her but she wouldn't be comforted, she was that upset.

Round us I could see the Boothes and Bells pulling down and I realised, with barely a few pounds earned, we were preparing to bolt. As the canvas tilts were struck, they were thrown mud-side out over the carriages and waggons, so we became anonymous in the grey dusk, and like a train of damaged snails we crept from the fairground. As we rolled to safety – my aunt at the reins and our windows covered with tarpaulin – I huddled alone in my bunk in darkness, wishing I was with Dorothy. I couldn't believe we'd ever be as close to each other again, after that happening.

I awoke the next dawn, crept outside barefoot so as not to disturb my father and aunt, and squatted in the long grass. I knew we must've travelled a good few miles from Weston Hill, as I didn't recognise where we were now. Our waggons had been parked up in a line that snaked along a narrow lane. I could see wisps of smoke rising from several of the stacks, hear the pops and crackles of rekindled fires, and smell the burning of pine logs. I wanted to find Dorothy and wake her. I heard a cough from the field beside me, so I walked to the gate and looked in; yet save for a lone sheep rubbing itself on the fence, the field was empty.

There were two trees standing a distance apart in the middle of the meadow. I stared at them a while, watching their upper branches bending in the wind. Then for no reason I can think of now, I threw up my arms and started running towards them, dew splashing up my bare legs. As I reached the first tree I caught a reflection of the early light in mid-air and stopped dead, and it was a good thing I did. A step further and I would've snapped my neck on the steel wire that was suspended between the trees. I caught my breath, then edged towards it and grabbed hold; it was a good inch or more thick. I tipped my head to look along its length, and it brought to my mind the month after my seventh birthday when I took my first steps on a rope.

That was at Bartholomew Fair, which by then had seen better times and the shows were sparse and cheerless. At the encampment next to ours, the children had strung a washing line close to the ground. Having seen the walker not long before, and heard my aunt's stories, I now knew what it was and was intrigued by it. I joined them one afternoon, taking my turn trying to walk along it, imagining myself as my mother. I was hopeless to begin with and the other children poked fun at me. But I was determined, and tried harder each time, till at last as evening came, I managed six steps without falling – better than all the others. The moment I stepped off the rope, I burst into tears and ran to my father's waggon. But they were tears of joy I shed.

Uncle James must've heard of it, as next day he brought me a leather globe.

– You should practise on this first, though don't let your father see you, he told me, rolling the ball towards me.

It came up to my knees and must've weighed nearly as much as me. I didn't ask why he had it or where he'd got it from. But for the next year, practise I did, secretly and at every chance – my uncle carrying the ball in his waggon whenever we moved on. It took all my concentration, and eventually I learnt to keep the ball steady under my feet.

I continued practising till the following summer, when we ventured to Appleby; it was then my father caught me, stole up and kicked the ball from under my feet whilst I was balancing. The ball fell into the river and that was it ruined. I was lucky my ankle ever healed at all.

Now, I had another chance – if I was quick before the encampment awoke. I climbed into the fork where the wire was anchored to the trunk, and stepped out before I was ready, falling at once. I tried again several times, falling repeatedly. I thought of how I'd learnt to balance on the globe, but the wire felt too different – cold to the touch, and sharp where it'd frayed. Eventually I managed three, four, then five steps each time before falling. I used my arms to balance but forgot to look ahead, and I was so rapt I didn't feel my soles being cut by the wire or notice them become slippery and warm with my blood – not till the pain finally reached me and I fell again. I sat on the grass a while and pulled a few tufts to clean my feet. I felt useless, stupid even to think I could do it. But I knew what was inside me now – the stories of my mother, the walker I'd seen with my own eyes, the joy of those months on the balance ball.

I tore a strip from the hem of my nightdress and bound my feet, then climbed into the tree again and onto the wire. This time, when I stretched out my arms I lifted my head too. I could now see beyond the meadow to a church, and a graveyard choked with yews. There were houses with smoking chimneys. There was another field beside it with horses, and dark clouds galloping above. I thought of the children in that sleeping village and wondered how they spent their days. And I took a step without realising. I noticed the far tree where the wire ended, its lower branches grazed to a line that mirrored my arms. And I lost count of my steps, forgetting the wire altogether. My gaze shifted to the church spire that tapered gravely into the sky. Suddenly it was as though I could no longer hear, and my legs seemed to stiffen; I felt queerly distant, as though I was in another's skin. And in that fleeting moment, as though a veil had lifted, came my first brief sense of poise.

Four

I was a few days off eleven, readying to remember my mother and Ellie once more – the fifth time I would've joined in that ritual at the roadside – when my father decided to leave Dartford Fair early and head south to the farms. I'd eaten a good breakfast of porridge with honey and was putting the final touches to my offering – a pair of wreaths woven from feathers I'd been collecting for the past year – when he told us we were moving on. Though the sun had now returned after a week of rain, and already it was beating fiercely upon us, the fairground was still a mire, awash in mud much like Weston Hill two years before. The gloom had kept the crowds away and my father had had enough. When I tried to mention the memorial, he stopped me before I could finish – he said the road was too poor now and would be impassable after the rain. They were building a new road further north, he told me, to allow more traffic and larger waggons. In years to come we would use that one, he said. He didn't say that we'd never pass my mother's grave again; he didn't need to.

– What about Blackheath? I asked him, which was where we should've been heading after Dartford.

The cycle of the fairs was so fixed and endless, most showfolk would do anything not to break it. Yet break it again my father did, just as he'd done after Ellie died.

– Blackheath is too hectic these days, too many new families, my father replied sharply, as though that was reason enough.

Too many new ideas, too many new and bigger rides – all of them more exciting, more costly to keep than ours, is what I thought. But I never said that to him.

– I don't like it there anyway, I told him instead, and he nodded, not asking me why.

– There's more money to be made on the farms in summertime, he said, and I nodded back, though in other years we'd only ever worked the hops, and the start of that harvest was still over a month away.

It was the cherry picking he'd set his mind on, to which we now headed after being pulled off the fairground by a pair of oxen. We travelled all that day and the next, rolling along sodden roads with a dozen living waggons and a few show carriages in tow. We had the whirligig and a set of chairoplanes with us, so there was a chance of earning a bit extra during our stay. But we'd not brought the menagerie; we'd left the beasts in good hands at Dartford so they might get shown at Hampstead if not at Blackheath. I still had Bess though, and she padded alongside my father, as he waved his walking stick in front of himself as if beating a path through bracken. And for as long as the wheels turned, which was late into the evening on that first day, I sat at the reins with my aunt and listened to her stories that now tumbled from her like a waterfall.

– I should tell you about your great-grandfather, she began on the second morning, patting her skirt over her lap as though that was where she kept the story. John Boothe was his name, and it's him started all this, she said.

– Did he have the first shows? Was he a walker like my mother? Or a lion tamer? I asked her.

My aunt chuckled at that, though I knew she meant no mocking by it. She shook her head and replied in a hushed voice.

– He was a horseman, a damn fine one at that. He's buried at St Dunstan's, not so far from Mile End. I'll bring you there one day. If you can find the largest stone in the south corner, then you'll be standing on his grave. And well he might turn in it, for his was once the largest in the whole graveyard, not just our ragtag bit of it. Eighty-five years he lived to, yet he was not long a grandfather before passing.

She told me of how he'd lost his first family – his sweetheart and firstborn taken by the consumption whilst he fought abroad in the cavalry; his second daughter felled by the pox a year after he'd returned and rescued her from a cruel uncle. Another year on – so he'd told his son Ned, who'd written it in his journal – John Boothe had set out one foggy morning upon Westminster Bridge, counting the dull lamps till he knew he was at its middle and so above its greatest arch, and begun hauling himself onto the balustrade.

– You might guess what he was planning, my aunt went on. Ready to throw himself into the slurry, he was. Then all of a sudden he heard a fella's voice booming out of the mist – like a horn across the battlefield, he said – and it's that what saved him. 'God tell me I'm not dreaming. Is that you Major Boothe?' he heard, and it must've goodly froze him where he lay, like a seal cowering under a club. He turned his head from the river and muttered into the dawn, '*Captain* Boothe, if you'd be so kind,' cos that's how far your great-grandfather had risen in the ranks, and as sure as eggs he weren't one given to sham. He saw a towering lump of a man standing beside him, offering his hand. He was top-hatted and had a waistcoat splayed over a belly that looked ripe with triplets. That fella was Sergeant Clark, who'd remembered his Captain being of higher rank, and he was delighted if a bit flummoxed by their meeting. Next to the Sergeant, with her hand tucked in his arm, stood a fine young woman – the Sergeant's daughter as it turned out. She was no older than my grandfather's first daughters would've been had they lived.

– So that was your grandmother? I said to my aunt when she stopped for breath, and she nodded, giving me a smile.

– He reckoned the moment he set eyes upon her, he knew that was the rest of his life taken care of, and he wasn't far wrong, my aunt said. He fell for her as quickly as he would've from that bridge. And though it took them twenty years of loving to start – till he was near enough sixty – they finally had three children one after the other, which makes him the oldest father there's been in our family.

– I'd like to see his grave sometime, I told her, thinking she'd finished her story, but she hadn't quite.

– He had Jack first, then my father and Georgiana, she carried on. They take up a good bit of our patch at St Dunstan's, though Jack's stone has no words on it bar his name. And you know that bit of copper your father wears round his wrist? That was my grandfather's. He'd been given it on the Continent as a battle charm. He reckoned it had kept him safe all that time he was out there. On his deathbed, he asked for it to be cut and resealed round my father's wrist. And then when he died it went to your father.

My aunt paused and gave a sigh, as though it were her own life she was remembering.

– Will that ring come to me one day? I whispered.

She shrugged and shook her head.

– Because I'm not a boy?

– There's no saying, she replied softly.

I decided to ask her right then about my mother's grave. I'd waited too many years to say it, fearing the answer.

– Why was my mother buried at that roadside? I blurted.

My words were barely out, when I knew by the set of my aunt's face she'd not meant her story to lead to that. She flinched at my question, and I knew I should stop myself, but I'd only one thought on my mind.

– Why does my mother not have a proper grave? I demanded, my heart pounding like a boxer's fist.

My aunt dropped the reins and snatched one of my hands, squeezing my fingers too tightly.

– Hush child, she snapped, her words shocking me, so that then I betrayed her as I never would've wished to.

I called to my father, knowing he would find a way to silence me as my aunt hadn't done.

– Why did you leave my mother where she died? I cried out.

My father was plodding ahead of us, now leaning heavily upon his cane like an old man. On hearing me, he spun towards us, took two strides round the horse, and swept his stick into the air like a baton, so I caught a glimpse of that copper bangle round his wrist. Whether by skill or chance, he only grazed my aunt's nose with the stick, but caught the side of my head with all his force. I know this cos my aunt told me it afterwards, though it took her a few attempts to do so. I only remember falling forwards, the rough grey of the mare's flank rising to meet me, a curtain of red falling over one eye. When I came to, my aunt was singing to me, just as she'd done the time I helped her with the gingerbread. I saw she'd a gash across the bridge of her nose, and a bruise that had spread from her left eye like an ink stain. At once she stopped singing and began telling me another story. I never told her how brave I thought her. And every day from then, no matter what my father threatened, she told me more, as though there was not enough time.

Five

Early the following summer, in my twelfth year, we were returning from a Whitsun Fair in Suffolk when the worst of fevers took me – bad enough for my father to stop the convoy and make camp, though it was barely midday.

I remember a sensation like hot liquid rising in my head, my blood scorching me, yet feeling frozen to the core, shivering like an abandoned cub. My aunt – it could only have been her – cocooned me in blankets and sponged my forehead. She gave me a draught, though the sugar couldn't mask the bitterness, and I sank into the deepest sleep.

I awoke to the cockerels crowing from their baskets in the undercarriage, with daylight bleeding round the curtain. I'd been sleeping against the timber slats that lined the waggon wall next to my bunk, and I could feel the ridges on my skin. There was a dampness about my body too, a dull ache in my belly. I'd sweated the infection, I thought. An urge made me run my hand between my legs, and when I drew it out I touched it to my mouth. At the taste of it, I sat up and wrenched the curtain aside. In the light I saw the stain on my fingers, as though I'd pulled a rusty stake from the ground. I tore away the bedding and my nightdress, then stood up in my bare feet. There was a dark smear on the inside of my leg and another on the sheet.

I screamed then. Just once. I'd never screamed before – not even for Ellie – and I never did after; not at my father, not at August Boothe, or the times I fell. Hearing my cry, my aunt threw open the partition and climbed out. Her breathing was laboured and I wondered if she'd caught my sickness. She took in my naked body, the blood, my tears, and silently slid the door behind her. She passed me a shift and wiped my mouth with the back of her hand.

– You'll be just fine, she said, in her special way so I'd believe her.

She opened the drawer beside the stove and took out a square of muslin, folding it twice into a pad.

– Put this down there, she whispered.

– Will it hurt for long? I asked her.

She shook her head, returned the muslin, and then helped me with my stays.

– You'll be right as rain in a day or two. You're growing, is all. A little early perhaps, but I was your age.

As she finished dressing me, I asked if it would happen again, which made her pause and look at me properly. If she was in pain, she never showed it.

– If you're lucky, it'll happen by the moon, though if it ever stops, you come and tell me.

Her final words to me, yet I felt sure she had more to tell.

There was a thump on the partition and she slid open the door again to let out my father. He was dressed in his moleskin suit he'd had tailored in Bethnal Green. He stepped down and pushed past without a good morning, and opened the waggon door. My aunt smiled at me and kissed my forehead before we followed outside. I burrowed my bare feet in the long grass, whilst my aunt busied herself with the hens, occasionally coughing into her palm.

If I'd known what was to come, I'd have told her then how much I loved her, but I just scrunched my toes and stretched them again to air them; then I returned to the waggon, not knowing her life was nearly over.

It was only proper that my father came across her first. He'd sent me for water, but my aunt wouldn't see me go in my condition, so she'd gone instead, taking our two largest buckets. When she didn't return, he started raging, cursing her for finding some local to pass the time with when our kettle needed filling, though she would never have done such a thing.

He took off in a huff, and soon he was gone as long as she. It was Joc Bell, Dorothy's father, who eventually found them; he's the last rogue on earth you'd want to see in your final moments – fierce as a terrier starved for the pit, with a prizefighter's nose and a jaw too big for his cheeks. My father sent him away to find a doctor. But there was nothing could be done for my aunt.

My uncle James got to me first and took me in his arms so I knew he had bad tidings. My father wouldn't be helped, and he sent the convoy to Wanstead rather than Barnet where we'd been due to go, saying he'd follow soon enough. I spent the journey on the floor of my uncle's waggon, doubled with stomach cramps, and that was all the time I had to get used to the changes.

My father arrived two days later with my aunt's body laid out on my bunk, her feet hanging over the edge and propped on a stool, the waggon smelling of dried flowers and scented candles. There'd been plenty mutterings that he wouldn't appear at all, that he'd bury her at the roadside like he had my mother and brother, instead of bringing her to the cemetery for a decent burial.

The mourners came from all over, and I joined the line shuffling to see her grey remains. I wondered who'd cut her hair short, like she'd never worn it, and why her skin looked so old – her being just thirty-six, my father said.

On the day of the funeral, we left at dawn and made fair speed to the City. At Bow, we slowed to a respectful pace before turning into Stepney Green. The plane trees alongside the road were wearing all their leaves, yet the top of the church tower was just visible in the distance. We'd once taken our shows to the Green for Eastertide, when every square inch from the railings to the hedgerows had been solid with folk, all craning for a glimpse of a showgirl, knife-thrower, or one-trick pony, performing on the roofs of painted waggons or in tiny stalls. Today though, save for the songbirds, the Green was deserted.

So it was, as she'd once promised, my aunt brought me to St Dunstan's. There must've been a hundred at the graveside to see her coffin tipped onto that line of us Boothes. I didn't weep then. I thought about my mother instead, and about Ellie, for whom I'd shed so many tears I thought my life's worth must already be spent. My aunt's death remained unexplained. A weak heart, someone reckoned – those legs and arms like twigs, too thin to let the blood pass.

– I died is all, is what she would've said.

After the burial when the mourners began to scatter, I picked my way through the headstones. Most were in fair condition, scrubbed for the occasion, but a few were still encrusted with moss. I wished my mother's was amongst them. I stopped at the largest and ran my thumb over the inscription. I knew it must be John Boothe's – my aunt's grandfather, my great-grandfather – laying there with his second wife and three of his children. I wanted my aunt to read the words to me, to tell me the names on the other stones. I wanted her to pick them out one by one and ask me if I remembered who they were and where they fitted in our story. That was when I finally wept, when I realised that her tales were told for good. I thought I'd never hear about her or the rest of my family again. She'd told me every story that I knew; *the tell,* is what she called it. Now those tales were mine to pass on, and already I had my own to add.

My father insisted the wake be at the encampment, not at some public house my aunt had never set foot in. So we returned to Wanstead, where the showmen had built a huge bonfire of fallen oak and beech they'd dragged across the Flats. We arrived at dusk as they were mounding it with brush, and when it was lit it raged and spat and devoured the kindling, till it settled enough to be cooked upon. I didn't recognise half the folk helping, but family weren't expected to ready their own loved one's send-off by themselves. There were vats of potatoes for boiling, a pig and lamb for roasting, and a couple of firkins on trestles. We ate at long tables, the meal lasting for several hours, and for all my fears I reckon I heard more stories about my aunt in that sitting than she'd told me herself in five years caring for me, and that's saying something.

Afterwards, we gathered at the fire, now a pile of glowing logs encircled with ash, and a strolling band struck a tune. All day and evening I'd been expecting my father to make a speech, and I thought this was the moment. But at the fireside he seemed entranced, and soon, from where I stood, I followed his gaze and lost myself in the licking flames and embers like fireflies.

Eventually the wind turned the smoke into my face. I closed my eyes and blocked the conversations round me, till only the heartstrings of a mandolin and peep-peep of a whistle reached me. When I opened them again, Dorothy was standing beside me and she'd slid her hand into mine. She didn't speak, and when I turned to her, the band fell silent. Then came a drum roll and Dorothy kicked off her slippers, and before I could stop her she stepped towards the flames, making me cry out, which told the gathering more than I'd have wanted. I saw her left foot touch the centre of the fire and her right follow through to the other side. Then her third step took her into my father's arms, her own father nowhere to be seen.

I'd forgotten I might do this one day, our ritual of jumping through fire that we were supposed to begin on our seventh birthday. It now felt too late, though plenty of folk do it all their lives, at weddings or funerals or whatever occasion they think demands it.

I suppose I panicked, not wishing for the attention. I stumbled through the flames, my hand covering my face, and at the far side a tankard was thrust at me from the shadows. I gulped the ale too quickly and spat it out, before returning the jug to a man standing beyond the firelight. He was tall and slender built like uncle James. He tipped his hat at me and took a pipe from his mouth; then he smiled, showing the gaps where his back teeth were missing. I nodded and he bowed, though he didn't step forward.

– You likely do not know of me, he whispered. I am your uncle August, your father's cousin.

He put out his hand and I took it too firmly.

– You are certainly your mother's daughter, no doubt about it, he said.

When he let go, he brought his hand to my face and brushed my cheek. I would've curtsied, but an arm came through mine, swinging me away for a dance. As my father drew me towards him, I knew at once from his breath – for the first time since losing my mother, he'd taken a drink.

Six

We usually only go to King Henry's Yard in Mile End in late November. We stay there till February, when the cycle of the fairs starts over and takes us first to King's Lynn for the Mart, then to the spring, Easter and Whitsun fairs, to Appleby in June to trade up our horses, then south again – it used to be to Fairlop, but now to wherever takes our fancy – before we head to Dartford.

But two years and two months from my aunt's passing, as July closed on the eve of a full moon, we found ourselves at the yard gate once more.

It was only my second time going there in the summer – the first being seven years before, the day after my seventh birthday. Now though, we'd only travelled from Blackheath, not from Dartford. The journey into the City had changed beyond reckoning in those years, with the running in of the railways like blackened scars, the extra bridges to cross, and terraces choking every street. Though it was a good day's roll across the River and out to Mile End, we still could've made it to the yard in daylight had we not met an unseasonal fog at Aldgate. It fell upon us in grey slabs, sending us off the main road. My father was leading the convoy as usual, and I was sitting up next to him. He drew the horses sharp, snorted louder than they did, and gave a shiver, pulling up his collar as though it were winter.

– We'll need someone to guide us, he said, laying the reins between us.

– I'll fetch uncle, I replied, knowing whom he meant.

I was fairly panting by the time I found James standing beside his waggon, cradling his newborn, and he looked up when he heard me.

– Someone under the wheels? he said, running a hand through his silver hair.

I shook my head, catching my breath.

– Father needs you to lead us in, I told him.

– Does he not have his own eyes tonight, James said, winking and rocking his arms.

The baby was his first – a daughter, not even named yet. He'd married Flo Freeman the year my aunt died. Flo already had three boys of her own, their father having been killed by a hansom, so this was her fourth.

Uncle James used to call me his little girl, when I was still under Ellie's wing. She loved you more than the stars, better than a mother would her own, he once told me. I often wonder what there was between them.

– I'll be right there, he now said, waving me away.

I returned to the front of the convoy and soon James arrived in his watch-coat. He carried a lamp on a pole, long enough so when he lifted it, the light could be seen above the roofs of the carriages. He called to my father, but didn't wait for a reply.

– You can walk with me, if you can keep up, he told me.

Indeed, I had to skip to stay alongside him, though the cobbles were treacherous in the damp. He had to lead us south first, before he could take us east below Commercial Road. We sank into narrow streets, the convoy stringing out with barely enough room to walk alongside. Blackened buildings loomed in the murk like devils. Their walls seemed to fold in upon us, and then fade again, as the fog lifted and thickened once more. When I turned, I could see only our horses, and my father and waggon in outline. Yet the crying of the wolves from the menagerie told me the convoy was together still, and their melancholy drew figures from the shadows, pitching questions from unseen mouths.

– Where would you be hurrying at this hour? came the first voice.

– Only to our beds, though it's not so late, James replied.

– And the lions are awake still, my father warned.

– P'raps you could stop and make us a show, said another.

And what might you do if we did, I thought. Draw a knife across our throats? Paw at me with cold hands?

– Not tonight. But catch us at Hampstead on the twentieth if you will, said my uncle.

Behind us, as the lion carriage rolled through, one of the beasts roared, and that finally did for the voices. But not till we reached the foot of Jubilee Street did I take my hand from my throat and draw breath. We turned north then into familiar streets, and as the fog began to lift, leaving a chill, friendly faces appeared in the doorways. Children bleary from sleep came to watch our passing, squatting on their front steps or pacing beside us, wondering what brought us at this time of year. We handed them what we had left of our barley sugar, and they gave us their grubby smiles in return.

The horses were exhausted now, from the heat of the day and the relentless cold night, and round us their damp breath pooled in clouds. They stamped their irons good and proper on the cobbles, flaring their nostrils in protest, so if there'd been any doubt of our arrival before, there surely weren't now, as at last Mile End reared before us.

The "Waste" is what we call the strip of rough ground that stretches along the north side of Mile End Road for almost a mile towards Bow. At the head of it sits King Henry's Yard, which on three sides has walls propped with timbers, the fourth side being the east gable of the King Henry Inn. Every winter when we arrive, we jockey a dozen or more living waggons into the yard, but the gate's too narrow for the shows and we've never dared widen it, for fear the walls will collapse. So we lay up the carriages outside, leaving space between them for the patching and painting needed during the wintering.

As we make ourselves at home, folk the country over turn their waggons north, south and all points, to descend upon the Waste – those few hundred yards of dirt – to transform it overnight into the greatest spectacle you'll ever see. Blink and it's littered with carts and tents, and shelters thrown up against the wind, as if they've always been there. Fires are lit to be kept in till spring, friendships are remade, old scores rekindled or settled, supplies bartered, and grazing fought over. The first of December is the start of the Winter Fair. It's my favourite time, those thirty-one nights. Not for me the long summers on the move. I yearn for winter, when we warm ourselves at huge braziers, the dead sky brought to life with limelight. I feel settled then, freed from the displacement of other seasons.

But back then, deep in summer's heart, we'd fallen to fallow times and returned there.

The new day brought the sun again and a knot of crossing-sweepers annoyed by our obstruction.

– We'll be gone in good time, I heard my father tell them, though I knew they wouldn't dare try keeping him to his word.

When I first stepped into the yard it took me a moment to recognise it. Over much of the ground, grass had grown to a few inches long, and was peppered with wild flowers, none of which we ever saw in winter. The air was heavy with pollen and the buzz of insects. The huge elder, usually barren and sad, was dangling young berries over the wall, hanging them out to ripen. A creeper bursting with crimson leaves had scaled the inn to the chimney pots and was all but burying them. Summer comes to the City too, I thought, bringing its own plenty. Then my father ended my daydream.

– When the waggon's in place, see to the stove and fetch the water, he said.

I thought of my aunt. If she'd been alive still, she'd have shrugged and squeezed my hand, gone to the pump herself whilst I prepared the range.

It took us the morning to site the rest of the waggons, to spoil that haven of flowers and bees. I shouldn't have skipped breakfast or worked without shoes. By midday my feet were blistered as if I'd been fire-walking, and my stomach gurgled like a drain. When we were done, I scaled the wall beside the gate and sat above the yard, looking out over the Waste. In four months' time, I thought, there wouldn't be a clear patch of ground to be seen. I pictured the horses in their blankets, the rowdy geese growing fat and gone again by Christmas Eve, the chimneys of wood stoves dripping with tar. And I told myself, I wouldn't miss it for anything. But once more my father intruded, looking up at me from where my feet were swinging, and in the instant before he spoke, I imagined myself fleeing along the top of the wall, balancing upon it as though it were a rope.

– The fire's still not made, he called to me.

– I'll do it now, I replied, though I thought – I've toiled all morning and brought the water but I won't tell you so.

– Go see Pritchard first, he said. Get something for the broth, and mind those bloody scales.

God damn Pritchard. She was the only butcher for a mile who'd serve us, though only cos her greed was greater than our name for thievery, undue though it was. We all knew she lumped her elbow on the meat whilst loading the weights. I took Bess with me; her charcoal fur had begun to sprout white hairs, but still she was almost lost against the grey cobbles. We crossed the road at the urinal, the stench far worse than in winter, and stopped for a moment at the derelict glass shop. The owner was long dead, but once upon a time, he'd made our paraffin lamps, before we switched to naphtha. I forget his name, but I know he lost all nine of his children in his lifetime – twin girls in a fire and the others to disease of one sort or another. Pritchard's was three doors along. I tied Bess to the railing, as I'd done on every visit since my aunt first sent me on that errand, and stepped through the open doorway, swatting at bluebottles.

– Leave it outside, Pritchard told me, as she always did, not looking up.

She was a foul creature, pale and fatty like the scraps she passed off as joints. I don't recall her ever having a good word for anyone. She even kept the hours of a miser, closing early in winter to save lamp oil. She made a show of wiping her hands on a bloodied rag, as though that would cleanse them, and took up a cleaver.

– What'll it be? she croaked.

– A pair of trotters is all, I told her.

And a bone for the dog, one you haven't pleasured yourself with, I thought.

She dropped the knife on the bench and grunted, as if to say I had a duty to buy more.

– Not your season for these parts, she said, but not as conversation.

I didn't tell her how long we'd be staying, how much trade she might expect. I weren't certain myself, though I knew Hampstead was less than three weeks away.

She wrapped the meat in wax paper, weighed it and held it out, her frown demanding payment. Bess began to bark then, which weren't like her. The butcher swung her nose at the window to see what the carry-on was.

– Go shut it up, she said, dismissing me.

I wished her a Happy Christmas and left before she could answer back. Outside, Bess was crouched, silent now, staring along the pavement. Coming at us at good speed was a figure in a long coat too warm for the day, tails flapping at his calves, dock boots clipping the cobbles. He was pulling a trolley that looked heavy but didn't seem to be causing him much effort. On it were several wooden poles sticking out the back, a bundle of ropes and a hemp sack bursting with something, a family of pythons perhaps. As he passed I could see his wiry black hair under a billycock, skin like burnt sugar, but his eyes were lowered and his only greeting an outward breath. All at once I bade him a good day, a fine day for a walk, a warm day for such speed, but to no reply. I called again but he weren't stopping. So I untied Bess and took after him, quick as I could on my blisters. He crossed the road where we had, paused at the yard and looked surprised to see it full, and carried on to Dog Row, where he stopped outside the doorway to the inn. Even then, I weren't sure.

Seven

For all my time spent in its yard, the King Henry Inn had remained something of a mystery. I'd only crossed its threshold once, at the end of the previous winter when my father took me there, the night before we set off to King's Lynn for the Mart. Bullard is still the landlord, and he wouldn't meet my eye that first time I stood at his bar. But his hand was quick when my father's back was turned, squeezing my arm, his gaze resting too readily on my breast. When I pushed his fingers away, he called me a whore and whispered he'd have me, no messing, if I ever turned my back on him; so I never have done.

The inn is a rambling pile, shaped like an L, caught between the yard and Dog Row, and partly hidden from the Mile End Road by an old stable. As a young 'un I'd wanted to sneak in to play skittles in the cellar, which was where the Bell's Penny Theatre stored their canvasses. But my father had told me not to go there alone, though he didn't say that again after my first visit. It's a public house, though the cattlemen seem to think it belongs only to them. Every market day morning they stop on their way to Islington, and every afternoon they return, once they've seen the last of their stock butchered and watched the cobbles run with its blood. But there are plenty other regulars besides, mostly costermongers, and a good few fairfolk through the winter.

Now, squatting on Dog Row nursing my feet, I watched the man arranging his trailer. After a while, he caught me staring and gave me a smile in return. I felt I should look away but I saw encouragement in his eyes. He chocked each of the wheels one after the other, and retied the four lines securing the load, holding my gaze as he did so, raising his eyebrows as he completed each task. When he was done he put his hands on his hips as a clown would, turned towards the door of the inn and bounded inside with a single leap. I held my breath and counted my age, then followed him into the gloom of pipe smoke and sweat. But the floor was too gritty for me to walk upon it barefoot, so I had to go outside again to retrieve my clogs from where I'd hidden them, feeling the beginning of a shower.

The bar was lined with drinkers resting their elbows, and one or two steadying themselves to piss into the trough below. As there had been on my first visit, there was a gang of waifs hustling for pennies. My father had warned me off them, telling me how they earned their keep. But I turned to one now – I think it was a girl – and asked after the man with dark skin. She nodded towards the back of the inn and put out a hand, but I'd nothing for her.

She meant the games room, a wooden building with eight sides in the old courtyard. You get to it along a narrow corridor with no windows and a lamp at each end. It's like a grotto and when I'd come with my father there'd been dancing, which had made the room seem larger. But now in the middle of the floor was a billiards table with several players gathered round it. The man had the cue and was readying for a shot when I called to him.

– Your load's getting wet in the rain, I said, but he ignored me.

I was about to say it again when I heard a voice from behind.

– He won't hear you sweetheart.

I turned to find a woman sat alone in one of the alcoves round the walls, which each had a table and two chairs and frosted screens for privacy.

– Come. I don't bite, she said.

We shook hands as I sat. She wore a black dress with a cream bodice tied loose at the front, and a rose in her hair –

which was dark and thick like mine, falling in curls down her back.

– Madame Rouge, pleasure to be acquainted.

She had an accent not of the fairs, unlike any I'd heard, and I didn't realise she was offering me a drink till she poured two shots from a bottle and raised her glass, tipping a few drops onto the floor before drinking it in a mouthful.

– And you, she said.

I nodded and gulped mine too. It burned my throat at first, but then slipped down like honey and warmed my gut.

– Your name? she tried again, about to pour two more shots.

– It's Lucky. Lucky Boothe. Pleased to meet you.

As I said it, she stopped and looked at me closely.

– Goodness! So it is. *The Ring Master's Daughter,* she said, as though announcing an act, leaning back and tugging her forelock.

– No one has called me that before, I told her, surprised by her words.

– But you do know what your father is? she said.

I nodded again. I'd heard his title often enough, bandied at the fireside and at the fairground gates when he was haggling over a lease. But I'd never called him it myself.

The woman half turned to the players, then winked at me.

– You like our black boy? she said, tipping her head towards the billiards. It's alright, he doesn't hear us.

– Nothing at all? Does he not speak either?

– Not a squeak. Just imagine, never saying your name or whispering his love. But he'll not speak ill either, or come telling his lies.

She turned again and watched him as he worked the table, so I did too, and soon enough he noticed us. Now, whenever he sank a ball, he tipped his head at me. When he missed, he smiled and rocked on his heels, and though the others could cheer or curse their own game, he seemed to enjoy himself as much in silence.

– I wager he likes you, Mme Rouge said at last. But mind, he reads lips as well as some do the bible.

– Who is he? I said.

– I think you know already.

– I think I've seen him before.

– On a rope perhaps.

– So it is him, I whispered. I was seven. He danced on the rope for me.

The memory of that night now returned – my numbness at losing Ellie and not understanding; the first sight of the walker, so strange and unfamiliar, not yet knowing this had been my mother's craft.

– You were there too? I added.

Mme Rouge nodded and smiled. She must've seen my father drag me from the tent; everyone had seen that.

– Virgil dances for us all, she whispered in reply.

I looked at the walker again and thought how used he must be to being watched.

– I don't think I could bear the attention, I said eventually, which brought a sigh from Mme Rouge.

– Then you'll never follow in our footsteps, she said wistfully.

– You're a walker too?

– I didn't catch my name from the bordello, if that's what you were thinking. I've walked for your Queen, and her beloved, God save them. I still have a letter from her. Not in her own hand of course, but her words all the same. Being I'm the only woman ever to attempt her *glorious fleuve*. Her *River*, she added, noticing my confusion.

– You've walked across the Thames? I gasped.

– Of course. Has anyone told you otherwise? Well alas, not all the way across. Not my fault, just a damned *contretemps*. Too much wind. And some rogue pinched the lead weights. You English are a sour lot. But I shall do it one day, you'll see.

She wagged her finger as though that would seal her success, then poured us both a third glass. I drank mine too quickly again and felt sick from not eating. I knew my father would be looking for me now; I'd been away too long and he would've found there was no fire or supper in the range. But I was still drawn to the walker, and to Mme Rouge's story.

– I should probably go, I said, without meaning it.

– Oh but you mustn't. Share a last drink with me, Mme Rouge spluttered. It makes me an honest woman. The rope is my life, you know; I have nothing else. And I don't come here every day, so that's destiny for you. Lucky as your name.

The next shot was to the brim and we chinked glasses like old friends. After she drank, she ducked her head towards me and put her hand to her mouth to whisper.

– Do you want to see me walk? It's a secret. Big surprise. I shall be at your Winter Fair, this very Christmas. But no one must know, especially not your father.

– Surely he could bear to see a tightrope walker now? So many years have passed, I said.

– Have you seen another since Virgil?

She knew I hadn't, and short of crippling me, my father had done everything to stop me learning the craft.

– Will Virgil walk with you? I said at last.

Mme Rouge shook her head, a little too fiercely.

– Once upon a time he might have. But let me tell you something, she said, covering my hand with hers. I knew your mother, and I can tell you she was the most heavenly creature ever to take to the rope. It killed my heart when she died. My skills are nothing to hers, and just a slip of a woman she was. Did he ever tell you, that damned father of yours? Didn't even give her a decent burial. You probably refused to listen, and I wouldn't blame you for that, with all

48

the nonsense he talks. You have her eyes for sure. Let me look at you. I wager yours are bluer still if that could be so.

She sat back again and rubbed a hand over her face as though clearing cobwebs. She looked tired, but I didn't want her to stop talking now.

– What was my mother like when she walked?

Mme Rouge pulled the rose from her hair and gave another sigh before answering.

– Always looking to the stars, that's what. I used to tell her, 'Don't look up or down, *mon ange*, look straight ahead.' And she'd nod and say *oui maman*, and look to the sky anyway. She once said to me, 'Let the sun blind me before it grows dark.' I reckon she knew what was coming to her, she was that close to the heavens.

Mme Rouge drank two more shots, and as her eyes began to roll and she started wagging her finger again, I realised I'd not long with her.

– He could teach you a thing or two, she now blurted, nodding at the walker. Don't expect any loving, mind. But you've time enough for that. Feet and stomach – that's how you reach him. And he loves a good story.

At that moment, my father appeared at the alcove.

– Well, well. If it isn't young Albert Boothe himself, Mme Rouge piped. Did I mention Limehouse? she added to me in a whisper. Plenty of work at the dock. *Buy yourself a flower.*

My father stepped towards us and before I could rise he slapped Mme Rouge across her cheek.

– It weren't her fault, I started to tell him, but he struck me harder and forced me to stand, upsetting the table.

He pushed me past the billiards, where now the men's backs were turned and the walker could only see the pocket beyond the end of his cue, the ball missing it and bouncing over the cushion. My father shoved me out into the old courtyard and through a gate I didn't know was there, before

I found myself in King Henry's Yard again, the drizzle now a downpour.

Eight

After the rain came a fortnight of heat to stifle us, and at once the yard smelt rank with the animals and so many of us crammed in, no scent of winter to mask it – no roasted chestnuts or whiff of naphtha. My head pounded, first from the drink, and then from the noise of repairs that were normally left till winter.

I was as good as kept chained for most of the two weeks we spent at Mile End, my father keeping me so close that I could barely cough without him knowing it. He'd parked up his waggon as far into the yard as he could, nearest the wall of the inn, so that even when he weren't watching I'd too many others to pass to reach the gate without being seen. And there were enough who sided with him to keep a constant guard, all those who thought me good only to mind the home, run errands and work a tired runt. But seeing the walker again, and hearing Mme Rouge's words, had stirred something within me.

It was seven years since I'd seen Virgil for the first time; five years since I'd walked on the tight-wire at Weston. The memories of both now returned, bringing with them a fresh desire. Then late one evening, good fortune served up a reward.

I was looking for a basket that had gone under our wheels, searching in the gap between the waggon and the wall, when I stepped on a length of clay pipe that lay in the grass. It rolled from beneath me and I fell against the brickwork, grazing my elbow. The next morning I tried walking on it and found I could balance, so I kept at it for the rest of the day. After two days I could manage all twelve feet of it without it moving. Then I spent all the hours I could on it, walking its length or balancing on the spot as I scrubbed the waggon paintwork and scraped the dirt from the undercarriage. My father didn't bother to check on me there, just as long as he could hear me working. So I passed my days like that, rousing my longing for the rope, filling my head with thoughts of Virgil, till I could no longer deny to myself what I dreamed of.

My father would leave the yard on odd occasions, usually just for an hour or two, and once for a whole morning. Whenever he did, I would try the hidden door to the inn's courtyard, hoping to find it unlocked. I tried to sneak beyond the main gate too and return to the taproom, but always there was an arm barring my way. Then, a day before we were due to leave for Hampstead, my uncle James came to me, his newborn strapped across his chest, wide-awake but silent.

– How's the painting going? he called out, though he could see me well enough as he craned his head round the side of the waggon.

I slipped off the pipe and grabbed what was nearest, an old hairbrush, and he laughed.

– Come and see your cousin.

I tossed the brush aside and stepped out.

– She's bonny, I said, stroking her forehead, and truly she was.

– She's going to be another Mary Bell, same as your mother. That's a good act you've got there.

My uncle took off his cap a moment and stroked his hair. Every so often he spoke of my mother; they'd grown up together, first cousins and only a year apart in age. I reckon he was still pained by her dying.

He took my hand and said he'd something to show me, leading me through the press of waggons that touched nose to tail filling the yard, and through the gate to the roadside. We got a good few looks from those that would've stopped me if I'd been on my own.

– Your father's away arranging the lease for the fair, James told me.

We came to the whirligig carriage first and he slowed his pace beside it, looking round as though he'd lost something, before squeezing my hand and walking us on.

– Hurry, he said, as if I'd given him cause to stop.

A little further, he paused a second time at the carriage that housed the lions, but still his ear was bent towards Dog Row. With a flick of his hand, he lifted the canvas at the rear and leant against the cage bars so that Mary's head slipped from the sling and fell between them. I put out a hand to cradle her, but my uncle got to her first.

– Don't worry, they're dozing, he said, nodding at three idle beasts lying in a dark corner of the cage; he turned to me then, as though remembering something. Did you ever hear of the trick Joe Bell once played? It happened before you were born. It's hard to imagine now, but his first boxing booth was just a square of dirt and a rope. He added the hoardings later so folk could only watch from the front and he could charge for the view. But the dodgers kept finding holes at the back, so one day he parked up the lion carriage alongside as a warning.

As my uncle spoke, he struck the bars with his knuckles and one of the lions snapped an eye open. I jumped in surprise and fell against the carriage behind me.

– There was a local girl, used to visit the almshouses, he went on. She wasn't too right in the head but she was the sweetest thing, full of joy. She was just passing one afternoon, not interested in the boxing. A lioness took a fancy to her, tore her face right off, it did. She was an awful sight after that, poor lass.

My uncle ran his hand along the bars and Mary stirred, though still he didn't move her. But the lion he'd disturbed now sprang to its feet and pounced towards us. I flinched before hearing the clanking of a chain as the beast reached the middle of the carriage and stopped. My heart thumped as though it might escape my chest, and only slowed once the lion sat again and dropped its head onto its paws. But my uncle had heard another sound and was already moving away. He began striding towards the yard again, calling to me over his shoulder as I hurried to follow.

– That girl didn't have a fair chance. I should've done the same to Joe Bell, cousin or not, stuck his head in the cage and see how he fared. I should've but I didn't. I wouldn't do it now as I've this one to look after, he said, lifting Mary out of her sling and above his head. I want to be around for her spreading her wings and I'll be no good if I'm hanging from a noose.

At the bottom of Dog Row he paused as he had before, and as I walked past him he caught my arm so that I stopped and spun round to face him.

– Your father's got the idea into his head that Dorothy's brother might be suited to you. I thought you should know.

He held my gaze for a moment, long enough for me to tell he wasn't joking.

Like it or not, Pip Bell has always been round about in my life, him being five years older and related same as Dorothy – though it was their father and my mother that were first cousins. Still, I'd not had an awful lot to do with him before the summer I was twelve, when I didn't know any better. I didn't know then either that he'd been taking his pleasure closer to home. The thought of lying with him again now sickened me.

– I don't know why I've just thought of this, James went on, as though to delay us further. But that balance ball I gave you when you were a child. That was your mother's. I don't know why I never said it before. Your father had no right ruining it like that.

I barely had time to consider his words before he turned me round, to see a figure approaching, pulling something behind him. It took me a moment to realise that it was Virgil trotting towards us, and that the sound was of his trolley wheels rumbling over the cobbles. At once my stomach lurched at the sight of him. When Virgil reached us he slowed to a walk and tipped his hat, beaming a perfect smile. He winked at me as he passed and then headed for the crossing, retracing where I'd followed him two weeks before. I watched him till he was out of sight, till I realised my uncle was trying to speak to me again.

– I was just saying, did you see his sack? It had RCD on it. Regent's Canal Dock. He must work at Limehouse. I've not been there in years.

– My father took me there once, I replied in a whisper, still staring in the direction Virgil had disappeared. Perhaps I'd like to see it again.

When I turned back to my uncle, I caught his smile and thought – is this the reason he brought me here, to have me follow Virgil? Does he mean for me to leave the fair?

It was then that the idea of running away lodged in me and began to take hold.

I stood inside my father's waggon and reached out to the walls as if they might tell me what to do next, though I knew in my heart that I was leaving.

Often when I needed to think, I took to cleaning the waggon – which I did most days when we weren't on the move. To the casual eye it would've seemed spotless, yet always I noticed some speck of dirt I'd missed in an awkward corner. I set about cleaning now as though I'd not done so for weeks – stripping to my shift before fetching a bucket of water and a brush. I started scrubbing the walls and floor, and used a footstool to reach the ceiling. I emptied and wiped out the cupboards, washed the cups and plates before replacing them; some of that china had belonged to my grandmother. I swept under my mattress and found the canvas bag I used for groceries. I vinegared the windows, polished the mirrors of the partition, and scraped soot from the runners on the sliding door. Then I found the stove blacking and spent the afternoon on my knees.

Sometimes I didn't feel it was me in those corners with my cloth and brush. My aunt once told me that before my father, a woman who'd taken in orphans had lived in the waggon. The partition weren't original, so it'd have looked different inside. Daytimes, she'd had them crawling over her like insects, my aunt said, and at night she'd tucked them in drawers or baskets, and slotted them onto shelves – the little 'uns up high, where the walls widened and the smoke and heat collected; they got the worst of the coughing fits but needed less bedclothes. There couldn't have been much room left for her to sleep. That was the story anyway. I'm sure that waggon held its past somehow.

I was crying when my father returned; I don't know what for. I was finishing round the back of the stove and expected him to bawl about it not being lit. But he just sat himself on my bunk.

– I'll make soup in a while, he said, though I'd never known him to cook.

He seldom sat with me either, and each time he did I was shocked by how quickly he seemed to be ageing – the darkness round his eyes, the greyness of his skin. I wondered what had brought this change in him now. There'd been a meeting, I knew that much. This should've been a busy month for us, yet we'd been laid up for the most of it. Uncle James had mentioned a few things; some of the bigger town fairs were in trouble, he'd told me, their charters threatened unless they could control the crowds. Country-folk were discovering trains, spending their weekends travelling pell-mell and panicking the authorities. The fairgrounds couldn't cope and the crowds were spilling onto the high streets in search of their fun. If the fairs were stopped, the crowds wouldn't come; that was the opinion of those that didn't want us.

We had our own problems too, father and I. My aunt's gingerbread had kept us in food and fuel and paid for the horses. But after my aunt died, my father wouldn't pay for any more ingredients or gather the extra firewood needed for the stoves, so I couldn't carry on making it. I was left just to clean the waggon and scrape together a meal once a day.

My father looked that tired now, I thought he might drop at any moment. He took a wine bottle from his coat and filled himself a goblet.

– Take a rest. You never stop. You're just like your mother was, he said, one of the few times he ever mentioned her.

I didn't look up, but gave the stove a final wipe before returning the paste to the drawer where my aunt had kept her bits and bobs; it was now stuffed with tools and lacquer for the coachwork.

– I should light the fire to fix the blacking, I said, but my father shifted along the bunk and told me to sit.

He reached to the shelf above him and from between two books drew out a folded paper. It must've always been there; I'd probably dusted over it a hundred times. He opened it now and handed it to me.

– You should have this, he said.

It was a poster with bold lettering, fragile and worn along the creases, so thin I could see light through it as though it were made of the finest eggshell. There were no pictures, but there was a mark at the top that I recognised from Dartford Fair. He took it from me again and began reading.

– 'Being for the benefit of Mister Freeman, twenty-fourth July, for one day only'.

The date of my birth and my mother's death; my father eyed me before carrying on.

– 'Mr Fanque performing daring feats on his steed. Songs of old from the Sisters of Limerick'. They were a fine trio, my father remembered.

He finished his drink and poured himself another.

– There were lots of other acts, tumblers from Astley's and trampolining and the like, he went on. But your mother was the biggest draw. She should've had top billing. 'Lady Mary Anne, femme on the high wire'. She borrowed your aunt's name, he said, returning the bill to me.

He fell silent then, and I studied the poster till he spoke again.

– I never wanted her to walk in her condition. I tried to stop her but she was stubborn. We argued, and she tripped and hurt her foot.

– But she walked anyway, and fell at the end? I said, and he nodded and gulped the rest of his wine.

– She was barely three feet above ground. I shouldn't have left her, but I was so bloody angry.

I stared at the bill a while longer, remembering the painting my aunt once showed me. Then I folded the paper and pushed it inside my skirt pocket.

– So you left her to give birth to me at a roadside? I said at last.

My father had closed his eyes now and the wine glass was slipping from his hand. I rescued the goblet and felt how cold his fingers were.

– I'll see to that stove, I whispered.

Nine

The day of our leaving, I was up with the dawn and the horses. They were skittish, sensing we were on the move. They'd become used to the unseasonal rest, thinking that cos we were at the yard again, they could relax now for a month or two, not just a fortnight. And it was always slow breaking camp from the yard – not like pulling down after a fair, blink and we were gone. We had to move each waggon out in turn to make space for the next to be loaded, and then wait till that was done, which made it worse for the beasts.

Since my aunt's passing, my father had been leaving it to me to pack the waggon, as he had the whole convoy to organise, to make sure everyone took their proper place in the order of the show carriages.

After taking Bess to the menagerie, I collected the hens into their baskets and secured them in the undercarriage, stowed the buckets and churns in the cratch, and the pots and kettle in the box below it. I slid open the window shutters and fastened them, removed the cowl from the stovepipe, and made the horse shafts ready. Inside, I cleared every surface into the cupboards and wrapped the best of the china in linen. I folded my bunk to the wall, wedged open the partition door, made the books safe with a rope across the front of the shelf, closed the hatches on the range and put a towel under the griddle to stop it rattling. Outside again, I raised the steps and checked the hens one last time, and as I stood once more I felt a blow to the back of my head. I turned and saw my father standing behind me, clutching the poster he'd given me the night before; it must've fallen from my pocket as I worked.

– Can't you keep it safe even for a moment? he yelled, tossing the bill onto the ground.

I felt a lump starting to sprout on my head, as I climbed back inside the waggon and noticed the bag I'd found the previous afternoon. I stuffed it with my nightdress, a blouse and skirt, a hunk of bread and cheese, and the poster from Dartford. I took the few shillings I'd kept from my takings with Bess and hid the bag behind the door, then returned outside to check on the horses. That's when I saw Dorothy loading her waggon, and I felt myself redden, felt sick in my stomach.

– I've hardly seen you these weeks, I called to her.

She turned to me but her eyes were distant.

– I've not been feeling well, she said flatly.

She continued tidying her baskets, so I helped her in silence till Pip Bell arrived with a strut, flashing gold on his fingers and stinking of the taproom.

– Just in time am I?

– To sit on your arse? I said.

– Not riding with us today then?

I shook my head and he made a face.

– Shame. Could've done with the company. Sis here's a bit down in the dumps.

Dorothy turned away when he said it. Company meant all manner of things to Pip Bell, so I didn't join them, though I wish I had for Dorothy's sake. Instead, I picked my way across the yard and met my father coming towards me, his arms laden with vegetables, looking like he was about to drop the lot.

– It's for that broth. I'll make it tonight when we're on the Heath, he said, as though nothing had passed between us that morning.

I rescued the load from him and carried it to the waggon. It took me a while to find a place for it all, such that I got to thinking again and had a moment of doubt. But soon my father was calling to me that we were ready to leave.

When it was our turn to move, my father set off on foot, inching the horses through the gate and nosing us towards Whitechapel. The other waggons had stopped on the roadside to let us pass, and soon we were at the front of the train. I wondered if I'd ever see the yard again; could I bear to miss it at Christmas, the smells and sounds of the Winter Fair?

I waited till we'd rolled awhile; I couldn't leave it too long, as my father would be stopping to sort the others into line.

– I think I'll ride with Dorothy, I told him, and he nodded without replying.

I threw my bag over my shoulder, stepped from the running board and began walking back towards Dorothy's waggon, which hadn't yet left the yard. But before I could meet Dorothy's eyes again, I turned and slipped into Dog Row. I walked past the doorway to the inn, along the outside wall of the taproom, and then without looking back I started to run. I ran till I could turn eastwards above the brewery – that great sprawl of buildings behind the high wall I've always wanted to climb. The smell of hot malt filled the air. It's a smell of my childhood. It stirred the memory of others that returned to me now: the smell of Bess – I should've taken her with me – her hot breath, her coat when it was damp, the dry turds in her cage after a summer's day on the move. The smell of my aunt's dead body, a bit like mushrooms. The smell of roasted chestnuts on the Waste.

Where the wall finally ended, I turned the corner and started heading south. At Mile End again, having run three sides of a square, I paused at the main road, from where I could just make out the rear of the convoy in the distance. It was only then, as I crossed the road without a care for passing hansoms, that I knew I was truly leaving, and I asked myself what I was doing and where I thought I was going. Another step and the convoy was out of sight; I was leaving it behind; I was running away to find Virgil.

– You for trade sweetheart? came a voice in my ear.

I swung round to face a boy – I'm sure no older than me – holding out a shilling, his eyes bloodshot and fixed upon mine, pupils like grains of dirt. I took a moment to fathom him, know that I should be elsewhere, before I started running again, hearing his laughter as I fled, each footfall taking me further from the convoy.

I had to pick my way through the back alleys of terraces till I found myself beyond Stepney Green. I'd collected a pair of children now, muddy-kneed from where they'd been tussling on the ground. They ran at my tail for a while, till I must've gone beyond the two or three streets of their neighbourhood and they tired of me.

Running kept me safe I reckon, amongst the press of folk in their Sunday best, though I turned a few heads and had one or two hands grab me. But none others gave chase, perhaps fearing I was being hounded by something worse than they. Eventually I came to St Dunstan's, to catch the last of the morning's worshippers leaving, and there I stopped running.

I found my aunt's grave easily enough, as even after two years it was still the newest in our plot, though the grass had grown high and there was no stone as yet. It was my father had to arrange it, but he'd barely spoken of her since she'd died. The graves round it looked untended now. I found what I thought was Jack Boothe's; I was sure it was his cos my aunt had said it only had a name, no year he was born or fancy words. I thought about his son, August Boothe. I was curious about him. I'd heard the odd story, though never from my aunt, and I often thought how strange it was – that I'd first met him the same night I first saw Virgil too. The second time – at my aunt's wake – I only saw him in the moment after my fire-walk, not before or later, not speaking to anyone, or drinking or eating.

I took a bite of bread, though it was dry and clogged my teeth, so I spat it out. I fingered Jack Boothe's stone one last time, touching each letter of his name, then as I turned to leave I spotted a flash of colour behind three stones that stood close together. I managed to slip behind them, and there I found a plain wooden cross as high as my knee, with no writing on it. The grass round it had been clipped short like a sailor's haircut, and the cross had a sheen as though it'd been lacquered. Beside it was a tiny vase holding a bright yellow rose, its petals open but beginning to wilt, its stem bending slightly as though seeking the sun. The vase was unglazed and looked hand-thrown. I turned it so that the rose caught a little more of the sunlight dappling through the oaks beyond the cemetery wall. It was then I saw the letters carved deep into the clay; a potter's mark, I thought at first, but surely that would be at the base of it. I took out the flower and flipped the vase over, spilling the water, but couldn't see another mark. I stood then, feeling chilled all of a sudden. I clutched the vase to my breast and looked round the graveyard to see if I was being watched, but there was no one now – just a hotchpotch of headstones blankly returning my stare.

I meant to prop the rose more carefully, but I grew agitated and desperate to be on the move again, so it fell over where I left it. I thought, what a mean act it would seem to whoever was tending the grave – stealing a worthless vase and casting the flower aside, but I took it anyway.

I left the cemetery to the south and I was back amongst the terraces, the rows upon rows of cramped houses with babies crying in tiny yards, women gossiping on their front steps, washing lines criss-crossing overhead. I ran through with barely a glance, street after street, holding the vase so tight I feared I might break it. Eventually I came to

Commercial Road, crossed at the toll gate, and then I could see the tops of the hoists and roofs of the sheds at Limehouse. It was here I'd once come with my father, and I recognised the puddled lanes that brought me at last to the Sea Purse on Queen Street, though the pub's door was now barred. Beyond it the road narrowed and ended at a footbridge, which crossed the lock that joined the Basin to the River. It led to the main gates of the Regent's Canal Dock, but they were shut too, fastened with a heavy chain, and there were no signs of life save for smoke rising from a guard's hut. I crouched on the bridge out of sight with my back to the railings, turned the vase in my hand once more before hiding it in my bag, and though I knew I shouldn't, I stretched out my legs and closed my eyes.

Ten

I don't know if it was the singing woke me, but I could hear it well enough when I came to, a lilting voice drifting from some way beyond the inn. I was stiff from lying awkwardly, damp from a shower that must've passed over, by the look of the clouds, so it took me a good while to rouse myself and get to my feet. I checked I still had my bag, the vase, that nothing about me was amiss, and then took a step towards the sound, not knowing where to start looking for Virgil.

I'd barely left the footbridge when the singing stopped and I heard the sloshing of water, the clank of metal, a door slamming. Passing the Sea Purse again, I thought of the evening five years previous I'd spent in its porch, waiting for my father. The front of the inn looked much as I remembered it, though dull without the crystal lamps lighting its windows. I couldn't recall the gate to the right of it though, solid timber, painted red. A barrel store, I decided, or the entrance to a penny gaff.

Near the inn was a lane, which my father had called The Opening and told me was a perilous place. It led to the River, to Narrow Street, and from it there now surged a foul smell that made me gag; what manner of shit and piss and rotting sea fare was causing it, I was loath to imagine. After it, terraces began on both sides, facing each other at a slant. With the quiet of the dock and inn, I didn't think it odd at first, the street being empty, front doors closed to the day. Then I noticed most of the houses were missing their windows – not just the panes gone but the frames too – leaving gaping holes like eye sockets.

There was only one house I could see that still had all its windows in place. I paused on the cobbles in front of it, my foot nudging a clutch of flower stems in the gutter. Then the rain began again, heavy this time. I should've knocked at the house; I would've at the fair – taken refuge in the first waggon showing a light. But I spotted a house across the way with no door, so I ran to it, getting soaked to the skin, shouting into the hallway as I stepped inside.

Other than an inn, I'd never been in a house before. I couldn't imagine having so much space out of the rain, though it wasn't so welcoming with the wind whipping through where the windows should've been, and the air acrid with pigeon shit. I only reached the first room off the hallway, the front room that faced the street. There was a simple hearth with the remnants of a past fire. The floor was bare earth and thick with soot. The brickwork was flaking and coated with white dust. I felt a wave of nausea rise through me from my gut. I realised it was my flow starting again, a sudden emptying – what felt like a whoosh of blood that was just a smear when I put my hand to it – and all I could manage was to stuff a rag there and wait for it to ease.

I know the singing brought me to this time, almost outside the window now, like a blackbird serenading.

– Roses, red, red roses, the voice came, over and over.

I was still standing, leaning against the brick opening through which I now peered. The sun was out again. The house with windows had its door open and it was from there that the singing was coming. I left the derelict and walked towards the voice. I could see a pair of legs poking out of the doorway onto the step and as I drew closer they began to twitch. If I'd been at the fairs I might've expected to find them unattached, such was our trickery. But it was a living thing making that sweet sound: a woman – very old she looked. She was sitting with a blanket up to her neck and a bucket of flowers at her feet, singing to the empty street.

– Roses, red, red roses, she trilled again.

I stopped before her and she looked up at me, sniffed the air, her eyes not quite meeting mine. She wore a scarf over her head that seemed so tight under her chin that it might hinder her voice.

– Will you buy a red rose, young lady, for your sweet beau?

– I've only a little money, I told her. My father calls me Rosie sometimes, though most call me Lucky.

She cupped her mouth as though to laugh.

– Well, you shall have a real rose dear, she said, reaching into the bucket.

She picked one, ran a finger along its stem to check for thorns, and held it out, but not quite to me. I stepped forward and took it, and thanked her. Her eyes jerked to the side and back again. Then I realised – she was blind as a newborn mouse.

– Lovely to meet you Rosie, she said, clasping my hand for a moment.

– And to meet you. Has it been a good day?

– Sundays are not so good, without the dockers, she replied, shaking her head and nudging the bucket with her foot.

I looked round at the neighbouring houses, all of them standing empty, like a row of abandoned nests.

– Being torn down for a bigger road, the old woman said, sensing my curiosity.

She didn't mention her own house. She beckoned me to join her, shuffling aside to make room for me on the step. I laid the rose beside me and studied the woman's face, though it seemed rude to do so. Her eyes roved as if following butterflies and her skin was so furrowed I could barely imagine how she might've once looked. She'd have some stories to tell, I thought. I'd met a few old hands in the fairs, but not many. "Old and blue at forty-two", the song went, though my great-grandfather had trumped that twice over.

– Do you sit here every day? I asked her.

– Every hour of God's daylight, except when he brings us rain, she replied, smiling as she said it. I hear all the comings and goings on weekdays but only rats farting on the Lord's day.

– Sundays must be lonely then. Have you always lived by yourself?

– I have the rats, she chuckled. I forget the others now.

– You must be well known to the dockers? I said, but she didn't answer.

How many of them she might know, I could only guess. She might recognise the fall of a heavy foot or a swagger, but she couldn't know them by their skin. If it was true that Virgil didn't speak, then no one could know him by his voice. If he still wore talc, like he had when I first encountered him, she might know him by his smell.

– Come, we need to get you into dry clothes, she said at last, though I'd not complained.

Her house was much better than the ruin, with plastered walls, clean stone flags, and a hallway smelling of lavender. She led me without feeling her way, into the first room, which seemed to be her bedroom. Its ceiling was so high I couldn't have reached it even standing on a chair.

– Find yourself something in there, she said, pointing to an ottoman beneath the window. I'll fetch us up some dinner.

– Please don't go to any trouble, I said, but that was her gone already.

I could barely lift the lid of the chest for the weight of it. From the smell inside, I reckoned it'd not been opened in a long while. The clothes were dry though, if a little moth-eaten. I found a dress that was too small, a blouse full of holes, and a woollen smock of about my size, which is what I decided upon. I got changed and laid my wet things over the back of a chair, then joined the old woman in the kitchen.

It seemed that she only had the downstairs; the floors above must've been someone else's, with an entrance round the back perhaps.

– Won't be long, she said, as I padded barefoot on the cold floor.

The kitchen was bigger than the whole of my father's waggon, with a fireplace you could step into and an iron crane for the kettle, shelves stacked full of china plates and knick-knacks, and cupboards for goodness knows what. The table was already laid with cutlery and plates, and a dish with sliced ham and a sprig of parsley.

She turned to me from the stove, holding a bowl of potatoes.

– Hope you don't mind cold meat? It's supposed to be summer after all.

Cold ham with potatoes. My aunt used to cook the same on Sundays and high days. Every winter she'd buy a flitch and try to make it last through to the next summer, cutting it first on the eve of our leaving Mile End in February.

After we ate, the old woman poured herself a brandy and we returned to the front step. The sky was pink in the evening sun, no sign of the earlier storm. There were occasional passers-by now – a pair of women arm in arm stealing into an alley, a gang of children beating a hoop along the cobbles, fighting for a turn. But otherwise the street was deserted.

It's never so quiet on the fairground, or in the yard at Mile End, or at any of the places where we stop. There's always talk to be had or overheard, an argument perhaps, folk practising their routines, the clatter of pots and pans in the endless rounds of baking, preserving, bottling – everything for sale, be it our finest fare or our skills.

I suddenly felt homesick for it, I suppose, though I didn't want to. But the yearning I had for Virgil was harder to ignore.

– You'll need to be up early to find him, the woman now said as if reading my thoughts, pointing a withered finger at me. You'll have to be at the bridge before it's light. They don't all come this way. There's a lane runs the other side of the houses, and another from the north.

I don't know how she guessed, but when she turned to me her eyes sought mine as well as they could.

– Why else would you be here child? You must be looking for some fella or other.

– There is someone, I began to say.

– Then I'm sure you'll find him, she said before I could finish. It's time I turned in, she added, looking up at the sky that was truly darkening now, as though ink was being poured upon it from above.

I helped her to her bed, though I knew she could've managed it herself. I was exhausted myself too, but I didn't reckon on sleeping soundly inside a house so soon, having only known a waggon before. So I found a coat in the hallway – one that was long enough to cover my legs and had a decent hood – and sat outside again as stars began to appear.

I sat for hours, my flow now a dull ache that I couldn't be rid of, till eventually the birds awoke and with their chorus came distant footfalls, before the first of the dockers trudged into view, their boots thudding inches from the doorstep. They passed like cattle, their jackets and trousers looking identical in the darkness, their soft chatter like lowing on the air; too early for bellowing or argument. Several must've seen me, noticed my face pale as the moon, but none made any remark, and none I could see wore Virgil's face under their caps. Eventually I pulled up my hood and fell in amongst them, following their trail towards the hiring, past the Sea Purse that was already open, candles ablaze in the windows.

Before the entrance to the footbridge there was now a heavy chain barring the way, with the front of the mob rammed against it and the crowd behind them arranging itself in untidy lines that stretched from one side of the street to the other. I could hear word going round that yesterday's storm had kept most of the ships at sea and there were only a handful of barges due, barely enough to keep a few dozen busy. Yet the dockers numbered in the hundreds, so most would miss out, I reckoned.

A man appeared behind the chain at last, carrying a crate which he turned upside down before climbing upon it. The crowd surged forward again, and the hiring began, the ganger pointing to the men he wanted, picking them out like beasts at market. It seemed random, I thought, but he must've had his favourites – the lucky ones ducking under the chain to be funnelled into the dock, the rest stepping back disappointed. It must be like this every day, I realised – so different to the fairground, where every man, woman and child has a job to do.

It seemed a treacherous place to linger, the press of unneeded men, stinking of sweat without a stroke of work done. Several headed for the inn; others huddled to while away the time till the next hiring. The early light gave shape to their faces, and it was a harsh sight. There were old and young alike, some looking drawn and spent, others fresh as the apprentices on the fairground. Bulbous noses, broken veins, skin scarred and scorched like crackling. Fair cheeks, a sparkle in an eye, a mouth with all its teeth. I caught the glance of a boy close by. He gave me a quizzical look, perhaps warning me that my clothes were scant disguise, that I should be gone before the day was truly upon us and others might notice.

I kept my head low as I inched round the edge of the crowd, pausing briefly at the Sea Purse. It was full now, the drinkers crowding from the bar to the windows. I turned and looked along Queen Street, towards a sea of men with their backs to me who'd seemingly given up already. It was slow following them. As I got nearer the flower seller's house I heard her voice again.

– Roses, red, red roses. Only a penny on Mondays. Will you buy one for your sweet belle?

She had three buckets at her feet, one already empty. Once in a while one of the dockers stopped and bought a rose, handed the old woman a coin and tucked the flower inside his jacket. A consolation for another day without work, to brighten the kitchen perhaps, or amends for some idle folly.

– You didn't see him then? the old woman called out, though I'd stopped several feet away to watch her.

I shook my head and approached, removing the coat I'd borrowed.

– They were too many, I replied, looking round at the hundreds of men still trudging towards the City. Where do they all go now?

– Home to their families if they have any sense. Some will return later. Come. Sit.

I joined her on the step again, using the coat as a cushion, and we sat in silence for a good while.

– I was a costermonger once. How about that! she began eventually, her breath sounding shallow. A few of us girls did it. Five o'clock every morning at the riverside. Load up the barrow, chat a while, find out whose thieving hands to watch out for, then down the lane to Shadwell. It was a bad day if I wasted a handful of fruit, the trade was that good.

She broke off for a moment to serve another customer, handing out a rose and brushing the thorns from where she'd peeled them into her lap.

– This was a wonderful street, right here, she went on. Every house was full. There were always children aplenty to cause mischief and run with each other. You can't imagine it now. We used to sling old mooring lines between the houses, tie them to the windows. All the children could rope-walk. We had a few arms and legs broken mind. Poor Louis was never quite right again.

– I walked on a tight-wire once, I blurted, interrupting her. I mean to do it again, now that I've no one to tell me otherwise. Wait, I said, rushing into the house to fetch my bag.

– You better be off again soon. It won't be long to the next hiring, she told me when I returned.

– Can I show you something first? I said, reaching into the bag and drawing out the vase.

– As well as you can to an old blind woman, she replied with a smile.

– I'm sorry. I know you can't see it, but here.

She took the vase and turned it over a couple of times. She found the opening, then the base and finally the inscription on the side, running her fingers back and forth over the mark.

– Where did you find this? she said at last.

– I was given it, I replied too quickly, feeling the blood rise in my face.

– Well it's a strange thing altogether. I can hear my father's voice as I read it.

She studied the vase a while longer, as if she could see it.

– *Mon ange,* is what it says, she whispered finally. *My angel.* But mind the time! You really must go.

She handed the vase back to me and turned away as another buyer approached – a maid clutching a folded parasol; behind the girl, in the distance, I could see the beginning of a crowd, returning for a second chance.

They came quickly now, thudding past the doorstep, close enough that I could've reached out and touched their boots. I put on the coat once more, pulled up the hood to cover my face, and took up my bag.

– Bless you, I said to the old woman, pecking her cheek.

I fell in alongside the dockers again, getting nudged by their elbows, smelling beer on several of them, hoping that by believing myself to be invisible, I would become so.

It seemed that a few ships had made it up the River in the calm of the morning, so there was now the promise of more barges and more work. Again there was a rush to the chain when the ganger appeared for the second time that day, stepping onto his box and scouring the lines of hungry men. Heads lifted and chests flared. The men that hadn't been favoured earlier had to show off their strength. I kept a good distance, squinting into the sunlight, pulling my hood further down. One after another, the men ducked under the chain or got turned away.

I almost missed Him then, his collar up and a cap hiding his face. I spotted him as he stepped from the red gate beside the Sea Purse; a moment later and I wouldn't have known where he'd come from, or I mightn't have seen him at all. I moved towards him but he whirled through the crowd like smoke, so quickly there was no chance of reaching him. He barely paused at the chain, nodded to the ganger and was gone over the bridge in a blink.

I suddenly felt without purpose amidst that anxious mob, so I slipped to the gate, tried it and found that it opened. I stepped through, and if I was seen, no one bothered to follow me. I closed the gate gently behind me and found myself in an alley alongside the pub. It opened onto a small wharf with a coal jetty – no tent of freaks or dancing girls as I'd imagined. From here I could see to the far side of the dock, where other piers reached out to the several barges that were now moored, some of them already crawling with dockers. But this part of the Basin seemed unused; I wondered why Virgil had been here. I reckoned he'd be working for several hours, so there was nothing to keep me. I'd have to return to the flower seller again and wait till the shift was done.

As I turned back to the alley, I saw in the far corner of the wharf a wooden lean-to propped against the wall of a larger building. It seemed out of place, like coming across a waggon where you wouldn't expect to find one. I looked round me, hoping I couldn't be seen, and then walked towards it. I put my ear to its door, peered through the only window, but it was curtained. I tried the door handle and it was unlocked. It didn't feel right to step inside unbidden. It weren't done in the fairs. A showman's waggon was private. You never entered without knocking. If there was a broom across the door, you didn't even knock as there might be sickness within, or a couple at each other's throats or in a cosy embrace and then it would be rocking gently. But in I went all the same.

The shack was cool inside and had a faint musky scent to it. After the old woman's house it felt no bigger than my father's waggon, though it surely was. Most of the floor was taken up by three chairs and an empty cable drum being used as a table. On it were a clean cup and plate and a candlestick with fresh candles. There was a sheaf of papers too, with a sketch at the top of the pile that showed a rope suspended over water. Below the window was a stove, and beside it a pair of walking slippers. I was certain now – I'd found Virgil's home.

At the back there was a narrow pallet with the bedding all neatly folded, next to it a sideboard with a wash-bowl and jug, a cutting board and knife, and a large earthenware pot. I lifted the lid and found a good amount of stew, the source of the smell. I dipped my finger. It was still warm. I found a spoon, pulled up a seat, and began helping myself. And that was me, my feet under Virgil's table.

Eleven

I awoke lying on the bed with Virgil standing over me. I must've fallen asleep after eating and slept the rest of the day – needing it after that restless night.

In my shock I opened my arms, Virgil giving me a puzzled look, and who could blame him? Then he smiled, which I was sure meant he recognised me. When I made to get up, he raised his hand and brought over a chair, and before he could sit I started babbling.

– I'm Lucky Boothe, I said. I'm from the fairs. I live at Mile End sometimes, in the yard at the King Henry. I was in the billiards room. I saw you on the tightrope when I was seven. You…

He put a finger to his lips and smiled again – a beautiful smile that made me feel safe, every tooth where it should be, each shining like a pearl. He took the pot to the stove, where he'd already lit a fire. Then he found a charred stick in the woodpile and began scratching on the flags beside the bed – six bold letters that I guessed must spell his name.

– Virgil! I said, as if I could read it. That's beautiful.

He nodded and sat beside me again. As close as he now was, I still couldn't tell his age. His eyes were so deep – like a well – that I could barely make out their colour. I could see his hair for the first time though, before having only seen him with a hat; it was black and wiry, with yellow streaks like tufts of straw that had blown in.

I took the stick and leant across him to score a line on the floor, then drew a figure above it and made a walking action with my fingers.

– I saw you on a rope when I was seven years old, I told him again. You're the only walker I've ever seen.

He sniggered, and then copied my movement with his fingers.

– That's it! You understand? My mother was a rope-walker too but I never knew her. I want you to teach me. It's in my heart to do it. Truly it is.

I thumped my chest as I said it, and Virgil put his hand to his own.

I couldn't be hushed then, though if he tired of me he never showed it. I told him about the time I first saw him, though not about Ellie. I told him about Sir Cooke, and when I described the band, I stood up and marched round the cable drum.

– They played like this, I said, miming the trombone. And then you came on stage, silent as a ghost. We all loved you.

I wrapped my arms round myself and Virgil smiled.

I told him about Bartholomew Fair, about the washing line and the balance ball, the emptiness after my father kicked it away. And Weston – the thrill of a real tight-wire – though I didn't say what my father did that time. I don't know what he made of any of it, but he seemed to understand somehow without hearing me, just as the flower seller could see things though she was blind. Perhaps he watched my lips, as Mme Rouge had said he might, or maybe he could hear a little after all.

By the end he was on his feet too, eyes closed, walking on tiptoes clutching at the ceiling. Then he bent and kissed my forehead and I wondered if he would linger, bring his mouth to mine. But he turned away and bounded to the stove to rescue the stew.

– Is it saved? Did I talk too long? I cried.

He didn't answer. He had his back to me still. When he turned I said it again and pretended to eat. He took the pot from the stove, removed the lid, and tipped it towards me, rubbing his stomach. Then he brought it to the cable drum and fetched me a plate and spoon from the sideboard. If he noticed there was less stew than when he'd left it, he gave no sign.

I watched his every movement as he ate, which he did with furious delight, head down, bent to the task. He didn't seem troubled by me, such that I wondered if he was often visited by strangers. I ate slowly and finished long after him, so it was then his turn to watch me. I could feel his eyes upon me, but whenever I glanced up he looked away, pretended to study the ceiling or the walls, but always with a smile ready on his lips. When I was done, he yawned and stretched his arms, straightened his back and lifted his head so his neck clicked like a series of locks. He piled the plates onto the sideboard but didn't clean them. From under the bed he drew out a blanket and a pile of canvas sacks, which he arranged on the floor at his feet. He was making a bed for me, I thought. But then he lay upon it himself, pulled the blanket over his head and waved goodnight.

I knew I'd been asleep too long in the day for it to come easily now, but I snuffed out the candles and crept into Virgil's bed. I'd have gladly made room for him beside me, opened my arms again and have him come to me. But it wasn't to be that soon. Yet, just being close to him stirred confusion in me, kindled a fire that Pip Bell had ignited two years before. As I lay listening to the sounds from outside – the wind howling through the derricks, water dripping into the dock – I churned with the memory of it.

It was the September of the year I lost my aunt, and as usual, we'd travelled to Oxford for St Giles. The fair was always rowdy and one of our best earners. On the Tuesday morning, the last day of the fair, my flow had returned – my fourth since starting three months before, arriving like clockwork, as the marker it would become to so many chapters in my life.

By the evening I was exhausted. My belly ached and my back hurt as though I'd been kicked, and I'd become short with Bess so there was little point in us dragging out our routine to the end. Then Pip Bell arrived, dressed to the nines in a tan suit and green shirt matching his eyes.

– All done, cousin? he said. Lots of fun to be had out there. I'm heading up the camps. You game?

I'd not spent much time with Pip Bell before, so I wasn't sure about going with him now. I was curious though, feeling a change in my body that I didn't yet understand.

As he waited for me to decide, Bess sloped behind him and nipped his ankle.

– That's it! I'm rescuing you from this crazed hound, he bellowed.

He grabbed my hand and pulled me towards him, as I yelped and he tucked his arm through mine. He led me onto the Banbury road, away from the fairground and Bess. The verge was dense with waggons and tents, and fires dotted in the scant spaces in between. The air smouldered with naphtha, like winter's glow on the Waste.

We passed a Dutch auction doing good trade and Pip slowed and rattled his coins, but must've thought better of it. Soon we came to a crossroads; Pip looked round him, then nudged me into an alley that led to a small green bordered by chestnut trees, with showmen huddled at tables under the branches. On the square of grass was a tiny stage draped with velvet and blanched with limelight. Pip left me for a moment and I lost sight of him in the gloom. He returned with a glass in each hand – my first taste of gin. I spat out the first sip, but the second seemed to dull my cramp.

– Ale, and now the hard stuff, he laughed. I saw August Boothe made sure you got a good sup at the funeral. Surprised your father let him come.

– I suppose he's a right to mourn. He's family after all, I said, but Pip huffed at that.

– I wouldn't have had him near it, he said.

– What do you know of him? No one seems to talk about him much.

– Only what I been told. He's Jack Boothe's son and it's reckoned he was born the same day as your father. He come from France when he was no age, shipped over with his father's corpse, and took to the Waste. His uncle Ned Boothe wouldn't see him starve, so he took him in.

– So he lived with my grandfather?

– He did for a year, thereabouts, so they say. You'll have to ask August Boothe what happened after, though he might not remember. You do know Jack Boothe was the older brother to your grandfather? August Boothe might just as easily have taken over the shows instead of your father. I'm sure he wouldn't lay no claim on it now though, but he might fancy claiming you, seeing he failed so miserable wooing your mother.

Pip smirked, pulling himself up straight.

– I'll go get us a refill, he said.

When he returned I tried to ask him more about August Boothe, but he was distracted now.

Sometime after the second gin I found myself squatting beneath the trees, staring out across a scrub. Not twenty feet into it, in a pool of tallow-light, a waggon was parked up with a woman sitting next to it. I could see her face from the side; her skin was black as oil, and she was fixing her hair that shone like gold. She washed her face with water from a horse bucket and set about doing her make-up, though it seemed she'd not even a cracked looking glass to see herself in. When she was done, she stood, and a dark fur fell from her shoulders. Under it she wore a white dress that was cut down her back to show her bony spine. I watched her a while longer, as she bent to fix one of her shoes, before she climbed into the waggon.

I found Pip again on the green, standing with the other showmen, toasting the success of the fair. Soon the lamps were put out till only one remained lighting the stage. There was a good deal of whistling as that same woman stepped from behind the velvet, swinging her hips as she crossed in front of us, carrying a stool as though it were a handbag.

Her mouth and cheeks were now rouged and her fingernails painted. Her eyes yawned, huge and brown like berries. She'd no music to accompany her, just a slow clap from the showmen. She was graceful I suppose, but oddly distant, undressing as if she was about to sleep, though she kept on her stockings and high heels. Then I realised she meant to tease the men, have them believe they could lie with her.

At last she stood, as good as naked. She moved the stool into the light at the front of the stage, swung her legs over it and spread them, showing her parts that must've had a dozen metal rings in them – a thing I'd never heard of, let alone seen before. She put her hand there and began moving it in time to the clapping, till the men started showering her with sovereigns and barking like stags. I felt a rush of heat between my legs and wondered at its meaning. And when the woman was done, when she'd turned and showed us her arse before leaving the stage, I turned to Pip – who'd watched it all without expression – as the last of the lamps was put out and we were plunged into darkness.

He bent towards me then, found my face and fixed his mouth over mine. He pressed a hand to my stays and the other where the blood was. My aunt's voice filled my head, telling me not to let him. Yet, I thought – I want this, and I reckoned Pip wouldn't stop whether I wanted it or not. We moved to the cover of the trees, the showmen's voices still close by. I lay on the grass and let him lift my skirts. He rubbed me again, smeared my chest with my blood and kissed me there; then he put it in me, his sticky hand stifling my cries of pain.

So it was that I began to learn the worth of my sex, what might be expected of me, and I made a promise then, that if I ever had to sell myself, it would not be for that.

Twelve

That first morning at the hut, I awoke to find Virgil gone and myself staring at the wooden ceiling a few feet above my head. I'd now truly slept a night away from the fair – not just stayed awake through the hours of darkness – and I felt excited that the threads of my old life were beginning to unravel, that I might be set free of my past that had so far only crushed me.

The hut smelt of damp clothes and old stew. The air was thick like a blanket, too hot to breathe. I opened the door to a haze of tiny flies like a storm of pepper, and stepped onto the empty quay under a cloudless sky. There was no one to be seen on the closest wharves across the Basin, but there were cries and shouts in the distance that told of plenty going on out of sight. I wanted to see the flower seller again, to thank her and explain where I'd gone. But I knew I should stay till Virgil returned. I was desperate for him to start teaching me to rope-walk, for that was what filled my thoughts now.

I washed myself, then tidied the hut, which took less time than my father's waggon, there was so little in it. I cleaned the plates, set the fire for the evening, made the bed and stowed Virgil's blanket and sacking. Then I sat with the window open and listened to the world going on round me. I could hear the noise of the Sea Purse, the laughter, squabbling and fighting, the smashing of glasses. I'm sure I could hear the second and maybe a third hiring too – a faint rumble at the middle and end of the morning. I wondered, however did they endure it, time and again having to turn away without dignity. Did Virgil have to suffer it too, or had he always had an arrangement? Did the foreman have Negro blood? A family connection perhaps.

Late in the afternoon, the hut door burst open and swung hard against the edge of the stove. I jumped in fright before I saw it was Virgil, struggling into the hut with a mattress and a bundle of clothing.

– You're home! I cried, the first words to pass my lips that day.

He looked pleased with himself, like a child with a winning ticket. I helped him put the mattress between the bed and the wall. He untied the work clothes that were wrapped round a pair of boots, pulled out a woollen jacket and held it up.

– For me? Thank you. But it's not so cold yet, I said.

As he lowered the jacket again, I heard something fall to the floor – a pair of scissors. I bent and picked them up, handed them to Virgil. He smiled and pretended to cut his own hair. I must've frowned, for he grabbed a set of overalls from the pile of clothes, shook them and held them to me.

– You want me to wear these? And you want to cut my hair?

He raised his eyebrows and nodded, pretended to dig in front of him.

– So I'll look like a boy and I can join you at work? I said, now understanding him. But when will you teach me to rope-walk? I cried, making the walking movement with my fingers again.

He sighed at that, drew imaginary circles in the air with his fingertip, then brought his palms together and tipped his head onto them three times. We'd need to sleep three more nights.

– Saturday we can rope-walk? I said, jumping like a clown.

He nodded again, but then dropped his shoulders and turned down the corners of his mouth.

– It's not so bad, I said. We'll work hard till then.

And it seemed only right that I should.

I drew up a chair and sat, my body rigid as though I was about to have a tooth pulled. But when Virgil took the scissors to me, his touch was as gentle and certain as my aunt's had been. My hair was matted and thick to my waist, and as he cut, the locks fell like dead branches, freeing me of the weight of my years. It might've shocked me more I suppose, had I let it. When he was finished, before he swept the pile of hair into the stove, I reached down and plucked a lock from the floor, twisted it in my fingers, then pushed it into my stays for safe keeping. I would keep it in the vase forever, I promised myself.

Virgil took a tiny bottle from his pocket, emptied it into his palm, and began to rub his hand through my stubble, massaging it gently as he did so. Then he fetched a lump of charcoal from the woodpile, drew it lightly across his fingernails and handed it to me.

– I'm too clean? I said. Not dirty enough like I've been working?

I used the coal to blacken my nails and hands, then rubbed them till most of the soot was gone but a stain remained. I tried the overalls, still wearing my dress, and they were a close fit, so I reckoned they'd be perfect by themselves.

Virgil took a step back and admired his effort.

– I look better now? I said, and he began patting his belly. And now you're hungry?

We made supper together – a broth of onions and potatoes, with fatty lumps of beef. Side by side, we peeled and chopped and tended the pot. When we ate, we did so slowly, watching each other, and I said little till we were finished.

– We make a good pair of cooks, I told him at last. I reckon you've had plenty practise, same as me. We're both alone aren't we? We only have ourselves. But perhaps now we have each other.

Virgil nodded, though I wasn't sure he understood this time. He gave a yawn and eyed the new mattress.

– Early to bed again? I said.

He had the mattress on the floor and was lying under his blanket before I could say much more, and it wasn't long till I heard a change in his breath. From where I was sat, I could make out every rise and fall of his chest. Eventually I lay on the bed beside him, listening to his and the other noises that came from the dock through the hours of darkness.

The next morning, I dressed in the work clothes whilst Virgil waited outside, his head turned away. I laced up my regulation boots, buttoned my jacket to hide my curves – though I wore no stays – and pulled down my cap to cover my eyes as Virgil had. When I stepped out of the hut, he held his arms apart and made a sound. *Lonnie*, is what I heard – the closest he ever got to saying my name – and I realised then, he did have speech of sorts.

– Lonnie it is, I replied.

I only had a few moments to become used to being dressed as a boy, just the time it took to walk along the alleyway beside the Sea Purse, open the gate and step into the hiring. It didn't feel so strange after the fairs, when as a young 'un I'd done the same to help in the chorus or replace an apprentice who was sick. But it wasn't so easy to hide my shape now I was older.

It was almost light and the day felt warm already, especially in those clothes. There were just as many dockers on the stones as before, and I was expecting every head to turn as we emerged, hundreds of pairs of eyes to fall upon me. But I was anonymous in my new garb, the same as any other docker – though I felt too slight beside them to be hired. I was sure I'd be left to fend for myself, turned away with the masses as Virgil flitted past as though winged. Yet suddenly I was on the footbridge, barely noticing the ganger, the chain, or any faces seeking mine. A blink and I'd been called on.

We filed into the dock area two abreast and were sent off to where we were needed. Virgil and I joined a crew of eleven others in the heart of the Basin. There was a coal barge already approaching and a hawser was thrown to us as we reached the quay. The air was thick with dust from the load. Virgil fetched up the rope several feet from the end and pretended to pull on it. He handed it to me, then fell in behind. I turned to see a third man lumbering from the crew to join us, his gaze fixed upon me.

– Name's Donald, he called out for my benefit, his voice as oily as the dock.

He was a great slab of a man, his face rough with pockmarks, his shoulders twice the width of mine. I had to turn away to avoid his eye and I didn't tell him my name.

We began hauling in the first barge, three of us to each of the two ropes. Virgil showed me how best to stand and grip the rope. The other half of the crew moved along the quay to haul another barge, the last man watching over us. When the boats were tied, a dozen or so other men clambered aboard and started removing the goods. I soon learnt that for every sort of cargo – coal or timber or bricks – there was a different crew that hauled it out from the hold. There were others still who loaded the ships moored out on the River, and foremen that ran the landing stages and stores. We were at the bottom of the heap, easily replaced if we fell by the way. Virgil seemed to know most of them though, whatever their trade, and they all had their own means of communicating with him – the cocking of a head, a hand signal, a raised eyebrow.

We landed dozens of barges on my first day, losing half of our crew in the afternoon, so we had to work twice as hard till dusk. By the end of it, my hands were covered with slime and muck, and raw from the tiny barnacles on the ropes that had ripped my skin with each pull, like splinters of glass.

It was a strain on the rest of my body too, the wrenching at my neck and shoulders, though my forearms didn't fare so badly, perhaps cos of all the use they'd had, scrubbing and painting my father's waggon. And it was stifling wearing so many clothes, but I was afraid to remove my jacket for fear of revealing my sex.

It felt odd not to be stared at, or at least only by Donald. So often in recent months, whether performing with Bess or walking through Mile End, I'd felt the gaze of others, as though it was my duty to give them something. But now being dressed as a boy, I found I could hide, and to begin with I enjoyed it. Yet I knew my destiny was to walk the rope inside a great tent, like Virgil, or across a fairground like my mother, to be caught in the spotlight with nowhere to turn.

My whole body ached as I walked home that first evening; I'd never worked so hard before. Virgil seemed full of energy alongside my feeble self, but I guessed he would tire again soon after eating. He set about lighting the stove and I washed at the sideboard whilst he kept his back turned. As he started on the supper, I lay in my shift trying to cool down. The next I remember, it was dawn. Virgil was dressed ready for work. He'd rigged a sheet as a curtain beside the wash-hand basin. I got up at once and kissed his cheek for doing it, stepped behind the screen and hurried into my work clothes, and gulped a forkful of the dinner I'd missed. Then it was off to the hiring again, as daylight was beginning to rise over the Basin, like stage-lights warming up when the naphtha is cold. Yet it wasn't smiling or painted faces that were found, but tired-looking ones, pallid, and already defeated.

This was how the days now blurred, such routine and drudgery that there was little to tell them apart.

Come the end of Friday, Virgil returned with me to the hut as usual. He lit the stove and tossed a couple of potatoes into the oven, but then left. I expected him to appear again at any moment, so I prepared dinner, tidied the hut and kept the stove alight. But he was gone till the early hours, opening the door quietly and creeping inside, lighting a candle that he shielded from me, though I lay awake still. He had a cloth bag slung over his shoulder and took from it a cheese round and an open bottle of wine, which he put on the table.

– Was it a good night? I whispered, but he didn't make any reply.

He slipped behind the curtain at the sideboard, and when he came out again in his nightclothes, he barely glanced at me before snuffing out the candle and slumping onto his mattress. I could tell from his breathing that he didn't sleep immediately, but turned over and sighed several times before I must've fallen asleep myself.

I awoke in the morning to find the door open and sunlight streaming in across my pillow. I jumped out of bed, fearing I'd missed the hiring, and ran outside in just my shift. It took me a moment to focus, squinting into the sun, till I could see Virgil at the wharf side, standing next to the trolley he'd had at Mile End, goodness knows where he'd brought it out from.

– Won't we be late? I called to him, pointing to the far quay.

When he saw me he shook his head and rushed over, hastening me back inside the hut.

– The docks are closed today! I remembered.

He nodded and smiled; I don't recall another Saturday when there was no work. Virgil looked anxious though, pulling out his shirt by his fingertips, pretending to have breasts, and nodding towards the Basin.

– You think someone might see us? I still have to dress as a boy?

He passed me a shirt and a pair of trousers, so I guessed I was right. He offered my work coat too, but I shook my head and tossed the jacket aside.

– It's too hot, I told him, pretending to pant like a dog.

I sat on the bed in a huff, pulling at the sheet below me with both hands, fed up already with having to hide myself.

It came to me then. I stood up and pulled off the bed sheet, folded it lengthways a couple of times, and wrapped it round my chest. Virgil looked puzzled for a moment, but then began rummaging in the bottom drawer of the sideboard. He pulled out a narrow bandage that fell from his grip and unrolled across the floor. He found several pins too and handed them to me with a shrug.

– That might do it, I said, pulling the curtain across so I could undress.

I re-rolled the bandage and began trying to bind myself, but it weren't so easy and the bandage kept slipping when I came to pin it. I peered round the curtain and saw that Virgil was still in the hut.

– Help me, I can't do this alone, I said, now maddened by the trouble of it.

He understood quickly enough when I stepped out and thrust my naked back towards him. I held the end of the bandage at my spine, brought the roll round my body and across my breasts, then handed it to Virgil. He pressed on the free end and began wrapping me like a mummy, as I took the roll from him on each pass across my chest. All the while, he held the bandage to my back with the flat of his hand. It was the longest anyone had touched me since that night with Pip Bell, and I tried not to recall it again – him kneeling behind me, his urgent thrusts making his belly slap against me.

I lost my concentration and dropped the roll, but Virgil caught it without letting go at my back. A few more turns and it was done. He pinned the bandage at either side under my arms. It felt tight, but not so that I couldn't still breathe easily.

– Now hand me the blouse, I said, turning to him.

I barely showed a swell when I stepped outside again, though there was only a lone guard in the distance to notice our effort.

Virgil returned to unloading his trolley. He drew out three poles and began lashing them together at one end. He beckoned to me and we lifted them till they were upright and spread like a tripod that stood a head taller than he did. Then we repeated it till we had two tripods standing a good twelve feet apart. His sack, it turned out, contained not a python but a walking rope, which he began letting out carefully onto the wharf. He tied one end to a bollard, passed it over the first tripod, lifted it over the next and finally tied it to a second bollard, taking up just enough rope so it hung slack. All the while, he worked as though with a precious silk, and I thought of him ruining his hands dragging those hawsers at the dock.

When he was done, he clambered barefoot up the first tripod and stepped onto the rope without pausing. At once he began moving as the rope did, swinging from side to side as it sagged nearly to the ground, shifting his weight and clutching at the air as though picking invisible fruit. Back and forth along the rope he went, never quite faltering but always seeming on the verge of it. I realised then that this was the source of his antics, the frenzy I'd seen him fake amidst the grace of his tightrope act. He practised with the rope slack – training at something harder to make his tightrope performance appear effortless. I wanted to call out and tell him that I understood, but I feared I might distract him.

He practised like this for an hour without rest, stripping off to just his slacks, and before my eyes he ripened in the sunlight, his skin dry but burnished like a ham glazed with the richest honey. His veins stood proud on his arms – not blue, but dark like the rest of him. I felt a yearning in my stomach, and it was only him finishing at last and waving at me to take my turn that calmed me.

To begin with I was too nervous to try more than a few steps, keeping in reach of the tripod in case I fell. It was so different to how I remembered the tight-wire at Weston. When I tried a second time, Virgil steadied the rope and stood at my feet to guide them, but still I kept close. Then he sat on the rope at one of the bollards so it pulled taut, and briefly it returned – the poise that had long ago visited me, which I'd rediscovered on the pipe at the Waste.

I was at it all day then whilst Virgil kept his weight on the rope, every so often lifting himself to ease the tension, till it was as slack as I could manage and I could walk to the middle without his help. I thought of Weston again, and Appleby – those times when my father had punished me; it pained me to think of the wasted years since, when I might have been following my dream.

*

Virgil left me again that night. I thought to follow him, but it felt wrong. So I minded the hut and ate the previous night's leftovers. As I sat in silence after eating, I remembered the pile of papers I'd noticed that first day. I thought – Virgil must've moved them when he found me. I'd always been good at hiding things in my father's waggon, and there weren't much more space in the hut, so I began searching. I tried the sideboard first, then under the bed, beside the woodpile, behind the stove, beneath the cable drum. There were no other cupboards or shelves, no trunks or suitcases, nowhere else to look, so I sat again, and as I did, I felt the familiar creak of the chair beneath me. I stood, took off the cushion and saw that the wooden base was deeper than I would've expected. I pulled on the front edge to see if it moved, and with a little force it opened like a lid to reveal a shallow box, holding Virgil's drawings.

Deep into the night I pored over his papers. There were hundreds of sketches of rigging and walks, a few in such tiny detail it was hard to fathom them. Some showed him inside wooden circuses and theatres so small the audience could've touched him. I decided this was where he went at night. I imagined us performing together one day, the crowd in love with us, hauling us onto their shoulders and passing us round.

I don't know how late it was when I lay down, but it was still balmy, and my own smell aroused me – a heady odour that made me want to quench myself with my own hand. At dawn when Virgil returned, I felt a longing for his weight upon me. But he didn't come to my bed that night either. I wondered how he thought of me – as a little sister perhaps, someone he should take care of and protect. Or was I simply not to his taste? Would he prefer a real boy? Perhaps I did seem just a child to him after all. Yet surely, I thought, we were not so many years apart that we couldn't share a bed and fold our limbs together.

As Virgil slept soundly, I tried to match my breath to his, that I might join him in his slumber, but I don't reckon I got a wink. When he rose again he dressed, cut himself a slice of black bread and a wedge of the cheese he'd brought home two nights before, and offered me the same.

– Hooray! No work on Sundays. So we can walk, I said, yawning and stretching my arms. How was the night? Did you perform somewhere splendid?

Again, he didn't answer that. He helped me with the binding and left me to change. Then we took to the quay under a sky as blue as I imagined the ocean, and practised on the rope all morning till I could no longer bear the heat.

– I know you could do this all day but I'm melting, I told him, fanning my face and pretending to faint.

He replied by moving his hand like a ripple upon water.

I nodded, grinning like a child.

– To the River, I said.

It was the first time in a week I'd left the Basin. There were a few folk wandering lazily on Queen Street, though not so many as to slow us. Just as at the docks, I found I could pass unnoticed, unremarked upon; a Negro and his companion is all we were and how we appeared to others. We passed the flower seller's but there was no sign of the old woman, and her door was shut. I felt sure that Virgil would know her too – you couldn't go that way and not meet her – but he made no sign of noticing her gone, keeping his eyes on the street. I took hold of him at one point, forgetting how I was dressed. It amused him I think, though he was quick to take his hand away. Then we came to the cobbled opening that led to Narrow Street, and for all that he might've understood me, I told him of how I'd gone there when I was nine.

I never asked my father why he took me that night. We'd arrived in Greenwich after seven long days travelling from Weston. We had a fortnight's lease on the fairground, but we hadn't a show on the first night. My father hired a boat across the River to the Sea Purse. He told me to wait in the porch and not go outside, whilst he attended to his business. He didn't drink back then, but whatever he was about, he'd not wanted me at his ankles. The lobby was so narrow that whenever someone came or went I had to press my back into the wall, else I'd feel a hand on me, or a face against mine.

It was probably only an hour, though it felt longer, when the pub started to empty and my father grabbed me to join the procession that swept us towards the River. It was like a circus parade – lantern-lit and with the men singing and rattling keys against their bottles – yet I don't recall hearing another child's or woman's voice.

The north bank was a stinking clutter of fish sheds and flour mills. Along the wharf's edge were dozens of wooden ladders that reached down into the River, all the way to the shore when it was uncovered by the tide, as it was that night. There was already a crowd gathering on the riverbed, round a circle of torches stuck in the sand like huge matchsticks.

My father nudged me towards one of the ladders.

– Get a good place. You might not get another chance to see this, he told me, though he'd not said what we were coming to see.

I felt every cold rung as I climbed down, every step feeding my curiosity. At last my feet touched the sand and my father pushed me on towards the front. I stopped at one of the torches and waited as the carnival raged round me. Eventually, on the far side of the ring, the crowd parted for a knot of men pushing two others with towels covering their heads. A cheer went up, followed by a sea of hands waving betting slips. Then the towels were pulled away and I saw that I weren't the only girl or woman there. Both the women were dark-skinned like gypsies, more beautiful than any of our womenfolk, looking delicate in the firelight. Their hair was as black as mine, but plaited and piled on their heads like nests of snakes. The men shoved them further into the ring, tore their blouses off so their chests were bared, and paraded them like sides of meat.

As the fight began I wanted to look away, but I just stood and stared, remembering my aunt's story of the lynching at Weston – of how she'd watched, unable to stop it. I saw every knuckle reach its mark, felt their blood spattering my skin, heard the snap of bone in their faces. I don't know how long it lasted, but they clawed and punched till one of them could no longer stand. Then the betting slips were in the air again, or hitting the ground depending on whom they favoured, and those who'd picked the winner turned to find the bookmaker. Still I didn't move, not till I saw both girls regain their feet; they were barely women after all. At once their eyes began to swell and grow dark, filling with tears as they nodded their respect to each other.

I never found out if my father took a bet. And if taking me had meant to be a lesson, to show me how I might otherwise fare in the world, then I was too young to learn it. Harder was the lesson at St Giles three years later – seeing how we treated our own, having our women splay themselves, that we might be filled with lust and set upon each other like dogs.

I didn't tell that last bit to Virgil; I only told him the drama of the fight.

Now, with the tide higher, it was hard to imagine one could ever see a beach down there. We stood beside the top of a ladder and gazed over the curve of the Pool, the water glimmering like silver, as if a giant had laid a cutlass before us. Virgil pointed to the far side where a steamer was being loaded, and walked his fingers in the air.

– You want to walk across the River? I said, and he nodded, beaming at me. Then we shall do it together, I told him, clapping my hands together.

He clapped too, so I'm sure he understood.

– I promise we'll do it one day. Let's go home and start practising.

Cooled now by a breeze that sloped off the water, bringing the River's stench, we made our sluggish way back to the dock. As soon as we arrived we took to the rope again, as though we were late for work and had a foreman at our backs. Virgil walked a few times before letting me practise for the rest of the evening, till at last, in the half-light, I managed to walk end to end, and Virgil looked at me, his eyes telling me what they could see – that it was now truly in my heart to master the rope.

Thirteen

It must've been a month after I arrived – a Saturday when our shift finished earlier than usual – that I finally visited the flower seller again. The weeks had slid by so quickly, one into another. We worked for six days a week, every hour of daylight, and had only Sundays to practise on the rope. Virgil disappeared every Friday and Saturday night, so Saturdays at the docks were the hardest for him, having to stay awake for the shift after barely an hour's sleep and still be able to perform in the evening. At least, that's what I thought. I so wanted to join him those nights, to see where he performed and to learn from him, but he never invited me and I didn't wish to intrude.

– I'm sorry I've not come sooner. I don't seem to have much time anymore, I told the old woman, sitting on the step beside her.

She smiled when I said this, plucked a rose from her bucket – one with its bud still tightly shut. She checked the stem for thorns, as she always did, peeled off the two or three she found, and handed the flower to me.

– When I still had eyes that worked, I used to sit and watch my roses until they opened. Now I just listen, waiting for the petals to unfold. I would tell you how it sounds, but I can't think of anything like it. So tell me what you've been about sweet Rosie, all got up in those old clothes, she chuckled, patting my leg.

I told her about meeting Virgil, losing my hair to find work at the docks, binding myself so I could wear less in the heat and still look like a boy. I told her about Donald, the sense of his gaze boring through my spine.

– He'll be wanting his way with you. You should take care around his type. You might be safer as a girl after all.

– And how are you keeping? I passed this way some time ago but didn't see you.

She gave a heavy sigh, like my aunt used to whenever she was upset with me.

– I have my moments. I miss the odd day now and then. How are the flowers? I don't trust who I get them from now. Some days I don't sell a single one. I'm sure they're past their best when I buy them.

– They look beautiful, I assured her, and mostly they did, only one or two starting to wilt.

– And you're finding your feet on the rope? she went on.

I nodded, though I hadn't mentioned it, but I was getting used to her now; a blind seer, I came to think of her as.

I'd only talked about Virgil, and how hard the work was. I didn't yet think of myself as a rope-walker, not enough to speak of it. But the flower seller seemed to know. When she'd spoken before of the children rope-walking between the houses, she'd not said if any were hers. And she told me nothing more now; we just sat till the light began to fail and I knew I should be hurrying home before Virgil left.

The night brought a storm from the north and it felt as though autumn had already taken hold. I didn't hear Virgil return, but awoke at first light to see him beckoning me out of the hut, grinning and hopping from one foot to the other. He was pointing to a barge floating a little way off from our wharf – from the look of it, one of the old fleet that were moored at the top end of the Basin, ready to be scrapped. The storm must've broken it loose and sent it adrift. But someone had tethered it to one of our bollards, the night watch perhaps. The rope lay slack, trailing through the water, so Virgil set about retying the line, heaving it till it was taut. He changed his boots for slippers, stretched his arms, and stepped onto the rope. Without looking back, he walked the ten yards to the barge, twirling an imaginary umbrella, as casual as though ambling across the footbridge to the docks. When he reached the boat he waved at me to follow, but he knew I couldn't, not yet. He was at it all day then, and I watched him from the quay in wonder, crying out every time the barge moved and the rope fell slack.

A few days later the boat began to sink, till its front was resting on the shallow bottom of the Basin and its rear poked above the water like a duck feeding, becoming an odd focus for our imagination.

In the month that followed, I spent every spare moment on the slack-rope, as Virgil walked over the water to and from the barge. In those hours of concentration and repeated failure, I achieved just enough to stop me from giving up. Eventually my legs grew strong, I learnt to empty my head, and I discovered a new balance of sorts. Then one Sunday morning Virgil brought home a length of bamboo.

– For me? I said to him, reaching my arms out.

He smiled and handed me the pole, then led me to the quayside. He faced me, took a step backward parallel to the water's edge, then nodded at me to follow. I imagined I had a rope at my feet. I kept an arm's length from him, every so often letting out a gasp when I thought he might misstep and slip into the Basin. He taught me to take slow, deep breaths, to feel them in my gut and release them on every step. Finally he guided me from solid ground onto the rope, stepping aside at the last moment. Now there was no question of faltering, no quayside to step onto if I got into difficulty, just inky waters you'd not wish to dip your fingers in let alone fall into. With the boat half sunk and not moving, the rope remained taut, and Virgil took up the last of the slack by sitting on the line at the bollard.

I fixed my gaze on the rear of the barge. The boat's paint was peeling, and there was a long red curl at the tip, reminding me of a pig's tail. It was the tiniest thing to focus on, yet I stared at it so intently I barely noticed my steps, till I reached the barge and saw Virgil jumping with excitement. He followed me out and then we took it in turns, back and forth as I gained my confidence, till I felt I could do it blindfold, though I daren't try.

I was about to step from the barge one last time when Virgil stopped me and pointed to the flag in the distance. The wind had risen suddenly and shifted the wreck just enough to make the rope slack. Virgil shrugged and sat down at the stern, patting the space beside him. As I joined him he pulled me close and put his mouth to my ear, muttering through his teeth.

– So we wait? I whispered, and he nodded.

The sun made its first showing, peeking from behind a cloud, catching the surface of the Basin so it glittered like the Queen's jewels. I looked out over the canal dock, to the River sweeping away to catch the Isle of Dogs in its crook. There was little heat yet we sat peaceful in our solitude, all round us the hoists lying idle, the jetties empty but for echoes. Even the railway was silenced, the viaduct arches watching over us like dull eyes. But the lead works lifted the spell, the stark chimneys belching in the distance.

When the wind died at last and the barge was stable once more, Virgil got to his feet again. There was still some slack in the rope but already he was at the edge about to step off. Though he walked in fits and jerks he made it look as if he had a pavement at his feet, not a rope just two inches wide. When he reached the wharf, he tightened the painter and then waved at me to follow. I took up the pole and stepped out. He guided me with his eyes, fixed upon me, like an owl's. Thirty steps and I was with him.

The weeks passed in a whisper then, as I prayed for Sundays to come quicker, when I could spend every waking moment on the rope. And so it became a part of me, like an extension of my feet, a heartstring that beat through my body. I grew to love it as much as I did being with Virgil, though still I wished for more.

At the end of autumn I fell into the Basin for the first and only time. I was close to the wharf and swallowed a bellyful of water that should've been the death of me. I was sick for a week; it turned my guts inside out, and I couldn't work. I lay on the floor of the hut with my head over a bucket and my legs flailing like the tail of a caught fish, clammy with sweat. The fever turned my thoughts to the Waste and I began to miss the life I'd had there; I even imagined walking at the Winter Fair with Mme Rouge.

As I recovered, the north winds began to bite, and to sap Virgil's strength. I returned to work still spent and by the end of the week I was exhausted. It was then that we were hauling a barge, overladen with a shipment of salt, five of us dragging the hawser round a bollard to bring the bow close enough to lock off the rope. With every heave came a shocking crack as floating ice shattered round the hull. Our gloves had holes and each time we unpeeled our fingers from the frozen rope, we left behind some of our skin.

Always Virgil had watched over me from behind, till that day when his hands grew so cold that he had to release the rope and step away for a moment, moving in front of me. As we finished landing the barge, two of the others who'd been behind me slipped away so I was left with only Donald at my back. At once I could smell his breath and hear his groans.

– I need some more weight back here, he said, as he gave a final tug on the rope, so that it slipped through my fingers and I fell against him.

He growled and reached to lift me. As he did so, his hand found a gap in the back of my overalls, and then my arse. He fingered it as though poking for grubs in the dirt. Virgil turned at that moment but saw only Donald helping me to my feet and patting my back with a grimace. The docker tied the rope without looking at me again, and I wondered – was that all he'd wanted; was he satisfied now?

It made me yearn even more for the Waste and King Henry's Yard, barely an hour's walk away. Already it was two weeks into the fair. I pictured the gingerbread sellers squabbling over sacks of flour, the Aunt Sally owners sending out for more clay. I reckoned that Pip Bell would've already stolen a few fortunes with his hat trick – only a wily one could beat that crooked hand. Then I remembered it was Friday, that Virgil would disappear; I couldn't spend another night in the hut alone.

I finished my shift without any more attention and joined Virgil to collect our wages. When we came to the Sea Purse I waved Virgil goodbye as he turned into the alley. He looked at me oddly, till I pretended to sniff a flower and he understood. As he pulled the gate behind him, I hurried to the flower seller, in time to catch her turning in for the night.

– All done for another day? she chirped as I neared, though she had her back to me.

– I'm sorry I didn't visit last week. I've been terribly sick.

I'd been seeing her most weeks. I worried about her in the cold, and whether her suppliers were cheating her, though the stock worsened for everyone as winter set in. It was always a relief, too, to hear a voice that wasn't a docker's. I would take her whatever treats Virgil had brought home the previous weekend that we'd not eaten ourselves; today it was pickled gherkins.

We sat in her kitchen as usual. There was a faint whiff of tobacco and I asked her if she'd taken up the pipe.

– I had a visitor. Someone wanting something or other, looking for someone; I can't recall. Those thighs are tough as tree trunks now, she said, prodding my legs where I was sat beside her.

She spoke less these days; the winter was getting to her, I think. She served me baked potato, saying she'd already eaten, and afterwards I helped her to bed and poured her a nightcap. When her eyelids began to flicker, I pulled her blanket over her and wished her sweet dreams.

I opened the front door to take in the night air and at once caught a flutter of white scarf like the one Virgil had begun wearing. I knew it was his, and he was moving at a fair pace. I stepped back into the hallway and glanced at the flower seller in her bed, her eyes closed now, her chest struggling with each breath. I blew her a kiss, stepped outside again into the road and started giving chase – at last doing what I'd been putting off for too many months.

I followed Virgil the length of Queen Street, deep into Shadwell. The streets were dark and crowded, so there was little chance of him noticing me. Eventually he paused at a square lump of a building, with a painting of a clipper above the entrance. Then he carried on round three sides to a yard at the rear, where a door was wedged open and the noise of a busy kitchen spilled from inside. When he disappeared through it, I reckoned that was as far as I could go, and I might've turned back and been none the wiser, but for spotting a rickety stair clawing the outside wall. I climbed it to an opening into a darkened corridor. A door led into a long narrow room that was carpeted and warm. It ran to the front of the building before turning out of view. There were men in uniform stood smoking under a chandelier, rubbing alongside walls hung with portraits that could've been of them. I meant to keep from sight but another door opened and an old sailor staggered through it, a card dropping from about him.

– Bring me a cigar boy, he mumbled through yellow teeth before joining the group.

I picked up the card, turned it over – it was white with a gilded edge and had the same picture of the clipper as the sign outside – then pocketed it.

I peered through the doorway to see a dining room filled with tables, most of them occupied. The rope must be somewhere else, I thought. There'll be a taproom or gambling den where Virgil performs, maybe a secret gallery in the basement. Perhaps they string a wire to the neighbouring building and he walks above the street; I felt sure I remembered a sketch of that. Or was it across the rooftop? But then I saw him, bowling through a swinging door carrying a tray of crystal. He now wore a white shirt, black trousers and bow tie, and his scarf was tied flat round his waist. I expected to see his feet in calico slippers but instead he wore black leather shoes, like polished ebony. He stopped at a table in the middle of the room and served the men, who may as well have spat at his feet for all the attention they gave him.

As Virgil stepped back from the table, he turned towards me and quick as I could, I closed the door, wondering if he'd seen me.

I ran home in the rain, my heart filling with love at every step. At the hut I began searching Virgil's papers again, wondering if it was only in those pages and my dreams that he'd flitted like a nightjar between enchanted halls, alighting upon a silver thread, mining the seam of our lives.

All that I'd imagined now dissolved, its place robbed by the monotony of his work, denying his true calling. And I loved him all the more for his sacrifice, though I knew not for what he toiled.

I lit the stove and every stub of candle I could find, cooked a stew from every vegetable and scrap of meat we had left, and set the table. I took off my binding, changed into my nightclothes and waited. When at last Virgil returned, I showed him the card I'd found and threw my arms round his neck.

– I followed you. I'm sorry, I whispered in his ear. You don't have to hide what you do. I wish you were rope-walking instead.

He pulled away gently and smiled, and I thought he might sit to eat, but he put his hands to my waist, lifted and carried me to the bed, and laid me down, then lay beside me.

We lay till the last of the candles burnt out – for an hour perhaps, just watching each other. Then as the first glimmer of dawn broke through the window, Virgil reached towards me and carefully unlaced my nightdress. He rested his face against my breast so that I could feel the warmth of his cheek. He stroked my belly as though I was with child. And when he lifted his head again, he closed his eyes, and I could see how he might've looked as a boy.

He pressed his mouth to mine, ran his tongue over my lips, and explored my mouth as though he were entering my body.

We kept our mouths together, falling drunk with the taste of each other, till my lips were so bruised they felt like the softest of ruddy fruits.

At last I took Virgil's hand and moved it to between my legs. Carefully he parted my flesh and dipped his fingers inside me – as gently as he'd delved into my mouth with his tongue. Then he lowered himself onto me, inside me, giving the softest cry – the only true sound I ever heard from his lips.

We didn't rise that day. We made love in between bouts of sleep. We ate in bed the meal I'd prepared the previous night. We discovered each other inch by inch, slowly, without words.

Fourteen

Monday's dawn was grey as the River. The high tide delivered a fleet of lighters into the dock, most of them piled with timber. Virgil held my hand fast till we reached the gate beside the Sea Purse. We kissed – our lips still warm from our lovemaking. Then we stepped out into the hiring, and suddenly I felt myself being swept onto the footbridge in a surge of bodies. I barely nodded at the ganger; I wondered if he even saw me. I pulled on my gloves, headed to where I was told, and turned to find Virgil not beside me. I spun round towards the footbridge but saw only Donald and was pushed on. I panicked; Virgil hadn't made it through, I thought, which made no sense – surely they wouldn't have turned him away. He must've forgotten something. They would let him in at the next hiring.

A boy I'd not seen before took my place at the front of the hawser and I took Virgil's, ahead of Donald. Virgil was the only docker I ever spoke to, so now I worked in silence and never learnt the boy's name. I wondered if Donald would try it with him too. When we stopped to let the men unload the barge, we sat apart and ate our ration alone. I was sure Virgil would appear at any moment with an explanation.

I had the idea again that we should return to the Waste for Christmas. We'd watch Mme Rouge perform and stay till New Year, then say farewell and board a ship to the Indies. I knew that Virgil hated the cold; it would suit him better in the heat. Then Donald's voice boomed through my daydream.

– Get up wench, he said, which made my heart stop and had me on my feet and back to my post before he could repeat it in someone's earshot.

I wondered – how long had he known I was a girl? From when he groped me, or had he guessed before?

I could hear him behind me, grunting like a pig, dropping curses like poison. He jerked the rope to make me fall again, then pulled me to my feet. He plunged his hand down the gap in my overalls and between my buttocks, finding my cunny this time. He fingered it a moment, drew out his hand, and pushed me away.

He had my scent now, and I knew that like a dog he'd not let go till he'd had his fill.

In my head I started running through everything I needed to do the moment the bell sounded: go to the hut in case Virgil had returned; change into my dress, put my overalls back on over it, and pack my things; then escape to the Waste and get help to find Virgil.

When the shift finished at last, I took my wages and joined the men filing across the footbridge in the rain, muttering hopes of more work the next day. I watched till Donald had turned from sight towards Shadwell, then I slipped into the alley towards the hut. I found it untouched, no sign of Virgil having been there since we'd left that morning.

I'd barely lit the first candle and stepped out of my overalls when the docker was at the door. He must've doubled-back after the corner. I was too slow reaching for the key and he was inside before I could stop him. He locked the door as I should've done, and looked me up and down. He could see the binding beneath my open shirt, my bare legs all bone and muscle. Before I could reach the stove he punched my face, his knuckles breaking the skin at the corner of my mouth. He kicked my shin and landed another blow above my eye. I was shocked by the speed and force of it. He pushed me across the floor to the sideboard. He doesn't much care for how I look, I thought, as he turned me away from him.

– I won't fight, I told him, but that made him angrier, made him punch the back of my head, as though he needed my struggle to arouse him.

He pulled at my shirt tail, tore my underwear to one side, and grabbed me round my neck. I could hear him loosening his fly and I waited till he'd found it in his overalls, felt him nudging me.

I'd spotted the glint of the blade from where it lay on the sideboard. Remembering what I'd once seen Pip Bell do, showing off with an Aunt Sally that was really a scarecrow, I swept the knife into my hand and swung against the docker's grip to face him. Did he think I turned to him in pleasure? Perhaps, but only for the second before I found his stomach with the blade, stuck it in to the handle and twisted it up towards his heart.

At once my hand was warm with his blood.

I didn't meet his eyes.

He slumped towards me and I had to step aside quickly, not to be pinned against the wall.

I didn't wait to see if he stirred after he fell.

I wiped my hand on the bed sheet and gathered my clothes, money, the Dartford poster, the vase and Virgil's papers into my bag.

I left the hut dressed in my overalls.

I locked the door behind me and tossed the key into the drink, losing a glove with it.

At the Sea Purse a few dockers were loitering, deciding which inn to head for next. I nodded and they wished me luck, as if I was off out for an evening's stroll.

I thought to myself – he might live if I tell someone. But he would surely tell someone if he lived.

Fifteen

I felt dirtied from the docker's touch. And all too soon after making love with Virgil; would he even want to lie with me again if he knew what had happened?

I was too shocked by what I'd done to think of the rest of it right away, so it was a while before the guilt took hold.

I wish I could've taken my troubles to the flower seller. She'd have known what to do even without me telling her, just by the pace of my approach, the shortness of my breath. But it didn't seem right to do so, to bring that burden upon her. I knew there was only one place I could go.

My leg was in pain from where the docker had kicked me, so I couldn't run and hasten my escape. Instead, I shuffled along Queen Street, and for the first time since arriving at the docks four months before, turned north into those same puddled alleys that would eventually lead me back to Mile End.

With my limp and my broken face, I feared I might look like one of the waifs from the King Henry. So I kept my head low, and carried my possessions against my chest as if together they would make a talisman, a charm born of a handful of useless objects.

Commercial Road took a patience to cross, but it wasn't till I reached Stepney that I began to feel choked by it all.

Behind one of the terraces, I found an empty coal shed with its door missing. I stepped inside and stripped off, discarding the overalls, tearing away the binding from my breast – though I'd forgotten my stays at the hut – and put on my summer things that were too thin for the cold. I swapped the boots for my clogs and ruffled my hair, which had grown a little since Virgil had last cut it. I winced when I touched the bruises. Then the docker's expression as he fell swam through my mind, and I retched at the thought of it, my stomach twisting like an old rag having the last drop of filth squeezed from it, though nothing came from my mouth.

A mother carrying groceries and a baby looked in at me as she passed – doubtless taking me for a whore rearranging herself, though I didn't care. I was just relieved to be myself again, leaving behind the trappings of the dock, stepping out in my own skin and no longer having to pretend to be a boy; for all the time it would last.

The streets were bustling, candles in windows and doors open to the night. Stepney Green was humming too, with children at play and folk gathered at a brazier where I warmed myself for a while. I knew what they'd be thinking of me, half-dressed and battered, but not a word passed between us.

As I stared at the coals, I felt sick again recalling the blood on the floor of the hut. I prayed that Virgil wouldn't return and discover the body, then with a jolt I realised he'd be taken as the murderer if he did. I stepped away to the edge of the Green and vomited into the hedge.

I sat on the grass and closed my eyes – I'm sure it was only for a moment. When I came to, my bag was gone. I jumped to my feet and walked back towards the brazier, looking all round me in the shadows. I found only the bill from Dartford on the ground. I picked it up, folded it carefully, and tucked it inside my dress.

It was all I had left now.

I couldn't face returning to King Henry's Yard just yet; I needed to think about the story I would tell – why I'd left, where I'd run to and why I'd decided to come back.

Instead, I turned east towards Bow, limping my way along the Waste, looking for where it ended; the Winter Fair seemed to draw out ever longer each year, and there were far more stalls and encampments now than I remembered from before.

I didn't have a plan. I thought I'd wait for a day or two before looking for Dorothy and James – the only kin I felt sure would take my side.

There was less trading and fewer shows in these parts, but the encampments were packed along the roadside shoulder to shoulder, lively with chatter and their fires glowing in the mist. I walked till I was exhausted, not even finding the end of the Waste, then turned back again, wondering where to stop for the night.

It was music that drew me at last – be it fate or luck or whatever you might call it. I walked towards the sound and came upon a band playing and a child balancing on a plank on the ground as though it were a tightrope. They had a good sized fire, with a kettle beside it on a prop fashioned from green branches and a cooking pot stood on bricks in the embers. Behind them sat a line of rod tents in an arc – canvas stretched over bent poles stuck into the earth – one of them lit inside by a single lantern. Through the tent opening I could make out four bedrolls and a square of carpet lining the porch. A string of bunting gave the camp a homely feel, and beyond it all was silhouetted a pair of carts parked up back to back, their horses picketed beside a trough.

The band was a dozen strong and included two boys on tambourine and the girl doing her imaginary rope-dance. The children were the spit of one another, and of the drummer who played standing up – all with red hair in tight curls. It was the drummer who saw me first and gave a wink that I took to mean I could approach, so I stepped into the circle next to an old coloured playing the double bass. The tune was so fast I couldn't grasp the rhythm; it weren't like anything I'd heard before. Even the girl had a job keeping up, and I was breathless myself when the beat slowed and the band stuttered to a halt.

– Would that be a young scavenger I see there? Been in the wars by the look of it, the drummer called out in the lull.

The children all turned to me and I began to step away, but the drummer was beside me, like that.

– You're fine where you are lass, don't mind me jestin', he said, nudging my ribs with his elbow.

He took the wedge from the prop and lowered the kettle over the heat, then offered his hand.

– Name's Earl. Same as the black fella t'other side of you, just to confuse. The boys are Thomas and Michael and that's Frances. Reckon you're older by a good amount. The rest can tell you theirs in their own time.

– I'm Lucky. Lucky Scott, I replied, though I don't know why; I'm sure I could've said Boothe or Bell and they wouldn't have known me from anyone.

– Pleased to be acquainted, Miss Scott. Will you have yourself a drink? You look like you could do with one. And a bit of a clean up too. Those bruises are sure to come up nasty. Bring a cold flannel Frances, he told the girl.

It was their first time at the Winter Fair, and only their second visit to the City, Earl told me. He didn't mention the King Henry, so I guessed they'd not ventured there – Bow Road having plenty enough inns of its own. When I'd dabbed my face and scrubbed my hands, Earl offered me tea with brandy, which he made for the men too, and with their instruments put aside, the fire became the focus.

It was only Earl made any effort with me. I saw now he had a scar on his cheek that looked recent, and pale spots like freckles. The other men were tight as thieves, and when one spoke they all did, their words flitting between them like a songbird deciding where to perch. With nothing in my stomach the brandy went to my head, so I was glad when Earl dragged the pot from the fire and sent the boy Michael for bowls and spoons.

– There's mutton stew if you fancy. Two days old and the better for it, he said.

I can say that was the best stew I'd tasted since my aunt had died and it took my mind off my situation for a moment. Earl ate next to me and pumped me gently without seeming rude; he was curious was all. I reckon he would've taken me in, right there and then, but for me making up some nonsense about being engaged to marry in five months, on my sixteenth birthday, all of which was a lie.

– Well that's a lucky fella alright. But if you don't mind me saying, he's a dolt for letting you out like that, Earl said, nodding at my skirt.

This time he sent Thomas, the youngest looking, to fetch me a blanket from the tent; there was no sign of a mother, I realised.

In the firelight, I noticed the coal dust still caught in my nails giving way to a brown crust, and the sensation returned of my fist in the warm pool of the docker's stomach. I felt I might retch again but I stopped myself, thinking of Virgil instead, trying to hold his face in my mind.

– And how soon before someone finds you? Earl said, making me jump.

I knew at once what he meant, though he thought it for the wrong reason – seeing my hair, and watching me eat as though I'd not done so for a month. Prison might be where I was headed, but I weren't there yet, and anyway I'd be more likely put to the rope for my crime than behind bars.

– No one's looking for me. I live on the Waste too, I replied at last, then thought, they mightn't know we call it that.

I decided I couldn't stay there for the night, even if Earl offered. I couldn't let any of the men give up their tents, and I didn't want to bed down with the children and their father, though he seemed a good sort. So I readied myself to leave, waiting for a chance to slip away without having to say my goodbyes. But with dinner done and the brandy being passed round the fire, the band took up their instruments again and began a slow march that made me think of the procession to my aunt's burial. The boys sat either side of me and banged their tambourines. The girl tiptoed on the plank as though in a daydream. When the bottle reached me I tapped it with a stone for a few bars. Then I took a swig – not too greedy but enough to help me forget – and soon I was going nowhere.

I awoke sweating under a pile of bedding. It took a while to let go my dream and know where I was, to remember what had happened the day before. The children were still sleeping and there was loud snoring coming from outside the tent. I crept to the doorway and unlaced the flap, and there was Earl lying under a blanket speckled with snow, his head turned to the fire. I might've snuck away then but for young Thomas waking and seeing me crouched at the entrance. He went from asleep to full volume in a blink.

– We still have our Margaret's dresses. Pop won't throw them. You could borrow one if you wanted, he said.

He'd a cheeky smile on a face full of freckles. I thanked him and whispered,

– Are you performing today?

– We're only practising, he shouted, which stirred his brother and sister. A foreign lady heard us and said we're good, and I'm the best, he carried on. We're playing for her but it's a secret. I can tell you it'll be Christmas Eve…

– And that be all you can tell, his father boomed from outside. You'll be telling me age next.

– Fifty-one if you're a day, the boy said, and I could hear Earl chuckling.

– The lady reckons her mother worked for Bonaparte, Earl said with a yawn. But we don't believe everything we're told, do we Thomas?

I guessed their secret of course, though I soon realised it weren't much of one at this end of the Waste. From the moment Earl rose, and for the rest of the morning as the band crawled from their beds, passers-by called out to him, so it seemed he was well known already.

– Will she be walking blindfold?

– Does she need a good man to hold her hand?

– Will you be having a go yourself, Earl?

And when someone told him that the authorities had refused the lady hanging her wire above the main road, he cursed the English as killjoys.

– It's Madame Rouge you're playing for, isn't it? I said at last, and he admitted it was.

He asked how I knew her, so I told him about the King Henry Inn and Virgil, as there no longer seemed any harm in it.

– She's the best rope-walker I've ever seen. Good as born on it, he said, with a wistful look.

He tried to chivvy the band then. It was a thankless task bringing them together. He'd get them all in one place for a moment, then lose one who'd forgotten something or sloped off – or in the case of the cornet player, had lost his wooden tooth and couldn't play without it. And then others would drift away and he'd have to start over. As he waited for a third time he asked if I was coming too, and I weren't so coy to refuse.

I'd already donned a woollen skirt, blouse and wide-brimmed hat that Earl had brought me from his cart. Now he offered a fur coat – just to borrow, mind, he said, though I could keep the rest of it if I wanted.

We must've made a pretty sight when we finally set off, me in my new garb and all of us hunched against the cold, trooping single file like our waggons in convoy, the band tuning their instruments as they walked. After a few hundred yards we turned into a tidy square – one I'd never visited,

Tredegar they called it. There was a green in the middle ringed with trees, and houses on three sides, though not like some of those terraces in Limehouse with ash piled beside their doorsteps and shit thrown from the windows to swell the heap. These were tall and stately, with whitewashed brickwork and leaded glass. There was one with a brass plate beside the front door, with a picture of a three-masted ship.

–That be a stevedore's mark, Earl told me, when he saw me studying it. They're the fellas unload the ships at the docks. Rough sort, but they turn a good penny, as you can see.

I smiled to myself when he said it, till it took my thoughts to the docker again, and to Virgil being gone. Then Earl saw Mme Rouge entering the square and called out to her. When she reached us, Earl embraced her and I removed my hat.

– I think you know this here Lucky Scott already, Earl said to her. Reckon she could do with a bit of mothering.

Mme Rouge frowned and looked me up and down as though buying a horse, but said nothing, turning to the band instead.

– We'll try the polka first today. I'm still not convinced about it, was all she said.

She was dressed in ballerina's fleshings and a slim jacket like a ship's captain might wear, with brass buttons and gold braids. She had her hair under a scarf, which altogether made it an odd look, though I could imagine how annoying it'd be to have a stray lock fall against one's cheek halfway through a walk.

She turned and strode away towards an oak in the middle of the green. I spotted the wire then, a glint of silver that stretched for a good thirty yards to a second tree, and maybe ten feet above the lawn. The band followed her and formed up along the start of the wire, six to each side, and Earl beckoned me to join them.

Mme Rouge pushed a ladder against the tree, changed into slippers, and climbed into the branches with all the routine of arriving to work at a factory. Instead of a pole she had a cane and umbrella for balance. Once she'd readied herself, she gave a nod to Earl, who raised a drumstick. On the first note, she stepped out with such speed it was as if a crazed puppeteer was working her, much like Virgil's dance, only more so: a few steps forward, slide back a few, forward again, her progress slow but frenzied. And to think, when I'd first met her, I'd imagined her act would be sedate and ordered.

She had a few tricks up her sleeve – juggling the props and balancing them on her head. But her showpiece was a pirouette, and it was quite a thing to see. First she spun on her left foot and returned perfectly to her starting position. Then she did the same on her right. The third time she lost her footing and I reckon we all drew breath. But at once she snapped open the umbrella and held it like a canopy to stop herself falling, and gave a smile that would win over the toughest crowd and convince them it was all part of the plan.

As she continued, with the band's gaze firmly upon her, I turned a moment to the houses overlooking us, and caught a face in a window. I feared we might be moved on, but instead Mme Rouge started to draw a crowd. When Earl noticed he gave them a smile and stood straighter, keeping the music rolling, thrashing his cymbal and snare, and occasionally waving a drumstick at the band. Beside him, his daughter shook maracas, her brothers their tambourines, and two of the men, thin as poles, played cornet and trombone. Facing them, the others played mandolin, fiddle, tin whistle, hand drum, accordion and double bass. Quite the little orchestra, they were.

Despite the cold, several of the audience were now sitting on the grass, fetching out knitting and picnics from their baskets, so I reckoned this had become a regular spectacle. It took Mme Rouge two polkas to reach the far end of the wire, the band having to play louder the further she walked. I thought she'd be too exhausted to make the return, but after a moment's rest in the branches she set out again, and I'm quite sure if she'd had feathers she would've preened them first. She waved for more music and the band struck up with the opening bars of the first tune. Immediately she repeated her pirouette, getting her first two perfect but faltering again on the third, though she didn't try to recover now. She had a technique for falling, almost too quick to see – folding her legs before curling her body. There were a few gasps, but only from the children, which got me imagining the older folk were the same as took their sewing to the hangings at Newgate.

I did fall into the dock once – when it was the foul water that could've done for me – and several times from the slack rope, though only from a foot or two onto the quayside. But I knew it was different falling from this height, that it was enough to end a livelihood or worse. After all, it'd cost my mother her life.

I'd have run to Mme Rouge then, but she called out saying she wasn't hurt. She removed her slippers, struggled to her feet and began walking back to us, swinging her jacket at her side, her blouse torn open. By the time she reached us, her breast was almost bared and she was puffing so hard I thought she might faint with the effort.

– Perhaps you could follow me with your instruments next time. You need to practise that anyway, she said to the band. I might leave out the final turn, she added, drawing several nods from them.

She came to me directly now. I stood a fair bit taller in my clogs than she did barefoot. I wanted to congratulate her, especially for the pirouettes, but she seemed not at all like she had in the King Henry those months before.

– Think you can do better? she snapped, biting her lower lip so a prick of blood welled like a tiny bud.

– I'm happy to watch, I replied, which was only partly true.

– Well I haven't time to dilly-dally. I have to practise too.

I wanted to ask her about the grave at St Dunstan's, tell her about my time with Virgil, and about the flower seller, but she raised her hand and continued.

– I'll say this now and be done with it. I've no truck with your family, she said, loud enough that the band could hear.

Earl stepped to her and touched her arm, but she was going to have her say, no doubt about it.

– How is it in English: blood is thicker than water? So why are you not with your father? He's lying sick and the shows are in a state. He won't thank me for my efforts, but you might help him if you tried. Tidy yourself up, you could find a husband soon enough, though God knows what you've done to get a beating like that.

I felt the attention now of every band member and wanted to leave at once, but Mme Rouge had backed me against the tree. There was an uneasy silence as she picked specks of dirt from her jacket and fixed her blouse. Then a thought seemed to come to her, her chill suddenly thawing, and she took my arm, turning me to face the band.

– Forgive me all, I've been rude, she said. I'm sure you know already, this *mademoiselle* is Lucky Boothe. But let me tell you what you don't know.

I could hear Earl trying to interrupt, but she cut him off, and I avoided his eye.

– She might have the misfortune of being of that family, but her mother was none other than Mary Bell. Don't be shaking your heads. Learn some history. That woman was the finest ever on the rope. I never saw another like her, French or otherwise. Believe me, I'm a duckling with a game leg to how she was.

She turned and whispered to me then, and I realised I'd been holding my breath.

– Your father doesn't see what's staring him in the face.

I tried to speak again but Mme Rouge turned her back to me and set about her make-up.

I looked towards Earl, but he was adjusting his drum, and the rest were now attending their own instruments, busily cleaning and retuning them, perhaps as confused as I was by the twists and turns of Mme Rouge's mood.

I didn't feel a whole lot welcome then. So, as I'd nearly done the night before – such that I would've missed all of this – I slunk off without remark, a tear coming to my eye, though for what I didn't yet know.

Sixteen

I reached the Waste as afternoon was beginning to fade – fires being kindled at every corner, pine cones popping like Chinese crackers, tallows being lit and wicks trimmed. The memory of the previous day still haunted me; as I walked, I kept repeating the movement I'd made with the knife – in, twist, and up; in, twist, and up – as if a sickness had gone into my arm. I thought about what Mme Rouge had said; I needed to know how ill my father was. But I didn't yet feel that I was returning home, though this was the place I loved to be in winter, the only place I really knew.

I passed a family of chestnut-roasters where the children were readying their barrows for their night's trade. From a fire opposite came the whiff of boiled eggs. But what made me pause came from the next camp – the smell of gingerbread. To this day, it still reminds me of my aunt, and of Ellie, and makes my throat quiver.

All along the drag, folk were practising their routines – juggling knives and fruit, swallowing swords, beating ponies till they got their sums right; all of this, our life as it goes on without an audience. Then as dusk gave way to naphtha, the Waste became awash with public, and those clowns and tumblers and jugglers laid their caps on the ground and took to their matchbox podiums under the moon, preparing to delight – for one night only, only for your eyes. Till the next night, of course.

As I came closer to the King Henry Inn and its yard, I began to see familiar faces and I lowered my hat to hide from them. There was old Willie Bell, bathing the performers in the fleeting glory of magnesium and limelight. He'd worked his pyrotechnic magic since a boy, losing a thumb and finger to his craft; seventy now but still spry as his grandson. You'd think his skin was blacker than Virgil's, but it was just gunpowder that had found its way into every pore. He could barely see anymore, his eyes seared by his handiwork, so I reached out and touched his arm as I passed. And then lo and behold there was his grandson – I forget his name – running a hat trick; I was surprised that Pip Bell was allowing such competition.

At last I reached the yard gate. It stood closed and near it was uncle James's waggon, candles in the window. It was beautiful how he kept it, the oak all polished, the crystal lamps gleaming and the brass buffed. It was his father had carved the horse shafts, and made the steps I now climbed gently as I could. I tapped lightly on the side of the waggon till I could hear footsteps; the door opened, and uncle's face appeared in the lamplight. His eyes ran over me and showed his confusion, before his wife spoke from inside.

– Who is it love? Don't be letting the cold in now.

He looked at me as if to ask – Should I let *you* in? But I knew from his smile that he'd already decided. He stepped back into the waggon, and I'm sure Flo was on her feet before she saw me. She thrust her baby at James before grabbing me to her, putting her hands to my cheeks and frowning at my bruises.

– Well what a thing for the wind to blow in. Thank the Lord for that, she whispered.

Then my uncle hugged me too and told me to sit.

– I'll fetch you some soup, he said. The boys are all out. They would've been excited to see you.

The waggon was warm inside and smelt faintly of cloves. There wasn't a partition like in my father's: James and Flo slept on a bed that slid out from the end wall, the three boys had a bed roll that fitted underneath and Mary had a cot. The stove was behind the door, and the table was where my bunk had been in my father's waggon. Above it was a shelf with china and horse brasses, a set of books I'd never seen opened, and a photograph of James's brother.

– So you have a new hair style. That's how they wear it up City nowadays is it? my uncle said.

His wife shushed him. She's a good sort, slight and plain but with a mouth you want to kiss the moment you see it. My uncle did a good thing marrying her and taking on her children.

– I've not been in the City, I told him.

– It's certainly no work of any tonsorialist I know, he quipped, which made Flo huff again.

– You don't have to tell us what's been happening to you, Flo interrupted. But is that causing you any pain? she said, touching her own forehead.

– It probably looks worse than it is, I replied. I tripped at the docks, is all.

Flo clasped her hands and gave a sigh.

– You've heard about your father then? she said.

– I've come home to see him. Does he have a sickness?

There was a pause before James replied.

– Of a sort, though I'm sure he won't die of it.

– He has a weakness for the drink, Flo cut in again. What are your plans now?

– We've got a spare bowtop you can stay in, James said before I could answer.

Flo turned abruptly to her husband, but he shook his head.

– Dorothy's gone, Flo said at last. Not long after you left. She took Bess. Her waggon is still here. She's gone to a good place, but she doesn't want anyone knowing where she is.

– She'll want to see me, I blurted, but I could tell from Flo's expression it wasn't that simple.

– Joe Bell's doing good trade, better than the rest of us anyway, my uncle said, changing the subject, though not sounding pleased about it. Everyone wants to box these days.

And Pip's sold his hat trick. Taken up bookmaking instead. That's where the money is I suppose. A few changes been happening, as you can tell.

– But my father. He's still taking charge?

– He drove everyone out the yard, my uncle replied, rubbing his eyes.

– And you all let him? I cried. Did he have a gun or something?

James shook his head.

– He's ill, Lucky. He didn't cope so well with you leaving, though he'll never admit it.

– But you surely knew where I was. Did you not think to look for me? I said, in tears now, as Flo came to my side and put her hands on my shoulders.

– And would you have come if we had found you? James said, taking up his spoon and running it round his empty bowl.

He looked at Mary, lying still in the cot but her eyes wide open taking it all in.

– I've been rope-walking, I said at last, avoiding his question.

– How have you been getting on? he said brightly.

– I'm pretty good on a slack rope. I need more time on the tightrope though.

– I'm glad you've been practising. Best not mention it to your father.

– He told me about my mother, I interrupted. Before I left, he gave me a poster.

– There's more to the story, Flo began, but my uncle stayed her.

– It's good what you've been doing, he said. The Penny Theatre will have their backdrops up in a day or two. You should go and see them. Now let's get your waggon warmed up.

In the morning I tried to rouse my father. There was no smoke from the chimney, no sound from inside the waggon as I approached. The yard was strewn with wood and iron, as if a carriage had been wrecked and its carcass dragged round like wildfowl. His waggon was slumped alone in a corner, low on one axle. The veneer was unfinished from the summer, and now the damp was in and the grain split.

I climbed to the door and opened it without knocking, stepped into the gloom, the stench of drainage hitting me at once.

– 'Tis me father, I called out.

Since I'd left, he'd removed the partition and the shelf above it – without a care it seemed, the splintered remains and shards of mirror lying on the floor. My bunk was gone too, a pile of bottles in its place.

– It's Rosie, father, I said again. I'm back now.

I could see the walls were rife with mould. The cupboards lay open and bare. I tore the curtains aside and pushed open the window.

– Are you ill, father? I said, to no reply. This place can't be doing you any good.

I looked round for the besom but found only a scrap of wood that might do the job. I swept the broken glass to the door, then dragged out a heap of spoiled clothes, a pair of boots with no soles, books from the missing shelf, their covers torn and pages sodden. I found a penny loaf covered with mould, rotting vegetables and something growing from the woodwork. Some of it I threw from the window, the rest I took outside, though I wished I could've just upended the waggon and let it all slide out.

I slowed as I neared my father, and for the first time he stirred more than just to turn in his sleep. There was a sheet on the floor with bloodstains, and under it a chamber pot. I eased it out and took it to the front step.

– Don't look down, I told myself, which made me smile.

There were other pots, choked with piss and shit, and one seemingly just for blood and phlegm, as though it was special, and I wondered – if this isn't a sickness, what does my uncle think it is?

When I was done inside, I dragged the whole stinking lot into a pile in the yard, threw on some broken timber, and looked for the paraffin. I found the can hanging in the undercarriage beside the hen baskets, the poor creatures forgotten and starved to death. I emptied it round the heap and fetched a flint from the stove.

My father opened his eyes then and lifted a hand.

– Mary, that you? he said, a whistle in his breath, and for a third time I told him.

– It's Rosie, your daughter.

I reckon it was an effort for him to say anything at all, and when he did manage to speak I wished he'd not.

– I have none, he said, and shut his eyes again.

The bonfire was alight quickly enough, flames and black smoke rising like a curtain over the dawn. I heaped more rubbish from the yard, and threw on the hen baskets too, which my aunt had woven when I was a child. Inside and out I found all manner of my father's soiled belongings – all of it too damaged to save – and though it pained me, I burned the lot till the waggon was good as stripped bare. I'd have torched the waggon too, had my father not lain inside it. But I made do with scrubbing it again, top to tail as I'd done before. I borrowed my uncle's pail and he must've seen me a dozen times going to the pump, but it weren't till late morning that he came with food, though he wouldn't go inside the waggon.

– There's enough for you both, he said, handing me a plate of stew. That's a good job you done, he added, looking round the yard, but there was no keeping him.

I found another plate, one I'd not thrown away in my haste, and placed it over the food to keep it warm. Then I began on my father. He was perched now on the edge of his bed, in just a vest and the trousers he'd slept in, looking as starved as the chickens had, his copper ring almost slipping off his wrist.

– You needn't have tidied today, he croaked.

– Call it an early spring-clean. Bit of Christmas cheer. You know what month it is? What you reckon: fresh clothes, sort that hair perhaps?

He still had his suit, rolled as a pillow, and agreed to be put in it once I'd washed and shaved him, and changed him as though he were an infant. When I was done, I found a fork and spoon and shared out the stew, handing him the bigger portion. The way he looked at it, I thought he was going to pick it up and throw it against the window, till I realised that he truly couldn't face it.

I ate in a rush, then moved my father's untouched plate to the stove, before returning to his side and taking his hand.

– I want to go and see the backcloths at the Penny Theatre, I said to him, hoping it might perk him up. I don't remember them; I was too young the last time they were showed. I want to see the one of your wedding.

He gave no sign of having heard me, so I went on.

– I've been learning the tightrope. It makes me happy. I want to walk at the fairs. It might help the Boothes & Bells. I know things aren't good. I want to help you.

And I could've carried on. I could've said – I've wanted to do this since I was seven; I tried for a year but you stopped me; I tried again but you hurt me more than you can imagine. I could've said – things are bad on the outside; it's you who's let it come to this; we'll all of us fall if you just lie here and rot. But I didn't say any of that.

– Tell me, when were the Boothes at their greatest? I cried, loud enough to be heard outside.

I knew his answer already – his two years married to my mother, though he didn't say it. He just slipped his hand from mine and turned towards the window.

Finally when he did speak, his voice came as flat as a priest's.

– It should've been you.

I know that's what he said – he was sat only a foot away – the words he'd buried for fourteen years. I gasped, breathing in sharply as though I might swallow his words to make them unsaid.

– Is that what you wish, that I'd died instead of her?

He might've nodded. But I was already up and at the door – only saw him lift his legs onto the bed, lay his head where there was no pillow and turn his face to the wall.

– Why did you never bring my mother home? I whispered into the silence.

I waited for an answer. A minute. Another. But he was done with me.

I was sick for five days after, though it felt like a month – something bad in my father's waggon, Flo reckoned. She'd not wanted me going near it; she'd pleaded with my uncle to go instead. But it was only me that could do it, step into that filth and try to raise my father from the dead. Flo nursed me in Dorothy's waggon, sponged my forehead, and brought me dry bread on the fifth day when at last I could keep something down. It'd kept my thoughts at bay at least, having my insides worrying me in every waking minute – keeping my mind from missing Virgil and what I'd done to that docker.

I thought it odd there weren't even a hint that Dorothy and Pip Bell had lived in that waggon. Yet they'd done so since Dorothy was six, when their mother's body finally gave in to the drink. The bed was narrow and hard and I shuddered at the thought of Dorothy having to share it with her brother for all those years. There was a tiny stove with no space for a pot, a box beside it that could barely hold enough wood for a day and musty drawers under the benches at the table. There'd been a window at the back above the bed platform, but it was gone now and timbered over, so daylight only came in when the door was open. The canvas roof and walls were still in fair condition, but the undercarriage was rotted through, so it would need a deal of work to repair the damned thing.

I came good on Christmas Eve, still a little weak, but able to walk at last. I stepped from the waggon onto the Mile End Road in the clothes Earl had given me, carrying his fur that I intended to return. At once I found myself amidst a whirl of merchants and wives in their finery – taking their seasonal stroll before braving our dim alleys for the one night they did so together, when the merchants would feign their surprise at every turn, and the wives blush when recognised by a passing showman.

I walked amongst them for a while, till I reached the first of several wooden hoardings and knew I was in the right place. The backcloths each stood eight feet tall and twelve feet wide, and stretched backwards in time into the mist towards Bow.

For decades they've been made. Each cloth tells the story of their year, showing us as we really are, so at least our public might think better of us, know that we suffer just as they, despite our jovial airs.

As I walked into my past, I found the canvas from the year I'd turned seven and I paused to study it. I weren't pictured in it, nor was Dorothy or the Cookes's tent. It showed a red barn and a group of fairfolk working as farm hands, with pigs and sheep and a few of our menagerie beasts. In the bottom corner was a milkmaid with her back turned, bent to her work at a cow's udder. She had yellow curls falling over her shoulders, and I knew if I could've seen her cheeks they would've been rosy and rich as cream, for it was Ellie whom the girl was meant to be.

I stood there a moment longer, blew Ellie a kiss and then continued back through my years – only one of which was missing – till I found the canvas of my birth year. I was saddened to find it in a poor state. It showed my mother, though her figure was all but lost to the damp, and me as a bundle of swaddling that had turned grey. I put my thumb to my mother's face – which was bigger than my whole hand – and wiped the mould from her brow, but the paint came away too and I made it worse. At least her eyes remained undamaged, if much paler than they were reckoned to have been. I wondered – do I really share them? I've only the word of others, as always. And then I thought – is it in these brush strokes that my mother truly rests? Is it here I must come to remember her – not Dartford, the place of her death, but the Waste, where she lived out her winters as I've done mine, where she learnt her trade, where I was given life in a cold embrace?

I moved on to the canvas for the year before I was born. It showed my grandfather Ned Boothe laid out under a blue silk. It was better preserved than the others; better looked after perhaps. He had two cherubs at his side that I guessed were meant to be my father and aunt as children, though the boy seemed the older of the two. There was no figure of a wife, just two men turning somersaults and a third child skating on a frozen river.

The next canvas along, and the final one I looked at, was the one I really sought – of my mother and father's wedding. In the foreground stood my mother dressed as an angel, with the wings of a swan outstretched as though she'd just landed or was readying to fly. She was on a low rope, with my father stood on the ground beside her, holding her hand, guiding her as she passed over a child lying asleep. Behind them, watching over them, the wedding party was fading into the fabric.

I stared at the painting for a good while. I studied the ghostly faces in the background and tried to remember their place on the family tree. My aunt had described it to me endlessly in her stories, and I pictured it now in my mind. At the crown of the tree was John Boothe, my great-grandfather, and at the bottom was my brother, unnamed. I knew where some of the rest sat, but I could never remember them all.

I imagined them now as players in the Penny Theatre, jostling for position on the tiny stage. I read them their lines, directed their actions, so they retold my story as I wanted it to be: My mother was alive, Ellie and Dorothy were my sisters, my father and I inseparable; Virgil was my lover.

But to what end? The backcloths tell the stories so much better than I. And they tell it how it is so.

I studied the wedding picture one last time. I pressed my nose to the canvas, kissed my mother's feet. Then I leant back, drew breath, and spat into my father's face.

Seventeen

It was one of those days that never got lighter than old soup, with a drizzle that fell in the afternoon without promise of ever ceasing. When I left the hoardings I turned into the Waste once more, and soon I happened upon the encampment belonging to the Freemans – Flo's greater family that numbered in the dozens.

Their waggons were at close quarters with barely room to have fires to cook on, but between them and the brewery buildings that loomed behind was a clear patch of ground. With the light so poor, I almost missed the tower that stood there. It rose as high as a house yet was all but lost against the grey wall. As I approached I realised it was a tripod like one of Virgil's, and I felt a pang of sorrow, thinking of him still missing, cold and frightened perhaps.

This tripod was much taller though, with iron braces so you could climb it like a ladder. Where the poles met at the top was sat a triangular platform with a pulley attached. A wire rose to it from a winch at the foot of the tower, then turned level and disappeared into the gloom.

From a distance, I followed the course of the wire till it cleared the camp and briefly I could get beneath it. It passed above a riding pen I had to skirt round, and over numerous stalls I'd not seen before: a peepshow with slides from a Negro war, a tent promising the World's Smallest Freak, and a shooting gallery with paintings of elephants and tigers as targets. I covered my ears beside that one, the marksmen cocking their rifles and snoots at me.

Soon I passed a set of ropes attached to the wire to steady it, and I guessed this was halfway to the next tower, which I found eventually in another clearing with food carts and a huge brazier. So this was to be Mme Rouge's route, and I felt sure it was here that she would perform her pirouettes.

I moved on till I reached a third tower, where the wire came to the ground again, to a huge pulley block secured by a metal stake buried in the earth. I reckoned Mme Rouge's walk would be two hundred feet end to end. I knew what excitement it would bring, yet I knew also that I'd not be able to enjoy it without Virgil. I'd dreamed we'd see this together, but now I knew not his whereabouts and feared I'd lost him forever.

I left the third tower and eventually came to the band's encampment, finding it empty, the shelters buttoned against the weather. My fingers were almost too cold to work, but I managed to undo the rope that stitched the front of Earl's tent, and return the fur.

As I backed from the porch, I heard a voice that made me flinch.

– Can I be helping you? said Pip Bell, before he saw it was me.

– I doubt it, I replied, turning to face him.

– Ah! The stranger returns. Nice get-up. The hair's suiting you. At least, I think so.

– What brings you to this end of the Waste? I heard you're running a turf these days. Plenty of fillies on your books?

He ignored me and looked towards the tower.

– We've got ourselves a walker. Should make us a few bob. It's been a while since we was robbed of our last one, he said, relishing the words.

– That's what your father says, is it? My mother was a chattel your family lost?

– I hear you been cleaning up the old man, he said, not answering me. Bit of a mess he's got himself into.

– And no one has thought to help him. What else would you have him suffer?

Pip smiled as if I was joking.

– You're hardly one to be sermonising. I'm guessing you didn't find everything when you sluiced him out. I'll bet he's still lying on it. Stuck it at me good and proper the last time I tried to visit. And trust me that will be the last.

I realised he meant my father's rifle. So he had dug it out. I'd not seen it in years and thought it long gone.

– Perhaps he believed you'd come to rob him.

– Of what? He's nothing left. Even his pride's in tatters, his own daughter lost to him. And to think he once wanted me to have you, not knowing I already had of course.

He turned to leave and I called out after him.

– What about Dorothy?

He looked at me over his shoulder, his eyes narrowing.

– Don't want to be found, is what.

– So who's she hiding from?

Pip smiled again, as if everything I said amused him.

– She might be better left alone.

He pulled up his collar and tipped his hat at me, and before I could speak again he was gone into the murk.

I returned to the second tower as dusk was falling. The hours to midnight dragged as wintertide nights had never done. I don't know what made me so restless; the growing crowd perhaps, pressing against me as though I were a leaning post. They prattled on as if waiting for a juggler or clown, and I wanted to scream – do you not know how this woman has toiled for her craft?

Though I was grateful it was busy and I might go unnoticed, I still imagined eyes upon me, faces from the docks. I knew that a night as big as this would bring folk from far and wide, and Limehouse was but a stone's throw. It was that thought that lingered with me when at last a bell sounded and the crowd hushed as if the Queen's own beauty sleep depended on it.

Then a call was passed down the Waste.

– Steady on the wire. Girl walking, came the cry.

A fog that had fallen like a cold blanket was lifting again now, and through it I could see the wire swaying above me. There was a distant chorus of applause, the first strains of the band. Then more waiting, as I craned my neck like a fledgling, eager for what was about to nourish my eyes. Finally Mme Rouge stepped into view, and bunches of tallows were raised to greet her. She was dressed like a girl half her age, her feet clad in dark slippers, gliding along the rope as though it were oiled. She wore thin stockings that showed her legs, and a navy blue dress that from below was too short to hide her knickers – blue, white and red like a flag, but not of our Queen. With all her brazenness, I wouldn't have blinked had she been naked above the waist, yet the dress just managed to cover her breasts. To my surprise she had a balancing pole, a long one that looked too heavy for her, but there was no sign of her cane or umbrella.

Though we could hear them well enough, the band was struggling to keep up for the crowd all thronging round them, and it weren't till Mme Rouge paused at the tower that they strode in front of us. Earl was leading, his snare drum and cymbal now slung from his neck on a silk. The children followed, and the rest in raggedy procession, with the double bass player arriving on a cart and looking fairly put out by it.

She didn't dance as I'd seen her practise, but laid her pole across the tripod and stepped onto the platform for a moment. Then she stepped out again, now holding a red flag in each hand, to a cheer that drowned the band. A few steps and suddenly she were lit up, and so was Willie Bell, perched inside the tower like an ancient monkey, a magnesium flare sputtering in each hand. In the glow I could see Mme Rouge's silvery mask, her necklace of blue stones, her pearl earrings like falling stars. She had a ring of white flowers in her hair and her lips were as red as a whore's.

What a beauty to behold. Before the flare was spent, she made two perfect pirouettes to more applause. When she began the third, I swear the music stopped an instant and the band drew breath. But they cheered with the rest of us when she completed it with a curtsy and stepped back to the platform with a final flutter of each flag.

She didn't stop long before she was out again the other side of the tower, carrying her pole once more, moving to the beat of the next reel. She had her back to the crowd now, and like that first time I saw Virgil, she faded from view till she was lost in the smoke – just three minutes was all we'd had. The band fought to follow her and I'd have joined them, but the mob closed round me too quickly, eyes on stalks, hungry for the next distraction. I wondered what might satisfy them now. Surely not some common tumbler or a lame hog telling the time. More of Willie Bell's antics perhaps. Or the twins joined at the scalp, or a native showing the rings through her parts.

It came without warning then – a squall that blew along the Waste, bringing hailstones, upsetting the stalls and whipping tent roofs into the air like rags. We were showered with sparks from the brazier, and on the wind came a cry of panic. The crowd heaved towards the noise so I joined the push, and above us the wire thrashed like a serpent's tail, as though God's own hand had plucked it.

Through the haze I saw a circle of torches and dozens of arms reaching up, Mme Rouge teetering above, not looking down.

Another squall ripped through us, took Mme Rouge's legs from under her. She was in the air for the blink of an eye, then she was lost in a tangle of arms. As I pushed forward, all talk was of her having struck the ground; for all that damned crowd, they hadn't even been able to break her fall. A few folk reeled towards me with bloodied heads, caught by the balancing pole.

When I reached Mme Rouge, she was lying on the ground, eyes closed, surrounded by onlookers. It was all I could manage to get my hand to hers and grip her cold fingers for an instant before I was jostled aside.

Already the story was being told all round me, and with each retelling it changed: it was the wind that swept her off her feet; a guy rope had been cut; she looked up; she looked down; she panicked when a squib was thrown at her.

She's fallen, is all I could think. Madame Rouge has fallen. That's all that mattered.

Eighteen

I looked out on Christmas morning to see the Waste blanketed in a fresh fall of snow. It was enough to return me to my bed, till James came to me at noon with two plates of Christmas dinner and a pomegranate wrapped in ribbon. I got dressed into every stitch of clothing I owned, not bothering to rekindle the stove, and took the fruit and one of the plates to my father, thinking I'd return later for my own. But I couldn't rouse him this time.

Instead, I visited Mme Rouge in the old part of the King Henry Inn, where she'd been carried four flights to a mean garret overlooking Dog Row and left like a bird with its wings clipped. I knocked and opened the door a crack.

– Come in child, I've nothing left worth hiding, she said.

She was propped on a narrow bed close to the window, taking a sip from a medicine bottle, which she afterwards stoppered with a cork. There were no chairs, so I sat in the dormer beside her and glanced at the view – row upon row of chimneys spiking the grey skyline, the terraces humped beneath.

I handed her the pomegranate.

– That's sweet of you. Earl gave me a pomander, and he's bringing goose and all the trimmings later. They have to sail back to Ireland in a fortnight, for a wedding or some such. I'm missing them already.

– How are you? I interrupted, fearing the moment to ask might pass.

She huffed and looked about her room casually, but I could tell she was in pain.

– I would've liked a daughter, she replied, as though that had been my question.

She reached for my hand and turned it over, then took the other and ran her thumb across my palm, tracing the lines with her nail.

– You'll keep walking, she said, though I weren't sure if she was telling or asking.

– I hope so, Madame Rouge. I know it's what my heart wants.

She sat straighter then, took another sip of medicine and her eyes grew wide for a moment.

– You know, you should call me Nat. That's my real name. Nat Parkes. It's a wondrous thing, the rope. There's nothing quite like it. I'll be up and about in a week or two. I need to practise. I shall be crossing the Thames at Easter. Look, it's written on my hand, March thirty-one. No mishaps this time. I'll guard those bloody guy ropes myself if I must. Perhaps you'll watch them for me?

She seemed as wistful now as the first day I'd met her – different again from Tredegar Square. I wondered if she'd known of Virgil's dream to cross the River; perhaps she'd once shared it with him, just as I had done before he disappeared.

– I'd so love to have seen that first walk, I told her, betraying my doubt without meaning to.

– But you can watch me at Easter, she cried. Forget the first attempt; it was a disaster. Have you never been to Cremorne Gardens at Chelsea? You must go and see it at once. There's a fine view of it to be had from the bridge. I'll be walking at dusk, at the height of the spring tide, the biggest of the year. The dancers will hasten the night and all its thrills. Oh, to have my youth again. They'll be planning the flotillas already. You should see the river in flood. I couldn't do it on the ebb, too afraid of the height. Silly isn't it, those few extra feet making all that difference? But I can't help looking down. The water draws me in. The closer I am to it and the more there is of it to catch me, the better.

On she went, speaking ever faster, the gaps between sips growing shorter. She described the pleasure gardens with so much excitement and in such detail. She spoke more openly than anyone in my family – than any of the showfolk in fact – such that I wondered if it was cos of her being foreign, or just the medicine.

– I could teach you. Once I'm done with the river. That'll be my last walk, I'm sure. I'm getting too old for it. Fifty is too old, isn't it? I could be your agent and send you off around the world, just as I would've your mother. Did you hear of my compatriot, Mister Bleedin' Blondin, crossing the great falls in America? They say he can do it blindfold. How about that. They'll be hankering for a woman to try it next. You should do it, before some Yankee does.

To hear Nat speak, you would've thought her about to jump through the dormer and dance on the slates before sailing to the Americas herself. But I feared the truth of it, and guessed that she was buoyed only by what was in that bottle.

– I've never even walked for an audience, let alone across some waterfall, I said at last.

– Pah! You mustn't fear your public, she snapped. They're on your side. Remember, they come to be entertained, not to see you quiver and shy away with dull eyes. If that's what they wanted, they'd pay some wretch tuppence to pull them off. Where I come from, there's women that walk over raging rivers, hundreds of feet in the air, pushing babies in barrows and juggling swords. Alas, it's not such a good time in this country for us women on the rope. You'll have heard of that poor mother I'm sure? Lord knows how many orphaned, and carrying another they say.

I shook my head again, but she waved me aside.

– I have a suggestion, an *assertion* no less. You should take to the rope as a boy. I'll wager every man and woman from here to Worcester will fall for you. Only a blind fool or heartless mother wouldn't.

– I'm not sure I can do that, I began, but she wouldn't hear of it.

– Trust me, they'll gather you to their hearts. They'll want to keep you from harm, lamb that you are. All those hungry men. They might take you for a boy at first, but then they'll see the *femme* in you and wonder if they have the same in themselves, though they'll never discover it. And knowing they can't have you, they'll spill gold at your feet instead of their seed.

– There's something I need to tell you, I tried to say, but again she dismissed me.

– When you walk upon the rope, think of it as a dance, she said. But be careful not to *think* it. Imagine yourself as a strapping lad on his wedding night, leading the first waltz, taking your sweet beau by the hand, slipping your arm behind her. You have to move her, as you want her to be moving in your bedchamber when the night is done. So don't tire her. Take charge and play her. Left, right, left, right, that's it. You know, I must apologise for the last time we met. I hope you understand I meant well. But we have a saying, us girls. "Love weakens us." Take heed of that. You must give your public a chance to love you and believe in your purity. I don't mean us to live as vestals – God knows I've done enough loving for us both. It's how they see you that's important. *La perception*. When you take your bow and step from the rope, they should imagine you walking alone to your chamber, undressing modestly behind a screen, and slipping between white sheets never sullied by a stranger. Don't follow my example though, least not how you saw me on Christmas Eve, all trussed up like a harlot. Do you understand? We have a task, to tame the rope as your uncles might a lion. But we have no smoke and mirrors to hide us.

I thought of Virgil, how he'd seemed to vanish from the tent that first time I saw him when I was a child.

– He just disappeared, the day before I saw you at the square, I blurted, and she knew at once whom I meant.

She dropped her arms to the sides of the pallet and sighed so loudly she could've been heard from the taproom.

– I'm sorry for you, but he'll come back, I know it. You shouldn't worry yourself. He'll be gone to sea or digging a canal some place.

– He was with me one minute, then gone the next.

– They nab them, men like that. They say they don't press anymore, but I know what goes on, especially for the coloureds. I did warn you though, you'll find no loving. And not because he won't; he's just never been shown how.

I didn't tell her how we'd spent our last weekend together, but I asked her if she knew where he'd come from. She took more of her medicine before answering and soon she was slurring her words and her eyes were growing heavy.

– I don't know for certain. I reckon his mother was a slave, probably owned by a Frenchman, and likely the father. That's what I think, for what it's worth. Did you know, we both saw him for the first time on the same night, under the same roof? Do you think you can fall in love when you're seven? It's funny what we think goes unnoticed. And that cousin of your father's, watching you like that. You should be careful around August Boothe.

She was shaking now and I put my hand to her forehead.

– Sleep a while. I'll come again later, I told her.

She managed a smile and waved me away playfully. I took the bottle from her fingers and placed it on the dresser beside her. I tucked her in best I could, taking care not to touch those shattered legs that I knew would never again carry her down stairs, let alone upon a rope or wire.

– One day I'll walk the River for you, I whispered as I left. For you and Virgil both.

I couldn't face returning to the bowtop, so I walked instead. I trudged in the snow without purpose, and an hour later found myself rattling the door of the police station on Leman Street. I don't know why I went there – perhaps to tell someone that Virgil and Dorothy were missing, or to confess to murder, if that's what it'd become. I was fortunate to find it barred against the night.

I sat on a low wall in front of the station, imagining the fat Bobbies snug in their parlours with a good brandy and a niece on each knee, till a woman dressed as though for an expedition shook me to, telling me I couldn't stay there, less I wanted to freeze to death. I'd not noticed the chill, or my hunger, but I soon felt the benefit when the woman took me to a nearby house and gave me thin soup and flip without spirit. I asked after Dorothy, saying she was my sister and had our dog with her. She smiled and led me outside again, past the theatre that stood there, and brought me to the door of a bleak looking building of grey stone with few windows. My mood was so low that I didn't argue when she handed me over to another woman, very tall and curt, who showed me to a huge room with a ceiling so high I couldn't make it out. There must've been hundreds of narrow bunks, all in neat rows, most already occupied with grey lumps bent to the dead air. I wasn't questioning anything now, and accepted the bunk I was offered as though I'd arranged it all beforehand. But rest didn't come easily and I spent the night picking at whatever was feeding on my skin, listening to the wheezes and cries of the other inhabitants. For some their sleep was so disturbed I'd have wished myself awake, had it been me.

They woke us before first light, rapping our beds with a baton. We lined up to scrub ourselves and for a scoop of porridge. I soon realised we were all women, and everywhere I looked I thought I saw Dorothy from behind, but every time I reached out and touched a shoulder, it was another's face that turned to me. I asked a few of them if they'd seen her, but none gave more than a shrug or shake of the head.

We were put on the street at dawn – those of us that weren't caught by the priest who lingered at the door – and I set off alone through Whitechapel. At every inn and hostelry I asked after Dorothy and Virgil, causing all manner of confusion as to which was who, had they eloped, and were all three of them black or just the dog. The places I went, they would've bought my cunny time over, or cut my throat for it, but I kept alert and washed over the City as if wearing a baby's smile.

It was to no good end though, and to keep my spirits up I tried to believe what Flo had said – that Dorothy at least, if not Virgil, was safe and hadn't been sold into the service of some foul master. I thought – if she's happy, she won't welcome me finding her with nothing to offer but coming back to the fair.

I returned to the refuge in the evening, reckoning that as I'd survived it once, another night wouldn't hurt. They'd only give us a bed for three nights in a week before turning us over to the workhouse, one of the older women told me. Yet it felt like a dangerous place and I didn't speak again. The second morning I left before the gruel and walked to Finsbury Circus. The streets were just waking and I sat watching the carriages come and go, in the lame hope that Dorothy might appear from one of the grand houses. But it was only City gents I saw, hurrying to gloomy offices to escape another day of festivities. So with Nat's words in my head I set out, crossing the River at the Tower, rounding my back to the cold, and tramping to Battersea without stopping, ignoring the taunts, the grubby clutches of passers-by.

I reached the bridge by late afternoon, and after resting briefly I took up my skirts and fell in amongst the hansoms that were moving at a crawl, the breeze off the River clearing the air. With all the traffic, it weren't safe to stop at the middle of the bridge, but I did anyway – saw the spire of the pagoda rising in the slanting light, and peeked through the timbers at the ebbing waters and mud banks littered with debris and empty skiffs.

All the while I'd been walking, I'd imagined the gardens alive with the pomp of a Christmas Fair, a thousand gas lights caught in mirrors dusted with snow, absinthe booths warmed by tallows, a great platform of gowned and suited dancers whirling against the chill. Every detail that Nat had painted, I'd plucked from its spring bed and repotted in winter's night. But as I stepped onto the King's Road and was greeted once more with the stench of horse shit, I saw that the gates to the pleasure gardens were chained. Through the bars I could see the ticket hut boarded over, and a tattered bill showing a balloon ride and a figure on a trapeze. The pavement outside was busy with gentlemen, the women on their arms smarter looking than in the east. The men eyed the gardens too, perhaps remembering warmer evenings when other ladies had quenched their laps. I felt uneasy then; there might be a shortage of girls, I thought, or a greedy chap fancying a trio.

I walked towards the bridge again, and turned into a wooded lane I'd noticed running alongside the gardens. Not ten yards in, a gap in the trees led to the fence. The railings seemed too narrow at first, but I thought – I've managed it elsewhere and I'm not so grown I can't at least try. I only took two attempts, turning my body sideways, dipping my chin to my shoulder and folding myself through.

I stepped over an empty rose bed to a fountain – a broad stone bowl breaking the backs of carved goddesses – then crossed a central path bringing me to a circus ring. I guessed this was where they held the trick-riding, though now it was thick with leaves and rubbish.

Beyond it began a line of great elms that bordered the park, watching naked as Cremorne slept. The gardens were far from how Nat had described them in their colour and spectacle, in the full bloom of flower and pleasure. Only the pavilion with its platform for dancing gave a hint of summer's splendour. Despite its lustres and gas jets having been removed for winter safe keeping, the ironwork remained in all its intricate detail, and to the side of it, the pagoda rose like a wedding cake, each of its tiers held up by Gothic pillars, grey as the sky yet ornamented as finely as any of our shows. I climbed it to the highest terrace, and if eyes fell upon me then I didn't feel them. I imagined Earl and his whole troupe up there, performing a jig as Mme Rouge teetered above.

Looking across the River it seemed an awful way from the south bank, and I wondered where the rope would pass, or if it would be a wire, or if anything of such length even existed. Would it make landfall where I was standing, or at the riverbank perhaps? I climbed down again and went to the water's edge, picturing it at full tide, lapping the pier. I imagined the dancers waltzing, the cries of children from the boats, fireworks above the bridge, and the walker flinging her arm in triumph. Neither the band nor penny steamers nor the din from the King's Road could compete with the crowd's roar. Yet suddenly it weren't Mme Rouge I pictured, but a woman a third her age, less rouge on her lips, short hair showing her ears with their peculiar curl. As she stepped from the rope, she was mobbed by the crowd, pressing closer, eager for a touch. For a moment I felt warmed inside by the thrill of it, but then I felt ashamed to be imagining myself in Nat's shoes. If I could've willed it to be her once more, I would have. But I knew it was over for Madame Rouge.

I felt a hand on my shoulder, landing like a bird, curious but cautious in the dusk. My first thought – a hopeful gent looking for a tug. But then, with that tender squeeze, I knew.

– I spoke with Miss Parkes, uncle James whispered as I turned.

– Then you made a good guess, I said.

– It's not my first visit. I have a cab waiting.

He took my hand and led me through the gardens in silence, back past the circus ring, to a workers' gate I hadn't noticed earlier, which he said was never locked. He helped me into the hansom; it was my first ride in one and he showed me how to fold the wooden doors over our legs. Once we were underway, he spoke again.

– I'm sorry about your friend.

– It's not your fault, I told him.

– I'm sorry anyway. We need another walker. For New Year.

– What did my father think to the last one?

– He didn't get out of his pit to see her.

– And no one spoke to him of it?

My uncle shook his head and turned his face to the night.

– Will she walk again? I whispered, though I knew the answer already.

– You saw her fall, he replied, turning back to me. You've seen the state of her. At least she has use of her hands. She likes to write letters.

It was clear to me now why he'd come. He wanted me to be Nat's replacement.

– So, will you do it? he said, the hope of a child in his voice.

I didn't reply immediately. It felt too soon to be speaking of it, the wire still warm from Nat's feet being upon it. And now it wasn't just her shoes I'd be stepping into; I'd be taking her place altogether.

I stared out from the carriage and watched the City pass by. Several of the shop windows were decked with tinsel and coloured lamps; it gave them a hint of warmth that they didn't have at other times, though nothing so alive as the Winter Fair at the Waste.

– I have to think on it. It's not so simple, I said at last, turning back to my uncle. What would my father do if he found out?

James sighed heavily, as though he'd already heard too much talk of his cousin.

– The crowd on Christmas Eve was our biggest in years. I'm not standing by any longer, letting your father drag the fair down. He has no authority if he chooses to remain in that mess. And it's a chance for you. You can have Madame Rouge's pole and costume, and we could follow you with a net. But I'm sure you won't need it. I know you can do it, and I know you must want to. Why else did you come to Cremorne?

Why indeed, I thought, if not to see for myself what Nat had dreamed of – perhaps Virgil too – the very thing to which I now aspired.

I didn't speak for the rest of the journey, not till after we'd returned to the Waste and I'd eaten with Flo; she was just relieved I'd not disappeared for longer. James showed me to the bowtop, the stove already in and candles lit. I'd been turning it over in my mind, the rights and wrongs of it. I knew what James was offering, what it would mean for me on one hand, and to my father on the other. I realised then that my uncle had been acting against my father ever since that day at Bartholomew Fair, when he gave me my mother's balance ball. He was determined to keep the craft of my mother alive, despite everything my father had done to bury it.

In the end, there was only one answer I could give.

– I'll have three days to practise and the day itself? I finally asked.

James hugged me to him and kissed both my cheeks.

– You'll be perfect, I know it.

– I shan't walk the whole wire and you'll have to lower it, I added quickly before he became too excited. I'll only walk between two of the towers; you can decide which. I can't wear Nat's outfit. And I'd rather have a lighter pole.

– I'll arrange it all. I'm sure we can drop it a few feet. And wear what you will, though I'd say women on the rope are none too favoured at the moment, another reason why we kept Madame Rouge a secret.

– She told me I should dress as a boy.

– Then perhaps you should take her advice, he said, kissing me once more before leaving me to my thoughts.

Nineteen

It was a day less than a fortnight since I'd walked across the dock with Virgil, yet already it felt like another life. The days ahead should've been filled with joy, doing what I'd always dreamed of. But I knew this chance had come at a dreadful price – Virgil having disappeared, Nat lying broken-boned in a meagre bed, fooling herself about her condition. And the memory of that docker was now tightening round my insides like a noose, and I couldn't speak of it to anyone.

I spent the next morning finding my footing on a wire strung low between two carriages. It was short enough that I could get across and back in less than a minute. I always counted my steps now; I got good with time and judging how far away things were, how long and high a rope was.

Round midday it started to rain, a proper downpour that brought my practise to a halt and looked to be setting in for the day. I visited Nat again, grabbing a sprig of holly from the taproom as I ran through the inn. She looked wide-awake when I reached her, though she was staring at the dormer as if she'd been talking to someone sat there. The room was now full of her belongings, stacked untidily round the walls in all manner of bags and boxes. I perched on the edge of the mattress and poked the holly stem through a hole in the bedpost, as she took my hand.

– Did you like them? The gardens? she whispered.

– They're beautiful, I said, wondering who'd told her. Have you seen them at this time of year though?

She shook her head and reached for her medicine, taking a long sip before offering it to me.

– What am I doing! she cried, stopping the bottle and tossing it onto the bedclothes. Cursed stuff, confusing my head.

She didn't mention her walk again, or the River. If I steered the conversation towards her, she as quickly returned it to me, like a game of tag.

– So what will *Mademoiselle Lucky* do now? Start her own routine?

– They've asked me for New Year's Eve, I told her too quickly.

– Steady on with my hand, she said, as I tightened my grip without realising. But that's wonderful news. You'll shine, I'm sure of it.

– You're not angry?

– How could I be, she said, throwing up her arms. I'm happy there's a silver lining to my rotten luck. You shall borrow my pole and props, and all my clothes if you wish, though you might do better with flannels and a shirt from your uncle. I fear I was a little outrageous, dressing my cunt in the tricolour. Oh, but listen to my language. Forgive me, child.

– Perhaps just the jacket, I said softly. I can't thank you enough.

– Nonsense! You can do it for me. And for your mother, God rest her soul. Get up there and show them what they've been missing all these years. I can't bear to see talent wasted, and all for the vanity of a dullard. Forgive me again. It's this damn tonic talking. But your father was always an arse. You could help him if only he'd let you.

She grew drowsy, whatever was in her bottle starting to take effect.

– I'll say one more thing, she said. Perhaps I've already told you. "Love ruins a woman's balance." Indeed, the rope is not a route to fortune, it *is* our fortune, she added.

– That's two things, I started to say, hoping to see her smile.

But she was fading again, her eyelids flickering, gently waving her hand at me to leave her.

The following dawn, two days to New Year's Eve, I arrived at the tower on the edge of the Freeman camp, and found Earl's band already huddled at a brazier tuning their instruments. They greeted me with smiles, and I thought – what a queer turn of events.

I glanced at each of them before I spoke.

– Can we start with a slow waltz rather than a polka? I said, which made Earl laugh and clap like a seal.

James arrived soon after with a knot of helpers and a new balancing pole; two of the apprentices would carry the pole to the top of the tower and the others would walk below me with a net, he told me. He must've known as well as I that there were sections where they wouldn't be able to follow, but neither of us mentioned it.

As I climbed the tower for the first time, I felt a sickness rising in my throat as though a lump of suet was caught there, pressing on my windpipe. I'd never climbed so high before; the yard wall was the highest I'd scaled. When I reached the platform I realised they'd not lowered the wire an inch. I began to wish I had a rope round me, somehow attached to the wire. But I knew such a thing could snag or trip me. It might break my fall, but it might also snap my ribs or wrap round my neck so I'd be hanged. Nat's words came to me then and I imagined beneath me a river in flood, a watery cradle to catch me if I fell.

The band had to start three times before I plucked the courage to take a step. With my knees bent I gripped the pole at my feet, then began to unfold, bringing it to my calves, my waist and then my chest, like a strongman lifting weights. Finally I stepped out, too cautious at first, but then in time to the waltz, sliding a foot forwards on every sixth beat. I thought – I won't try any backwards moves like I saw Nat do, not at such height with just a flimsy net to catch me. And so Nat's magic waters ebbed and I faltered, and more of her words rang in my head: *Don't think it.*

I retreated to the tower, the wind behind me, and stood on the platform, waiting for my breath to slow. Suddenly the memory of my walk near Weston Hill when I was nine years old came to me – standing on the fork of the tree, the stiffening of my legs, the sense of emptiness as though my spirit had fled. I didn't care to remember it too often – falling at my father's feet, feeling the wind in the grass before his foot caught my jaw and then my spine. An accident, he'd later said.

Then I thought of Virgil, how perfectly he'd walked without hearing.

I signalled to Earl to play from the beginning and I repeated my routine of lifting the pole. I closed my eyes and for the first time felt a pulse travelling through the wire, a gentle thrum that stirred my soles. It came in waves, and after each wave was a lull, and in each lull I took a step. I felt my grip on the pole loosen, as if it were a flower I was loathe to crush. I can't say if my feet found the beat of the music again, but they discovered a rhythm all the same. Eventually I opened my eyes and I faltered once more, the pole dipping to one side so that I nearly dropped it; yet I was close enough to the second tower to lunge at it, and fall clumsily onto the platform, catching my skirt.

I had to rest a good while before I could move again, but eventually I climbed from the tower, leaving the pole behind, and at the bottom met James, who at once took me to the bowtop.

Later, when I'd thawed and the blood had returned to my feet, he asked me about the walk.

– You looked like you'd seen a ghost when you came off the tower. And you didn't say a word when I spoke to you. Could you even hear me?

– I don't know. But I know I was thinking too much and that did for my concentration, I told him.

– Well, for a moment you walked like an angel, he went on, looking like he might cry. Where did you learn that?

– I only remember taking a few steps. And I remember the wind, I replied, which was the truth of it.

He brought me the clothes I'd asked for, left me to dress as a boy, and then came to take me to the tower again. As I stepped from the bowtop, the feeling returned of being invisible, and I felt glad of it.

I walked several times more that day and didn't fall once. The next day I tried walking with a scarf over my eyes, but decided I preferred just to close them. And I carried on practising till long after dark, so that Willie Bell could test his flares.

After each time I climbed down from the tower – so James told me – I was white as a lamb and couldn't speak, and I wondered what sacrifice I was about to make.

Twenty

The year's last morn, I visited Nat again. When I opened the door I found her hauling herself from her bed on a leather strap hanging from the ceiling.

– Earl rigged it. It's to help me keep up my strength, she said gaily, looking surprised to see me.

I felt I'd interrupted some private ritual. I asked her if she'd seen another doctor.

– No bastard will come before New Year, she told me.

She'd two bottles of medicine now and every few minutes took a sip from each.

– So you have it all planned, I hope? I never did try it blindfold, except once with a fella on the Left Bank, but that's another story.

– How do you know about that? I asked her, though I guessed it was Earl had seen me and told her.

– The little things we think go unnoticed eh? she said with a smile. I so wish I could be there.

– Could someone not bring you down for midnight?

– I don't think I'm going anywhere for at least another day or so, not with this mess to sort out, she said, patting her bedclothes. I'll see the fireworks from the window and that'll do me. There'll be plenty more occasions to watch you, I'm quite certain of that.

– But you know I owe you everything, I blurted. You led me to Virgil after all.

– Don't be ridiculous. You owe me nothing.

– I'll come for you tomorrow. I'll take you to my waggon, and on Wednesday we'll go to the infirmary. My uncle will arrange it.

– Ah, yes. James Bell, she sighed. He's a fine man and he cares for you dearly. Now, mind you get some rest, and I'll see you again next year! You're going to be loved. You'll set them alight. Just remember – focus!

She waved me away, as she always did, saying she needed to doze.

– Can I ask one last thing?

She held up a finger and smiled.

– I happened upon a wooden cross at St Dunstan's.

She opened her whole hand then and raised her eyebrows.

– It was you who took the pot? she cried. Well I'm glad it was. It was just a silly thing I was given. But I needed to remember your mother. It brought it all back to me, meeting you in the inn. I just wanted somewhere to put my memories of her. I do love that churchyard. And truly it's where she belongs, not on some country lane, trodden by filthy cattle. Now, you must go.

I couldn't bear to tell her I'd lost the vase, and I didn't want to leave her, but I pulled another blanket over her legs, then took to the stairs – moving so slow I'd forgotten where I was going by the time I reached the bottom. The inn was already filling with merrymakers, though it was barely just getting light, and I knew it would only get busier later, staying that way till well into the New Year.

I left the King Henry and paused at the yard gate that stood slightly ajar. I could see that the door to my father's waggon was lying open. I stepped into the yard and found it otherwise empty. He'd been keeping the stove in the last few days, James had told me, and rousing himself in daylight, which was progress of sorts. I climbed the waggon steps and peered inside. It looked much the same as when I'd last visited, though there wasn't much left now to be put out of place. But it seemed he had come by a small bench, which he'd fixed where my bunk had once been – the only thing he'd done. It struck me then how final this made it, the changes wrought by my leaving.

I warmed my hands at the range. There was a pot of grey porridge, but I didn't want even a taste of it churning inside me for the hours till I walked.

– So you got your wish, came my father's voice, cold and flat.

He stepped into the waggon, his limp more obvious than he usually allowed it to show. He took off his cap, his once fine head of hair grown thin and greasy. I moved away from the stove so he could check on it.

– Can't you at least be happy for me? It might help our fortune, I said to him.

– It never brought anything but ill luck before, he snapped.

– Perhaps I can turn the tide.

– And risk your life for it?

– Why, do you think it of any consequence?

I had to ask him then; it'd preyed upon me so long:

– How many times did my mother fall when she was a tightrope walker?

He poked the ashes and took an age to reply, as though there were too many occasions to recall.

– Only the once I saw. And it wasn't really her fault, he muttered at last.

– Before it, when you argued, she didn't just trip? I said.

He faced me for a moment and I held his gaze, before he turned to the stove again and checked it a second time.

– Will you wish me well? Will you come and see me? I tried.

He riddled the ashes again, and put on more wood than was needed. As I watched, listening to his silence, it was all I could do to stop myself grabbing the poker from him and cracking it over his skull.

The wind turned in the afternoon, rushing in from the south as though from another season. I wanted to sneak one last practise without help. As I climbed to the top of the tower, it felt warmer the higher I went. In the failing daylight I looked out over the closing night of the fair – folk just awakening, starting to prepare for a final spectacle. Stalls were being uncovered once more, chestnut carts pushed into place, costumes dusted down from the previous night's antics – the last time they would be used before their annual repair, or retirement as rags.

I walked unnoticed now, with the fairfolk going about their business and no public yet to speak of. And with no net below me, no band to drown my quickening breath, I came to understand – a little late perhaps – that I had to make every step count. Practise or no, if I fell I might die, or end up like Nat in some dreadful state. I might be thirty feet above ground or at head height, but it should make no difference. I could be trussed in a ball gown or dinner suit, or naked but for a wig. The clouds might open and sunlight strike my face, or I might be part of one of Willie Bell's set pieces. None of it should matter, if I took every step as if my life depended on it.

And when the time came, I made sure it was no different to when I'd practised. A quarter to midnight, wearing cream flannels, a flat cap, jacket, white shirt and bow tie, I climbed the tower again, the Freeman boys carrying up my pole for me. I took a while to gather myself at the top. There must've been so much noise but I don't recall it. I remembered what Nat had told me – about the women on the continent with their wheelbarrows, about our duty to perform, to be the symbol of the crowd's fears whilst encouraging their desires.

But when I closed my eyes and stepped out, I cleared my head of thoughts. And it was not to any cue that I moved, as I heard nothing of the band. I knew only where to place my feet, to keep my legs slightly bent and my head up. I moved with each lull that cycled through the wire, felt the changes in the wind through the hairs on my face, sensed the firecrackers by the sulphur in my nostrils. Later, I learnt how close the rockets had flown, how brilliant the flares had burned and obscured me for the minute to midnight. So much for no smoke and mirrors.

When I reached the second tower, I opened my eyes and at once was assaulted by the sounds of the Waste. The church bells chimed the hour, fireworks exploded, and when I stepped onto the platform and raised the pole above my head, I heard the laughter and cries of children with no one hushing them. And once more I gazed upon that ribbon of life stretching east and west as far as I could see, from the King Henry to Bow, peppered with the glow of encampment fires, and naphtha lamps footlighting every tiny stage. And I thought – down there, in light and in shadow, all manner of life could be found. Always there were new joys, and horrors besides. Take three steps in any direction and you could behold unfathomable skills. They would seem so accomplished you'd take them as natural without knowing of the thousands of hours spent learning them. At every corner you could find wit and ingenuity beyond measure. And I felt a part of it now. Yet peer beyond the wrong canvas or waggon door and you might find discord, resentment or small-mindedness. It might last for a fair, a season, or an entire generation.

Suddenly I felt fearful of what lay ahead of me, the changes I would bring about by what I'd done. Then just as abruptly came the emptiness, the knowing that my elation – like Mme Rouge's medicine – could only buoy me for so long.

I needed the boys to guide me down the tower; I'd have lost my footing without them, I'm sure of it. Uncle James met me at the bottom and pressed me to him, and though I've always loved him as I should, I wished in that instant he were Virgil and so I spoiled the moment like a fly in good wine.

– You were magnificent; perfect, he told me, struggling to get his words out for all his excitement.

I pulled away too quickly, complaining that my flannels felt tight.

– I need to get out of these damn clothes, I said, like an ungrateful child, and at once my uncle's face fell, his happiness bruised.

But before he could say more, a garland appeared round my neck and I felt myself lifted above the crowd; it was the Freeman lads, bearing me on a bed of hands, much as they might a corpse.

In the light of the torches that lit the path to Dorothy's old bowtop, I caught sight of my father for an instant, but he gave no acknowledgement.

Inside the waggon, the stove was roaring. A flagon of port glowed ruby in the candlelight. There was a wooden platter with a whole goose swimming in fat and surrounded with vegetables, a basket of bread and a jug of gravy – all of it laid out on the table and decorated with holly. In front of the raised bed, hanging from a dressmaker's dummy, was a navy blue dress and matching boa, and a lace headpiece with white feathers. I knew at once who'd arranged it, and I wished all the good luck in the world to be heaped upon her, to speed her recovery.

The boys left me to change, though I could hear them outside keeping the crowd at bay. The clothes fitted as though tailored. I dabbed a little rouge on my cheeks, wrapped the boa round my neck so I wouldn't trip on it, and opened the waggon door to find James arguing with the well-wishers.

– Back inside for goodness sake, he said.

– I want to see Nat, I told him.

He took a moment to understand, then grabbed my hand.

– I'll come with you. You won't get far on your own.

Indeed, it took an age to fight through the crowd, my uncle leading and trying to protect me. There was no doubting my sex now, and at every turn I was accosted for an embrace or kiss, till it felt as if my cheeks were public property, such that when I reached the King Henry, I was near drowning in spittle and lip-paint. And I thought – if this is what success brings, I might prefer to walk in solitude.

The inn was bursting, every window and door thrown open and the horde spilling out like worms escaping from a tin. Even the ground floor of the old wing was busy with a dance; I felt sure we could fetch Nat to see it.

As I edged through the revellers, I realised I was now no longer being molested, and that to these folk at least – for all they'd not made it beyond those walls in so many days – I was just plain Lucky Boothe, come to visit her poor friend once more.

I lost James, so I took to the stairs alone, elated that I'd finally done a thing I could feel proud of, and had Nat to share in my happiness. As I bounded up the several flights, I thought of that day near Weston Hill, when I saw my father at the edge of the field, when I stepped from the wire joyous at what I'd done and I ran to him, when he pushed me so that I fell to the ground, when my heart was truly broken. I wanted to return to the moment just before it, as though it had never happened, so that I could reach out to someone else without fear.

At the top of the stairs I threw open the garret door, though I knew it was rude to do so, but it was New Year after all.

– I did it Nat, I cried, lifting my arms as if I was a child again. I did it!

And the moment dissolved just like that.

After, I wondered – had I knocked first and got no answer, would I've still barged in? Probably, cos I'm like that. But once I had, could I've turned away sooner? Probably not. Anyway, what is seen can never be unseen: the battered fighters on the riverbank; the dancer's cunny at St Giles; Ellie's smile before it left her. Why can I never look away? Do my eyes see things before I understand them, so that with every passing second it's already too late?

My mind caught up, told me that it was indeed Nat's face I was staring at, purple and twisted, the leather strap tight round her neck and cutting into her cheek, as she dangled limp from the ceiling.

James reached me then, put his arms round my waist, and pulled me backwards through the doorway, as I kicked and bleated like a calf.

Right under our noses, Nat had gone and done what she'd always intended, once her legs could no longer carry her – by age or accident or the rot of medicine. And us poor fools, eager to meet her every wish, had given her enough rope to end it.

Part Two

Twenty-one

My aunt once told me, it says on John Boothe's gravestone he was born on New Year's Day, 1740. So always at the start of the year I'd wished a thought to heaven; now, with Nat's death, I had another to send. There's nothing to say he was born on the Thames though – which he was – and I don't mean in a house on a bridge over it, or on a barge or some such. He popped out right there on the ice, when the River was frozen and half the City was celebrating. There'd been a souvenir to prove it, my aunt had said, though it was lost along the way – a gilded card hand-printed upon the River itself, giving his birthplace as "Number Two Starling, London Bridge".

The story goes, John Boothe saw a half dozen of those River fairs in his lifetime; his son Ned remembered the last one, where he bought his own memento for sixpence, which told his age as twelve and occupation as circus boy. He'd wanted it to say showman, but I guess the printer thought him too young for such airs. That card did survive, along with Ned Boothe's journal from which my aunt used to read me stories. Before she died, she took it from my father's bookshelf and gave it to my uncle James for safe keeping. So perhaps she'd known she weren't long for this life.

Of that last fair, my grandfather Ned Boothe wrote of a great fog falling over their yard at Westminster and lingering for a week. When it lifted, the whole City was a sheet of ice so you couldn't tell where the cobbles ended and the Thames began. The hackneys plied the River instead of the highways, which riled the watermen, as that was their earnings lost till the thaw. So they tried their hands at fairground tricks and selling ale and mutton pie, which got the showmen all ruffled. But it was only a few days it lasted, and with the crowds as big as they were, there must've been trade enough for them all.

The way Ned Boothe described those fairs, they didn't seem a whole lot different to ours on the Waste – a ribbon of roundabouts and swing boats and booths for every fancy. They used sails as tents; they upturned rowing boats and propped them as stalls, covering the hulls with mill blankets to keep out the frost. They cut holes in the ice to fish, though I can't imagine they caught much. Ned Boothe remembered skating with his sister, and the time they'd raced from their tent to the bridge. Georgie had won but couldn't stop, catching a pillar and breaking her ankle. It kept her on crutches for months, and she walked with a stick the rest of her days. Us women, seems we've a history of crippling ourselves. He wrote too of seeing lions and an elephant roaming the ice, though it might've been a fantasy or Wombwell's Menagerie showing off their new stock. But that winter, with his brother Jack having sailed to France, Ned Boothe was now second only to his father, and with their tumbling act, they turned their biggest profit at that fair. My aunt reckoned that's what gave Ned the taste for it. By spring they had their own menagerie, so maybe there's truth in his story after all.

– Father and son, they worked themselves to the bone. And that's how it should be, my aunt had said.

It must've been another ten years till John Boothe's heart finally gave up. My aunt and father both were born in time for him to see them, his first grandchildren, though I don't know a thing about their mother, not even a name. I don't think she survived long after my father coming and there's nothing in any of Ned Boothe's stories, so I reckon his heart was broken by it.

Ned Boothe must've had that pair of nippers running round his feet when August Boothe, my father's cousin, landed on his front step aged two and nothing. That's supposing Ned had a waggon by then and weren't still living in a tent. He was at King Henry's Yard anyway, though it was summer. As Pip Bell had told me, Ned took the boy in, and ever since August Boothe has made a habit of arriving unexpected, without a scrap of history to be sure of.

He must've been watching me on New Year's Eve, though I didn't see him – not even after, when I was borne through the crowd like a prince. It was another three days before he made himself known, when the excitement had passed and I reckoned my performance was already forgotten beyond the Waste.

He found me in the garret at the King Henry – wrung out from weeping day and night since New Year's morn – trying to sort through Nat's things. I'd come across a poster like the one from Dartford my father had given me; it was folded inside the lid of a tin box that was full to the brim with photographs, each in its own papery envelope. Elsewhere were piles of letters – too many for me to know what to do with.

I was so lost to the task, I didn't hear him climb the stairs and open the door.

– That was a very fine walk, came his first words, catching me unawares.

He offered his hand but mine were full with tying Nat's papers in a bundle. I dropped the lot and cursed myself before accepting.

– Apologies if I startled you. I do hope you remember me?

– Of course, you're my father's cousin.

– Please! Call me August, he said.

I squatted to pick up the papers and he joined me at once on his knees.

– This is rather a lot of letters, he said, fingering the pile. She must have been a popular lady. And so many from France. I was there once. I never much cared for the place.

He smiled when he said this. He was dressed in a thick woollen suit, long coat and stout shoes. He kept his collar up and cravat tight round his neck, and only removed his hat to greet me. He had a pipe in his hand too; it had a long ivory stem and amber mouthpiece, and I wondered if it was the same he'd poked me with as a child.

I'd never been in his company long enough to note his features, apart from his missing back teeth. He had a nose like a beak and gaunt cheeks. His skin weren't as pale as mine or my father's, and he'd no taint of illness or complaint. You'd call him quite hearty I suppose, as though he'd seen the sun more recent than our last summer. His eyes were too green though, as if they belonged in a different face. And even now he seemed so tall.

– I was wondering what this is, I said, holding up the fairground poster.

He took it in his fingers as if it were a delicate leaf, checked the back though there was nothing on it, and turned it over again.

– I shall have to translate, he said, holding the poster at eye level and studying the words a moment. "For your *délectation* and wonder, for this three nights only", he began. "Madame Duparc, most eminent *funambule*, by appointment his majesty, Emperor of the French".

– Do you know who that was?

He leafed through some of Nat's papers before replying.

– From the look of this lot, I would say she was your friend's mother.

– She never mentioned her to me, I said, though I remembered how Earl had joked with his son about Napoleon Bonaparte. Did you ever meet Madame Rouge? I added.

He stood up and moved to the window without answering.

– She had a fine view, he said then, seeming to mean it. So will you follow in her footsteps? Your own mother's footsteps in fact. Though not literally I hope. I could help. I know a great many people outside of the fairs.

– The fair is my home, I told him, piqued by his mention of my mother.

– But not always, from what I have heard. Not that I blame you. I would never have made a showman myself. I am more your impresario type, if you understand me.

– You didn't feel the family bond, I said, which made him smile.

He pocketed his pipe without lighting it, and began rummaging in Nat's trunk, though I didn't want him to – but what could I say? I had no better claim.

He turned so his back was to me, as if sensing my unease, yet continued to speak.

– I happen to be on excellent terms with the proprietor of Worcester. I had a hand in Vauxhall too. And then there is Monsieur Blondin. You have heard of him? I saw him walk the Great Falls, September last. He has the perfect system. Soon he will sail for England. I shall host him at Crystal Palace in June. He will want to meet all the young women following on the heels of his fashion, no doubt about that, he said, turning round again. So how about you? You do know you have a following already?

He drew a newspaper from his coat and dropped it onto the bed. The front page had a bold headline, with a sketch beneath showing two stone towers like monuments and a figure in a long skirt balancing on a wire between them.

– The press have taken a bit of licence as usual, but there was no fooling the public. You would be a boon to pantomime.

He began looking through Nat's photographs, taking a good deal of interest in some. I thought them such an odd thing, making time stand still. He studied more of the letters too, before replacing it all and turning back to me.

– So how about it? I could arrange some engagements for the spring. What do you think to that?

– I think we'll have moved on.

– You could stay in London. I have a lady with fine lodgings in Stepney. I think you would like her. She cooks the best roast potatoes and refuses to tell me where she gets her beef. You can practise on the Green. I know the keeper.

– I don't know, I said, and he gave me that smile again.

Why not just go, I asked myself. I'd run away once already, and there was even less to keep me at the fairs now, with Dorothy gone and Nat dead. But I was still holding out hope for my father – that he might realise what I'd done and believe that I could do it again, that it could help him.

– Think on it, August Boothe said at last, taking out his pipe once more and tapping the end of it against his temple. But not too long, he added. Mrs Ducking's rooms are at a premium.

He took his leave then, and I thought – how will I give him my answer? I guessed he'd find me in his own good time. And I found myself wishing to hasten it.

Twenty-two

A week after New Year I'd still not tidied the bowtop. There must've been a dozen squeezed into the waggon that night of my walk – some of the band and a few others I didn't recognise; they'd come as soon as news spread, tucked into the goose and drunk themselves into a stupor, whilst I lay on the front step sobbing more than I'd ever done before.

Now, the leftovers were reeking, the floor felt even stickier underfoot, and there wasn't a clean plate to eat from. As I looked about me, thinking I should begin clearing up, there came a knock on the waggon step and my father's face appeared in the doorway.

– Not interrupting? he said, before climbing inside.

He was wearing his moleskin three-piece, looking unusually cheery. I cleared the table and benches. He didn't seem to notice the mess.

– You're feeling better then? I said to him as we sat opposite one another.

– Much better. Fit as a flea in fact, and I should be grateful to you for it.

That was as much thanks as I got as he glanced round the bowtop. I was curious to know if he'd seen inside it before. He knew most of the living waggons in our families – had taken a drink or meal in some, held a meeting or fought his corner in others – but this one had only ever had Pip Bell and Dorothy live in it, so I wondered if he'd ever had reason to visit before.

– And you're bearing up? my father continued before I could ask.

– That's about the measure of it, I replied.

– I'm sorry about Miss Parkes, he said.

For what, I thought: her dying, my finding her, my loss?

– I am too, I told him. I'm sorry she couldn't see there was anything left for her. She could've taught me so much.

He played with his bangle a moment, running his fingers too easily underneath it, though for years he'd complained of it being too tight. He took a deep breath.

– You did well at New Year, he said at last.

I gulped – loud enough for him to hear me – and savoured his words. I knew how much he still blamed my mother's death on her craft – such that he couldn't bear even the presence of a tightrope walker. I wanted to tell him – of all the mouths I'd wished to hear those words from, I'd most longed to hear them from his. But the moment passed.

He slipped his thumb into his waistcoat pocket and hooked out a tiny parcel.

– I came to give you this.

He placed on the table a scrap of velvet tied with silk. I pulled the knot and the cloth fell open. I knew at once what it was. A pair of claws, milk-white with veins of amber, each with its base and inside edge dressed with silver, the two of them held end to end by a tiny clasp, so they made the shape of a crescent moon – a twin tiger-claw brooch, like the single claw Sir Cooke had worn after Ellie's death.

– It belonged to your mother. It's worth rather more than this old thing, my father said, twisting the copper bangle round his wrist. It's time you had it. Perhaps it'll bring you better luck than it did her.

I lifted the brooch above the table and turned it in my palm, fingering the decoration, as delicate as the skeleton of a leaf. My father closed his hand over mine and sighed.

– It's yours, if you promise me one thing. To not follow your mother's path. It'll ruin you. Find yourself a young man to wed and share the brooch with. You could do worse than Pip Bell, you know.

I flinched, though I kept my hand where it was for the moment. He was offering me both claws, both parts of the brooch. He wished to give me away to the world, to a marriage not of my choosing.

I considered his words for a moment longer. Then I drew my hand from his, so he had to catch the brooch to stop it falling.

– I can't accept it, I said, and lifted my head to face him.

My father slumped backwards and thrust the trinket into his pocket without wrapping it, then pushed against the table so he could stand.

– You'll not walk for this fair again whilst I'm alive, he said, in a voice I barely recognised.

– Your cousin, I began, but he didn't let me finish.

– James Bell is done with his meddling, my father barked, looming over me.

– I don't mean Uncle James, I interrupted, and I watched the hairs on my father's neck jump to attention. August Boothe wants to hire me, I went on, my words falling upon my father like lead.

He turned away for an instant, then twisted sharply back to me. He took a moment to form his words, but finally when he did so there was no doubting him.

– If you choose him, it's at the expense of all else that you know. He's no part of this family or this fair. He'll ruin you just as he ruins everything that he touches.

My father turned his back, wrenched open the waggon door and stepped out into the snow.

Twenty-three

Nat's funeral was as dreadful an occasion as could be. By the time it was arranged, Earl and the band had left for Ireland, unable to afford to change their plans. There were just a handful of mourners at Bow and no wake. I wished Nat could've been buried at St Dunstan's – even if with the other suicides beyond the main graveyard. But it seems she'd made more enemies than friends on the Waste. Only now did I realise how much she'd been thought an outsider, despite her being courted as our new rope-walker. I thought – what misery it is to die without family, knowing that none of one's blood flows in another.

August Boothe came though, which surprised me; he was the only Boothe or Bell to attend – the only soul I recognised. Perhaps he came because he knew I'd be there.

– Have you arrived at a decision as yet? he asked, stepping up next to me at the graveside, as Nat's body was lowered into a paupers' pit.

I didn't reply then, feeling it was wrong to speak at that moment.

Once the gravedigger had shovelled in a meagre covering of earth, I crossed myself and turned away from the miserable ceremony. August Boothe followed and after a few steps repeated his question. I looked over my shoulder, saw the already empty graveside, and thought – if I defied my father and walked at the fairs for a second time, would I be treated any different to this, in life or death?

– Tell me again where I might stay, I now replied, and August Boothe visibly perked himself.

– With a rather wonderful lady by the name of Mrs Ducking, said he. She will treat you better than a mother and make quick work of anyone that might be searching for you.

I turned to him and he met my glance with a raised brow. He could only mean my family, I thought; he couldn't know of my predicament elsewhere.

– I've made my decision, I replied at last. We leave the yard at the start of February. Come for me then.

The rest of the month brought all manner of talk about Nat's death. Even the newspapers had an opinion of it that folk at the Waste were keen to share with me.

The press had seldom bothered with the fairs before, but now it seemed they were snapping like dogs – condemning Nat for risking her life so publicly, then taking it by her own hand. I wondered what purpose their words could serve, these outsiders who'd never known or cared about her, when all Nat had wanted was to feed herself and follow her heart. Could she not have found some other occupation, better suited to her sex – is what they asked – which meant they would rather she'd been a whore, or chained to the nursery or parlour, with a husband to provide and make the pot boil. Yet these were the same folk who'd stared in wonder at her and been thrilled by the feats for which they now condemned her for performing.

But their reports did the opposite of deterring me.

There was also a rumour of Virgil being sighted, which had me rushing to St Katharine's to check a schooner just returned from Belgium. The dock was a sordid place, more so even than Limehouse, with an air of death about it. I found the boat eventually, amongst a score of others all flying different flags. Most of its crew were coloured but Virgil's face weren't amongst them, so I left disappointed.

I was desperate too to hear word from Dorothy, but none came and I felt helpless at the thought of looking for her again, when it seemed she didn't wish to be found.

The days dragged as I brooded, despite the plenty of activity round me. I didn't speak with my father again, and even Uncle James was frosty on the few occasions we spoke, though he didn't try to dissuade me. It seemed there weren't many people with a good word to say about August Boothe, but they weren't offering me nothing better.

At last came February fourth, the day the fairs were due to leave for King's Lynn, the day August Boothe had arranged for my lodgings to begin. I took up my bag, shut the door to the bowtop and stepped out from the Waste. It was the queerest thing witnessing the convoy preparing and not joining it, for a second time in six months.

I hadn't seen Pip Bell since before Nat's fall, but there was no avoiding him now, first to be ready, slowing as he led his waggon past me. He was dressed in a fawn suit, with a gold watch chain hanging from his waistcoat. His fingernails were scrubbed, a mark of his clean living as a bookmaker. He'd grown a pointed beard and I wondered who for, if not for himself.

– Moving on cousin? New horizons! he sneered.

– I think you'll find it's you moving and me staying put, I replied.

He grabbed his tuft and pulled at it, and I thought – well that must be its purpose.

– August Boothe get you under his thumb at last?

– Giving me a chance, is all.

– Too good for the fairs are we?

– I've not seen you mucking out the lions lately. Or swabbing the blood from your boxing ring, though you profit by it.

– You heard about the walker in Brum? he went on, ignoring my remark. Her fella spliced the rope to save a few

178

bob. Sixty feet she fell. Belly split like a watermelon. Five weans and another on the way. Reckon you'd do better as a kitchen slave.

– You almost sound like you care, I said. I'll take my chances if it's all the same to you. If August Boothe can manage the Crystal Palace, Cremorne Gardens and Worcester, I'm sure he can manage Lucky Boothe, I added, stretching the truth as I knew it.

– Well, good riddance, though I wouldn't be so sure about him, Pip Bell replied, turning away and geeing his horse.

*

I didn't wait longer; I couldn't bear to wave off Flo and Mary and the children. I walked onto Mile End Road and into the path of a hansom. The driver bellowed as his horse reared, and when its front hooves fell again the left grazed my shin. I escaped behind the carriage and across the road before the driver could curse me a second time, and found myself at the old glass workshop. Smedes was the maker's name; I remember it now. I stood at the window, wiped the grime from the pane and peered inside, and I swear for a second I saw the old fella sitting in his chair, hunched over his eyeglass, till I felt an arm slide into mine and I turned to find August Boothe towering over me.

– I was rather afraid I might have missed you. It really would not do having you walk alone to your new lodgings. Shall I take your bag?

– I can manage, I said, easing my arm free.

– I would have hailed a cab but there was a bit of commotion, he said. And what with the Boothes and Bells about to cause chaos. Bit of a homecoming for me, this place, he went on, looking about him. Back yard of less happy times. Same for you perhaps?

– Shall we just go? I replied, anxious to stay ahead of the convoy as it began leaving.

We had to pause at the gates of a brewery yard, for the draymen that passed in and out as though on elastic, shouldering their barrels to the carts lined up on the roadside. Then we moved on till we came to the corner with Stepney Green, and August Boothe turned into the doorway of the White Horse Inn.

– Coming? he said, offering his arm.

Inside, it was quite different to the King Henry. I felt the warmth of its two log fires. The floor was swept, no brick dust crunching underfoot. There was a row of high stools at the bar. The chatter of drinkers was a polite murmur, not base and shrill like the cattlemen and the girls who hung at their boots.

August Boothe seemed well known to the landlady; she'd set a tray by the time we reached the bar.

– Tea or lemonade? he asked me.

– Lemonade will be fine.

– Indeed. It would not do in your profession to drink anything stronger. Personally, I cannot stomach the stuff. Causes me convulsions. Your mother thought it amusing. She believed I was cursed.

I turned away, his remembering my mother stirring me again. I wondered how we might look, the two of us sitting there at the bar – not like man and wife for sure. Should I turn to the men at the window tables, the two ladies in the snug, and tell them he's my uncle, not my client or owner? I hoped the landlady knew the truth of it and would put them right when we were gone. Still, I drank the lemonade too quickly and August Boothe took that as time to leave, though he'd barely taken a mouthful of his tea.

– Must not keep the lady waiting, he said, before bidding his farewells, catching the eye of several of the drinkers as we left.

From the inn we turned into Stepney Green and stopped eventually outside the door to number seventeen. There was a stench of night soil from the neighbouring houses, buckets with ill-fitting lids cluttering their front doors. But the steps to this house were clear and as spotless as the inside of any waggon in the fairs.

– This is us, August Boothe said, though really he meant me.

It felt strange to be standing again before those houses, the backdrop to so many memories: the fair on the Green, following my aunt's coffin to St Dunstan's, running to the docks and finding Virgil.

He had a key to the door, though he rapped hard and called out as he unlocked it. We stepped into a hallway that smelt of lavender – reminding me of the flower seller's – with white walls, a high ceiling, and a wooden floor so polished there was not a mark upon it.

– As you know, Mrs Ducking is your housekeeper, August Boothe said, opening the first door we came to. She lives upstairs with her husband, though you will likely never see him. I imagine she will be gone to market now. She will cook your meals morning and evening. There is a privy outside, and a copper if you need it, but check with her first as she has her routines.

The room was darker than the hallway, though it had a bay window overlooking the Green. At once I felt the weight of the floors above me, the ceiling pushing down. There was a fire set in the grate and beside it a coal scuttle. The bed was behind a screen and weren't too narrow; there was a wardrobe and a dresser with a mirror, an armchair with a bright cover, and a stool at a table just big enough for two to eat at. So much space and barely a scrap of my own to put in it.

– I believe you are the only guest in the house tonight, though that will change, but this is the only bedroom downstairs, so you are well away from it all. Consider this on account, August Boothe said, handing me five shillings. With room and board it comes to fifteen shillings per week. I shall keep all monies from your first engagements until I am paid off, and after that I shall take expenses and my fee and you shall have the rest. Any questions? Be sure to make yourself known when Mrs Ducking returns. I shall see you again when I have organised a rope.

He left, and I sat for a moment on the edge of the armchair, not yet allowing myself to relax into it. I felt as though I'd been thrust into a new life, just like that, no family or friends, just some vague dream looming over me. I emptied my bag onto the bed. I hung my spare dress – the one from Mme Rouge – on the outside of the wardrobe, as there didn't seem much point in putting it inside, and I unfolded the poster from Dartford onto the mirror, poking the top edge into the frame to hold it. Was this my home now, I wondered. Could it really be?

Twenty-four

That first week in Stepney, I felt truly severed from all that had gone before. I knew I had to put the months just passed firmly from my mind, but I battled with my thoughts till it pained me. With too much time to think, I kept returning to Nat. I couldn't help but dwell upon the moment when I found her, though I struggled to recall anything of what I'd seen – like losing the thread of a dream upon waking. I was glad of that at least, not having to suffer the image in every troubled moment.

It didn't start too well with Mrs Ducking either. She told me all about it when we spoke for the first time, three days after I'd arrived.

– That afternoon Mr Boothe bring you, she began, I come home and find you stone cold on the bed and no sign of your uncle. There's no waking you, and you're the same when I bring you supper that evening. Next morning you've not touched the plate, and you're staring out the window, not answering. I almost fall over you an hour later, outside on the front step – you on your knees scraping coal dust into your skirt. God knows why. Just as one of my guests is arriving and all.

After that, she told me, she took me back inside and tried to get a meal down me, but right away I was sick from it.

Finally, on the third morning, she was stood over me at the table in my room, waiting to see if I could finish a sandwich.

– I've been thinking to meself, that Mr Boothe, he's sent me a bad 'un, she said to me, though I could tell she wasn't too angry cos she was smiling as she said it.

– I'm just a bit out of sorts is all, I replied.

She gave me a wink, probably thinking it was my time of the month, but it weren't that.

– Well if you take a good breakfast, I'll not force dinner down you and we'll see about supper, she said. I won't have food wasted but I won't be letting you starve on my watch either.

She said August Boothe was paying her to feed me three meals a day, so she'd do my washing whenever I wanted, instead of making me dinner. And that was the start of me not eating enough, readying myself for returning to the rope.

– I'll do my best and keep any strangers away, she went on. There's already a few been sniffing at the door, wondering what a pretty young lady like yourself is doing alone around here. "I don't keep that kind of house", I tell them, but they still hang about and you've only been here three days. I'll have a word with Mr Boothe about it.

She truly was as good as a mother to me then, though she couldn't have been more unlike Ellie or my aunt. She was only my height, but stout as a horse with thick arms and a good roll of fat round her neck so her chin never showed. When I asked her how she knew my uncle, she winked again and told me she'd known him a good while.

– Must be nigh on twenty years, though it feels like yesterday, she sighed. Before you were born of course. Your uncle came here when he was about seventeen – at least that's how old he thought he was; he'd no one to tell him for certain. He only found out later he was born on the exact same day as your father, though hundreds of miles away.

– I was told it was in France.

– Foreign parts, is what Mr Boothe told me.

– And is his mother dead?

– I don't know that, and I don't know if he knows his-self; he never speaks of it. He met your mother when he came here though; I know that much. He was a mite bewitched by her, to say the least, though I'm not saying she encouraged him. It was before your father anyway. That's what Mr Boothe told me.

– It feels odd, you knowing these things, and yet we've only just met, I said to her.

– Well I can't be sorry for that; it's how life is sometimes. I can still remember your aunt's funeral, coming right past this window. Mr Boothe stayed here that night. Must be a few years ago now?

– Four years, though I don't recall him at the church, only at the wake at Wanstead. Do you remember when my mother died too?

– Goodness no child, she said. I didn't even know her. I only heard of her from Mr Boothe. He didn't stay here much after your mother and father wed. He was back and forth to Paris, I don't know what for, but he said your aunt was there as well sometimes.

And so I learnt that my aunt had left the fairs too, for a while at least – just as I was doing now.

After seven days August Boothe came, and what a relief it was – I was feeling that alone, and all the while turning over Mrs Ducking's stories in my head. I opened my door to him and he stepped from the hallway, handing me a parcel.

– How are you keeping? Mrs Ducking feeding you properly? No problems with the other guests?

– I never seen anyone, and I'm keeping fine, I replied, as I knew he would've already asked her, and she would've told him – she's good as gold, keeps to herself, and cleans her plate at every meal.

– You have your first engagement, August Boothe went on, perching on my bed and crossing his legs purposefully, his gaze falling upon the Dartford bill.

I sat on the stool, but jumped up again like a jack-in-the-box.

– It's too soon, I've not touched a rope since New Year, I can't do it, I said in a panic, and he held up his hand to stop me.

– Relax; it's not until Easter Sunday. At Highbury Barn. It will be very prestigious. The top agents will be there.

I thought of Mme Rouge, her plan to make another go at crossing the River. She must've known it was a dream, a fantasy to ease her final days.

– But Easter's months away, I cried, and my uncle laughed at that.

– Make up your mind. It's seven weeks yesterday to be exact. They are rather fond of their *funambules* at Highbury, so much so they have a permanent tightrope. Two hundred feet of it, so I am told, and sixty feet high.

– That's far too high. I'd never survive a fall, I said with a shudder.

– They probably exaggerate. Nearer thirty perhaps. In any case, you cannot think that way.

– But where will I practise?

– That is all arranged too. I shall leave you to dress, and then we can take a short walk.

I took the package behind the changing screen and untied it on the bed. I pulled out a shirt and jacket and held them to my chest. There was a pair of trousers, fleshings and slippers too, all of which I tried and were a good size. I decided to wear the fleshings and when I was ready, August Boothe took up my slippers, led me from the house and across the road. I'd not set foot in the Green that whole week. I realised then how poorly I must've been not to have wanted to – being it was a place of good memories, of better times when the fair had breathed life, though now there seemed to be none, save for a solitary snowdrop that nodded its milky head to welcome me.

On the far side of the park, we found a rope rigged between two planes that stood bare and upright as sentries. It was perhaps fifty feet long and not quite as high as Nat's wire at the square – enough to hurt if I fell awkwardly, though not so high as to cripple me. If I stayed true to my belief that every walk counted no matter how high or low, then it was enough to prepare me for Highbury.

– I have made some arrangements, August Boothe said, handing me the slippers. The rope will be left alone. But if there is any damage done, be quick to tell me. You'll find a pole and ladder hidden behind the bush. Return them each time you finish. And be sure to keep up your strength.

I must've barely noticed him leaving, as I was climbing the tree before I remembered to kick off my clogs, so impatient was I to return to what I knew. I put on the slippers and sat in the branches; the bark was smooth and damp, so I had to grip firmly to stop myself falling. With my left foot I pushed on the rope to judge the tension; I reckoned on needing it tighter, but I knew I'd not the strength to retie it. I curled forward so my chin was touching my knee, and turned my head to one side to stare along the rope – just as I'd done with the wire at Weston all those years before. I studied the rope in front of my face as if through a lens, picking out every fibre on the surface.

I stood again and found my balance, drew in the air that tasted of the rot of winter. I took a step forward onto the rope and my legs failed me for a moment, expecting something more perhaps, till at last they accepted the new weight of me.

From then, each morning that weren't too wet or icy, I took to the Green at dawn. I rope-walked till I no longer could, till the skies or failing light stopped me, though I took a good deal of persuading to give up on a day. Though Mrs Ducking's tongue was sharp enough to keep her doorstep quiet, it couldn't save me from becoming a curiosity in the park, and I'm sure folk started visiting the Green merely to watch me, not even bringing a nipper or dog to pretend otherwise.

The days rolled by like that, one into another. I suffered a good few falls till I found my focus and could walk the length of the rope without faltering. Some afternoons I felt faint from not eating and had to rest till my strength returned. But I kept at it, and eventually I could walk out and back again without opening my eyes. And just as August Boothe said – though frankly I'll never know how – no one ever touched the rope, let alone tried to steal it.

Twenty-five

Spring saw off the last of the snowdrops and fetched up a crop of new shoots. August Boothe came by every week and always asked how the food was. He brought me a lighter pole so I could practise for longer as the days started to draw out, though it made me walk more slowly.

I found myself looking forward to his visits; he always had an encouraging word, though he showed no affection – not like Uncle James or my aunt.

With just a week till Easter, he told me I'd need a costume and he'd have Mrs Ducking take my measurements. That evening she came to my room, tape in hand, though I'm sure she could've guessed as well without it.

– Good God, there's nothing of you, she said, when I stepped from the changing screen, barefoot and wearing just a shift.

– I've always been this size, I lied. I just look bigger in my clothes.

She was right though; my ribs were sticking out as if about to escape, and my breasts had shrunk so they were almost flat like Dorothy's. But the thinner I'd become, the more like a bird, settling on the rope like a whisper. Even the pangs of hunger had lessened and I didn't tell Mrs Ducking how erratic my flow had become, and that it was so light now I could still rope-walk through the worst of it.

On the Friday morning, August Boothe arrived with the new outfit and a hansom to take us to Highbury for my first day of practise. The journey was an ordeal, the roads choked for the holiday and fine weather, but my first sight of the gardens made up for it. As the cab set us down at the head of the park, I could see stretching away on both sides vast beds bursting with tulips – blankets of red, yellow, pink and lilac, like a giant patchwork. Between the beds were arches grown over with rose bushes not yet in bloom, and beneath them tables set for lovers to take in the view. The rope spanned the middle of the park, suspended high above the lawn from wooden towers that looked permanent, just as August Boothe had said. As we walked towards the nearest one, a man a little short for his suit came running to us and I feared he might trip on his hems, though it would've made a good clown act.

– Good morning, good morning. Owner of the modest Highbury Barn at your service, he said, grabbing our palms as if gold might appear in them if he shook hard enough.

– And Lucky Boothe at your service, August Boothe told him, bowing slightly.

– An excellent name, if I may say, the man said turning to me. And only our second walker this season, he added, touching his ample nose. We're all terribly excited. And dressing as a boy to escape attention – a fine idea indeed. It might fool the press for a day or two. Well, you know where it all is and the visitors have been warned, so help yourself. And if you do fall into the flowers, be sure to pick one for your dearest.

He smiled till I returned it, and left without giving his name. Then the helpers arrived, a girl and boy, both wearing boots that looked much too clumsy to climb in. They brought with them the heavier of the balancing poles from the Green, and before I could greet them they began scaling the tower as though it were a mere climbing frame.

– The changing tent is the other side of the hedge, August Boothe told me, pointing with his pipe. I have some business to attend to, then I shall arrange lunch.

– I've already had breakfast. I'll not eat again before I walk, I told him.

– Very well. Just lemonade it is then. I shall see you after you perform. Our cab is due at six thirty, on the dot.

The costume was another good fit and elegantly finished, the waistcoat finer than any I'd seen, even on a showman. The flannels were white like a swan, as was the shirt, and to hide my face there was a black tricorn with silver lace trimming that made me think of Sir Cooke, and so of Ellie. I was a good while climbing the tower and even longer settling at the top, though it was cooler up there than I'd expected. But eventually I cleared my head, ignored my rumbling belly, and stepped out.

At once I imagined myself walking at Stepney Green, surrounded by planes newly in leaf, under the gaze of a dozen onlookers, poised just a few feet above the ground. I imagined it, and in no time found my way to midway along the rope, where I squatted on the pole to rest, then made the second half with my eyes closed. I crossed five times like that, the heavier pole hastening me, till the wind whipped up for a moment, bringing a shower and sending me down the tower again. I stood a while at the base of it, watching the visitors hurrying for shelter, one of them asking me where he might buy an umbrella and looking bemused when he heard my voice. Then the weather truly turned and that was the day abandoned, a grim northerly blowing us back to the City.

I was exhausted when night came but sleep wouldn't rescue me, no matter how dull I tried to turn my thoughts. If I slept at all it can only have been in the half-seconds between trying to fall asleep, and the night dragged like a leg in chains.

In the morning, we had another slow carriage ride, the sight of the beautiful gardens once more. The weather was kinder and I practised for the rest of the day till long into the evening, gas lamps lighting my way. August Boothe never showed any sign of impatience, though he had to turn away a few hansoms till I was done.

It was past ten o'clock before we left and when I arrived home – for that is what it now was – Mrs Ducking was still up, a little worried I think. I waited till August Boothe had left us before asking Mrs Ducking if she had any scissors. She fetched me a pair without question, perhaps just relieved that I was still in one piece. In my room, I stripped till I was naked, and in the light of a single candle looked at myself in the mirror, placing my hands round my waist. I took up the scissors and drew the point across my stomach – not breaking the skin but flinching at the touch of the cold blades. Then down between my legs, I started to cut the hairs that grew there, till there was only stubble left. Finally I brought the scissors to my head and began cropping my hair to the scalp.

I thought of how Virgil had sheared me all those months before and I felt the change of it once again. Then at last I found the sleep that had been eluding me.

Easter morning, August Boothe was at my door not so early. He barely glanced at my hair, but took my bag, though it only held my costume.

– That is quite as calm out there as we could hope for, he told me, his words reminding me of how my aunt used to speak.

I stepped outside to a waiting cab and the twitching of nets. Three such mornings and I was now the subject of some attention – that slip of a girl trying to pass for a boy, only leaving home by hansom, never on foot, and only with that man she says is her uncle. That was the gossip round about, according to Mrs Ducking; but I knew it wouldn't last beyond the weekend, when I'd become my old self again, up at every dawn and walking alone to the Green.

Sunday's journey was quicker, the route taking us past an empty King Henry's Yard and up Dog Row towards

Islington; I thought of all the times I'd trudged those cobbles with groceries, in rain or shine or deep in snow.

When we arrived, there was a line of empty carriages already parked up, the drivers all standing on the pavement chatting and smoking. Inside the gardens, hundreds of chairs had been arranged in a crescent on the grass, facing a stage that was set for a concert – all of it a good way from the tightrope.

I performed in the orchestra's interval. At the crash of a cymbal sounding the break, I closed my eyes, imagined Mme Rouge's hand calmly leading me, and took my first step. There was not a breath of wind and the rope barely moved beneath my feet, no hum as had guided me at the Waste. It was over so quickly – with little of the noise and excitement of New Year's Eve – that at first I weren't certain if anyone had seen me at all. Yet there was a good cheer as I climbed down the tower, though no one seemed to notice me miss the final step, my feet landing heavily on the ground, jolting my spine.

When August Boothe found me, I was already out of my costume and waiting in the garden of the tavern.

– You were quite a hit, he said excitedly, waving a clutch of cards and taking a seat opposite me.

He laid them on the table and took a diary from his jacket, thumbing the pages.

– First we have next Saturday at Barnet. Then Sunday at Mitcham. The thirteenth at Epping Forest. And a private do in Hampstead on the twenty-third. How does that sound for starters? At this rate we shall have filled April by the end of the week. You are going to be a busy bee.

Before I could answer, I was brought a glass of lemonade and August Boothe had his usual pot of tea; I'd not yet seen him drink anything else. I would've liked something stronger, to quell the pain that had started in my back. But

I'd barely taken a sip when he handed me five shillings that I weren't yet due, and dismissed me with a final word.

– I need to confirm some more engagements, he said, and nodded to where a carriage was waiting.

I'd not taken a cab alone before and it felt odd, having a horse and driver just for me. We sped into the City as darkness fell and I thought about the performance – my first since the Waste. I should've felt more excited, but I was still saddened by Nat dying without realising the dream she'd shared with me.

As we turned into the Mile End Road, I thumped on the ceiling to get the driver's attention.

– Drop me at the White Horse, I called out, as he lifted the trap door without looking down.

The carriage drew to a stop outside the inn. With aching legs and back, I stepped down and turned to pay the driver, but his attention was already on another customer, so I guessed August Boothe had already paid him.

The taproom was busier than before, though I found an empty alcove. The landlady brought me wine, and I thanked and paid her, then pushed the bottle and glass aside so I could rest my head and chest on the table, my arms dangling to the floor, not caring how I looked. I must've lain a good while like that before I sat upright again, reached for the bottle and drank half the wine straight from it in one go. Then I calmed myself and finished the second half more slowly, a glass at a time. At the last dregs, I looked up to see a woman standing beside the next alcove, squinting at me in the gloom. I thought she was beckoning me at first, as if asking for a dance, but she was just grabbing the partition to stop herself falling.

I suddenly pictured Nat in her final seconds – in the moment before James arrived – the clearest I'd remembered it. I saw her reaching out to me, not quite dead, and me not moving, not understanding she wanted saving.

Twenty-six

For two days after Highbury, I lay in bed wondering if I'd gotten into a fight at the White Horse, for all my head and back ached. On the third morning, Mrs Ducking suggested a hot bath.

– I've never had one before, I told her.

– Then it's surely time you did. However have you got to such an age? she cried.

– We don't carry so much water that we can sit round in it. We wash in rivers mostly, I said, and she gave me a curious look.

I surprised myself at my answer, speaking as though I was still at the fairs, or taking a short rest from it.

– You need a little luxury now and then. Stay in bed and I'll come for you when it's ready, Mrs Ducking said, leaving the door ajar.

The copper was in the scullery next to my room and the bathtub was beyond that; I'd only ever seen it piled with firewood and never known it used before, so it couldn't have been a pleasure she enjoyed often either. The pump was on the street, two doors away, so it took her plenty of toing and froing to fill the copper, then fetch pots of boiling water to the bath. She talked all the while, and every so often I caught a snippet.

– I was born in your room. My mother kept this house for forty-one years. I've always lived in these parts, I heard her say.

It turned out too, she'd never set foot west of Aldgate or east of Bow Cemetery, and had never seen the River either. Nothing for me there, she said. She seemed to know the Waste well enough though.

– All ready, duck, she said at last, returning to my room. The size of you, you should be light enough for me to lift without any bother, she added, scooping an arm beneath my hips and another round my shoulders.

It was a comfort to feel her touch, though it made me think of Virgil, which didn't seem right. She carried me with my head in the crook of her arm and my belly beneath her hefty breasts – that must've fairly slowed her when she climbed the stairs or walked any distance. I could see the stubble on her chin and a mole on her left cheek with hairs poking from it like bristles. I could've peered up her nostrils if I'd wanted.

– I reckon I should put you back on full rations before you waste away, she said, when we reached the tub.

She made such easy work of slipping off my nightdress without putting me down that I was sure she must've had children, though she'd never mentioned any. She'd not spoken of Mr Ducking either and it seemed rude to ask. She kept my head supported, and I barely felt a twinge, till she laid me into the water and I flinched at the heat of it. It was the strangest feeling that took me a while to get used to.

– You must've been bathed as a baby, she said, but I said I didn't think so.

I didn't tell her I could barely remember a thing from before I was seven, that most of it had gone with Ellie's passing, and now I'd only stories to go by. Yet her words did stir a memory of sitting in a basin on the ground beside a campfire some place, but that's all there was.

Mrs Ducking hung a block behind my head to stop me slipping below the water, tipped in a cup of salt, and then was away again to the copper. I lay for the rest of the morning in silence, till the water had cooled so much that Mrs Ducking could no longer replenish it quickly enough. When at last she lifted me out, she wrapped me in a towel like a child and set me on my feet, my skin hanging from me like an old prune.

– Can you walk without my help? she asked.

I wanted to say I could, that the bath had worked and I was cured, but I was afraid to try in case I fell. The pain was still there, unlike any I'd ever had – like a slow hammering on the bottom of my spine. It made me think of my father kicking me at Weston Hill.

I wanted to make it to my room by myself, so I held the towel to my body with one hand, gripped the edge of the tub with the other, and took a step. I reached the hallway and then used the wall to guide me. One foot in front of the other is all it takes, I told myself – those steps out of infanthood, never forgotten. My feet carried me now to my bed, though Mrs Ducking urged me to try the chair, so I might get up again without her help. But lie down I did, staying wide awake till late in the afternoon when August Boothe visited.

He appeared at my door bearing a silver jug – for making coffee in, he said. It had a wooden handle on the side and a lid with a hinge, and was in need of a good polish. He said it was French, though he couldn't recall how he'd come by it. He asked Mrs Ducking to bring a tea tray and kettle and I reckon she must've been goodly sick of boiling up water by then. He made coffee for me, black and very strong, and tea for himself that he also took without milk.

– That should perk you up, he said, though I gagged at the bitterness of it. I am sure you will be glad to hear you now only have Barnet this weekend, he went on, producing his diary. Mitcham have cancelled – some furore over that accident in Birmingham. The press are still making a meal of it. Even a fool would think – no wonder, if the rope were no better than a wash line. I sent a new plan for a wire, which would have cost me more, but they will still not hear of it. So be it. But we need you back on the rope, young lady.

– Tomorrow perhaps, I said.

– This evening would be better, he pressed. The other news I have is that Epping is now on the Saturday and Sunday. And on May Day you shall perform in Oxford, alongside the river. Also, on the first of June, Monsieur Blondin shall be at the Crystal Palace. I thought we might have you at the entrance, on a slack rope perhaps. How does all that sound?

The rope at Barnet was only slightly higher than at the Green, and I wondered if August Boothe had asked for it to be lowered, guessing my state of health. It was rigged alongside the cattle market, where stalls were selling sweets and china dolls. Nearby was a set of chairoplanes and a dobbie roundabout just like ours. My audience was a ragged bunch, none much older than ten or eleven, and they showed little interest other than to pelt me with clods of earth. Towards the end I slipped, though I managed to stay on the rope, pausing to find my balance and finish the walk, but I knew then how much harder I'd need to practise.

On our return, having told August Boothe about my pain, he took me directly to the White Horse. He sat me at a table and ordered me a jug of wine, the first time he'd done so. Then he left me and I didn't see him again that night.

In the next alcove were two women, handsomely dressed and made-up as though for an outing to a show. The one nearest spotted me and I looked away at once, but then she called out so loud I couldn't ignore her.

– Come park your bum with us. No good drinking alone, not at your age, she cried.

I was reluctant but she insisted, so I brought my wine to their table and drew up a chair.

– I'm Ruby and this here's Pearl, the first woman said.

They each offered a hand, both long-fingered and heavy with rings. I shook them in turn.

– I'm Lucky Boothe, I said, which sent Ruby's eyebrows aflutter.

– Pray, what does a girl with a name like that get up to?

– I'm a tightrope walker, I replied, and I reckon it was the first time I'd told it to someone I didn't know.

Pearl sat up and clapped.

– That calls for a celebration, she said, and waved to the landlady. I simply adore a walker. If my feet weren't planted on the stage, on a rope is where they'd be, without doubt. I envy your very soul and heart.

– Pearl gets a little excited, Ruby cut in, patting her companion's arm.

– How often do you perform? Pearl carried on, putting her hand to Ruby's mouth.

A boy brought champagne and poured us each a glass.

– Lovely to meet you Lucky, Ruby said, raising her flute.

We toasted each other and at once my spirits were lifted.

– I practise every day and perform most weekends, I said, my seasoned voice coming so easily.

– It must help being slight. But why do you keep your hair so short? Ruby said.

– So it doesn't fall into my eyes, I replied, which was the easiest answer I could give.

– When can we see more of you? I'm desperate to see a walker in the flesh, Pearl said, and it was Ruby who stopped Pearl's mouth this time.

– I'm over at the Green most days, I said, pointing towards the window. I'd need to ask my uncle when I'm performing next. I've no head for dates. I'm sure it's soon.

– That's a handsome gent you have for a kin. I'm impressed to see such a fella taking care of his own. Wherever did you find him?

Ruby nudged Pearl, then took my hand in hers.

– He's a good sort, I'm sure. I don't listen to gossip. Now tell us all about rope-walking.

I must've right prattled on then, the champagne taking effect, and soon there was a fresh bottle in the bucket. I told the women about my walk at Mile End, how I'd prepared myself for it, and how I'd felt when I came to do it for real. I didn't mention closing my eyes though, or the thrum of the wire; those secrets belonged to me. At some point Pearl moved to my side and rested her leg over mine – Ruby seeming unable to tame her friend any longer. Then I suppose the drink began to wear off and suddenly I felt the pain in my back return, which stole my breath and made my eyes water.

– I'm sorry. I've come over so tired all of a sudden, I told them, and all I wanted was to cross my arms on the table and lay my head down.

The next I knew of it, I was awaking in a bed in the centre of an attic room, wearing a nightdress not my own. There was a small window and through a crack in the curtains I could see the black of the night not yet done. I remembered the pain, and realised it must've now eased. I turned back the quilt and strained to see in the candlelight. The women were flopped on a couch, wrapped together under a sheet like sisters. Behind them a door stood open into a closet and for a moment I thought I saw a face reflected in the mirror above the basin, yet I was certain there could be no one else in the room. Ruby opened an eye then.

– Feeling better sweetheart? she said through a yawn. You took quite a turn. You were rocking so much we had to leave you to it.

I looked round me and noticed how huge the bed was, with pillows and space enough for four to sleep in it.

– We gave you a little something for the pain.

I nodded, but at first I couldn't reply. I felt as though my jaws were wired shut and my mouth stuffed with cotton. I waited for the sensation to pass and then opened my lips, sucking for air like a newborn.

– I'll fix us a nightcap, Ruby said, untangling herself from Pearl, who'd been purring in her lap and remained sound asleep when moved.

She stood, wearing not a stitch, and crossed the room in front of me.

– We're upstairs at the White Horse if you're wondering. You're quite safe.

In the taproom Ruby's hair had been hidden beneath a wide hat, but now I saw her locks were blonde as could be. Her skin was dark and tight over her breasts, her nipples standing up like top hats; her cunny was as hairless as my own now was, and had a birthmark above it, like a splash of blood curling towards her stomach. She threw on a silk gown and poured two drinks from a sideboard that was edge to edge with bottles, decanters and all manner of tiny pots and brushes for make-up. Round the bed were several chairs piled with clothes. There were dresses hanging from the picture rails, shoes lined up below the window, and in one corner a tower of trunks plastered with shipping labels. Ruby perched on the bed and handed me a brandy glass, more like half-full than just a sup, and I swirled the liquid round the bowl like I'd seen others do.

– You were telling us about your hair, she said, reaching out and running her fingers over my scalp.

– I suppose it is a little severe, I whispered, able to speak at last.

– Not at all, I love it. You might've gathered we're in theatre. We're actors. Not the music hall kind though. We've been doing a three-month run at the Garrick. Do you know it?

– On Leman Street? I've passed by it before once or twice, I said, recalling Christmas Day with a pang of longing.

– That's it. Delightful place. I'm sure they could use a rope act.

– You should come to our winter fair. We've got penny theatres and sideshows, and it lasts for a whole month.

– We'll book a room at once. I love a good fair, Ruby gushed.

I felt a warmth for the Waste then, to think I could still be a part of it.

– They might have me walk again at New Year.

– It's in the diary young lady, Ruby said, pointing to her forehead. You are the sweetest thing.

I felt the pain in my back again and flinched, upsetting my drink. Ruby reached behind her and took a dark bottle from the table. She prised out the stopper with her thumbnail and splashed a dose of liquid into my glass.

– Knock it back, love. It dulls every ache and pain that life throws at you, even the curse, she told me with a smile.

She lifted the glass to my lips and helped me drink. Soon her voice was fading – the last I would hear it – though her words stayed ringing in my head till they seemed to chime with my thoughts and join me on a journey into my dreams.

Twenty-seven

– Is that you awake at last? Mr Boothe has already stopped by twice today, Mrs Ducking called out as she thumped down the stairs.

She'd heard me stagger outside to the privy and was waiting at my door, holding a tray, when I returned.

– You've slept for two days and not eaten a thing. He says you've got Epping this weekend and need to practise. Now, I'm not his messenger but I reckon he has a right to be concerned.

– I feel fine. I ate something bad at the weekend, is all.

– Well I'm supposed to know you're safe and not lying somewhere in a gutter.

– It was only one night and my uncle knew where I was. Anyway I'm not a child and he's not my keeper.

– But he does pay the bills, so in my book he calls the tune. I've brought you some porridge and we'll start over. I won't have bad feelings in my house.

It was Tuesday afternoon. I'd awoken Sunday night on the floor of my room, a bottle in my hand, wondering how I'd got there. I quickly discovered how the medicine eased my back-pain and dulled what little appetite I had left, so I kept supping it till I don't know what brought me round, and here I was now facing a bowl of gruel, my stomach tightening at the sight of it.

– You must eat something, Miss Boothe. I shall have to tell Mr Boothe what's been happening. Our arrangement is over I'm afraid. I won't see you starve yourself, not for love nor that damned rope.

– I'll try, Mrs Ducking, I promise. Please leave me a moment to dress.

As soon as I heard her clogs on the scullery flags, I lifted the floorboard at the foot of the bed, which I'd seen was loose when I was lying on it, and scooped most of the porridge below it. Then I ate what was left, though my belly complained at even a tiny mouthful. Once I was sure I'd kept it down, I looked out my outfit, which I found crumpled under the bed, and got myself dressed to practise. As I did so, I caught myself in the mirror and saw how grey my complexion was. I touched my mother's poster that was still fixed there; how long might it last in my possession, I wondered. I had so little I'd been able to keep hold of. One way or another, I'd let it all go.

With Mrs Ducking hastening me, I made it to the Green by late afternoon and practised till dusk, though I strayed no further than in reach of the tree, each time taking just a few steps before turning round. I returned to the White Horse that night and asked after Ruby and Pearl. The landlady didn't know them by that name, but she knew whom I meant, and told me they'd moved on – she didn't know to where.

The next day I fared better, and by the end of the morning I'd walked the whole rope, barely noticing it beneath my feet. I managed it dozens of times over the following days, and before I knew it I was standing beside a gnarled oak at High Beech, telling August Boothe the rope was too low.

– It's worse than at Barnet. They'll think I'm a fool. There's no danger if I fall, even if I walk on my head.

– I would dearly love to see that one day. But for now we must do as our proprietor wants. You are here to please, whatever the circumstances.

I tried to remind myself that I should perform the same no matter the height. Yet it was too easy and the crowd showed more interest in the ale and suckling pig. I thought – I should snatch a child onto my shoulders, and juggle swords like the French women do. Then I might pique the crowd's morbid urge.

But as August Boothe had said, I had a paymaster to serve, who didn't think of moving the rope for the second day. So I walked then as I did before, no harder than climbing steps, and once again the crowd's attention fell elsewhere. Yet the proprietor came to me after and pumped my hand as if we were old friends.

– Excellent performance once again, full of grace. I tried it as a young man, so I know what it is to make it look effortless.

I curtsied, but the owner waved it aside, smoothing his scraps of hair across his scalp.

– I should be bowing to you. I have a jousting tournament on Dartford Hill, Saturday next. I should like you to walk at it. The same arrangement as today, Mr Boothe? he said, turning to my uncle and shaking his hand.

I gasped at the owner's mention of Dartford, which August Boothe took to be my excitement at the offer; he nudged me and gave me his smile that showed his missing back teeth, as if to say it was all part of his plan.

It was close to midday and the sun was beating upon us, as we neared Dartford in a sweat, rattling along the old road that was still good enough for a single carriage – despite what my father had told me all those years before.

All morning, since leaving at dawn, I'd been pondering the coming performance – at the site of my mother's last rope-walk, cut down in the peak of her craft. And eventually – as I knew we would – we passed my mother's grave, which I'd not seen in five years. I wanted to slow the carriage but August Boothe had only just nodded asleep. So I made do with looking out the window, seeing the oak where the bowtop had been set alight, and the rusting remnant of waggon that was the only gravestone my father had afforded his wife.

As the verge disappeared from view, I took out the medicine bottle to suck down the last drops. I'd almost finished it now and the relief from it had been lessening the more I took, though every so often it offered a glimpse of a lost memory, had me scratching for a fragment – a moment of happiness perhaps – like a pearl hiding in an empty shell.

At last the carriage came to a halt and August Boothe awoke with a start, fumbling for his top hat.

– I think we might have arrived.

– I think so too, I agreed, speaking carefully so that my voice didn't betray me.

I stepped from the carriage, keeping a firm hold on the side rail, and took in the scene laid before me. The plain was barely recognisable without the encampments and waggons and trappings of the fair. Lines of ribbon now marked a narrow arena down the middle of the heath, with empty stalls at the far end awaiting their owners. Beyond was the rope and tripods, where I would entertain the crowd coming to gamble on the skills of trick riders and their steeds.

– Your pole should already be here, my uncle told me. You can begin practising as soon as you are dressed. You should manage to get a few hours of daylight yet. And that will be yours for the weekend, he added, pointing out a small waggon behind the stalls. Now, I have some business.

– I know, I said, interrupting him. I'll get dressed and get on with it shall I?

Feeling the heat of the journey and the medicine taking effect, I stripped off as soon as I was inside the waggon. It was plain and unlived-in, with just a chair, empty bunk, and a tiny sideboard with a washbowl half-full with tepid water. I scrubbed my whole body, starting at my feet and ankles, running the cloth up my shins and tracing the line of bone, rubbing the backs of my knees and the little flesh I still had on my calves. I rested my hand on the top of my thigh and massaged round my groin, wondering when the bleeding might return. I touched my belly, and each of my ribs that stuck out like the rungs of a ladder. I stroked my forearm, rubbing the thin veins, then cupped my breasts and held them a while, pinching one of my nipples till it was sore.

A knock on the front step brought me up sharp.

– I'll be right there, I said, and heard an unfamiliar reply.

When I opened the door the next sound to reach me was the canter of horses from the plain, their distant whickering floating upon the breeze. It stayed with me as I walked to the first tripod, climbed its slender rungs, and took to the rope – a gentle cadence that pulled me along as if I were a pony trap on the lightest of springs.

I counted every step, notching my passage in the soles of my feet as if marking time. Sixty-one steps out, sixty-two back. I walked again and counted the same. And a third time, wondering where the extra step came from, trying to discover the moment I gained it. It could only be as I turned, and that thought was the devil that tripped me, made me falter and later blame it on a sickness when the truth would've been easier to admit. I landed on that damned ankle and it sent a jolt to my spine. A faint, August Boothe told the proprietor. The show was off, too dangerous to attempt.

– She will be a lucky girl not to have broken something, I heard him say, the owner still keen for me to perform the next day.

They carried me to the waggon, laid me on the bare bunk and drew the curtain. August Boothe ordered a doctor from Dartford, who arrived in a huff, long after dark. He had a bulging nose and brown spots on his yellow face.

– Unlikely to be a fracture, he said, barely touching my ankle and not looking at me.

But when we were alone, he bent over me and laid his cold hands on my thighs, making me shudder. I grabbed the empty medicine bottle and shook it in front of his face.

– Who gave you that? the doctor barked.

– A friend. It keeps the pain at bay. My back isn't so strong.

– Because you're starved, he said, tugging the skin at my waist. There's more meat on a flea.

– Might you give me enough to see me through the night, I said, but he didn't reply.

He sat on the edge of the bunk and rummaged in his case, an ancient leather thing he could've had from birth for how old it looked.

– I'll give you something to rub on it, he said.

– What good will that do, I spat.

Then it happened so quickly. I sat up and touched his leg by accident. He caught my eye and quick as that, unbuttoned his fly as he footed the chair against the door. He took my hand and gripped it round his cock, though there was not so much of it. I pulled him till he came in my palm, and he stood and wiped himself with a handkerchief. Then he returned to looking in his bag, and without having to search for long he fetched out a slim bottle, no more than a jack's worth, but enough for a few days. He dropped it into my lap and drew the curtain on me without another word.

As he left, he spoke to my uncle on the step.

– A week's rest should do it, he told him, and I heard the chink of sovereigns, night visits being a costly business.

Twenty-eight

I passed that night in Dartford in a fug, convinced I was lying on the spot where my mother had fallen at the end of her final rope-walk. I imagined her quarrelling with my father before it – him pushing her, causing her to trip and twist her ankle. She must've been quite a size with two in her belly, and good at concealing it. I'd seen a painting of her on the rope that showed her swell, but I knew it could've only been made after her last performance, in the knowledge of what had followed. Cos to my mother's last breath, we'd stayed hidden – my brother and I – beneath the great walking dress she wore, with a bustle big enough to hide a horse and draw a good laugh, the crowd never wise to what lay beneath her cottons and silks. But it wasn't long before my mother's fate became known to all who cared to learn of it – her blood spilt on the soil, another attraction passed, as fleeting as the fairs themselves. And in her place lay me, one moment safe in the airless, noiseless and watery warm, the next dragged into the cold, gasping and grasping for life, vying for survival. Why do I seldom talk of my twin? I have no place for him inside me, is why. No name. Just lonely words drifting like vagrants: Husk. Blue. Still.

*

August Boothe cancelled Hampstead and Oxford and brought me home to Mrs Ducking, telling her in my earshot to keep a close eye on me. She began bathing me every other day, and took to locking the front door in the hope of keeping me safe. But whenever she left the house on errands, I slipped into Stepney, limping round the streets in search of my medicine – that tonic that I couldn't name, but only describe by its look and taste and how it made me feel.

My hunt took me to Mile End, not a dozen steps beyond the old glass maker's – spitting distance across the main road from the King Henry Inn. It was a tiny chemist's shop. The owner was Raggett, and he was an ugly fool. He could barely see over the till and had one leg shorter than the other so he stood lopsided. With that and his monocle, and a belly that could feed a pig for a week, we could've charged a pretty penny to show him in the fairs. On the first occasion I visited, he was happy to take one of Mrs Ducking's silver spoons in exchange for a quarter pint of the stuff. But later, nothing but my mouth would satisfy him – sticking himself in there, stroking my chin and calling me his little gypsy boy.

Eventually, buoyed much as Nat had been in her final days, on a wave that I knew might drop me at any moment, I returned to the Green and to the sanctuary of the rope. August Boothe hadn't visited me for a month, but he must've gotten word I was practising again, cos he arrived at the Green on just my second day back, looking pleased with himself.

– You found everything in order, I trust?

I nodded as I readied myself to step out, realising I'd taken it for granted the rope would be here on my return.

I walked to the far tree in silence, my uncle following me below, a few paces behind.

– Bravo! he called out as I finished, taking my balancing pole from me before I climbed down to rest. I am having a slack rope brought here later today, he said, handing me a towel to wipe the sweat from my hands. Crystal Palace is two weeks tomorrow – Saturday first, in case you had forgotten.

– I remember, I replied, though in truth I'd thought it another month away.

– We need to be prepared. Crossing the Falls of Niagara has made Monsieur Blondin the most respected rope-walker the world over.

Then I will hardly impress him on a ten foot slack rope, I thought to myself.

– I'll begin the moment the rope arrives, I replied.

I practised every day from then, except once when the pain in my back was too great for the medicine to lift me from my bed.

My head was filled with thoughts of Virgil, the slack rope reminding me of the Basin; all those Sundays spent with him teaching me. It surprised me again, how different it was to the tightrope, having to start over learning how to balance.

Which left me little time to anticipate Monsieur Blondin.

It was a perfect summer's morning. August Boothe sent a hansom pulled by a mare black as night with pink ribbons in its mane. It was her birthday, the driver told me, and I shed a tear at the thought he might care so.

Crystal Palace was a sight to lift even the lowest of spirits. The carriage turned a corner and there it loomed before me – a great sweep of glass and metal, rising from the ground like a monument of ice. Around it were numerous fountains that dwarfed any of those at Cremorne. Huge balustrades marched across the lawns into the distance. There were statues of beasts so lifelike they might've broken out of a menagerie.

All round me, a raft of eager souls were descending upon the arena, clutching their two-and-six to enter – so many of them, and of all ages, they must've been scouring the riverbed and filching from their grandmothers for the flood of shillings and half-crowns that poured into the turnstiles. Not even the promise of gladiators being torn apart by lions could've brought them any quicker.

The slack rope upon which I was to perform was rigged on the concourse outside the main palace entrance, quite dwarfed by the walls of glass; I'd be like a flea in a life-size circus, I thought.

August Boothe met me and handed me a ticket.

– This will get you a good view from the gallery, he said. Be quick getting ready. I shall be bringing in the Monsieur very soon.

I changed in an alcove at the edge of the concourse, rather too close to the queuing crowd. I wiped the sweat from my feet, adjusted my cap, and took to the rope. I made a poor effort to begin with – faltering too many times to pretend it was part of the act – though the crowd were far more concerned with getting inside.

But then the queue fell silent, everyone turning their backs to me. I was midway along the rope and paused, almost completely still. I took two steps forward, caught a glimpse of August Boothe, and met the eyes of the man walking beside him, who only reached the height of his shoulders. The man nodded in my direction and the crowd looked towards me again. I turned on the spot – a perfect pirouette that I hadn't practised. The crowd cheered and applauded as I reached the far tripod. Then the queue was moving again, the rattle of coins filling the air, and my uncle and Monsieur Blondin were gone from sight.

I jumped from the rope, recovered my clogs, and slipped ahead of the queue into the Palace, climbing the stairs to the upper gallery, to where the press and privileged were gathering. The view gave a sickening sense of the chasm Blondin was about to walk above – a hundred feet to earth from the middle of the rope, I reckoned, and higher still at each end.

At the strike of four o'clock, the strains of the Coldstream band faded and Blondin stepped from a curtain atop the nearest tower. Behind him, to a fanfare, a huge canvas was unfurled, showing a waterfall and above it in the mist a walker on a tightrope. Blondin nodded to every corner of the hall and a roar of voices greeted him. He was dressed in a plain blouse that stopped at the elbows, scarlet breeches, and pale fleshings. His only ornament was a feather headdress and a row of medals across his chest. He lifted his pole now – a red and white striped one that I took a fancy to – and began descending the rope for the ten or so yards before it became level.

– Three hundred feet across, my neighbour whispered to me in a frail voice, with a look that hinted she wouldn't be upset if he didn't make it.

His walk was as much a dance as Virgil's, at every step lifting his knee to above his waist and occasionally throwing a foot out to one side. At midway along the rope he paused, then all but sprinted to the far platform as though on a running track. He rested there for just a moment, but I knew what those seconds would mean to him, before he set out once more down the incline. He walked backwards this time, and I do believe every one of those ten thousand breaths was held for him. Stopping at the middle, he crouched, then lay on his back, his pole beneath his neck, and let out a great yawn. It broke the spell and let us all breathe again and smile nervously at his antics. But instead of getting up, he rolled over so his face was touching the rope. He tossed his cap so it floated into the audience, gripped the balancing pole, and then drew himself up into a perfect headstand, which brought the loudest applause yet and not a few cries of disbelief. Back on his feet again, he returned to the first platform, slipped behind the curtain, and I was sure then he must be done. Yet he was out again in seconds, wearing a sack over his head and body, his arms poking through holes in the sides. He repeated his routine to such stunned silence you'd have thought the palace was empty. At the end of it he pulled off the sack to reveal a bandage covering his eyes, and the crowd roared, as he tore that off too and took his bows, waving again to every corner and throwing kisses to us all.

When I next heard the clock strike, I could barely believe half an hour had passed. The band piped up with a few rounds of God Save the Queen and only then did I realise Her Majesty must be there too, tucked in the Royal Box with her beloved. When I made to join the applause I found a hand gripping my forearm and I turned to the woman beside me, who was still staring ahead to where Blondin no longer was.

– God bring St Vitus upon us. Do it again young man. Please do it again, she pleaded.

I good as had to prise off her fingers as she cried out, though there was no leaving the gallery even when I was free. The crowd were remaining firm in their seats, or standing beside or on them, none wanting to miss the exchanges now raging all round. At once, everyone was an expert on Blondin, his name falling from lips like an old friend's. This was how he'd managed it; that was the best moment; that was the slip he'd not meant. It made me impatient to return to the rope, towards ever-greater peril.

It was August Boothe who freed me at last, pushing towards me along the aisles and grabbing my wrist, more excited than I'd ever seen him.

– What a marvel. A sensation. Truly the finest in the world, did you not think? he said, and what could I do but agree, and know it was beyond anything to which I could dare aspire.

We took a short ride to a hotel, a neat cream-coloured building standing in a vast rose garden. My uncle whisked me into a lounge where Blondin was already taking tea, holding forth amongst a gaggle of women.

I could see him properly now. His eyes were small and close-set, his moustache wide and bristly, his goatee beard trimmed like Pip Bell's. He'd changed into a white waistcoat and jacket with more medals attached, a pale shirt and bow tie, grey flannels and brown leather shoes polished like a veneer. He leant on his cane, holding his top hat in the same hand and a teacup in the other. He spoke in French, I guessed, and I wondered if any of the women could understand. August Boothe brought me into the circle and exchanged a few words, before Blondin turned to me and the ladies huffed.

– Monsieur is interested to hear of your progress, my uncle said, so I curtsied, which seemed the right thing to do.

– I'm a little out of practise on the slack rope, I said.

August Boothe translated at once, yet Blondin took a while to reply, holding out his cup for a waiter to refill it. When he did speak he made my uncle laugh.

– He says you need only imagine there is no rope at your feet.

I smiled and turned away shyly to Blondin's admirers, but they were now busy stuffing their mouths with sponge cake and helping themselves to more tea. I wanted to make the most of this encounter, fearing it might not be repeated. I thought back to those first steps at Bartholomew Fair when I was seven. And I remembered all the things I'd wanted to ask Virgil and Nat: where should I focus when I falter; how should I breathe when my lungs are full with the cold; which part of my foot should I turn on? Then I fell upon a question I thought the cleverest.

What do you see when you wear a blindfold?

What a great discussion we could have, comparing the strangeness that lingers behind one's eyes, how different night is to day.

I was about to ask it, had the words poised on my tongue, ready to smile at my own wit, when I blurted another question altogether.

– But why ever do we do it? I said, and without needing it translated, Blondin roared with laughter.

He carried the whole room with his cheer. Even August Boothe was amused and nodded to me several times as though I'd won a great argument. At last the Frenchman collected himself, raised a hand to silence his followers, and replied in perfect English.

– Why indeed, he said, patting my arm like a father might. We do it because we cannot possibly *not* do it.

Twenty-nine

I took a spate of engagements for the next six weeks, roused now as much by meeting Blondin as by the medicine. I must've visited two dozen towns and cities and travelled hundreds of miles, though I can only recall Cambridge for its river and the awful journey, and Reading for the children cutting the guy ropes. I know that in one week I walked in eight different towns, so that my performances became my practise. I only riled Mrs Ducking once when I forgot to tell her of a midweek show, when she'd made a bath ready and found me gone before I could take it.

I was paid handsomely at the end of it all, my debt to my uncle finally cleared, such that I could now afford my tonic without stealing or selling my body for it, as I'd once promised myself I never would. I should've guessed the chemist would prefer me penniless and desperate though.

When you opened the door to Raggett's shop, there was a huge bell that rattled and brought him scuttling from the back room. But the day I barged in with shillings in hand, he was already behind his counter, and I saw his face light up before he noticed the coins. His eye with the lens always roved more, but perhaps only cos you could see it better. He gave me a looking up and down, which should've warned me well enough.

– I've run out down below. Be a love and fetch me a new flask, he said, pointing to the highest shelf in the glass cabinet behind him.

I stepped across to his side of the counter and as I looked up he grabbed me by the little hair I had and pushed me to my knees. He had it out and in my mouth before I could speak, which was when August Boothe strode into the shop.

He couldn't have seen me at first, but he must've seen Raggett's face all screwed up, and it didn't take him long to fathom. He stepped through the counter as if it weren't there, showering me with glass and splinters, picked up a paperweight and swiped it against the chemist's cheek, who took a fair tumble as I spat him out.

My uncle pulled me to my feet and marched me out the door, took me to the White Horse and ordered me a brandy.

– He forced me, I began, but my uncle put up his hand.

– I leave this evening with Monsieur Blondin, he said. I was coming to the Green to let you know. I shall be gone for a week. I suggest you rest.

I should've sought out another supply at once, cos the next day the pain returned as if someone was hammering a nail into my hip. I lay on my bed looking at the ceiling, imagining faces and creatures in the plasterwork. By and by, my room grew busy with visitors: Ellie, my aunt, Nat. My mother too. I don't know why they chose that time to visit. Did they mean me to feel guilty for surviving them, for living beyond my time?

They urged me outside, across the road and on to the Green. I lay beside the far hedgerow, staring up at the sky's vast blue canvas. I lay there so long, so still, I'm sure my blood stopped flowing, growing stagnant in my veins. Then night fell and I was pricked like a pincushion by the light of a million stars. By dawn the dead were gone – in their place a procession of memories that passed in front of me as if painted on a huge scroll, being unwound like the scenery of the penny theatres. With the parting of the night's curtain, I knew that nothing was forgotten, that all joys and pains remained if I truly wanted to recount them. The trees, the bushes at my side, the tripods and rope, they took on a size of their own, so the mightiest planes now brushed heads with dandelions, and the tightrope scraped the heavens so I could balance upon it and sweep clouds from the sky. And if I stepped off I might plummet like a gravestone or spin to earth like a seedling on the wind.

I heard a voice and saw Mrs Ducking standing over me as the sun rose behind her.

– For goodness sake, I've been worrying myself sick all night, she said, and then I knew what I should do.

I let Mrs Ducking take me home but I wouldn't stop for breakfast.

– I need to go to Blackheath, I told her.

– But you've been awake all night and not eaten.

– I need to visit the fair, I insisted.

I swapped my blouse for a clean one, took my bag and found a hansom at Mile End. I often travelled alone now but it felt different this time. The journey was so familiar but the sounds and smells seemed changed; perhaps I just noticed them differently – the din of steam engines whenever the cab neared a station; the stench of all those people pressed together in the heat.

When I arrived at the fair it seemed altered too, the crowds sparser than in previous years. I took a sip of medicine and roamed awhile without recognising anyone, till at last I spotted James walking away from a ring of waggons. I didn't call out; though it'd been six months, it wasn't him I'd come to see.

My father's waggon was outside the circle, as I'd feared it would now be. The door was open but there was a broom across it. I rapped on the window anyway and climbed to the top step before I heard his voice.

– Busy, whoever it is, he called out.

He was slumped, wine glass in hand, on the tiny bench that had replaced my bunk. I almost didn't notice the girl, as there was barely room for two on the seat. She lay under a blanket, her legs tucked out of sight. He was holding one side of her, as if she'd fall if he let go. When she saw me, she moved off at once, keeping the blanket wrapped round her, and took to the floor, her hair tumbling about her shoulders in yellow curls. No older than me, I reckoned.

– I said I was busy, my father repeated, reaching for a bottle from beside the bench. You look awful. He been hitting you?

– Not at all. He's a perfect gentleman, I said. I'm just under the weather. I've been working every day for two months.

– He's made a slave of you then, my father scoffed.

– I've been rope-walking, I said. I'm good at it. I pay my own way now. I've saved a little already.

– Every fairground wants a walker, these days. It's the bane of my life.

– I'm sure it's because of Monsieur Blondin, I said. I met him at Crystal Palace.

– A bloody charlatan, so I've heard. Bet he's never worked a proper fairground crowd. Anyway, we've got Della now, he said, turning to the girl, who shot me an awkward look. We found her in King's Lynn. Never seen a hill before she came away with us, but swims like a seal. And just orphaned. Isn't that right Della?

The girl nodded and I felt for her, to be introduced so.

– Della fancies her chances on the tightrope. We're starting her next week at Astley's old place. You should come along, you might learn something. It's never too late.

– I was always too soon for you, I replied. That, and you'd rather I'd never been born at all, as you once told me.

My father put the wine glass to his lips and sipped noisily, not answering.

It was then I saw it – when the girl reached for her own glass and let the blanket slip from her shoulders; it was pinned clumsily to the collar of her blouse as if a mere trinket.

– So it's hers now is it? I blurted.

220

My father frowned at the girl before spotting the tiger claw.

– She wears it rather well I think, he said. Anyway, I seem to remember you didn't want it, so your sentiment seems an odd one.

– You denied it to me for wanting to become a walker. Yet now you give it to her for attempting the same craft. Surely that is what is odd.

The girl started unpinning the brooch but my father stayed her.

– Keep it on, damn you. My daughter's just leaving.

– Do you treat all your new hands this way? I said, not moving.

– Bit of discipline doesn't do any harm.

– I meant, sharing your bed with them.

My father sighed and shook his head.

– Don't you have to be somewhere? That cousin of mine not got you slaving for him today?

– Like I said, I've been working for two months, I replied. I'm resting now. Looking for other employment perhaps.

My father eyed me for a moment, then turned away, staring into space as though reckoning something.

– Come back up here, he said at last to Della, patting his lap. My daughter really is leaving now.

I didn't wait to be told a third time. I stepped from the running board, wondering if I'd ever set foot on it again. I heard a slap, a whimper from the girl. I closed my eyes for a moment, then walked into the fair.

Thirty

August Boothe returned only for one day. He was bound next for Dublin and then Edinburgh. He said that before finding me any new engagements he wanted me properly recovered, though he didn't say from what. And though we'd never spoken of it, he brought me two quarts of the medicine and told me to reduce the dose a little each day.

In the weeks that followed, I sank into a torpor that kept me in bed every day till gone noon, before spending my few waking hours on the Green, when it was warm enough to lie in just a shift. But I didn't take to the rope again, not then.

As my uncle had instructed, I began eking out the medicine, taking less each time. My mind would uncloud for a moment, revealing the things I'd allowed to slip: searching for Virgil; getting word to Dorothy; visiting the flower seller again; discovering whether that dock-rat had truly died by my hand. They were like so many loose threads, and I felt if I let just one go beyond reach again, I would lose them all.

Eventually, the tonic was doing little more than painting a dull veneer over my world. By then I was counting the drops as if crazed. Ten hundred. Nine hundred and fifty. Eight hundred and seventy-five. Once, I only managed to count out three hundred and spent that day doubled in bed with such pains in my stomach.

I stopped sleeping and the only food I could manage was a plain soup that Mrs Ducking brought me. She wanted to fetch a doctor but I persuaded her not to. At some point she took the mirror from my room – perhaps not wanting me pained by how I looked, or fearing I'd break it and injure myself.

The less medicine I took, the fiercer the visions became, and the more strange my memories. Repeatedly I saw Nat's face, sometimes drained and contorted, sometimes still alive – pleading for my help, caught in the strop she'd used to regain her strength, with me in reach of saving her. Had I not moved cos my soles were still warm from her tight-wire and now I had a taste for her garland? Had I not tried to save her cos of what I might lose? Could it really have been so?

I met Ellie in my nightmares too, and cursed her for abandoning me when she found true love. Could I have seen the pulley falling, and thrust my tray forwards causing her to step back? Might I have thought – if I can't have you to myself, then no one can? I'm sure there was such a rumour at the time. Did they have no shame, placing such burden upon a child?

What a relief then, taking a thousand drops of the stuff and returning to its pleasures, escaping the starkness of my thoughts.

Yet, a chink had been revealed in its armour, a glimpse of a world of no medicine, so that after a vision that kept me awake for two days I took just a hundred drops and plunged into sleep for I don't know how long. The next I knew of it, Mrs Ducking was standing beside me with her hand resting on my back, and I was eating as if my life depended on it. Inside me I could feel every movement, every twist and turn of every grain and morsel as it passed through my gut, till I could stomach no more and I shitted a stream of the stuff into the pot beneath my bed.

I began September as bright as a lamb, clean of that damned pollution. At last I could see beyond my imaginings. I took delight in every fading flower, the sharpness of every blade of grass. My sense of smell returned too, so I took in the scent of summer's passing and the stirring of autumn. Mrs Ducking thought me much improved and thanked God for my recovery. I took to having my weekly bath again and began eating a solid meal every other day, till my stomach could cope with more.

As I grew stronger I felt ready to return to the Green, though I feared it might tempt me back into familiar ways. But when finally I arrived there, I found the rope adorned with silk ribbon, dozens of short strips draped along its length, hanging like delicate fingers and waving in the breeze like a welcome. I climbed the tree at once and stepped onto the rope as if after an hour's rest rather than a month in that hopeless pit, and though it took the day to manage the whole rope without falling, I had an audience by the end of it, pausing from their Sunday strolls. And when they applauded and children threw their hats into the air, I felt a queer sensation rising in my stomach.

Hunger. It had returned.

When I arrived back at Mrs Ducking's that evening, she invited me upstairs into her parlour. It was my first time stepping above the ground floor. The room was generous, with a narrow bed at one end, and the remnants of a fire in the grate.

– I only heat this room nowadays, she said, when she saw me looking. It was a bit cool two nights ago; I can feel it starting to turn.

– It's very cosy, I told her, though it smelt of old cabbage.

– When my husband was alive we kept fires in every room, she went on. Ten year ago we had a dozen staying that were building the railway. I slaved around the clock, not a day's rest in two years, that's how long they stayed. They weren't a bad sort. We certainly had worse, before and after. I don't mean you, of course.

– I didn't know Mr Ducking had passed away, I gasped, though I'd never seen or heard tale of the man till now.

– Oh goodness, he died months ago, she replied, as casual as that. Soon after Easter it was. I've had an empty place at my table ever since.

I reached for her hand, feeling ashamed I'd not known, that in my busyness I'd missed her husband's body being carried downstairs and carted away. But she made it seem of so little consequence – all in a day's work.

– Every winter we used to watch the fair pass my sister's house, she went on. She lived three streets away. My two boys, they'd wait up until dawn if the waggons were late coming. That was before you were born.

– We came in the summer too, a couple of times, I said. The first time, I was seven. I suppose that was a long time after. Are your boys nearby? Do you have grandchildren?

Mrs Ducking shook her head and busied herself setting the table.

– Mine were not so long on this earth, she said, taking a deep breath. Twins, both died of the pox, a day each side of their tenth birthday.

– I'm sorry, I told her, but she just shrugged and said it was all a very long time ago.

The table had cork mats instead of a cloth, the surface so polished you could see the cutlery reflected in it. She brought out a whole roast chicken, a heap of potatoes, vegetables and stuffing, and a jug of gravy as brown as the table. I set upon it at once, hoping I wasn't being rude in my haste, and what with all she'd just told me.

– Do you have any other guests at the moment? I asked between mouthfuls, and she put down her knife and fork and dabbed her mouth before answering.

– The last one's just left, she said. I feel I'm getting too old for it. And I reckon you're quite enough for me to be looking after.

– I don't wish to be a burden. I'm better now and I'm going to stay that way, I told her.

– I shall look after you as long as is needed, she insisted.

I took all my meals with her then. I adored her parlour with its cast fireplace and oak mantle full of china, the wing-backed chairs with lace shoulders, the wall of books. I'd have imagined it very different had I given it a thought, but I never had; Mrs Ducking had brought me my meals, washed my sheets and bathed me, and I'd not considered her life beyond that.

I began practising every day again, and eating enough for two, till my stomach started to swell and my breasts found a hint of their shape once more. My hair grew back and my bleeding returned, though the pain was little more than an itch to what I'd suffered coming off the poison.

When my uncle finally came back, I realised I'd been practising so hard but with nothing to work towards; I was just walking for my own pleasure and healing. I was so glad to see him I threw my arms round his neck, taking him quite by surprise, and he nodded to Mrs Ducking, as if to say they'd conspired in my recovery and the job was now done.

– It's a joy indeed to see you looking so well, he said.

– And to see you, I told him, cos truly he looked hearty for his jaunt.

– I shall get straight to business. I spotted a vacancy in *The Era*. Worcester on the twenty-eighth of this month. I cannot fathom them for not contacting me directly, but I applied as soon as I saw the notice. You would be walking for seventy yards at forty feet. I've asked for fifteen pounds, a fair price I think you would agree.

– I'm more than ready, I said, but he put a finger to my lips.

– You can never be so. You have two weeks. Monsieur Blondin sends his regards.

Thirty-one

Being well again, I could think about the months just passed – not only the better moments like meeting Blondin, but that last clash with my father. It enraged me so, that I now resolved to forge a path of my own, to remember what Nat and Virgil had taught me, and finally to honour my mother's legacy.

I began by shedding my boyish skin; it had become another burden and I needed to bury it along with my bad memories, like of the docker. Mrs Ducking helped me. She fashioned my hair and bleached it till there was not a strand of gypsy black to be seen. She came with me to Aldgate and chose my costume – a cream dress with lace flounces, and matching bodice.

– This'll get 'em talking, she said, lacing me in till I could barely breathe.

I bought a second dress, cheaper but cut the same as the first, to practise in. We found kohl for my eyes, carmine for my lips, and a pot of nail polish at a price Mrs Ducking couldn't believe.

– It's a good thing your uncle pays you handsomely, she said, which made me a little sore.

– I feel I take all the risk for it, I retorted, a little sharply perhaps, as she quickly apologised.

My last day of practise before Worcester, August Boothe came to the Green. I was trying a pirouette near the end of the rope when he stepped into view. He clapped after I managed it twice; I didn't attempt a third.

– I want to change my stage name, I told him, as he helped me from the ladder.

– And your sex? he replied, looking me up and down.

– I won't take another step dressed as a boy.

He smiled and fingered the fabric of my new outfit.

– You have excellent taste.

– I want to be known as Mademoiselle Rouge.

My uncle took out his pipe and began shaking his head.

– It is much too late to change the posters. They will already be on every wall and lamp post in Worcester.

– Then they must be replaced, else I shan't walk. You can say that the Boothe boy is ill or something, but lo and behold, you've found another at the eleventh hour. A *Female Blondin*. How does that sound?

August Boothe looked away for a moment, towards the far tree where the rope was anchored.

– That perhaps you should not tempt Lucky Boothe's demise so easily, he replied at last, turning back to me with a smile. But to answer your question fully, it sounds like a name I wish I had coined myself. Female Blondin, indeed. I like it very much. I shall send word and see what can be done. If we can make them think you are someone else, then we have nothing to lose.

I clapped my hands. My first triumph, if a small one.

We journeyed the next day by train, my first time on one. It seemed an awful luxury, but my uncle insisted it was cheaper and quicker than the stagecoach. When we arrived at Worcester station, the first thing I saw was a poster of a woman rope-walker, pasted over a torn bill.

– They are changing as many as they can, August Boothe told me, pointing to my name.

I asked him to read it and he bent till his eyes were level with the print.

– It says, "Mademoiselle Rouge, famous Female Blondin, most fearless rope dancer extant, performing her daring exploit, a terrific ascent of the rope accompanied by spectacular fireworks." So how does *that* sound? he said with a flourish.

– A little terrifying and fearsome, I admitted. Though just as exciting as the Frenchman I hope. How high is it again?

– Perhaps fifty feet. I'm sure no more than that.

There was a hansom waiting for us, and a cart to take our luggage and my balancing pole. It was already dusk when we passed the Pleasure Gardens, slowing at the entrance – a huge pair of iron gates that were now shut. Through them I could see a long straight drive, and at the end of it, a squat glass building aglow in the last of the sun, like a broken-off chunk of the Crystal Palace.

– Perhaps a little fear is healthy, I said, as the glasshouse changed colour.

August Boothe sniffed and pointed to one of the gate pillars, which had a poster the same as we'd seen at the station, only larger.

– Let us hope the gamble pays, he said, tapping the roof of the cab for the driver to continue.

In the early morning, the air sharp in my chest, I paced the length of the Arboretum to become familiar with my surroundings. I discovered great avenues and terraces flanked by colonnades, flowerbeds in every direction, a green for bowling and another for archery. I found hothouses and bandstands, a marionette theatre, an orangery, and empty stalls with pictures promising tea and cake. At the centre was a great stone fountain dripping with moss and ferns. None of it quite had the mystery or grandeur of Cremorne, but the gardens were something to behold all the same.

I'd just two hours to prepare before the gates were thrown open. I was not allowed on the main rope yet, but had to practise on a short rig a few feet above ground, such that the prospect of the walk itself began to panic me. I forgot the hours I'd spent on the Green, and convinced myself I'd gone stale – that the medicine had destroyed my poise. I couldn't eat and had to dress myself three times before I was happy with the effect. But in my muddle came an idea, when the headscarf I was trying out – to decide whether it fitted with my costume, – fell down my forehead over my eyes. I thought – I've managed it before, so why not try it again?

At four o'clock I started climbing the tower in a stiff breeze. When I reached the platform the wind seemed to lessen and I looked out over the gathering crowd. I'd not expected so many, thinking most would wait till my second performance at nightfall when the arena would be ablaze with gaslights. But I was mistaken. Soon I could barely make myself heard to my helpers above the din from below, and I took to miming my instructions for readying the pole.

I was a good while preparing myself, and the crowd swelled with every passing minute. I wondered what had brought them in such numbers. Had they seen the new poster and been curious of this cuckoo in the nest? Then I realised – how stupid of me – they were flocking to witness one of the fairer sex; we'd become something of a rarity on the rope.

Before I stepped out, I tied the blindfold round my eyes to ensure the right tension, then dropped it to my neck, which is when I looked directly down and sensed I was now at a height beyond that which I could fathom. The short descent to where the first guys were attached and the rope levelled was not as steep as I'd feared though. I took a breath there, then lifted my balancing pole to my chest and stepped forwards to a great roar.

I walked at a steady pace, counting my steps, and stopped at the middle of the rope. I might've tried a pirouette had I felt ready. But instead, I grabbed hold my scarf and pulled it up till it covered my eyes. When the crowd saw this they started to applaud – too politely, expecting the worst.

Upon my first blind step, it flooded back to me – the loss of hearing, the feel of the rope through my feet: I was walking in Cambridge above Jesus Lock, waving at the boatmen; I was dressed in flannels on my first day at the

Green; I was practising at dusk on the wire above the Waste; in the meadow near Weston Hill; on the washing rope at Bartholomew Fair. I recalled every slip and misjudged footfall, as though they were imprisoned in my feet and with every step I now took, another was set free, leaving me to walk a perfect line.

When I reached the far tower, I feared the noise from the crowd might unsettle me. I threw off the blindfold, handed the pole to my helpers, and began climbing down at speed. At the bottom, August Boothe was waiting.

– Truly magnificent, he said, clasping my hand. The press are humming. They'll be over you like a rash. Perhaps I should speak for you.

– I'll speak for myself; I'm not afraid of them, I told him, and as I did, a throng of reporters fell upon us and not even both our voices were enough to satisfy them.

They hounded us the length of the Arboretum, sporting similar brown suits and felt hats, only the cut and how well they wore them setting them apart. As I reached my changing tent beside the first tower, one of the more dapper finally caught me, my uncle still fending off the others.

– Phelps, Worcester Herald, he said, then fired a series of questions: What's your age? Where you from? Is that your husband or fiancé?

I replied as quickly as I could and all the while he scribbled into a notebook.

– And where else have you performed? he asked, which made me pause before replying.

– Till two days ago I was known as Lucky Boothe, I told him, taking a deep breath after I said it.

– The fairground boy? he said, looking up from his notebook.

– There can't be many folk believed that.

– It made good copy, he replied, raising his eyebrows. So, how about the esteemed Lucky Boothe's favourite walks?

I reeled off as many places as I could remember, and a few engagements I hadn't kept, till he seemed satisfied.

– And what makes you now call yourself Mademoiselle Rouge?

– Madame Rouge was a friend of mine. I walk in her memory. And now you know I can do so even with a cunt between my legs.

He stopped writing and broke into a smile.

– That would make an excellent headline too, were it printable. But wait! he called, as I pushed into the tent. There's more I need to ask for my readers.

I paused and turned back to him.

– I've another performance to get ready for. But perhaps we could meet after, I said, letting the canvas close on him.

My uncle weren't keen to allow it, but agreed the reporter could join us at the hotel at the end of the evening. Before that, I walked a second time, without blindfold, as it was good as dark now anyway, amidst fireworks set off from both towers. On returning to the first tower I was handed a shorter pole with a flare at each end, and so I stepped out for my encore, my arms wide, looking as though I had magnesium spitting from my fingertips.

– That was a very grand finale, Mr Phelps told me after, sitting in the hotel bar, overlooking the river.

I took a sip of the lemonade my uncle had insisted upon and winced at the sweetness of it. I reached for the reporter's tumbler of gin and poured half of it into my glass, which made him laugh.

– You certainly have plenty to celebrate, he said, glancing at August Boothe at the next table, where he was deep in conversation with Blondin's agent.

The taproom was little bigger than Mrs Ducking's parlour, though the ceiling was higher. It had a carpet the same dark red as its walls – and most of the furniture in fact

– and I thought, if you wore the same colour you'd be quite lost in it.

– So you're making your own way in the world? A brave stance for a young lady, if I may say so.

– Are we back to the interview now? I replied, which made Phelps chuckle again. I'm no different to other women in the fairs. We all have our duties.

– Tell me then, what was yours? he asked, taking up his pen and notebook.

The question stumped me somewhat, and Phelps sat back and flattened his tie as I pondered what to say.

– You're not with your family now, apart from your *uncle*? he continued, when I didn't reply.

– My father's cousin, to be exact. They were born the same day: one in Paris, the other in Whitechapel.

– An intriguing coincidence then. Specially for two such important men in your life.

– I've made my own way with hard work and practise. My uncle gave me a chance, is all I would say. But it's just me on that rope in the end. Had I fallen tonight from that height, I would surely have died.

– I don't doubt that, Phelps said, scribbling into his book. Indeed, I've witnessed such a fall.

I thought Phelps too young to be a reporter, clean-shaven and his hair glossy with oil. But he was sharp enough for it. Doubtless he reckoned there was another in my life, but he didn't press me. Instead, he asked how I'd come by my name, my real name, Lucky Boothe.

– Ellie Scott, who raised me, called me that, I told him.

– Not your mother then?

– Ellie was killed when I was seven and I don't recall much before it. But I can tell you something from every day since, I said, which was almost true.

I could've told him the few stories I had from before Ellie died, but to what end? I could've said – my father cast me out after I took his wife from him with a tug to her gut. I could've told him the story that'd done the rounds at the time, the one that Pip Bell enjoyed telling: that Katherine Scott had taken a glass shard to my mother's belly and slit her open, before plucking me out by my ankles and giving me a good slap on the arse; though I've always reckoned I fought my own way out.

I must've shed a tear, thinking of it all, as Phelps touched my hand and told me he was sorry for prying, though I thought that was precisely what he was meant to do. But I weren't about to give any more, not for nothing anyway.

Thirty-two

If summer dragged in a haze of that damned tonic, autumn now passed as quickly as my hair grew out, looking quite odd till it returned to black. I fell accustomed to the hustle and bustle of always performing, barely knowing the hour let alone the day. The Female Blondin, my very own invention, proved a sensation. Suddenly it seemed that Mademoiselle Rouge was known to every household in the land, her image plastered on every news-stand, though I'd not yet performed north of York or west of Reading. It turned out Phelps had inky fingers in a host of newspapers, not just the *Worcester Herald*. Between his and August Boothe's connections, I was busy every night and most daytimes for two months, with barely a murmur from the authorities – the Queen now having graver concerns than the exploits of a mere fairground girl walking the tightrope.

I lived out of a wooden suitcase August Boothe had bought me, and got too familiar with the insides of dull hotels and boarding houses, so Mrs Ducking and I became strangers again, occasionally passing late at night but mostly not at all. The novelty of the railways didn't last either, and I yearned to be horse-drawn once more. I must've earned a pretty penny those weeks, yet so much went as expenses; I was travelling further afield, I had to pay Phelps for the bookings he found, and I was still paying for my room in Stepney as well as all the hotels along the way.

As had happened before, the performances became my only practise, with hardly a spare hour between. No sooner had I undressed from a walk, I was whisked to one railway station and delivered to another, in a compartment thick with soot, and before long I was thinking the docks hadn't been such hard work after all.

When the weather turned, the outside engagements stopped and for all of November I performed inside – anywhere that was big enough to accommodate a tightrope. I even appeared at the Garrick and asked after Ruby and Pearl, but I was met with blank faces.

I was surprised at how many circus buildings there now were – places we'd been passing for years that had always looked drab and unwelcoming. Newly minted, they reminded me of Virgil's sketches, and I felt saddened at having lost all those pictures and plans he'd so painstakingly drawn.

I learnt how to perform close to an audience, to step quickly past anyone that looked about to touch me, and avoid the distraction of those trying to catch my eye.

Phelps came to know me rather well, noticing my every mood, when I cried or laughed. And always he respected me for my craft.

– You inhabit the dreams of every man that encounters you, he once told me. I wager it's your face they see when they return home and bear down on their wives.

– But I have no wish for such attention.

– Yet you have no control over how people react, he said.

*

At the end of it all, the end of November in fact, I was returning from Hammersmith where I'd done a week in the same theatre, four shows a day. It was early evening and I was slumped alone in a hansom, barely able to lift an eyelid. I must've travelled like this a good many times in those weeks, half-asleep if not entirely so, and I reckon it was only by August Boothe insisting I had the same driver every time that I escaped trouble. The cab had just reached Fenchurch when the smell hit me. It was such a jolt to my senses – a familiar exotic balm of animal shit and sweat – that I sat up at once and threw the blanket from my legs. The driver slowed the horse as we approached a bend in the road, and suddenly into view came the rear of the fair convoy – with the arse of one of Wombwell's elephants stuck out from a carriage like a monstrous face. The driver drew the cab to a halt and opened the roof hatch, as he bit the cork free from a flask and spat it into his lap, then sucked on the bottle.

– Reckon you'll be quicker walking from here, he called down to me, before taking another swig and stopping the bottle without offering it.

Indeed, the convoy was taking up the whole width of the road, every waggon and show carriage carrying a red lantern, like a string of Christmas candles stretching as far as I could see. The Boothes and Bells would be amongst it – I was sure of that – but this was an entire fair before me, goodness knows how many families and shows. I knew they must be headed for Mile End, as there was nowhere else nearby for such numbers to descend upon. I knew also I might once again join them, help them transform the Waste into the month-long Winter Fair, the same as had fed my soul for all my childhood.

My two lives now collided, like twins parted at birth. I'd found success of sorts, courting adoring crowds day and night; the fame meant little to me, but the craft had become my lifeline. I could ignore the rumours – of my addiction to opium, as I now knew the tonic to be; that I had a Ruby or Pearl in every town; that I only went with men during my cycle. In truth, I'd turned to no man or woman for love since Virgil, and only for opium before I could buy it myself.

I had to ask myself though – am I truly in charge of my trade? Do I even know my fee? I only see what August Boothe pays me. Might there still be a place for me elsewhere – in the fair perhaps?

– I'll say goodbye, I called to the driver at last, waiting for him to release the doors before I flung them away from my feet, knowing he'd be happy to see me gone and not stuck as the convoy crept to Mile End without a care.

I stepped from the board, my legs feeling like a stack of cards ready to collapse. The driver handed me my case and wished me luck. I tramped up the line of show carriages, counting fifteen in the menagerie alone, before reaching the Freemans, where I jumped onto the back of the first living waggon, using the corner post as a handhold. The driver must've felt it and at once he craned from his perch. I recognised him as one of George Freeman's sons, though I can't recall his name.

– Jesus! If it's not Lucky Boothe herself, he cried out, making his passenger lean over too and give me a good looking up and down.

– Is my uncle James ahead? I called to them.

– He'll be up there somewhere. The Cookes are leading us, mind. Come up if you're wanting.

I jumped down and skipped to the front of the waggon, slinging my case at the driver's feet before he lifted me beside him and shunted his companion to make room.

– We're not long over London Bridge. Took half the bleedin' day, with all the traffic, he told me.

I smiled to myself, reckoning there would've been far more folk behind them cursing, though I didn't say it.

– We've come from Elephant and Castle, he went on. Been there two weeks, repairing the shows. So you're coming to walk for us again?

– I'm not sure my father would allow it, I replied, shaking my head. And anyway, did he not find another girl?

It was the woman who piped up now.

– Weren't a useful toenail on that one. Good for lying down and not much else.

The driver laughed and pretended to be shocked.

– Women sure got a tongue on them, he said, before turning to me. She got in the family way, he mouthed, as if it might not be common knowledge. Not your father's, though I don't know how he could be certain, forgive me for saying. Went home to King's Lynn anyways. North End girl she was. But you've been busy. Can't roll two yards without seeing your name, whatever you call yourself these days.

– And good for you, putting a skirt on. Did us all a favour, the woman chipped in.

– So do the Freemans still have the wire? I asked.

– Right in front of your eyes, the driver said, nodding to the waggon ahead. And we've not had a pair of feet on it since your own. We're still carrying it though, bloody thing taking up a whole carriage. My father tried to sell it to yours, but he was wanting none of it, not that he's in charge of much these days, though he's afforded a new waggon somehow; been towing it all summer since Blackheath, not sure what for.

The convoy came to a halt then, where the road narrowed towards Aldgate. I was glad of the distraction, cos I felt a blow hearing those words, realising what my father had lost by his own bloody-mindedness – those shows and reputation hewn by his grandfather with sweat and toil. And now he was wasting what little he had on a waggon he didn't need.

I bid the couple good night and began walking again beside the line of carriages that had now fallen into single file, ready to snake forward once more. I came to the Bells eventually, waving to those that noticed me in the dark, and calling to James as I passed him with a swagger.

– Hey stranger! What's the hurry? he cried out when I didn't stop.

I came upon our old whirligig, pulling a new waggon behind, and then saw my father's. So it was true: he no longer headed the convoy. He was nudging forwards like the rest of them, following each lurch of the carriage in front. I gave him a good fright, stepping up to his riding bench and plumping down beside him. He didn't speak immediately, making out he was concentrating, though all he had to mind was the back end of the Cookes's train. But when we'd remained idle for a few minutes, he let go the reins and gave a sigh.

– Full of surprises, I'll say that for you, he said.

– I was just passing. Thought I'd pop in to say hello. Actually I had a cab, but there's no chance of overtaking you lot tonight. Do you never get any trouble, holding the traffic up like this?

My father allowed himself a smile at that. He pushed his hand into his coat and drew something out, dropping it into my lap.

– For God's sake take this away from me, he said. It's been burning a hole in my pocket.

I looked down. It was the brooch, or half of it at least, a single tiger claw. I glanced at his chest to see if he was wearing the other, but there was nothing on his jacket or collars. I closed my hand over it, taking care not to crush it. My father yawned and stretched his arms so his sleeves rode up; no sign of his copper band either.

– You won't mention Pip Bell again? I said.

He shook his head and forced a laugh.

– You're looking a sight healthier than last time, he said, dropping his arms again and turning to me.

– You're looking well yourself.

– So you never found the Negro?

– No. And Dorothy never came home?

I knew he wouldn't have tried to find her; he didn't consider her his concern. And could I really say I'd done much more, for her or Virgil?

– I was wondering, might you have me walk again at New Year? I now blurted.

He didn't reply at once, so I knew he'd already considered it. But he sat as if pondering it for the first time. I turned the tiger claw twice in my palm before I broke the silence.

– I've still got a room in Stepney, I said, rising from my seat.

He put his hand on my arm and stayed me.

– I don't recall it was me had you walk last time, he said, which I thought was the end of it, but he went on. We have a new waggon, first of its kind.

He winked at me. I'm sure he'd never done so before.

– I think I passed it, I said.

– Needs three horses on the hills.

I took up the brooch and fixed it to my blouse, turning it so it looked like the top half of a waxing moon.

– So might I use it as a dressing room? I said at last.

My father nodded, looking straight ahead.

– At the least, he replied.

– Then I might prefer it for a few weeks whilst I practise, I told him, leaning back in my seat, wondering how comfortable I should make myself.

Thirty-three

We were in sight of the King Henry Inn, when up ahead I saw a waggon pull out of the convoy and turn into the yard; then another; then several small show carriages followed. It was too dark to make them out, and I wondered whom of us Boothes and Bells they might be, most of our shows being too wide to fit through the entrance.

As we reached the gate, I was ready for my father to turn our waggon to the left but he remained looking straight ahead, our course not altering.

– You're riding past the yard, I told him, pointlessly.

He turned to me for a moment, seeming about to speak, but looked forwards again.

– We're not pulling on? I said, realising now what was happening.

My father nodded and lifted the reins to keep the horses moving.

– It's time the Cookes had it, he replied.

The Boothes and Bells had always taken possession of the yard – for all of my lifetime, and for countless years before that. Now there was no choice in the matter – is what my father really meant.

We rolled on for another hundred feet or so, to where it became wide enough for my father to park up his waggon and have a slip of ground between it and the roadside. The new waggon was towed beyond, where the verge widened even more, and our show carriages were taken further still.

My father chocked the wheels and settled his horses, then took up a lantern and my suitcase and told me to follow him to the new waggon, which had been parked up beside our trusty old whirligig.

– I can't believe this thing's still going, my father said, patting its side as though it were a favourite beast.

He ran his hand along the timbers and gave one of the wheels a gentle kick.

– Could do with a lick of paint, I said.

– It's still a profitable ride, he replied, dropping his head and moving on to the living waggon.

I gave him a smile, but he didn't see it. Often I've tried to ignore the changing of our fortunes, if nothing else to save my father the shame. Though I was once blamed for so much – merely by being the one that survived – I knew the truth to be different, that it was really my father who was failing, and had been since the day I was born.

The waggon had six lamps fixed inside and my father now lit them all. It was well furnished with cupboards and drawers, and lacquered shelves with carved ends. The woodwork was inlaid with brass, the mirrors etched with silver, all of it polished to a sheen. There was a sash window on each side, with sliding shutters on the outside. There was a partition across the middle separating the living space from the raised bed, just as there'd once been in my father's waggon. The ceiling was yellow, and on it was painted a wreath of roses circling a pair of swans touching beaks, their feathers like snow. The stove was set in a tiled nook along one of the walls, rather than behind the door. There was a mantelpiece above and a lamp to either side. I was afraid to touch any of it, in case I broke something.

– So what do you think to your new home? my father said, trimming the lamp wicks.

As he spoke, I heard a cockerel crow – too late for this day, too early for the next; I turned away so as to hide my tears.

– I think it rather fine, I whispered eventually. A little too good for me perhaps.

– Nonsense. Only the best for the Ring Master's daughter, he said, not finding my eye.

– Does it really belong to us? Do you mean to keep it? I asked him, still doubtful.

– Of course. I shook on it at the coachworks, he said.

Which meant he was yet to pay for it.

I reached for the tiger claw pinned to my chest. I knew well enough its worth. Might he have traded the other half as down payment, I wondered. And what of this change in him, coming about in my absence; should I be suspicious of it?

– How is James, and Flo and Mary? I said at last, not wishing to pry further.

– Looking forward to seeing you, I reckon.

– I chose August Boothe over the fairs. I'm surprised anyone is looking forward to seeing me.

– Well, there's no denying that. Though perhaps you're not wholly to blame.

My father sat on the bench opposite the fireplace and eyed the stove as though he'd not seen one before. He bent forward, lifted the hotplate, and played with the lever at the base of the chimney.

– It's a bit new fangled. Seems a shame to dirty it. I reckon you've got the finest waggon on the Waste now though. Let's get this thing going. My throat's awful dry.

It was a week till August Boothe came. Seems I'd timed my leaving with him having business away. He probably thought I'd chosen it so, yet I'd been so busy performing I'd struggled to remember my own diary, let alone his.

The morning was frigid and I'd not kept the stove in overnight, so I was still wrapped up in bed when I heard his voice outside. I eased open a window to hear better and the cold air slapped my face.

– I don't claim to own her, I could hear him saying, his voice sounding different. But I damn well pay for her food and lodging, her clothes, hansoms and trains, whatever luxuries she wants.

– Then you flatter her with things she has no need of, I heard my father reply. Just as you once tried with my wife, though she saw through your charms quickly enough.

There was a pause before August Boothe replied, a shifting of feet on the gravel.

– I don't dwell on the past, Albert, he then said. Your daughter accepts willingly enough what I give her. But it can't be paid for if she's not earning.

– Well I'm sure you have it all in writing, signed and sealed.

– Are you mocking Lucky's reading skills? August Boothe said, lowering his voice.

– I mean to put that right, my father replied.

– And you've waited how long? To think I once coveted all of this. Is there nothing you've not left to ruin. You're no better than a gypsy.

– I believe that may be truer for you than me, though we share some of our blood, my father said.

There was silence then, like a standoff. But at last August Boothe continued and once more I bent my ear to the open sash.

– So must I go to every waggon to find her? Or will you just tell me where she is?

– If I see her, I'll let her know you came by. She knows where to find you?

Did my father know that I didn't, I wondered. Did he know that August Boothe had never shared with me anything of himself, except his travels with Blondin?

– Whose is the new waggon next to that ridiculous ride? Pretty little thing.

– It's to be burnt, my father said. There was a death in it.

– Shame. It looks new. Might I see inside?

– You know the lore. No one sets foot in it again.

– And do remind me, which of your lores lets you take to your bed those girls you call women?

– Was my daughter old enough when you took her?

– You did nothing to stop her leaving, any more than when she ran to the Negro. I've never laid a finger on her, nor would I.

– Indeed. Why would you? Least, so I've been told.

I heard a door slam, footsteps on the cobbles. Then, clear as day, the cocking of a rifle – a sound I knew from the shooting galleries.

I threw a coat over my nightdress and eased open the waggon door, to hear a third, harsher voice.

– I reckon it time you be on your way.

Pip Bell, dressed in a black suit, was pointing a rifle at August Boothe, who stood with his back to me, my father standing to the side between them.

– I should apologise about that Spooner chap, August Boothe began saying. He wasn't the pug I'd been led to believe. I'll happily reimburse...

– I don't care about the fight, Pip interrupted. I want you off the Waste. You don't belong here.

August Boothe raised his hand as if to object, and I imagined his next words – I was living here a lifetime before you were born, young man. But Pip tightened his grip on the barrel and August Boothe didn't reply.

– Easy, son, my father said, glancing at Pip and then me.

August Boothe noticed me now.

– Ah! Very fetching, for a ghost, he said, looking me up and down. Could you not wear one of the many dresses I lent you?

– I've only what I was standing in the night I left and none more, though I'm sure I earned you enough for the rest of them. Anyway, you've doubtless taken them all back now.

– You overestimate your worth, he snorted. A while longer and I could have got a handsome price for you at

Worcester. But no matter. And remind me, you've returned here for what reason?

– I needed to rest. I was losing my poise, I told him. I'd have fallen again if I'd carried on much longer like that. And this is my home. I know that now.

He huffed and rounded his shoulders to the wind.

– It's a poor choice, I fear. You'll not walk at Worcester again. Mrs Ducking was upset, of course.

He turned away slowly and lifted his arms, till Pip lowered the rifle.

– Be off with you now, my father said.

– Just like when we were young 'uns, hey Albert? August Boothe replied. I'm more family than any of you. I could've claimed all of this nonsense if I'd wanted. But I care for none of it. Rotten, is what it is. Good riddance to the lot of you.

He spat his parting words, turning and slipping through the press of waggons till he was gone from sight.

I don't know what business Pip Bell had had with August Boothe to bring him out like that, gun at the ready, but he made himself scarce after, is what I do know. I lay low myself for a few days – my father and James checking on me – only venturing out at night, and then only within shouting distance of our waggons.

The Winter Fair went on much as normal, though catching its breath when word of the Prince's passing reached us, the news spreading as quickly as the fever that took him. James came to my waggon that day, seeming quite upset by it, warming his hands at the stove in silence.

– I started thinking we should cancel the fair, he muttered eventually, as he fingered the bits and bobs on the mantelpiece, stuff that I'd found on the Waste over the previous nights.

– Not a good idea, I said flatly.

I had my few other belongings back too, my father having collected them from Mrs Ducking; he wouldn't have me return there and I was saddened not to visit her again. There wasn't much of worth other than my mother's poster from Dartford, which was now tucked into one of the mirror panels on the partition; it had become even more fragile and I wanted to be able to see it every day before it perished completely. James stooped a moment to study it.

– Such a fateful day. It still surprises me your father kept it.

– I've little else of hers. Let me enjoy it at least.

He straightened and turned to me.

– Of course, I'm sorry. Your mother was dear to us all, you know. In fact, it's your walk I wanted to speak to you about. With everything going on, we won't be able to rig the wire till the twenty-sixth. I'm worried it's not enough time for you to practise. What do you think?

– That you don't want me to do it, I replied, taking his hand. And that you listen too much to rumour, perhaps.

– If you'd fallen at Worcester it would've killed you, he blurted, waving his open hand at me. Though it was magnificent to watch, he added in a whisper.

– You were there?

He nodded.

– I saw you a couple of times. You have your mother's gift, no doubt about it.

He'd been spying on me; it was odd to hear him admit it.

– Then let me do the walk. My father seems in favour of it, though he never quite manages to say so.

James burst into laughter at that, and grabbed the mantelpiece as if he needed its support; he might be a little drunk, I thought.

– Believe me, you Boothes are harder to read than old headstones, he said.

– The walk will be fine and it will bring the crowds, I told him firmly.

– Yes, you're right, of course. Help them forget their woes for a few hours. We'll get to work when Christmas is done.

Climbing the tower, taking those first steps, it was almost too painful – my belly still tight from the meal Flo had cooked for us the day before; my father had joined us then too, the first Christmas dinner I can recall sharing with him.

Now, on the wire, there was no more hiding.

My father kept watch over me as I practised every day, though August Boothe didn't appear again. I found myself seeking Virgil's face in the crowds below, praying he might return to the King Henry.

On the morning of New Year's Eve, at the foot of the middle tower, my father showed me Willie Bell's latest handiwork – a huge wooden frame with dozens of short flares lying horizontal rather than upright, fixed to it in a pattern and joined by a continuous ribbon of black powder fuse.

– What do you think to it? my father said.

– What is it? A lot of flares pointing at us?

– It spells your name, or at least part of one of your names, he replied with a smile.

I stepped back and looked at the pattern of fireworks again, trying to make out the shapes. My father took up a stick and began pointing.

– This is R, as in red. This is O for open. And U, and G and E. That spells Rouge. Willie's not tried it before. So what do you think?

– I think it will look beautiful. What colour is it?

– Well, red, of course.

– Just red?

– Just red, my father nodded.

A good-sized crowd gathered for my midnight walk. From the platform atop the first tower, I looked out over the Waste, the new white dress bought for me by my father billowing at my feet, the tiger claw brooch pinned above my breast. I saw hundreds of fingers of smoke rising from wood stoves, the roofs of stalls and waggons still frosted white, narrow paths running between them like veins of ice.

Before I set out, I remembered Nat – Madame Rouge, who'd shared with me the secrets of her craft – and John Boothe my great-grandfather, who'd started us all on this curious journey. I thought of my mother, who'd planted the desire in me, and touched her brooch. And I sent a prayer for Virgil and Dorothy too, hoping it might one day find them.

My first steps drew a huge cheer from the crowd that made me wobble for an instant, my pole dipping to one side.

When the bells struck the hour, I was at the middle tower, where far below Willie Bell was at work, sparking his flares that spelt my name and almost smoked me out, shooting rockets past me as though I was the target.

The sound was deafening and it was all I could do to block it out long enough to reach the far tower, rest a while, then begin my return.

I ended my walk at the middle tower, too tired to reach the starting point, and at once a ring of torches formed at the base of it to light my descent.

It was my father who carried me to my waggon this time, fending off the clutches of the crowd. The apprentices ran beside us and I could hear their buckets filling with coins till they could run no more.

The next morning, my father came to my door again, clutching an envelope like a child with a treat.

– It's an invitation, he told me, breathless and excited. It's from the new mayor at Lynn, *"requesting Mademoiselle Rouge to open and close the February Mart"*.

I took out the letter and glanced over the script as if I could read it. The edges of the paper were gilded, and at the top was a crest, a tiny painting in black and white showing an old merry-go-round, like the one the Bells had owned for two summers.

– It's the greatest honour to be asked, my father said, with a spark in his eyes that I'd not seen before. They're offering *fifty* pounds. We'd be lucky if all our shows earned us that over the fortnight. Will you do it? he said, reaching for my hand, asking me as he'd never done before, to walk the tightrope.

– Of course I'll do it, I whispered. Of course I will.

Thirty-four

We came to King's Lynn cowering in a blizzard, having travelled eight days in rain. My waggon was slower than it might've been – too heavy the opinion was, too sluggish in the mud. It lost a wheel at St Germans and took half a day to fix, so that was it fallen from favour, though I was still in love with it, its luxury beyond my imagining. When we made it to the city at last, we found the streets running like a river. The authorities led us to North End and told us to park up there till the flooding eased. Come the 13th it did, and with the stink of fish in our nostrils, we moved to the market place to take our pitches alongside the local shows that'd already had the pick of the spots.

In the afternoon, my father oversaw the rigging of the wire, his first proper hand in my walking. I stepped from my waggon to hear him questioning the height of the cable, the size of the anchors, the number of guys and weights. He didn't reckon the tower built in front of the Exchange Building was strong enough. He thought the span across the market place was too long for me to walk without somewhere to rest. There were too many big rides below me. The pole was too heavy but not long enough, the wire not tight enough.

I padded up to him in my slippers that mopped up the lying water like sponges, and slid my hand into his as he argued with one of the riggers.

– I'd like to start practising. How soon can it be ready? I said to them both, pressing my thumb into my father's palm to silence him.

The rigger turned to me, her eyebrows lifting with relief.

– We could be done in an hour, she said, if we could be left alone to get on with the job, is what she hinted.

– Come on. I want to see how it looks from up there, I said to my father, grabbing his arm.

The balcony of the Exchange was where I would ready myself. From there, I could step across to the platform at the top of the tower and begin walking right away. When we reached it, my father produced a fishing line and lead from his coat, and leaning out over the balustrade, he lowered it to the cobbles, counting off the distance.

– Thirty-four feet. They told me it was thirty, he said, reeling in the line again.

– It was fifty at Worcester.

– That's of no comfort. August Boothe had no right.

– I'm in more danger riding a hansom. In any case, it's my decision to do it, and thirty-four or thirty makes no difference.

My father sighed as I swung my legs over the railing and jumped across to the platform. When he made to follow me, I offered him my hand. As he stepped, he looked down and his face turned ashen.

– It's not so easy after all, he stuttered, as he joined me.

– Just keep looking up, I told him. Find something to focus on. There's a church spire, I said, pointing to where it rose behind the market place, its tip pricking the velvet sky.

I could feel the breeze peeling off from the harbour, cold and steady. My father took a deep breath and knelt at the wire at our feet. He grabbed hold of it where it passed above the middle of the platform. He tried to shake it, as if testing its strength, but it was even thicker than the one at the Waste and remained quite rigid.

– The rigger said it's from the docks, the same as they use for the big ships, my father told me, though it was he that needed reassuring.

I put my weight on the wire and it hung firm beneath me.

– It's not going anywhere. I could be pushing a barrow of bricks and it wouldn't give an inch, I said.

– And you're quite sure about this damned pole? my father went on, fetching it from the edge of the balcony and handing it to me.

I stepped onto the wire again and tried it without leaving the platform.

– It feels about right, I told him. Anyway, I find I walk faster with a heavier pole.

My feet were cold and wet, reminding me of Weston – my bloodied soles, finding my focus for the first time. I've often thought – had my legs not worked as they did that day, had I not been visited by that queer sense of loneliness, I might never have walked at all, and my father would've found me in the field simply gazing at the wire, my lesson from Appleby seemingly learnt. It would've saved me from his blows, the years of hurt and discomfort. And I knew now, the fact that we were sharing this moment at all, was a miracle in itself.

There was a gust of wind and suddenly we could see flames rising from North End.

– They're burning their old boats, my father said. They were telling us last night, they moved them from the quay on the floodwater. They usually have to drag them all the way.

– Why do they have to burn them at all?

– It's their custom, just as we have ours. They give thanks to the old fishing season and welcome the new. One of your mother's cousins is married to a North-Ender. They live there still.

– And what of Della? I blurted, without really meaning to, though I was curious whether she was down there some place within the walls of the town.

– I'm sorry about that day, he said. It wasn't a good time for me. Though perhaps you brought me to my senses. I'm told she's heavy with child. It's not mine.

– This family is tangled enough without it, I said.

My father took my hand again and looked towards the flames.

– You know, I loved your mother rather too much I think. I couldn't bear the loss of her. I realise now I'm only just awakening from it. It's as if I've been asleep all these years. I've not been seeing the life going on in front of me.

– I would like to have known her. I have so few stories of her, I whispered.

We got the signal from the riggers; I lifted the pole to my chest, took a long breath, stepped onto the wire. It felt solid beneath the thin soles of my slippers. The daylight was almost done, the moon already showing its face, looming large as it rose, just a day off full. I took a few steps in its glow, my father's voice becoming faint. I felt strong and calm. I looked down and saw the dark tilts stretched over the walk-up rides in case of rain. When I turned on the wire towards the platform again, I saw that I'd walked out twenty feet or so. I saw panic in my father's face, giving way to doubt when I nodded to him, and finally his relief when I smiled.

I awoke late the next morning to such commotion outside – waggon doors banging, the hammering of metal stakes, laughter and arguing beneath my window. But it was the womenfolk that roused me eventually with their wolf-whistles that you'd sooner expect from men.

I tossed the bedclothes off me and stood up too quickly, taking a moment to find my balance. I pulled open the curtains on both sides of the waggon in time to see my father and uncle James approaching from opposite directions, each dressed in their finest suit. I waved at them both and flung the door open to welcome them; I don't think either knew the other was coming. The night had chased away the last of the rain and now sunshine was drenching the Mart. I looked out from the doorway and up at the silver cord stretched across the square, lying as still as if it were a solid rail suspended there.

– How are you feeling, Lucky? Are you nearly ready? my father said, the first time I can remember him using my name.

I bent and kissed his head, without telling him why.

– Have you eaten? James said, not understanding my gesture.

– I never eat before I walk, and I feel quite rested. I'll get changed and be there.

– Whenever you're ready, my father said, squeezing my hand before leading my uncle away with him.

I didn't tarry. I knew I'd slept too long and that they'd come because I was late and they were worried. There was a good deal depending on my walk – the coffers of the Boothes & Bells not the least of it. I decided on the white dress from New Year, and slipped it over my shift. I threw on a coat, found a woollen hat and scarf, my clogs, and stepped from the waggon clutching my damp slippers, as the market clock struck twelve.

At once, a hush fell over the fair, as the town's officials gathered in their pomp. I watched the bishop, with his curious hat and jewelled staff, step up to make his speech, the mayor and crier either side of him in their black gowns and chains of gold hoops. The blessing lasted too long as usual, though the women round me did their best to honour it with their silence if not their full attention, continuing to mouth their gossip at one another. But they joined the crowd heartily enough for the final amen and the applause.

The ribbon was cut and the worthy took to the fairground for the half hour before the public were allowed to join them – the bishop and his party heading for the shooting gallery, the others scattering amongst the stalls or seeking out the Siamese twins. Everyone else having to wait, they turned their gaze skyward to the wire, anticipating the next act, delaying their own pleasure a while longer.

I had to move quickly then to reach the Exchange. I skirted round the edge of the market place to avoid the press of bodies, entered the lobby where a porter was beckoning me, and took the stairs two at a time, to find James already on the platform, positioning my pole.

– Your father is at the other end, he said, pointing to the second tower that was just visible on the far side of the square. I think we're almost ready for you.

He might just as well have commanded the heavens then, for all of a sudden the wind picked up, rain clouds closed out the sun, and a chill came upon the air. I looked over the market place, which at once became a sea of hats and coats, and collars being turned up against the cold. At the first drops of rain, umbrellas snapped open amidst the roofs of the stalls and rides and waggons, completing the canopy over the fairground, like stepping stones across the square.

I took several minutes to prepare, to slow my breathing, relax my wrists and ankles – enough time for the sun to find its way out again briefly, making the wire glisten, and painting a rainbow in a perfect arc beyond the church spire, its ends falling at the rooftops of distant houses as if the effect was planned by some trickery or other. Umbrellas were lowered again, and heads turned upwards like scores of baby blackbirds waiting to be fed.

I made as perfect a walk then as I've ever done – without falter or bad step, keeping a slow, steady rhythm. I paused at the middle and looked down, heard the distant cheers, saw the waving hands of children wrapped in furs. Then I focused on the far platform, my father standing motionless gripping the safety rail. The second tower stood in front of The Gryffin Hotel, the platform almost at its roof line. As I neared it, I could see a line of dormers peeking out from garret rooms, with tiny sashes and squares of leaded roof above them. As my gaze passed over them, I caught a movement in one of the windows, then the lowering of a sash, and a face appearing.

It wasn't so abrupt as to unsettle me, though I stopped dead at that moment, my balancing pole dipping and giving away my distraction.

I saw His wiry hair, those wind-blown yellow streaks. I saw His gentle smile that I would know anywhere.

I held my breath till I thought I might faint.

He'd been gone a year and two months. He looked no different now to when I lost him, when I let go his hand and he slipped into the dawn. I never once believed he'd left me of his own will; I always felt sure he'd been snatched. I'd had to stifle my doubts – that the docks had become a cage to him, that he'd felt crushed in that tiny hut, in that stiff suit serving old sailors who would've sooner pissed on him. And always I knew in my heart, I would never truly know his thoughts.

Yet come back now he had, just as Nat had promised he would.

Thirty-five

So often I've awoken not recalling the hour of finding sleep, not remembering my dreams, sometimes not recognising my surroundings such that they only fall into place once I'm fully awake. Now, as my eyes cleared and adjusted to the daylight pouring through the curtains, I could make out a jacket hanging on the wall, a narrow unmade bed pushed close to the one I was lying in, pairs of different sized shoes, hinting that the room was shared.

The door opened. Virgil with a towel round his waist filled the doorway. He gave me his broadest smile, closed the door and let the towel slip to the floor. I edged against the cold wall so he could lie beside me, offered him the cover, but he shook his head, waved his hands in front of his face. His skin was bone-dry yet threw out heat as though from a recent bath. He propped his head on one hand, licked his other thumb and touched it to the corner of my mouth, brushed his fingers over my lips. He gave me his puzzled look and tried to speak. He mouthed the words, I shook my head, he tried again. I'd forgotten how to understand him. He tried a third and fourth time, and on the fifth I got it.

– How are you? he was trying to ask me, nothing more.

– I'm Lucky, is how I am, I whispered. Cos you've come back to me.

I made the walking movement with my fingers and he sniggered like he used to. I opened my arms to him; he paused a moment, then bent and kissed my forehead. I unbuttoned my shift, took his hand and put it to my breast. He ran his finger across my cheek, tracing a scratch, touched his lips to it when I winced.

I remembered then: Tears of hope blinding me, I'd finished my walk to great applause, rushed down the ladder as though the tower were on fire, my father following me in his confusion. Slipping at the last step, I'd caught my face on a splinter. I shook off my father – hoping he'd stay to meet the mayor and such and accept their thanks – ran into the hotel and swept up the stairs, five flights to the garrets. Into his arms. Our mouths locking, his tongue tasting just as I remembered. Our limbs folding together.

And how did he really look? Just as he did that last morning when I gazed up at him, lying on the bed in his hut, my lips bruised from the hours of being upon his. Back then, we'd found every way to bring our mouths together, every way to taste each other, ways that no one else knew of – that's what I'd believed.

That's how he now looked, his hair a little shorter perhaps.

I pulled him towards me, clasped him round his back, felt once more the lumps on his skin that I'd found earlier. And once again, he didn't flinch when I followed their length, the peaks and troughs. They began at each shoulder, crossed in the small of his back and ended across his buttocks. At first I'd thought there were dozens, but then I could feel that the welts were separate, so he must've taken just a few lashes each side, else they'd have melted into a single messy scar. They were the only evidence of our lost year, but they were enough to tell me not to ask more.

Our mouths met now, so familiar. He kissed between my breasts. I felt him grow against me, my wetness coming in an instant, and I drew him inside me once more.

When he lifted his weight from me, I cupped my hand between my legs and wished it safe there. He stood, falling limp, his body showing no dampness from our embrace; whatever heat was needed to make him sweat, I'd never witnessed it. He took a shirt from the back of a chair and retrieved a wooden suitcase similar to mine from under the second bed. He lifted the top layer of clothes and took out a pair of black trousers from beneath.

– We could be married, I cried all of a sudden, and he turned to me again; I never really knew if he could hear me or not, but he could often sense when I was speaking. Do you know what that means? I said.

I jumped from the bed and stood naked next to him. I plucked a few of my hairs and wrapped them round one of his fingers like a ring; I did the same to one of mine. I took the slip off a pillow and laid it over my head as a veil, linked my arm in his and pretended to dance a jig.

– And then we could do a rope-walk together, I said, walking the fingers of both my hands in the air again.

Virgil smiled, but then made a sad face and pulled away. He pointed to his right foot; I'd not noticed it till now. There were black stumps where his big toe and first toe should've been, and the others were crushed against each other where his foot was turned in and upwards. I sank to my knees and kissed his ankle, kissed where his toes weren't, brushed my lips along the ridges of his sole. He put his hands into my hair and I looked up at him. He shrugged but shed no tears for his loss, his craft snatched from him, hobbled for God knows what paltry reason.

So I cried for him myself, my countless questions dissolving unanswered in my tears.

We came to my father's waggon arm in arm – me in my white walking dress, Virgil in the black suit and white shirt of his employment at the Gryffin Hotel, his lame foot barely noticeable. Though I don't believe Virgil could really fathom it, he was coming to ask my father for my hand.

Flo had cooked a meal and set my father's table, as it was still a chore he struggled with – preferring to eat at the invitation of others. He was on his way back from repairing a ride, Flo told me, though James arrived as we did and greeted Virgil like a long-lost brother.

– You've finally brought her to her senses then? James said, patting Virgil on the back.

Virgil nodded, though I knew he hadn't understood, and I realised then how seldom I'd seen Virgil with anyone but myself and the dockers we'd worked with.

Flo put her fingers to her mouth and pretended to eat.

– Hope you like beef, she said to us all, pulling out a chair each for Virgil and me, scowling at James for not doing it.

– Perfect timing, James then said, as we heard footsteps outside.

My father beamed from the doorway, dressed in his overalls, spitting on his hands and rubbing them together to clean them.

– Not late I hope?

Virgil rose to greet him and my father took his hand excitedly.

– Glad to meet you properly at long last. It seems you bring a smile to Lucky where no one else manages.

– Which is why I wish to marry him, I blurted, not wanting to delay asking.

– I thought we had to make it through to dessert before he could ask that, my father replied, filling our wine glasses.

– Better said now and celebrate for longer, James said. I'll raise a toast to that, if I'm not being presumptuous Albert?

My father paused as though he had to consider it, but then raised his glass too and I squeezed Virgil's hand.

– To Lucky and Virgil! they all said, Flo dabbing her eye with a napkin.

– When will it be? Might you marry here in Lynn? she said.

– Of course. When the Mart is over, we could arrange it. Do you think, father?

– Well, we've been invited to Bristol from here. They want you to walk at the zoo in Clifton, though not till Easter. So you could marry before we leave, or wait and have it on the Down in spring.

I pondered for a moment, before remembering it was Virgil's decision too, turning to ask him; his clown's smile, his raised forehead, told me all I needed.

– We'd rather it was sooner.

– Then Virgil will need this, my father said, taking a parcel of velvet from his waistcoat, pressing it into Virgil's hand and closing his fingers over it.

Thirty-six

For the two weeks of the Mart, we spent every spare moment together. Come midday on the last day, there was already a good crowd gathered, with all the shows charging half price for the afternoon, so the market square was full when I ventured out from the hotel. I was still flushed from lovemaking, still warm from a final embrace before Virgil had dressed for work – patting the tiger claw where it was pinned behind his jacket lapel, where only he and I knew it was – and then rushed away to the kitchens.

– Don't forget my walk, I'd called after him, though I knew he couldn't hear, and I was sure he'd remember.

I stopped at my waggon for my coat and headscarf, and looked out across the square. The Siamese had a long queue as usual, and the Negro showing her cunny for a shilling – which sometimes seemed a damn sight easier way to make a living than rope-walking.

I began heading for the Exchange to start my practise, though my performance wasn't till midnight – the end of the fair. But I barely got past the first stall when a figure stepped into my path and blocked my way with a cane. August Boothe – looking drawn and greyer than normal, yet wearing the same smile as when he used to come to the Green to see me practising, when I would finally notice him and know he'd been watching me a while.

– Quite a show you made here the other week, he began, reaching for his pipe and lighting it for the first time in my company. You should be more careful climbing down though. I'm told by friends of mine who take to the mountains, that most of their mishaps befall them in the final part of their descent. Concentration wanes, I suppose.

264

Rushing to the next big thing. Remember that New Year at the Waste when they carried you above their heads? That's the best way.

– I try not to dwell on that night. It doesn't hold the happiest of memories, I said curtly, hoping he might stop speaking and let me pass.

– Yet it should do, as should this day. Can I walk you to the Exchange?

He offered his arm but I ignored it, trying to edge round him.

– Why have you even come here? You never visited the Mart before.

– I have a new girl in training, so I'm taking notes. And on the contrary, this is my fifth or sixth time, he said, adjusting his cravat. I saw every one of your mother's attempts.

If he told me that now cos he thought I didn't know my mother had walked at the Mart, then he was right; I couldn't recall it ever being talked about. But I wouldn't let him draw me in, not even to ask about his new walker.

– So you'll know well enough that I need to prepare, I snapped. And I'm perfectly able to get there alone.

I heard my father's voice then and turned to see him walking towards me.

– Lucky! You alright? he was calling out.

When I turned back to August Boothe he was gone – like smoke in a gust – slipped away into the knot of stalls.

– Lucky? my father repeated, as he reached me. What is it?

– Nothing. I was just...

– Are you off to rehearse? I'll come with you.

He took my hand and led me along the edge of the square, every showman nodding or having a smile for him. I looked over my shoulder several times, but didn't see August

Boothe again. At the Exchange, my father chatted with a new porter.

– This is Lucky Boothe, my daughter, he told him. You won't see a better rope-walker in this land, and only fifteen years of age. Been learning it since she was a child.

– Pleased to be acquainted, the porter replied. Though pardon my saying, but it seems a perilous thing for a girl of any age.

– My daughter assures me it's all up here, my father said, tapping the side of his head. It's quite beyond me. I'm no good with heights.

My father stayed with me for the afternoon, as I walked out and back from the balcony, no more than thirty steps each time. I found it hard to concentrate and not think about August Boothe. I didn't want to tell my father, or ask him about my mother performing there. But I kept a good eye on the fairground below, checking for anyone standing still and looking up for too long. Yet I only recognised Willie Bell and his grandson, scuttling between the towers with armfuls of rockets and flares.

I didn't see Virgil either; his shift didn't finish till quarter to midnight – just time for him to climb the second tower and watch me from there, as he promised he would.

I set out on the wire, the lightest of breeze cooling my face, though nothing could quench the heat in my heart – the fire of my love for Virgil, rekindled inside me. I found again the steady rhythm of my opening walk a fortnight before, and not even the darkness unnerved me, nor the fireworks, the noise, or smoke. I walked to the far tower, my balancing pole as flat as the horizon, my eyes and heart opening for Virgil as I approached. But I saw only my father, the two apprentices who would carry down my pole when I was done, and Willie Bell's grandson sparking a flare to light my finale.

As I took my last step, I frowned at my father and he gave a shrug of his shoulders. I let go of the pole and accepted the coat that he thrust at me.

– Virgil? I said.

– He must've been held up at the hotel, my father replied, shaking his head. He probably watched from below. You were magnificent.

I looked to the hotel roof, saw the garret dormers like black sores on the tiles, none of the rooms lit, the curtain on Virgil's window still drawn open.

– Yes, he'll be on the ground, I agreed, and began climbing down before my father could stop me.

James was at the foot of the tower, and beside him Flo with Mary on her hip.

– Virgil? I said to them, but I could see at once they didn't know what I was asking.

I ran into the hotel – to the dining room, but it was closed; to the kitchens, but there was only a cook chopping onions.

– Virgil? I said to him.

– Left an hour ago, he muttered, not looking up from his board.

I took to the stairs so quickly that I barely noticed the steps, as though it was a ramp I was running up. I'd lost my slippers by the time I reached the room, bursting through the door. There was no sign of Virgil, no suit hanging on the wall, no suitcase under the beds.

– Virgil? I cried out.

Am I in the wrong room, I thought.

– Virgil? I screamed into the corridor.

There were three other rooms on the landing and I tried every door and every door opened and every room was empty. We'd been quite alone up there for those two weeks and I'd not even realised it. Then I heard a footfall.

– Virgil? I cried out again, pulling at my hair.

I smelt the pipe smoke a moment before I saw it curling from August Boothe's mouth, as he appeared at the top of the stairs, his smirk too much for me to bear.

My heart emptied. I dropped my arms to my side, let my head fall forward, all my fight escaping me, the tears coming so quickly.

– What have you done? I whispered. Why do you hate me so?

August Boothe shook his head and leant against his cane.

– Not you, my dear. Just a little matter of a docker down Limehouse way, he said, taking a last suck on his pipe before tapping it out onto the floor. You see, they believe your Negro fellow did it. And when they found the glove they thought he'd done his mate too and tossed the body into the drink. Two a penny, dock boys. They would hardly drag the Basin for that. But the ganger's brother – they couldn't let his murder go unavenged. They're all family down there, you know – the barge owners, the wharfagers, the landlord at the Sea Purse. The call-on is just a farce. They squeeze those wretches for every drop of blood they have. It's quite clever I suppose, making them fight each other to be worked like animals and throw their pittance back across the bar the moment they're handed it. Not my style though. I'm sure even the fairground is a more civilised place, wouldn't you say? Anyway, he's been wanted for a while and by good chance he's landed at my feet.

So this was the truth of it – the docker had died by my hand. I wanted to run then.

– I've forgotten the poor chap's name, August Boothe went on, filling his pipe afresh. Duncan, I think. No, Donald – that's the fellow. He got a hatchet buried in him. Must have been someone strong to floor a brute like that. There's no way a fair lady could've managed it. The old girl sends her regards by the way. I think she rather misses your visits.

– The flower seller? You spoke to her? I said, struggling for my words.

He laughed and made to speak again.

– Your chap. Virgil, or whatever he calls himself at the moment. He fled when I showed him the wanted notice. Must've thought I was judge, jury and hangman rolled into one.

– Did you touch him? I whispered again. Please tell me you didn't hurt him.

– I wouldn't hurt a fly, he said, raising his hands in defence.

I fell silent as my rage took over me, every ounce of my hatred, every last drop of my sorrow.

I ran at August Boothe with all the force I could muster, head down like a bull, slamming into his stomach before he had time to let go his cane and protect himself. He stumbled backwards from the top stair and fell. That's all I saw.

I grabbed an oil lamp from where it hung in the corridor and threw it after him. The glass shattered and flames spewed out, catching the carpet in seconds. I gulped for air but suddenly there was only black smoke, filling my lungs, searing my eyes, stealing my voice.

Part Three

Thirty-seven

I awoke in my waggon, the air strangely acrid, sensing we'd been parked up a while. Flo was in bed beside me and Mary was in a basket on the floor, a beam of early sunlight warming her face. I stretched my legs under the covers and at once Flo opened her eyes and touched my arm.

– How do you feel sweetheart?

I opened my mouth; all I wanted to ask was – Virgil? But it wouldn't come.

– You've had an awful shock, Flo whispered, putting her hand to my forehead; she moved closer and kissed my cheek. We've been travelling for a week, she told me.

She sat up and waited for me to respond, but I was too confused.

– We're not making great progress, she went on. The roads are in a state after the rain and wheels keep breaking; we had five go in one day. We stopped at an inn for the night and then one of the zebras died, so we're staying on a few days. The landlord's that pleased for our custom, he's let us bury the poor animal in his paddock.

As she spoke, I felt my stomach heave; before I could warn her, I vomited down my front and over the bedclothes, though Flo moved quickly enough to avoid the worst of it. At once she took Mary to her sister's waggon, fetched a cloth and bowl of water, and returned to clean me up.

– It's all the travel catching up with you, she said.

My father came then, tried to hide his concern when he saw me, but I saw the stopped frown, the slight shaking of his head; I don't think he could bear seeing me broken-hearted. He sat at the bedside and took my hand like he'd never done when I was a child.

– You feeling better, love? At least you're awake at last, he said, his gaze falling above my eyes.

I knew something was wrong, and swept my hand over my scalp.

– It's alright. You lost a bit of hair in the fire. It's not so bad.

The fire: that's what I could smell all about me. I began recalling fragments of it – the lamp breaking, the smoke engulfing me.

– Have you told her anything? my father said, turning to Flo.

– Not much, she replied.

– They couldn't stop it but they think everyone got out, he said, turning back to me. The hotel burnt to the ground though. Do you know where Virgil went?

I shook my head, retched again but had nothing left to bring up. I wanted to weep, but even my tears were dry.

*

I bled that evening, my stomach closing like a draw-string bag. I took it to be my courses returning; I never knew when to expect it anymore. Flo found me a square of muslin – just as my aunt had done when it first happened all those years before – and she stayed with me again, bringing me a second pillow and telling me to rest, though I'd slept too much.

The next morning at sunrise, I dressed and stepped outside for the first time since leaving the Mart. Flo was already at her chores, Mary toddling at her side, their waggon parked up behind mine.

– Good to see you up and about, Flo said, drawing Mary to her. There's porridge on the fire if you fancy. The boys are with James in Skegness; did I tell you that? They'll join us on the twenty-second, if we make it there by then.

I frowned at her, shook my head.

– You don't remember? We're going to Bristol, to the zoo at Clifton. They want you to walk there at Easter. If you're feeling up to it, of course.

How can I think of that now, I wanted to say. I have to stop Virgil being taken in for the docker's death; he'll surely be hanged if he's caught. There's nothing else for it but to hand myself in.

That's what I was thinking. I'd need my voice to do it though, if anyone was to believe me; I'd need to be able to tell what had happened, down to every last detail.

I found a hedge behind the inn to squat beside, then walked towards the ploughed fields beyond, upsetting several rooks that cawed at me. The dawn smelt of dead crops, the rot of winter. Dew settled on my lips. I coughed and spluttered, trying to clear my lungs; I stopped and held my sides when the cramp returned. I walked on and soon the sun peeked above the low cloud. But I didn't want to see it, bringing its promise of spring. I wanted to suffer; I wanted black clouds overhead, hailstones to fall upon me in torrents, thunder to deafen me, lightning to strike me dead. It hurt more to be under a heavenly sky, remembering what I'd lost and seeing what beauty remained despite of it. But that damned sunlight won through, teasing the first snowdrops from the earth, bringing a cruel scent. I jumped a stile, tore my palms on winter thorns, drank stream water that tasted of cattle, and grew a blister on my sole. I carried darkness in my heart and too many questions in my head.

When I returned to Flo, I ate a little of the porridge and managed to keep it down. I spent the rest of the day sitting where the zebra had been buried, willing the grass to grow back in its shape, as had once happened with an elephant at Blackheath. There was so much activity round me – waggons getting fixed, clothes being washed and put out to dry alongside muddy tarpaulins, props being repainted. So much to be done. But I felt hollow, stripped bare without

Virgil at my side, still not believing he'd been torn from me a second time.

I decided to tell Flo that night – at least some of what had happened – once Mary was fed and asleep.

She sat cross-legged facing me on the bed.

– What do you remember? she began.

I still couldn't make any sound with my voice, so I had to shape the words with a silent mouth.

August Boothe. August Boothe. August Boothe. Three times I tried, before she understood.

– Why do you mention him? He's not been seen since the Waste, she said, but I shook my head violently. Steady on! You saw him at the Mart? Who was rope-walking? Your mother? Mary walked at the Mart; is that what August Boothe told you?

Flo sank back and sighed with the effort of trying to understand me. I knew how hard it could be – those months I'd spent with Virgil.

– He was obsessed with your mother; you know that, don't you? she went on. I'm quite certain Mary never performed in King's Lynn. I don't even recall seeing a rope-walker there before you. That man is a rogue.

I managed to tell her that August Boothe had been in the hotel when the fire started, that he'd fallen down the stairs and might've been hurt. Did no one see him?

– I'll speak to your father about it, she said, but I didn't want that, covering my face with my hands to let her know.

I killed a man, I now tried to say. I killed a man.

Flo frowned at me but I could tell she understood right away this time.

– No one is dead, she whispered. Everyone got out. Besides, there weren't that many. They were mostly outside. They'd been watching you. You were wonderful.

Shaking my head again: Not then. At the docks. I killed a man at the docks. You saw how I was when I came back to the Waste, the bruises and cuts. I have a confession to make. I killed a man.

Flo shrank from me, untangled her legs and stood up. She grabbed hold of my shoulders, brought her face to mine, tears coming to her eyes. What a pretty mouth she has, I thought. She dropped her head and turned away to check on Mary.

I pretended to write on my hand. Flo closed her eyes for a moment. Then she nodded and was gone to her waggon to fetch paper and a pen.

She sat before me again and touched a finger to my lips, dipped her nib into the ink.

– Now, tell me everything about it. Slowly, from the beginning.

She wrote down every word of my silent confession, till it filled three pages. She read it back to me twice and rewrote it. She stayed calm like she always did, waiting patiently whenever I paused, not judging me or looking shocked at what I told her. At the end, she put the pen in my hand, which felt odd, and made me scrawl a mark at the bottom of the page. Then she folded the paper into an envelope and took something from her pocket – bright red, a stick of wax, she told me. She held it over the candle flame till it began to melt, then let the wax drop onto the back of the envelope. She asked for my tiger claw and pressed it for an instant into the puddle on the flap. She blew on the wax till it was dry and slid the envelope inside her blouse.

To what end, all of this? I wondered.

Thirty-eight

The morning we left the inn, a clear sky beckoning us onward, my voice had still not returned and I could do little but lie in bed, hoping I'd recover soon.

But not an hour into the journey I started bleeding again, heavily this time, and I was certain now it wasn't just my courses. I felt as though I was being punched in the stomach. I couldn't call out but I thumped on the wall of the waggon till Flo arrived – her cousin, who was leading my horses, fetching her to me. She made me sit up in case I was sick; then seeing the blood, jammed a pillowslip between my legs.

– You know what it is? she said, calmly taking my hand, though she couldn't hide her worry.

She found a bed sheet and threw it into a heap on the floor, making me crouch over it – I was passing that much blood now, and awful clots like lumps of liver. The waggon began rocking over the ruts, so Flo called to her cousin to pull out of the convoy.

– I'm so sorry, she cried, squeezing my hand, mopping my brow.

The bleeding eased soon after we stopped, so I lay on the bed again. Flo wiped me down and laid her hands gently on my belly. She'd had four of her own, so I was glad it was her who was with me.

– It's Virgil's? she whispered.

It couldn't be anyone else's, so I didn't understand why she was asking me that, though I couldn't believe that something of Virgil's would be fighting me so.

– Am I losing it? I croaked, just enough to be heard.

– I think you might be, Flo replied. I'm so sorry, sweetheart.

And I know she was; she showed it in every furrowing of her forehead, every lowering of her eyelids as though they were too heavy, every effort she made to speak when she could no longer bear to. She knew, same as everybody, the day Virgil had returned to me, and it wasn't long enough ago that there could much inside me to survive.

*

Flo spent as much time with me as she could after that, to be sure I was healing. I felt guilty for bringing it all to her door; I wished it could've been different. I was run out of sorrow though – all gone on myself and Virgil and what had happened. I know I could've died without Flo's help. There was no more bleeding, so I was certain I'd lost whoever it was inside me. She didn't speak of my confession again, and I put August Boothe from my mind, but I couldn't keep Virgil out; the shame of losing what might've become our child.

Another week and we arrived at Clifton. We'd never travelled so slowly nor encountered such terrible roads, so many of them washed away by a month of rain.

– You're looking a mite better, Flo said when she came to park up the waggon for me, chocking the wheels and letting down the steps. I don't think you've been here before. The Down goes on for miles. When you get your strength back we can explore it together. Mary will love it.

She set about unpacking the waggon – unbolting the cupboards, opening the range, setting up the table.

– Your father's popping by in a moment. Shall I help you with your clothes?

I let her remove my shift and wash my face, freshen me up. She found me a dress – one that I used to practise in. She didn't try to get me to talk; she was good like that. She didn't stay once my father arrived though; I knew she hadn't told him any of it.

– We're not far from the zoo, he began, settling himself at the table and eyeing the kettle. They want you to walk across the boating lake. Your Blondin chap did it last year. It's four weeks away, so plenty of time. Do you want to talk about anything? Virgil? The fire? You took in a lot of smoke. I'm sure Virgil will find us soon. You can be wed here after all. How's your voice?

I answered with a shrug. Even if I could've spoken, I had no words for him, his hopefulness coming from I don't know where.

– James will be with us by the weekend, he went on cheerily. He's bringing a new tightrope. There's a couple of Bell children just turned seven, so there'll be a banquet and fire jump and all the rest of it. We can rig the rope if you want and you can make a little show?

I stared at my hands in my lap; I could still see specks of soot in my fingernails. I thought – I have no voice, no lover, no child. My father rose and took up the kettle, stepped outside to fill it.

I spent the Saturday morning helping Flo, preparing lacquer for the woodwork she'd begun stripping at the inn. She was distracted of course, with her family soon to arrive. I helped in silence, till in the early afternoon her boys and James rolled onto the plain, a dozen waggons and carriages following them, Pip Bell's included. When all their reuniting and tears were done, James came to me, hugged me and put his mouth to my ear.

– It's going to be alright, he whispered. I'll tell you about it very soon.

He had a pair of suckling pigs for the feast, which he said had been won in a bet, and right away he rolled out the new rope and made a great fuss of rigging it between two oaks.

My father insisted it should be no more than head height, and whilst they argued over guy ropes and pulley blocks, I slipped away to my waggon, leaving a broom outside across my door.

I knew I'd be expected to walk the rope that evening, but I was too wrung with nerves to think of doing it. Surely Flo would tell them that I shouldn't; make some excuse for me. My insides felt like they were twisting into a knot, drawing my skin into me, as though I might fold in on myself and be swallowed by my own stomach.

Eventually I could hear the beginnings of the feast – the rattle of cooking pots, the laughter of the young 'uns as they ran in packs between the waggons, the tuning of a fiddle and guitar. Then the spitting of the fire being lit; I buried my head under my pillow when I heard that – I couldn't bear the sound.

There was a tapping at my window. I wished I could shout to send the visitor away.

– Lucky. I need to talk to you, my uncle James called through the pane, a note of apology in his voice.

He said it twice till I reached for the latch and pulled up the sash an inch without opening the curtain.

– I've some news from our travels. I think you should hear it.

I knew he wouldn't be bothering me with gossip or trifle – he was too considerate for that – so I got up and opened the door to him. I hadn't noticed earlier how pale he was looking, not holding himself tall like he always did. And his hair was getting too long and looking unkempt. He took off his boots and coat and slumped on the bench at the table.

– Bloody nice waggon you've got here, he said, looking about him as though he'd forgotten it. You're a lucky girl, you are.

I nodded, gave a shrug, which was all I could do now. Luck comes and goes in this family, I thought to myself. Mostly goes.

– So I'll get to the point. Your Virgil was seen near Skegness.

– Is he well? I croaked at once, the first words to pass my lips in three weeks, surprising me as much as James.

– I didn't believe for a moment that you could stop speaking for long, he said. Well that's good. Take your time. I believe he's well, yes. But he's on the run, scared witless for the both of you. He thinks he'll bring danger to you if he comes near.

Just as suddenly, my throat went dry again.

– He didn't do anything wrong, I mouthed; and a second time till my uncle understood.

– I know. I could tell right away. So do you really have no voice?

– You?

– Yes. It was me that saw him. He sought me out in fact. He tried to explain what August Boothe had said, him being wanted and everything. The pair of you; you're a bundle of hard work.

James winked and touched my shoulder. I don't reckon he could do harm to anyone, though he might've been driven close to it a few times. He and Flo both – they're like a stick of rock with goodness running through it.

– Flo mentioned the letter, he went on. She has it safe. That was brave of you. It could save Virgil's neck, if it comes to that. I don't need to hear the details – you've told it all to Flo. And I promise, no one will get to you here in the fairs. We're putting everyone on their guard, telling them there's a feud between August Boothe and your father. Folk don't need much persuading when it comes to those two. There's always been bad blood between them. Your father doesn't know the truth of it though. Better we leave it that way.

– Thank you, I managed to say, the words dying in my throat, knowing that James didn't know the full truth of it either.

I grabbed his hand and squeezed it, to make sure he was watching me.

– I can't walk tonight. But help me walk again, I mouthed. And bring Virgil back to me. I have nothing else.

Thirty-nine

The morning after the banquet, I stepped from my waggon in white flannels and blouse, glad of a leaden sky instead of the glare of sunshine that I still wasn't ready for. James took me to the tightrope. Seems he and my father had agreed on eight feet – not too high but enough so it could still be walked under. I got some looks from the showmen and women nearby as I changed into my slippers and checked the rigging. I sensed an atmosphere too – mutterings that I was refusing to talk rather than not able.

I didn't climb onto the rope right away, so that made folk watch me even harder. I didn't yet believe I could do it again.

– Take your time, James told me. I'll leave you to it for now.

I spent a couple of days taking my time, just walking under the rope, back and forth between the two trees, counting my steps – seventy-five, the same in each direction, which reassured me. I walked with the balancing pole too, getting used to the weight of it. On the third day I mustered the courage to climb up, and the moment I was there, I scoffed at myself for having made so much of it, walking across and back without faltering.

I practised every day then, a little more each day, always with one eye on the edge of the encampment, waiting. I carried on helping Flo with her repairs, till eventually she said I should stop and concentrate on the rope-walking. She was sure I was recovered now, though she still looked out for me; she knew it wasn't just my body that needed healing. I was sick twice more in those weeks but blamed it on the water from the heath. There weren't no more bleeding and I felt quite at peace, no longer blaming myself. My voice still eluded me though.

On the last Thursday, my father and several other showmen carted the rope to the zoo and rigged it across the lake between two lookout towers that must've been twenty feet high, with stairs for the public to climb, though they were closed now. When they were done staking the guy ropes to the embankment, they hung our bunting from them and made it our own, and I felt at home amid the yowl and roar of that huge menageric.

Then, early on Good Friday, sun poured into my waggon and awoke me slowly. I lay there for an age thinking about the day ahead. When I rose at last, I washed, and dressed several times before deciding on a plain blouse and skirt. My hair was all grown back from the fire now, and I tied it in a ponytail to keep it from my eyes. I couldn't eat a morsel, yet I forgot the pangs of hunger the moment I reached the top of the tower and felt the wind in my face.

I spent a good while preparing; this was my first performance since the Mart. I knew I'd have the lake below me for most of it, but knew also it was too shallow if I fell. So I thought of those first steps at Bartholomew Fair, of the joy they'd brought. I thought of my first New Year's Eve walk at the Waste; my realising that whatever the height, I had to make every step count. I focused on the flags atop the elephant house waving in the breeze, and told myself I didn't have two hundred or three hundred steps to take, but just six, all perfectly placed, one after the other. Then six more. And another six after that. With this in my mind, and the noon sun beating down on me, I stepped out.

The crowd were mostly children and seemed puzzled by my lone figure suspended in the air. Perhaps they wanted the sky to turn blood red or the earth to tremble. Or maybe they just thought me foolish. I should've borrowed a monkey from the zoo, put it in a suit and billycock and given it a cane to twirl, just to get a laugh. I walked across and back twice cos I felt so good, though I'd only been asked to do it once. At the end of it, I passed my pole to the helpers, but they fumbled and it tipped from the platform and plunged to the earth like a spear. When I reached the bottom of the tower my father showed me the pole, its nose buried several feet into the muddy bank, not two yards from a line of children queuing for lemonade.

– That was *lucky*, he said, breaking into a smile and reaching for my hand. Come, there's someone wants to meet you.

I was so hot now I just wanted to duck my head in the lake, but my father was already leading me towards the bandstand, where two men were stood in conversation, looking uncomfortable in suits and top hats. Returned once again to the world of toadies and cads, I thought. Could not even my father keep me from them? As we neared I saw there was a third man crouched behind, tying his laces. When he noticed us he stood at once, as if we'd caught him at something, and beamed us a smile. He was red-faced, round like a barrel and barely my height, not even reaching the shoulders of the other men. His jacket was too long and his trousers had patches of dirt on both knees.

– Wonderful! Truly splendid, he said, showering me with spittle, offering a damp hand that I shook limply. Young Dorothy has been telling me all about you, he went on, and suddenly he had my attention.

– This is Mr Smith from Cremorne Gardens, my father told me, raising his brow. It seems that our Dorothy is now one of his housemaids. And this is my daughter, Lucky Boothe, he said, turning to the man.

– So I've been told. *Lucky* Boothe, indeed. Or should I say *Mademoiselle Rouge*? Edward T. Smith at your service, he said, taking my hand again and kissing my knuckles. Have you ever considered walking across our great river?

I could only nod like a fool till my father answered for me.

– I'm afraid Lucky has lost her voice to a cold, but I'm sure she's very interested, he said.

– Well, it's an ambition of mine to see it done. It's rumoured it was tried once, though I'm sure the claim is exaggerated. If you'd consider it, I'm offering to engage you to cross the river from Battersea to Cremorne. It'll be a first for man or woman, and all the better for being in my tenure. I propose the date of our closing night, twenty-seventh September. That will give me five months to bang heads with the authorities. There'll be one or two things to arrange of course, fireworks and such. Mister Pablo Fanque is taking to the ring for the weekend. I'm offering the sum of fifty pounds and hope it doesn't break me, though I'm certain we'll draw a crowd of ten thousand for such a feat. I'll leave you my card and you can give me your answer when you've decided.

He said all of this with a smile and a bow at the end of it, handing his card to my father. And still I could only mouth my thanks, which he waved aside.

– These gentlemen are my witness, he said.

He beamed again, turned and walked away alone, shuffling with one of his shoes still loose. The two men cast him a curious glance. A few more steps round the bandstand and he was gone.

I was quite in a fluster now, desperate for my voice to return. I wanted to scream Dorothy's name. I wanted us to rush to Cremorne at once, though I knew that wasn't possible.

– It's almost too much to believe, my father said when we were back at the encampment. Such an opportunity. And to hear good news of your cousin. Do you think you can do it?

Of course I can, I mouthed. I want to do it more than anything, I thought to myself.

– I'll get word to Mr Smith at once. The Boothes will go down in history for this.

I had to walk again on the Saturday and Easter Sunday. On Monday we struck camp and set off to Swindon for their May Day fair. I was desperate to perform again but there was no call for a walker, so I practised at the encampment instead. The Bells staged a boxing tournament and we showed the whirligig and menagerie, though after the beasts at Clifton ours seemed a lame effort. It was mostly railwaymen and their families that came – rather like being in the King Henry Inn at Mile End, where you'd be forgiven for thinking all City folk raise livestock or push barrows for a living.

The afternoon of the fair was when I realised I still had something inside me. I was sick twice that morning, and I noticed a bulge in my stomach, but thought I was just bloated from drinking stream water again. Then I was playing tag with Mary and felt flushed with the effort. But it was when I was tidying the waggon to the clack of the Aunt Sally that the noise suddenly felt too much and I just wanted to curl up and sleep. I slipped off my clogs and skirt, and lay on the bed. When I lifted my blouse, I knew; I could no longer deny it. Where before I'd had nothing to grasp but skin and ribs, I now had enough belly to need both my hands to cover it. I began rubbing it, gently at first, in circles getting larger. I pressed it till it hurt and I thought I might vomit again. There was a knock and before I could call out, James opened the door. He looked awkward to find me undressed, as I pulled the bed sheet quickly over my body.

– Beg pardon, he said, tipping his head. I was wondering if you'd mind having Mary for a while? Flo's tending a camel that's taken ill, and myself and the boys are needed on the rides.

I nodded and he thanked me, stepping aside to let the child in.

When James had left, Mary toddled over to me and I took her hand. I rested it on my stomach and she laid her head there, facing me. I eased the sheet away and felt her ear touch my skin. I mouthed to her at first, then tried carefully to make a sound, not wanting to strain my voice if it came.

– Do you hear it? I managed to whisper.

Mary gurgled, her eyes dancing like a drowsy fly; she had a way of looking sometimes that made it hard to catch her attention.

– I reckon you might have a little cousin on the way, I whispered again, stroking the down on her cheek.

She climbed into the berth and nestled against me to sleep, which was how Flo found us, however many hours later when the evening was drawing in.

– I'm sorry about the time, she said, out of breath and her hair smelling of dampness and filth. We lost the camel I'm afraid. There's something rife amongst them. Now two of the lions have stopped eating. I pray we don't lose any more. Your father's in a terrible state.

She pulled off her boots at the door and grabbed one of the cloths from above the stove to give her hands a good wipe, then lit a stub of candle and stepped towards me, bending to kiss Mary's head.

– My voice is coming back, I whispered.

– I'm so glad, she replied, and I met her eyes and saw them begin to water.

I knew then, that Flo cared for me as only my aunt and Ellie had before. I knew I should tell her, but I knew too that she'd want me to stop rope-walking. I couldn't give her the burden of it, with her knowing that I'd be too stubborn to listen to reason.

She touched my forehead and scooped Mary into her arms. When she was gone, I put my hands to my belly again. I lay listening to the closing minutes of the fair, watching the candle burn to the wick, till just the shadows from the naphtha lamps outside played over the walls and ceiling of the waggon. I could hear the shooting gallery in the distance, the final gunshots and cheering. And from the sound of it, the last boxing bout had drawn a good crowd – Pip Bell doubtless making a tidy sum, whoever the winner. I wondered what odds he'd give me if he knew what I was planning, and how they'd change if he learnt of my condition.

Forty

I have an urge to see my grandfather's journal again, bring its leather skin to my nose, tease its pages between my fingers. I know from my aunt's stories that her father told things just how they were. One day I'd like to learn how to read it, perhaps how to write down my own stories. But I worry that day might never come, so I'm telling all of this to you now just in case, cos I know you're in there and listening. And just like my aunt once told me, I reckon you'll do better hearing the truth, warts and all, so one day you might understand.

We've lost the menagerie. All of the animals sickened, bar a couple of lionesses that have now been shot anyway, to save them the slow death the others suffered. Everyone was blaming the zoo, saying it must've been one of the beasts they'd bought at Bristol docks that was infected, till we remembered our zebra that died before we arrived there. We've now heard that every fair that went to King's Lynn has lost its stock. Wombwell's is the only menagerie left, them having missed the Mart this year.

Our convoy has split again; some are heading to Winchester and the rest are travelling to Kent with my father – to work the orchards before making ready for Dartford Fair. But first, you and I are going to Cremorne Gardens with uncle James; my father's mood is too low for him to manage it.

– Take good care of my daughter, he tells James, as he helps me into a hansom at Richmond Park, though he hardly needs to say it.

– We'll see you tonight at Greenwich, my uncle replies, grabbing my father's arm to reassure him.

It should be less than an hour to Cremorne if the roads are clear, James tells me. I keep rubbing my stomach, forgetting that he's sitting next to me; he's sure to work it out if I don't stop doing it.

– You asked me if you could see this, he says, as we leave the park through the east gate.

He hands me a parcel with brown wrapping. I know what it must be, though I hold it as if it's a mysterious treasure just unearthed.

– Thank you, I whisper.

It's four years since I last saw it. It's smaller than I remember, and the covering is darker – like old blood rather than new. I trace the letters stamped on the front: N for Ned and B for Boothe. I've always thought it odd that my aunt entrusted it to James and not to my father.

I open the journal and there's the young man with striped trousers and bare chest, balancing on a leather ball, a tiny fly squashed upon his face.

– Your great-grandfather, James says, peering over my shoulder.

– Aunty read to me from this most days till she was gone.

– She loved you dearly, you know; it's a terrible thing she died so young.

– It seems us women are ill-fated.

– Not this one, James says, patting my leg.

I want to move his hand to my belly, spread his fingers across it and let him feel what's beneath them. But I can't do that.

I turn the pages of the journal, trying to focus on the dark script – so tiny, it's as if a beetle stepped in ink and then walked back and forth across the page. But I fear the marks will never give up their secrets to me.

The hansom rounds a corner sharply and jolts me against the side, so the journal slips from my lap. James catches it and returns it to me.

– Why did Dorothy run away? I ask him suddenly, a question I've let go unanswered for too long.

He thumbs a patch of grime from his square of window and looks out at the city morning rushing by. I can tell he doesn't want to reply, but how can I not ask now?

– She didn't run away, he says finally, without turning back to me. She was sent away to be looked after.

– She's always been more than able to look after herself.

– Yes, Lucky. But she had more to deal with, not just herself.

He pauses and glances at me before carrying on.

– She was with child, he says.

James looks at me again, but not at my stomach; he hasn't guessed. I sit on my hands to stop myself touching it.

– Was?

– For God's sake, Lucky. She couldn't possibly have kept it. Don't be judging us, he blurts.

– You haven't told me anything yet, I say.

– The child was her brother's. That damned weasel.

– Pip Bell?

James nods and turns away again. I feel sick in my stomach, but not in the way I've become used to. I left Dorothy when she most needed me, is all I can think of.

– Then for certain, she'll not want to see me, I cry, the first time I've raised my voice since it returned.

– She must've spoken well of you to Edward Smith, else he wouldn't have offered to hire you. He's no fool; he's owned half of the West End in his time. Dorothy wants nothing more to do with the fairs though.

– Because no one did anything to stop it? Could you not have helped her rather than sent her away? Does my father know any of this?

– What would you have him do if he did know? The boy's not worth hanging for.

– Why did Pip defend my father at the Waste?

– It might've looked that way, James says. I reckon he heard the argument and took the rifle from your father's waggon; Albert was none too pleased about that. Pip Bell must've had his own score to settle with August Boothe.

– I think you are all cowards, I say at last, resting my head against the window, pulling my hand out from under my leg and laying it on my belly, no longer caring whether my uncle notices.

I don't speak again, even when we arrive at the entrance to the gardens. The gates are chained but I can see through them to the pay-box, now freshly painted and showing new posters. I can see too, stretching into the distance, the jets and lustres of a thousand gas lamps restored to their glory. Cremorne has awakened from its long winter, drawing me into its clutches as though it was written in my first teacup that I should return here.

I hear the clunk of the cab doors unlocking at my feet and stand to step out.

– I'll be keeping an eye out. I don't think Dorothy will manage seeing two of us at once, James says, not getting up.

I don't reply, struggling with what he's told me – though it's not really him that's done bad. But I reckon he, like others of the Bells, could've done more to help Dorothy earlier.

I find the workers' gate unlocked and push it open, the squeak from the hinges startling a dove from its nest – little more than a few twigs piled where a branch forks, looking barely strong enough to hold the bird's weight. As it rises it drops a feather, and I reach up and pluck it from the air, which makes me smile, as I've never even managed to catch a falling leaf before.

I walk along an avenue of elm and poplar now dense with greenery, the echo of traffic from the King's Road growing distant. Every few yards, on one side then the other, a stone goddess watches over me, bearing a gas-lamp as a crown. At the end of it, I find the circus ring again and it's been cleared of rubbish – the sand raked smooth as ice, not a hoof mark or footprint to be seen. It's too tempting to resist, like at the bakery in Mile End where I was often sent on errand – the loaves laid out so neatly that I'd want to push one and send them all out of line. I step into the ring and begin walking in a spiral, dragging my foot from side to side, leaving a trail like a grass snake in a dune. I take a while to reach the middle, and only then do I notice her, standing where I'd started. She's wearing a red coat to her ankles, which makes her look even taller if that's possible, and gives a glow to her face.

– Hello Lucky, Dorothy calls out, as casual as if we've already seen each other earlier in the day.

I start towards her, lurching as I reach her so she has to grab me. She feels so full and strong, she must fear I'll break in her grip.

– So you're not a ghost then, she says, pushing me away to look at me properly.

– No, not a ghost, I reply, releasing her too. You're looking well.

– I'm doing fine.

We move from the circus ring and walk between geranium-beds already in bloom. I have to take her hand to slow her, and as we round a path towards the River, I stumble for a moment, feeling faint.

– It was a bumpy cab ride, I explain, holding onto her arm.

– It's not far, she says.

She leads me to an old hunting lodge, its back wall strangled by ivy, like at the King Henry Inn – the greenery so thick, a chimney could fall in and not be seen again. We step inside, through a scullery with polished flags and the biggest copper I've ever seen, to a parlour with a good-sized hearth. When Dorothy takes off her coat I see her outfit, a black dress with white trimming and a pinny round her waist.

– I clean at the big house, she says when she notices me looking. And I work on the gate in the evenings during the season. We opened on Good Friday. Take a seat.

– I came here, Christmas before last, I tell her.

– I might not have been living here then, she replies flatly.

– I was looking for you. I wanted you to return to us.

– But you'd already run away, she says, taking a cloth to the china on the mantelpiece, though it looks spotless already.

– Sometimes I think I shouldn't have. I wish you'd written. James could've read to me. He's waiting at the front gate.

– I don't want to see him just yet. Did he tell you I stole Bess? She died, I'm afraid. Will you have some tea? You are staying for a while?

– I'm not sure what I'm doing, I whisper as Dorothy disappears to the kitchen; I'm saddened to hear of the bitch, but animals come and go much like we do.

I stand at the empty grate and fiddle with the ornaments, finding not a speck of dust on any of them. I move to the bay window and look out on a privet maze where a blackbird is scratching in the leaves. When I turn back to the room again, I see a young woman dressed like Dorothy slipping through. She nods and smiles but I'm sure only cos she knows I've spotted her.

– That was Hilda, Dorothy says when she returns with the tea tray, blushing as she sets it on the low table in the circle of armchairs. There's four of us live here. We look after ourselves mostly, but we get a meal a day from the big house.

– And that's where Mr Smith lives?

– He owns all of this. We don't see much of him, he's so busy. He's a decent man, pays us fairly and never raises his voice.

– How did you come to be here? I ask her, which makes her reach for the teapot and start pouring, though her hand is shaking so much I have to take over.

– There was nothing else I could do, she replies at last.

– I know, I shouldn't have left you, I say, returning the pot to the table.

I take her hand and stroke the back of it, her skin still smooth despite the work it's been put to, and tears come to her now.

– My family are no good. I so missed my mother when she went. I know you miss yours and you never even knew her; that's harder, I suppose. I went to a place for girls who'd done the same as me. I cried all the time I was there.

– I understand. James told me today. But it's not your fault, it was done to you, I tell her, thinking of the refuge in Whitechapel, the two nights I spent there, when she might've been nearby after all.

– Mr Smith does good works. He was visiting the house when I was recovering. He spoke to me like we were equal. I thought he wanted something else, you know. But he seemed so kind. He is kind.

– He offered you a job?

– Not right away, but he said something might come up.

– You should've told someone earlier about your brother, I say, the first time I've properly mentioned it. Uncle James would've listened to you.

– We were just young 'uns, Dorothy says, welling up again.

– I went back to the Waste that Christmas. James and Flo told me you were safe but that's all they said.

– Don't blame them, or yourself Lucky. I'm alright now. Mr Smith came again after a fortnight and took me with him. I didn't tell anyone where I was going. I didn't want Pip following me, nor my father.

We fall silent a moment. Dorothy's done well to find this situation. She has a new life and she's safe. We've got so much to talk about – I've got so much to tell her – but there's one thing clawing at my mind that I've got to ask first.

– That other uncle of mine. Has he ever come here? I whisper, as though he might be listening.

Dorothy leans forward and puts down her cup. She makes no pretence of not knowing whom I mean.

– You mustn't be angry. I promise, I'm no good at it. He came here a few months ago, just after New Year. He knows Mr Smith. They both lost money at Vauxhall when the gardens closed. He told me you'd been rope-walking for him. I was so glad to hear word of you, I suppose I got carried away by him.

– He didn't try anything else? I start to say.

– No, nothing like that. He said you'd given up with the walking. He wanted me to try but I was hopeless. We've got a wire in the gardens you can practise on when you're ready. You are going to do the walk aren't you?

– I hope so, yes. But I need to tell you something: I have a lover, or I had a lover. It's hard to explain. His name's Virgil. He's in hiding and I know August Boothe had a hand in making him run away; he admitted as much to me. Has he visited again?

– I can't remember the last time. February perhaps. He told me his mother tried to walk across the river once.

I stare at Dorothy, wondering if I've heard her right, my hand reaching for my belly as a reflex.

– But that's impossible, I tell her, my mouth falling open. He's never spoken of his mother. And I've only ever heard of one woman who's attempted the Thames.

– He said she was from the continent, Dorothy goes on, standing up to clear the table. Died last year of a fever or something.

I let Dorothy's words sink in, a plug of bile gathering in my throat. I think of August Boothe in Nat's room, rifling through her things as though a stranger's, saying how much he disliked her country; I remember now – he offered to look after her trunk, and I never questioned why, nor saw it again. And I think of him standing beside me at Bow, watching Nat's corpse being tipped into a paupers' pit.

– Are you alright Lucky? Dorothy says, bringing me to. Apparently his mother didn't manage it. Too windy or something. Mr Smith reckons she never even started out. You must try it though.

I swallow painfully and clench my fist in my lap. I think of all the times Nat could've told me. She only mentioned August Boothe once, like a warning. I begin to wonder – did she know herself? I can only guess at what circumstance brought August Boothe to England – taken from his mother at birth perhaps; he's certainly always known who his father was. Yet, there's a chance Nat didn't know that August Boothe was her son; it's not a lot to hold on to, but it's all I have left.

It comes quick now, rising from my stomach and stopping my breath. I make it out of the parlour, but heave onto the flags in the passage.

– Come and sit back down; I'll fetch a cloth, Dorothy says, squeezing past me with the tea tray.

– Bring a mop and I'll clean it up, I say.

– Just sit. I'll do it. You can stay the night if you need to.

– We're supposed to be going to Kent, I tell her, when she returns.

– Then you must come back soon.

I stand again, a little unsteady, and hug her to me for a moment.

– I will come back, I whisper to her.

And then I say to myself – I'll come again and walk across the River. I'll do it for you and Virgil. For Madame Rouge. For my father.

Dorothy sees me off from the riding ring. I don't speak to my uncle James when I find him again outside at the main gate. We travel to Greenwich in silence and I keep to myself for the three days that follow till we reach Kent.

We arrive at the orchard on the full moon. Beside the first row of apple trees, their blossom all fallen now, my father sets alight the last menagerie carriage. Our stories tell that it caught fire once before, decades ago when my grandfather owned it. He rebuilt every inch of it and repainted it a dozen times – so many layers, so many lives sharing its splendour. Now, it burns in minutes like tinder, leaving a pile of ash and a hushed mood.

When the ceremony is over, Flo comes to my waggon with a plate of dinner; we've not spoken since my visit to Cremorne Gardens.

– I'm not hungry, I say to her.

– Maybe later then, she says, laying the plate on the sideboard. I wanted to ask how Dorothy was when you saw her?

I take a deep breath, thinking how to answer. I want to blame someone for how Dorothy was treated, but I know in truth it's Pip Bell I'd have to confront and I haven't the energy left for that. I'm glad he's gone to Winchester and not joined us, though I feel like a coward too for thinking it.

– Dorothy is well, I say at last, knowing that what happened in the past was out of Flo's hands. She's happy and she's well looked after.

– Well I'm very glad for that, Flo says. And you're going to do this walk across the Thames? It seems terribly dangerous.

– Yes, I'm going to do it. I won't fall, but if I do it'll be into water and I'll be rescued. I only wish I could do it sooner. The end of September seems a lifetime away.

– And you're quite recovered? Do you want me to look at you?

I shrink from her, hoping she doesn't notice.

– I'm fine, I say to her. You know, we're just like spring flowers, Dorothy and I.

Bouncing back. Blooming for another year.

Forty-one

I've had three months of barely holding a crumb down, though I've kept you secret, even from Flo. You've been thrashing about inside me so much, like you're turning somersaults, I reckon you're already in training to be a tumbler. Better that than a rope-walker anyway. I'm beginning to understand now – though far too late – why my father tried to stop me knowing of my mother's craft. It's no better than opium, the pleasure and the pain. But it's what I have and what I live for. I only pray I can keep you safe.

We've been working the fruit farms for most of these weeks. Every morning at dawn, and at dusk when I've been able to, I've been practising on the rope. Sundays, I've been spending all day on it, whatever the weather, whilst father's been going off some place, I don't know where. Flo's often round about but she hasn't noticed any change in me, or has chosen not to say anything. There's been no word of Virgil, but no sign of August Boothe either, so I'm glad of that at least. There was talk of me performing at Dartford Fair, but it came to nothing. It went poorly for us without our animals to show, and afterwards only a few folk carried on to Blackheath.

At last, the time's come to move on and head to Cremorne, so I can start my preparations. It feels like the entire fair's been holding its breath all summer waiting for my walk; there's almost too much depending on it, but I know I can do it.

The first morning of September, all packed and our goodbyes to the farm folk done, six waggons including my father's and mine begin to roll. James and Flo will follow in a week, and the rest will join us in time for my performance, so they can keep working the harvest for as long as possible.

I don't ride on my waggon to start with, but walk alongside the horse that's pulling it, keeping close behind my father's. The mare ignores my whispers and pocketful of oats – too fed and watered already, I suppose. I think my father is leading us wrong at first, cutting west through the lanes instead of north to the main road, till we round a bend and arrive at a familiar crossroads. At once I feel myself returned to my aunt's stories. Another few minutes and my father slows and steers his waggon to the roadside, so all of us behind do the same. And now I see it – the verge opposite with its grass freshly cut, a new wooden cross with a neat mound of stones at its base giving life to a crop of sunflowers.

– Been having a late spring-clean, my father says, striding across to the memorial.

I follow and step up beside him, admiring his work.

– It's beautiful, I say, which it is.

I run my fingers over the shapes cut into the dark wood. My father reaches out too and pats the side of the cross with his palm, so his sleeve falls back and I can see he's wearing the copper band again; I can't recall the last time I saw it.

– I didn't know you could carve, I say to him.

– I'd hardly call it that, he snorts. Just your mother's name and a few swirls.

– Well it's beautiful all the same.

– I didn't put anything about your brother. I didn't know what to write.

– It's beautiful just as it is. Perhaps one day you could teach me to do it.

I touch my father's arm and we stand in silence a moment. Truly, he and I have travelled full circle now, in all manner of ways, old and new.

– Shall we go on? he says at last, turning to me, waiting for my nod.

We've taken two days to reach the ruined gardens at Vauxhall. Mr Smith has told us we should pull on there till he's ready for us to move to Cremorne. Just inside the broken gates, there's a patch of ground that's been cleared of brambles and smells of rotting leaves, and that's where we park up. The moment we're unloaded, my father and two others set about rigging the practise rope. They fix one end to an old oak, then run it between fallen statues, behind a crumbling bandstand throttled with weeds, and over a huge mound of shrubs piled ready for burning. Where the rope ends, the trees are too thin, so they tension it round a colonnade. I climb up and take to it at once, getting a round of applause after my first try.

Soon, passers-by are stopping at the gate to watch, so it's not long before word reaches the receiver; Mr Smith hasn't thought to mention us to him. When he arrives – a gruff fella with poor skin and a threadbare suit – he takes a dim view of our presence, till my father explains our purpose and the man tells of childhood visits to Astley's Amphitheatre. He watches me practising for a while, before leaving us to it, accepting our promise to be gone in three days, though we know it might be a fortnight.

My condition should be plain for everyone to see now, but I've been eating little and wearing baggy clothes, so I look no different at first glance. Occasionally I fear that one of the Bell women has guessed, but none speaks of it. As for the men, if it's not being dangled in their faces, they don't notice the thickening of a bosom beneath a blouse too big, the ripening of a complexion, the rising of a milky scent. I'm desperate to see Dorothy though, to tell her. So I send word, assuring her that Pip and her father aren't with us. On Saturday afternoon, she comes.

304

When my father sees her, he hugs her like I've not seen him do before; she looks uncomfortable with it, and I don't blame her – we both could've done with such affection a long time ago.

– The waggons seem so small now, she says, as she ducks through the door and unfolds herself to sit. How ever did I manage?

I think of her bowtop with its sagging roof and mean bed.

– This is a palace compared to what we once had, I say to her. But yes, it is a wonder how any of us cope, especially once you've known something else.

– Mr Smith still teases me about it. He says he can hear me rattling around in the lodge like a bead in a tin. He jokes about moving me to one of the huts in the garden. But I keep telling him – I'm not really no gypsy nor showgirl; my mother never set foot in a waggon before she met my father. My room's not much bigger than this but I've a whole house around me. We can leave our sewing out or do a puzzle over a weekend. I forget where I've left my shoes sometimes. I reckon I've lost something in every room twice over, moving things upstairs from downstairs and back again.

I feel such joy to see her, to hear her rattling on. As she does, I take a seat across from her and begin unbuttoning my blouse, lifting my stays to better show my belly. I'm sure she would've noticed eventually, and I know it'll be difficult for her, what with losing her own, though she could never have kept it.

– Dorothy! I say suddenly, which stops her and makes her look up.

– Oh! is all she manages at first, turning away for a moment.

– We're going to have company, I say, beaming at her.

– How soon? she says, trying to stop her tears.

– I don't know. Three months perhaps.

She wipes her eyes and brushes aside her fringe, rubs her palms together to make them warm, and holds them out towards me.

– Can I touch? she asks, her hands already on me. Definitely a girl, she says, after stroking me a couple of times.

– There's a chance you might be right, I say with a smile.

– It's the walker's then? What was his name again?

– Virgil. Yes, it's his.

I rebutton my blouse and now it's my turn to conceal my tears, but there's no hiding from Dorothy.

– Dear God, I'm sorry, she says. I'm sure Virgil will return. I know what love is now too.

She stops herself and her cheeks redden; she's said more than she meant to, but I've had long enough since my last visit to work it out.

– Hilda's very pretty. She has skin like yours. Can I ask you something? I whisper.

Dorothy puts her finger to her lips, letting me know she'll talk about it when she's ready.

– You must come and see the preparations, she now says, changing the subject. They've been building for weeks. I still can't believe it's happening, and all for you. It's going to be glorious. You'll be famous across Europe. All over the world. But what I am saying? she cries, jumping up from her seat. You can't possibly do it in your condition. I'm confused now. You shouldn't be doing it at all.

– I'll be fine, I say, holding up my hand to stop her. I'm sure it's not coming for a while.

I stand and reach into the wardrobe for the dress that's to be my costume. It's too big for me, so it'll hide my swell perfectly.

– From now on, I'm going to wear this all the time, I tell her, climbing into it. I had it made for me in Dartford. I think my mother wore something similar when she was carrying.

I'll be wearing it for my walk across the River, so no one should think it odd if I say I'm trying to get a feel for it now. And then they won't notice when I start showing.

Dorothy puts her hands to my stomach again, now hidden under the dark folds of heavy cotton.

– There'll be thousands of boats looking out for you, she says, a little nervously.

– So there'll be no space left when I fall into the water. I was hoping for a soft landing, I jest.

– You've not just yourself to think of now, she snaps. You've responsibilities, and people who love you.

– Take me with you then. Take me back to Cremorne.

– Of course. We'll live as sisters again, Dorothy whispers.

I pack my bag with a spare blouse and skirt, my slippers and flannels, and the tiger claw brooch; my mother's poster is too fragile to move though, so I touch it for luck and say goodbye to it for now. When we stop at my father's waggon, he's sorting the takings from the fruit picking.

– I'd rather you stay and practise here, my father says when I tell him.

I know he still wants to keep an eye on me, though there's been no sight of August Boothe in over six months; if he knew the truth of my situation, he certainly wouldn't let me go.

– It's only for a couple of weeks, I say. Dorothy will keep me safe. And anyway you'll be pulling on there too any day now.

– Perhaps I'll speak to Mr Smith about us coming sooner.

He hands me the cab fare and a little extra; I can see he wants to give us both a hug, but Dorothy's edging away. So he just waves to us, wishing us luck.

Though it's nearly dark when we arrive, Dorothy's so excited she wants to show me the River at once, but with the moon in cloud there's little to see except silhouettes and shadows. So we return to the lodge and take our supper with

Hilda; though I'm sure she never looks up from her bowl, I can feel her eyes upon me for every second of the meal. She's paler than I remember, yet just as pretty – the kind of face you wouldn't wish on your enemy, for all the attention it must suffer.

– You can have my bed, Dorothy tells me when the meal's done and we're rested.

She shows me upstairs to her room, which I reckon might be smaller than my waggon after all, though it only has a bed and dresser and a single chair, so there's still space to move in. The window's wedged ajar and has no curtain or shutter, so it sits like a black square on the wall, sucking away the candlelight. The bed's wide, with lilac sheets that match the walls, and it's still warm enough not to need blankets. She brings me a nightgown as I've forgotten my own. It's soft like feathers and smells of lemon, and is much too short below the waist to be hers.

– I've some oil you could use on your belly, she says, as I lie down.

She fetches a bottle from the dresser and before I button the gown, she sets about massaging my stomach. She brings a candle closer and traces with her finger the dull line that falls from my navel.

– Can I listen? she says, turning away from me and putting an ear to my stomach, resting her hand above my groin. She's kicking. I can feel her. Do you think she's saying hello?

She makes to sit up but I stay her, wanting her there a while longer. I run my fingers through her hair and stroke her forehead.

– I'm so happy to be here, I tell her at last.

She sits up and turns to me with a worried look.

– You will be careful won't you? There are so many things to live for.

I nod, her words reminding me of Ruby and Pearl, the warmth of their vast bed, the pleasures I imagined them enjoying. And I know she's right. There is still life to be shared.

Forty-two

Dorothy rouses me with her clattering in the scullery, then her footsteps on the stairs. I can hear the dawn chorus.

– Are you awake? We should go to the river, she whispers round the bedroom door. The tide is at its lowest for months.

My eyes are still half-closed and gummed with sleep as she prods me out of bed, slips my shoes onto my feet, and leads me downstairs. She wraps a coat over my nightgown and we step outside, tasting autumn in the air – late fruits and decay falling upon the tongue at once. Dorothy takes a deep breath, grabs my hand and starts towards the maze.

– It's the quickest route. I'll show you. Straight through from one side to the other.

I would never find all the gaps in the hedges alone. I have to remind her of my condition to slow her. As we reach the River's edge, I double over to catch my breath. Then as I stand again, I see it – the riverbed exposed left and right for as far as can be seen, and for several yards towards the middle. I reckon if the south bank were visible too, it would look the same. As the water grows slack and the mist rises, the River gives up its secrets. Rubbish washed down with the tide lies beached on the sand like a shed skin, and amongst it there are treasures on display. I want to give stories to it all: weapons dropped by fleeing murderers, the spoils of botched burglaries, coins thrown for luck – all of it caught in the early sun. And now a half-dozen mudlarks go to work, hunched over with their faces almost touching the sand, filling their sacks with loot just found, or stolen from one another at knifepoint, loading their backs till they can carry no more.

– Isn't it beautiful? Dorothy whispers, bringing me round.

She's staring now at the pier that lets from the gardens midway along its riverfront. There, rising to perhaps a hundred feet, is a tower formed of two immense props, crossed at the top and cradling a tiny platform. Each beam is guyed by several ropes along its length, holding it still as a church spire. Behind, the wooden bridge with its ramshackle supports looks about to give in to the weight of traffic already upon it.

– And there's the other, Dorothy says, pointing to the far side of the River.

What she sees now is only what she knows to be there. It takes several more minutes of the mist rising before I can see the second tower on the south bank, perfectly mirroring the first.

– And there's to be a third, in the middle of the river, Dorothy adds excitedly. Goodness knows how they'll build it. Mr Smith is spending a fortune. Can you believe it? And all for you.

I cover Dorothy's hand and squeeze it gently. I turn to her, see her mouth part and her bottom lip start to quiver. A tear falls onto her cheek; she cries so much in my company. She doesn't reach to wipe it. I lean towards her and kiss it away.

– It's for all of us, I say.

She takes my arm and turns me away to face the pagoda.

– Let's go up and see the view.

I'm about to tell her I've seen it before, but she knows that already, and anyway I need to see it again. We climb to the highest level and as we reach the top, we hear the first strike of Sunday bells from a church tower still lost in the fog. We look to where the rope will pass and fall to the gardens, the scent of lavender already rising from a dozen bowers. It'll be steep – perhaps the most difficult part of the walk – and over buildings and solid ground, more demanding than climbing at the start, cos I'll be tired. Here I will set down after my greatest feat, buoyed in my heart, though sorrowed by absence. I might be showered with gifts and praise, but for what good without Virgil at my side?

My thoughts now fly to Madame Rouge, my aunt, and Ellie. To my father, and Dorothy, beside me again at last. And to you inside me, waiting to join me in the world.

Before Dorothy begins her shift, she shows me the tight-wire set alongside a line of poplar. It stands at less than head height and stretches for a hundred feet over several sections. Dorothy has learnt from Mr Smith's men that I will walk for two thousand feet across the River, which makes the practise wire seem scant preparation.

When Dorothy is gone to the main house, I return to the lodge to fetch my slippers. At the back door I encounter Hilda for only the third time. We both pause on the threshold, neither of us moving aside for the other. Hilda reaches for a lock of hair that's fallen onto her brow and pushes it back under her cap. Then she breaks into a giggle – which relieves me somewhat – and steps back into the scullery.

– Dorothy is very dear to me, she says, not meeting my eye. I have no kin. She'll not come to any harm with me. I can promise you that.

– She's dear to me also, I reply, touching Hilda's arm. I'm glad you have each other.

Hilda curtsies, as if forgetting we're equals, and slips past me without speaking again.

When I begin practising, the gardens have already opened to the public. The day is cloudless, and warm by mid-morning, and for much of it I perform for an audience of polite and finely-clothed children, not a jeer or lump of mud thrown. I walk without fault, from end to end and back again, over and over, my costume dress hanging to my calves – hiding my curves, my bump, my fears. I practise without stopping or eating, till dusk falls and the families begin leaving – the gardens closing early on Sunday evenings, so there isn't the urgency as on other days, to encourage them home before they might encounter the visitors of the night.

I step down from my final walk as Dorothy arrives.

– *Mademoiselle Lucky.* Your dinner is served, she announces with a flourish.

We walk hand in hand to the lodge, past the tiers of supper-boxes where evening meals are being finished.

– I spoke with Hilda, I say. You must tell her not to fear my being here; it won't be for long.

– But you'll stay till the birth at least? Dorothy says as we enter the house.

– I belong with my father now. I've a child on the way and no husband. It's hardly a good situation.

– What good have men ever done us, Dorothy blurts, but then smiles, leading me to the parlour.

There are five of us at dinner, including Hilda and the other two maids, and the table is lively with their chatter and laughter. Only on Sunday evenings, when Mr Smith prefers to serve his family himself, are they all free to eat together. I'd been hoping to meet the proprietor again but Dorothy says he's to travel for a fortnight and won't return till shortly before the walk.

– Don't worry. He has all the preparations in order, Hilda reassures me. He's very particular and organised, is Mr Smith. I'm sure he won't miss a single detail.

After the meal – a fine mutton stew as good as I ate at Earl's encampment, that lifetime ago on the Waste – I excuse myself, feeling quite exhausted by the day. Hilda is relaxed with me now, smiling as I leave the parlour with Dorothy at my side.

I climb the stairs slowly to Dorothy's room, flop on the bed, and Dorothy sits beside me on the only chair.

– Can I tell you a story? she begins.
– Of course, I say. I love stories.

Forty-three

For two and a half weeks, I've watched the festival build round me – dozens of stalls assembled, huge braziers wheeled into place, yards upon yards of bunting sewn and hung. Hedges have been trimmed and shaped, borders weeded, lawns cut, the maze cleared of dead leaves and litter. Metalwork has been scraped and repainted, the fumes filling the air so you can still taste it; even the main house has been hurriedly whitewashed by an army of boys. Mr Pablo Fanque has arrived – fresh from a visit to Norwich – with a fanfare and a convoy of gay carriages, and is setting up in the circus ring. Boats are now gathering at the pier to be decorated, the third tower has emerged from the middle of the River, and beacons have been raised along the embankment and filled with straw and wood.

All the while, I've been walking back and forth along the wire, sometimes with an audience, other times not. My father has visited twice and I've assured him all is well. In truth though, I've found spots of blood between my legs; I've been doubled over with cramp that's felt like a band of leather tightening round my belly; I've been sweating as though I'm in the Tropics. Though I've barely been eating, my bulge has continued to grow, so I've had to keep my shape hidden under my walking dress. Whenever I've felt unwell or about to cry, I've slunk under a willow and hidden amongst its weeping branches. Night-times, I've lain alongside Dorothy and we've shared our stories.

With two days to go, the Boothes and Bells and Freemans and Cookes, all of whom have been gathering at Vauxhall, roll up at Cremorne and make camp to the west of the gardens. At once, Flo comes to find me at the lodge. She and

James have only just arrived from Kent – towing a cart piled high with early apples – having stayed on at the orchard after all.

– Forgive us for not coming when we promised, she says, standing in the parlour, eyeing my dress.

– I'm being well looked after, I tell her, as Dorothy steps into the room and slips her arm through mine.

There's an uneasy silence, till Dorothy parts from me and lets Flo embrace her.

– You're both looking well for having each other again, Flo says at last. And your father seems very happy, Lucky. He says he's been busy finding bookings for you. He reckons you'll never be short of work once you've walked across the river. It'll be a boost for us all. Losing the animals has been such a blow.

– I have to manage this walk first. But yes – it's sure to be the start of something new, I say to her.

My father visits a third time whilst I'm practising and sits watching me for the afternoon. He calls out to me whenever I'm walking past him. He tells me the folk at Clifton Zoo want me to walk there again as soon as I'm done at Cremorne. A pleasure garden in Brighton is booking acts for November fifth. And he reckons I should consider Worcester for New Year, rather than Mile End, which I could do on Christmas Eve instead. His words start to blur, and by the end of it I'm more exhausted from the listening than walking.

*

This final Friday, I watch the rope being rigged across the water. They've had to wait till now so as not to hinder the River traffic any sooner. They run the rope out from a great drum that's been brought by barge and unloaded onto the south bank. With the might of a steam tug, the free end of the rope is hauled by a wire to the top of the first tower, then pulled to mid-river and hoisted to the second. Finally it's brought to the north bank, over the third tower, then lowered and wound onto a second drum anchored in the gardens behind the pagoda. Four hours it takes, which gives me a welcome rest from practising. The guy ropes are to be fixed in the morning, my father tells me, to keep the River clear for as long as possible, and save the lead weights from being stolen.

With the rope set and the day almost done, my father announces a banquet, and I step from the practise wire for the last time.

By dusk there are hundreds gathered at the encampment, in a huge meadow beyond the gardens. Dorothy sits with me at the head of a raised table, where we can be seen by everyone. But now, on account of her father and Pip being rumoured to have arrived, I'm looking out for Dorothy as much as she is for me. I have my father beside me and she has James.

A good while into the meal, my father stands and makes a speech that heaps even more attention upon us, and I wish myself to be anywhere else.

– I look at these two beside me and mourn the years lost, he begins, which makes me and Dorothy stare harder at our food. We've seen difficult times, and I'm first to admit I should've done more, he goes on. I've ignored my daughter's talent for too long. I suspect I've been blind to other things too, he says, glancing at Dorothy and then to the crowd. But this is a time to celebrate. I only wish Lucky's mother could be here to see it. My kin, raise your glasses, he cries out. To Lucky. My dearest Rosie.

How do I spend this final night? Not in the warmth of my cousin's bed; our stories are told for now. Not gorging upon suckling pig, nor in a fug of gin or brandy, though something clouds me. With celebrations raging round me, and Dorothy returned to the safety of Hilda's arms, I sneak away to my waggon, which I've not visited since leaving Vauxhall. The door opens too easily and I pause to look for a candle, before I hear his voice, smell the damp tobacco.

– Better we speak in darkness, August Boothe says. Close the door. Take a seat.

I remain in the open doorway waiting for my eyes to adjust, till I can make him out at the far end of the waggon, sitting on my bed, his hand covering the side of his face that's towards me.

– What are you doing here? There's a whole fair outside would see you dead, I say, which seems to amuse him.

– And why on earth would that be? I've made rich men of many of them, though I doubt any would admit to it. So much of it done with your help, of course. A little wager here, a little wager there.

– I want you to leave.

– I suppose young Dorothy has been telling you all kinds of things. I shouldn't have mentioned to her about the old dear.

– You didn't much care for your mother?

– Nor her for me, he spits. I wasn't even sure till I read the letters.

– And did she know who you were?

He doesn't answer, but I've heard enough.

– I'm going, I say, as if it's his waggon I'm leaving and not mine.

– Wait! How's the little fellow? he calls out, dropping his hand and rising quickly from his seat.

I catch sight of his cheek, the skin red and blistered like a side of pork not yet ready on the spit. It's the same on his nose and the edge of his ear too. He turns away when he realises I can see.

– So what was it all for? I say bitterly. A mother you never loved? For my mother – who never loved you? Is that enough to waste a life over?

I slam the door before he can reply and walk directly out of the encampment. The King's Road is choked with omnibuses ferrying home the evening's visitors, and I catch a good amount of attention as I stumble as though drugged, not knowing where I'm headed. I walk till I fetch up in a churchyard, find myself at the end of a line of graves, too exhausted to walk further, and there I lose the night.

*

I awaken at first light, my dress dishevelled, a man standing over me, resting the tip of a spade on the earth beside my head.

– About time, the man says.

I feel as if there's someone lying beside me, their hand on my shoulder, trying to make me turn to them, but I can't move my head. The man bends over me and reaches under my armpit.

– Get up! You can't stay here. I've a grave to dig, I hear him say. There's plenty houses up the road for your sort.

I understand his words now, as I will myself properly awake and see that I am quite alone on the ground.

– I'm not of any sort, I croak. I'm walking across the River today. Please help me stand.

– Think I fell out me ma yesterday? he snorts.

He lifts me, lets me gather myself, then nudges me to the gates and onto the pavement.

When I reach the camp, I find it in a state of panic, folk too tearful to speak and looking like they've been up all night. My father sees me first and I'm glad of that.

– I was only going for a walk, I cry, as he hugs me to him and helps me towards my waggon. I didn't realise how tired I was. I fell asleep in a park. It was stupid of me.

– You're safe; that's all that matters. We need to get you fed and rested, and out of these wet clothes. I'll get Flo to heat a basin for you. Your feet look like they need a good soak.

– It'll be quicker at Dorothy's, I tell him, crossing my arms over my chest.

We climb the steps to the waggon; as my father reaches for the door handle, I stop and pull away from him.

– What is it? Was someone here?

I begin to nod, but already the memory seems of a ghost, much as the rest of the night is now dissolving like a dream.

– No. Nobody was here, I say at last. I just want to wait outside for Dorothy.

The encampment falls calm once more. I can hear fires being coaxed and breakfasts prepared, replacing the hullabaloo. Dorothy finds me on the step and I tell her what little I can remember of the night.

– You gave us a good scare, she says. You are a strange one, Lucky Boothe.

– We're a strange pair.

– Well I'm sure something good will come of it all.

– I need to prepare myself.

– Then you should rest. Come to the lodge and I'll get you bathed.

I grab her hand and bring it to my lips.

– I don't deserve you, Dorothy Bell.

– We don't deserve each other.

– I should never have run away.

– Perhaps we should've gone together. Anyway, which time are you meaning? she says, smiling and stroking my cheek. If you hadn't left, I'd still be with the fairs. I have a better life here at Cremorne.

– And what of your brother and father?

– They've not come near me. Perhaps someone's had a word.

– I'm glad of that. I'll need to get this dress cleaned and dried. Could you do it for me? This damned thing's weighing me down all of a sudden, I say, touching my stomach.

Dorothy eyes me as if it's her I've cursed.

– You mustn't speak like that, she says. It'll bring the worst of luck.

– Surely I've already had the worst of it. Last night August Boothe was sitting right there in my waggon and now I can't bear to go inside.

Dorothy climbs off the steps and stands up.

– You need to eat, she tells me.

I join her and we stare at one another for a moment. She has lines round her eyes that make her look older than she is, reminding me of Ellie. Dorothy's hurting too; I know that. She's had enough loss of her own.

Forty-four

I know it now, that there is no true rehearsal for the River, only hours of practise that might resemble what one feels on the day, but can never truly prepare one for it. There is no readying oneself for that endless rope, strung out to such unimaginable length, towering from such height, with its dozens of guys like a giant cat's cradle. There is no preparation for the bluster of the crowd, the clash of oars holding a hundred boats steady, the wind funnelling up the channel chasing the tide like a raging tiger.

Six hundred and fifty yards. Two thousand steps, my father reckons, if I walk heel to toe.

– You'll have to take it in strides if you don't want to be up there all day, he tells me before I begin my climb.

An immense throng has gathered for my performance. They crowd both riverbanks; they cram every steamboat, lighter and schooner till close to sinking. There are rowing boats with sun canopies, others with sails. I see the oddest sight: a skiff with a crystal chandelier suspended above the middle, hanging like a kettle on a crane. Folk stand on sterns and bows, teetering above the water. A few are swimming, already fallen perhaps, or taking a treacherous dip. On the bridge, they jostle for every square inch of cobble beneath their feet, as though at the hiring at the docks. They hustle for the best vantage point, block each other's view. And as I make my approach to the start of the climb – you still bound inside me – they collect in a huge and deafening burst of applause.

I've often imagined doing this walk in winter – the River a sea of ice, shimmering violet as a bluebell glade, the air so cold that it turns my breath to frost and makes my fingers stick to the balancing pole, as once happened at the Basin.

Yet, we're at the turning of the seasons, clinging to the last of summer's heat, my outfit much too heavy for it. And whoever you are, I know you're safe in the airless, noiseless, watery warm inside me. I haven't a comical bustle in which to keep you, but I have the dark folds of my dress, hiding you from all but Dorothy, though I'm sure others are about to notice.

There's so much noise now, it could drown the sound of a steam train – laughter, shouting, gasping and screaming.

Laughter greets the first steps of my ascent, as if I'm setting out on an afternoon stroll in a light breeze, rather than climbing to a hundred feet with nothing but two inches of rope between me and the ground.

– Steady on the rope. Girl walking, comes a distant cry.

At the platform, which is nothing more than a narrow ledge, it's shouting that reaches me from below. It rings in my ears as I take those first steps above the River, till it becomes a roar that awakes you in my belly. Those steps I've practised a thousand times – just six steps, one after the other. I think to myself, I could do this blindfold and not hear a thing, but somehow it helps, this crazed accompaniment.

Gasping is what I hear when I falter halfway to the second tower – rising from the middle of the River like some strange monument – when I feel you tugging at my groin for the first time, as though you are desperate to see daylight. Too soon, I tell you. I stoop and bring the balancing pole across my knees, glance down and see the mass of boats like miniatures upon the water. Maybe the crowd thinks it's part of the act; certainly they breathe a sigh when I stand again, step forward once more – six steps, another six steps, all the way to the second platform.

Am I too long resting there? Long enough for it to grow dusk and chilly before I step out once again.

The second half of my walk brings the screams, as the crowd sees the guy lines go slack ahead of me, and realises now that this is no casual turn. The rope starts to swing in the breeze, and a struggle begins ashore to tighten the remainder of it. I cry out, but I am a hundred feet beyond help. So I crouch, fearing that if I stand again I might slip, one leg each side of the rope, and fall upon your tender skull.

I should return to the middle tower, but instead I shuffle towards the next guy rope. When I reach it, I let go my pole – let it plunge to the waters far below – and collapse onto the main rope. I grasp one of the lines that feels no more than a bootlace, wrap my legs round it, and make a graceless slide to the water, the cord burning my skin. I land on a tiny craft that at once whisks me to the pier, where Mr Smith and the crowd all round him cheer my failure so loudly it brings me to tears.

– An incredibly brave attempt. Quite spectacular. Very brave indeed, he calls out to me, lifting his hat.

– I'll try it again, I plead.

But already he's turning away and my father and Dorothy are pushing forward.

– You cannot. Not in that condition, my father cries.

I look at Dorothy but she shakes her head. She hasn't told him, I'm sure of it.

– You're shivering and exhausted. You cannot try it again. The river will be down soon.

– Lift me up, I need to piss, I tell him, and he helps me from the boat onto the end of the pier.

– I'll take you, Dorothy says, grabbing my arm.

She knows that I wish to speak to Mr Smith. We hurry as quickly as the crowd will part for us. I'm breathless when we reach him.

– Sir, do you have minute? I say, panting like a runt.

Hearing my voice, he stops and turns.

– Of course my dear, he says, reaching for my hand and kissing it. How good it is to see you safe.

– I want to try again, I tell him. I'll do it after nightfall when the tide has turned. Load your fireworks onto the boats and set them off from the River instead of the lawn. Start the beacons early. Then there'll be light enough for me to be seen.

He ponders this for a moment, before tipping his head towards me.

– And for you to see, my dear? he asks.

– It'll be enough, I tell him, with such conviction that I'm sure he cannot refuse.

Yet I bend towards him and whisper in his ear, and he takes but a second to understand.

– So be it, he says, nodding sternly. I shall make the arrangements and have it announced at the circus. Is eleven-fifty too late? You will truly be the last act of the season. The finale, no less.

– Eleven-fifty it is, I reply, squeezing Dorothy's hand.

Forty-five

None that I love see me off, for if all goes to plan, I'll reach the gardens quicker than they could row a boat in this bedlam, or cross the bridge through the crowd; seven minutes at best, perhaps nearer ten. Instead, they gather at the pier on the opposite bank, awaiting my landfall – the Boothes and Bells, the Freemans and Cookes, and a good few others besides.

As I begin my ascent a second time, the River is in flood, just as Madame Rouge imagined it. Flares are sparked from the flotilla till it seems every boat has one, like batons being passed from one riverbank to the other. I barely pause at the first platform, but step across it and continue walking. I fix my gaze on the middle tower that's bathed in red smoke. It takes all of my attention, so I don't notice the spectacle growing round me – the blues, silver and gold exploding above me, beside me, at my feet, setting my ears popping. But as I approach the tower I do notice it fall into darkness for a moment, the flares spent, as though I've been chasing a rainbow to its end. The pole grows heavy, so I rest on the ledge a while.

I step out for the second half and soon I've gone further than on my first attempt. It feels now like I'm heading for home. I can picture the Waste at Christmas, my waggon parked up on the Mile End Road, snow banked to the top step. There's a pot of broth bubbling on the range and I'm sat in candlelight with a child in my arms, its soft lips clamped round my finger. The thought carries me over the third tower and to the start of my descent, towards the blazing beacons.

I've now walked at my greatest height.

I've crossed the River Thames on a tightrope.

Mademoiselle Rouge has triumphed.

I must still be at seventy feet or more as I descend over the pier, so I can't see my father watching, nor Dorothy, Flo or James, nor any of the Cookes or Freemans. But I imagine them standing with their necks craned, my father hugging Dorothy to him. I can't see the platform of dancers either, the swells and their ladies in evening dress, beckoning the night. But as I pass above the pagoda, its top barely twenty feet below, I'm close enough to make out three men standing alone on the highest tier, a single lantern lighting their faces: August Boothe, terribly scarred, with his pipe, cane, and crooked smile; two Bobbies in brass-buttoned tailcoats, top hats under their arms. In my panic, I think – I could take a single step to the side and fall to the earth just like that, feel the rush of air against my cheek and spill my blood, join Madame Rouge, my aunt, my dear Ellie, my mother.

But then I hear the strike of midnight, and your struggle to live begins. I know you must be good, for only something pure could survive inside me for so long. I know too that I've carried Virgil with me – that we've walked the River together, as I promised him we would. I wonder if you are now peeking out at my stockinged legs as white as milk, my slippered feet, the rope no wider than my sole, drawn tight as a bowstring and dissolving into the dark. Is that your first breath warming the tops of my legs? Can you see below to the upturned faces of eager children, their mothers shielding their cheeks against the night's chill? If you'd looked down earlier, you might've seen the bevy of boats struggling against the current, their decks bathed in magnesium and packed with other faces; or you might've marvelled at the bridge and wondered how it could remain standing with those tens of hundreds at its railings.

And for what do they now cheer, if not their utmost belief in me, oblivious to what is still hidden? Will they leave satisfied, their hearts filled with delight, or will they want more? And what of the River, Madame Rouge's beloved *fleuve?* Is it really anything more than a foul slurry?

I descend now to the bowling green that's ringed with torches, the noise of the crowd like nothing I've heard before, the pain of your coming like nothing I've ever felt. I roll onto the damp grass and at once Dorothy is with me, taking my hand.

– You did it! You crossed the Thames on a tightrope.

I have only a weak smile to give her in return.

I see my father and Flo stepping up, their faces cracked with confusion and worry. Flo kneels beside Dorothy and puts her hand to my forehead. She knows now of course.

– In God's name, why didn't you tell me? I have the letter, she sobs, putting her hand to her breast.

Then, out of my dreams steps another, and bends towards me. Skin like butterscotch. Hair with yellow streaks. Scent of talc. A brooch, milk-white with amber threads, like a tiger's claw, pinned to the outside of his lapel.

He reaches for my free hand, and lays it with his own against my cheek.

– Virgil! I whisper.

You come too quickly now, in a sea of muddled faces, and I wonder – when will the pain and cheering stop?

I see Dorothy lift you, give you a slap on the arse to bring your first breath.

She'll be a mother to you always and love you better than a mother might her own.

She will, if you let her.

As she lays you upon me, I smell your milky warmth, and my eyes do fall upon your beautiful form, your skin like burnt sugar. I'm sure yours open too, dark pools like your father's. I'm sure I meet your gaze and think to myself – perhaps now, for my own father, you will be the son he's never had, a Master for his Ring.

I'm sorry I have no fight left in me, that you are born in blood, as I once was. I'm sorry I'll never watch you grow, never hold your hand to avoid a hansom or cover your nose to the stench of the River.

But you have my story; you have your father and mine, and you have Dorothy.

Don't worry about me. Just remember what your great-aunt would've said:

I died, is all.

Cheers!

With much love to Lara and Jali, for their patience and not asking too many questions; to Lara also for her steadfast corrections.

With love and thanks to Caroline Kalberer at the Ry, for her limitless generosity and the perfect place to write.

An early draft of this novel was written in 2012-13 with the assistance of an Arts Council England Grants for the Arts award, as part of the Escalator Literature programme – with particular thanks to Laura Stimson and Sam Ruddock at Writers' Centre Norwich, and to my mentor Michelle Spring. A later draft was work-shopped at the Unthank School of Writing, Norwich – with thanks to Sarah Bower and Ashley Stokes.

Many thanks also to Kate Worsley for her incisive editorial comments, and to Victoria Hattersley and Saffron Myhill-Hunt for proofreading. All flaws my own.

And huge thanks to Mark Copeland at insectcircus.co.uk for his fabulous cover design.

This novel is a work of fiction. It is not intended to be representative, or be an accurate portrayal, of showmen or women, fairfolk or their traditions. Nor do I claim intimate knowledge or experience of tightrope walking; I reserve the greatest respect for those who practise this ancient craft. I am though greatly indebted to a number of sources for inspiration, including: *Fairground Strollers & Showfolk*, and *Fairfield Folk – A History of the British Fairground and Its People*, both by Frances Brown; *Seventy Years a Showman*, by 'Lord' George

Sanger; *The Tightrope Walker*, by Hermine Demoriane; *Showmen – The Voice of Travelling Fair People*, by Sally Festing; *Black Victorians/Black Victoriana*, edited by Gretchen Holbrook Gerzina; *The Rose, The Shamrock & The Thistle*, published by Caledonian Press; *Old Ordnance Survey Maps*, by Alan Godfrey. It goes without saying that sites on *T'Internet* were also a great source of information, foremost being: *The National Fairground Archive*; *The Blondin Memorial Trust*; *British History Online; The Internet Archive; The Victorian Dictionary*. I was also greatly inspired by visiting the Gordon Boswell Romany Museum, Spalding, with thanks to Margaret and Lenda Boswell for their time and stories.

I'm also grateful for the body of work of singer-songwriter and exquisite teller of stories, Laura Marling, which proved a curious but faithful companion to my six years spent writing this novel.

And with much love to mum and dad.

The publication of this novel is a bit of an experiment. Constructive/deconstructive comments most welcome to: hello@northcitypress.co.uk

Historical Notes

Although the character of Lucky Boothe is entirely fictitious, real people and events inspired her creation, and I confess to having taken considerable liberties with names, dates, places and times. I wish now to set right a few of these historical facts:

The two-thousand foot long rope-walk across the River Thames, from Battersea to Cremorne Gardens, as described in the novel, was successfully completed by the "Female Blondin" Miss Selina Young (aka Madame Genevieve), on 19th August 1861. She'd had to abandon her first attempt on 12th August following the theft of lead weights from some of the guy ropes, which had caused the main rope to sway too fiercely for her to complete the second half of her walk. Her successful crossing was reported to have taken her just seven minutes. An artist's impression from the 24th August 1861 edition of *The Illustrated London News* is reproduced below.

Miss Selina Young was the granddaughter of a well-known showman, James Bishop. On 14th August 1862, she fell whilst rope-walking at Highbury Barn, North London, and was crippled for life. With an unfathomable lack of respect for her unique achievement of crossing the Thames the previous year, the press now pilloried Miss Young for being, in their opinion, vain and ambitious.

The tragic accident in Birmingham, alluded to in the novel, occurred on 20th July 1863 at Aston Park, when Mrs Edward Powell was performing for the annual Foresters' Fair. A mother of seven, and in the late stage of pregnancy, she fell to her death when the rope she was performing on broke at one end. An inquest returned a verdict of accidental death, caused by dry rot in the rope's core. This incident also drew considerable attention from the press, and was discussed in the House of Lords (*Hansard HL Deb 23 July 1863 vol 172 cc1230-2*). Furthermore, it sparked a letter from Queen Victoria to Birmingham's Mayor, expressing "her personal feelings of horror that one of her subjects – a female – should have been sacrificed to the gratification of the demoralising taste, unfortunately prevalent, for exhibitions attended with the greatest danger to the performers." She added her hope that the Mayor would prevent future such exhibitions from happening.

These two incidents were reviewed in considerable detail in an article entitled 'Our "Six-Hundred-Thousand"', p169 of *The Rose, The Shamrock & The Thistle*, vol. iv, Nov 1863–Apr 1864, published by Caledonian Press, a facsimile of which can be found online. *The Rose, The Shamrock & The Thistle* was a woman-run periodical, which was first published in May 1862 and ran for the next two years, featuring articles on women's employment and current events.

In other news: The French tightrope walker, Madame Saqui, was known as "The first funambule of his Majesty the Emperor", and accompanied Napoleon Bonaparte on the battlefield, to entertain soldiers between assaults. She continued to perform into her sixties, and died in 1866 aged eighty.

Madame Saqui's compatriot, Charles Blondin, performed at Crystal Palace on 1st June 1861, at the request of the Prince of Wales (later King Edward VII), who had previously witnessed one of Blondin's numerous traverses of Niagara Falls.

Edward T. Smith was a "serial impresario" and probably the most successful manager of Cremorne Gardens, Chelsea, between 1861 and 1867.

THE FEMALE BLONDIN CROSSING THE THAMES FROM BATTERSEA TO CHELSEA ON A TIGHT ROPE.—SEE SUPPLEMENT, PAGE 341.